Warwickshire County Council

L|L			
3/18			
7 Jan			
6	4			
30/1/24			

This item is to be returned or renewed before the latest date above. It may be borrowed for a further period if not in demand. **To renew your books:**

- **Phone the 24/7 Renewal Line 01926 499273 or**
- **Visit www.warwickshire.gov.uk/libraries**

Discover • Imagine • Learn • *with libraries*

Warwickshire County Council

Working for Warwickshire

THE SHIPBUILDER'S DAUGHTER

Glasgow, 1928. Margaret lost both of her brothers in the Great War and is now the last remaining child of wealthy and powerful shipyard owner William Bannatyne. Without a male heir to carry on the family business, William expects his daughter to marry well and provide him with a grandson to inherit his business. Margaret loves her father but she has ambitions of her own: to become a doctor. Her father lets Margaret finish her training, but he doesn't count on her meeting Alasdair Morrison, a union man at the shipyard. Suddenly she's faced with an impossible, heartbreaking choice ... will she choose love or obligation?

THE SHIPBUILDER'S DAUGHTER

THE SHIPBUILDER'S DAUGHTER

by

Emma Fraser

Magna Large Print Books
Long Preston, North Yorkshire,
BD23 4ND, England.

British Library Cataloguing in Publication Data.

A catalogue record of this book is
available from the British Library

ISBN 978-0-7505-4524-2

First published in Great Britain in 2017 by Sphere

Copyright © Emma Fraser 2017

Cover design © Ellen Rockell – LBBG
Cover illustration Portrait © Colin Thomas
Background © Shutterstock by arrangement with
Little, Brown Book Group UK

The moral right of the author has been asserted

Published in Large Print 2018 by arrangement with
Little, Brown Book Group Limited

Magna Large Print is an imprint of Library Magna Books Ltd.

Printed and bound in Great Britain by
T.J. (International) Ltd., Cornwall, PL28 8RW

To my Hebridean family, past and present.

Prologue

Glasgow, 1920

The scream was like nothing Margaret had ever heard before and seemed to go on forever. She dropped her book and clapped her hands over her ears. Almost worse was the awful silence that descended a few moments later.

Her heart hammering, she ran to the window and looked outside. Although her father's office was on the third floor, only a fraction of the shipyard was visible; the rest, sprawling alongside the Clyde, was hidden from view. Beneath her a crowd was gathering, converging on something she couldn't quite see through the grimy window.

She used the sleeve of her dress in an attempt to clear a patch, but all she managed to do was smudge it more. As urgent shouts filled the silence of moments before, she sped downstairs, emerging into the soot-filled air, her breath coming in painful gasps. She hesitated, suddenly reluctant to discover what horror had precipitated the blood-curdling screams.

'Where are you going, Miss Bannatyne?' a man asked, grabbing her by the elbow.

'What's happened? Is it my father?'

His lip curled. 'No, it's not your father. What would he be doing down here? It's an accident. Nothing unusual, but not summat a young lass

11

like you should see. Better go back indoors.'

She shook his arm away. 'Let me go!' She couldn't just go back inside – she had to see for herself.

Eyes fixed on the huddle of men obscuring her view, she threaded her way through the grime-stained figures, their stale sweat mingling with the smell of burning coal, welded steel and other odours too foreign to identify, until she was standing inside the circle of onlookers. One of the workers, his face deathly pale, lay on the ground, pinned down by several steel girders. Blood seeped from beneath him, staining the dust red and, just visible through his torn trousers, white bone glistened through a ragged gash in his lower leg. Margaret clamped her hand over her mouth to stop herself from crying out. Part of her wanted to turn away, to slip back through the mass of bodies and return to the safety of her father's office, but another, stronger part couldn't tear her eyes away from the scene unfolding in front of her.

The injured man groaned, sweat trickling down his face and pooling in the hollow of his neck. He looked up at his colleagues with frightened, pain-filled eyes. 'Help me. For God's sake.'

His pleas galvanised the group into action. Several men jostled past her, almost pushing her to the ground. One of them crouched by his side and grabbed the end of the girder. He turned back to the watching men. 'We need to get the weight off him. Come on, men, put your backs into it.'

'Stop!'

The shout, loud enough to be heard over the clanging metal, stopped the men in their tracks.

Way above her head, so high up she had to crane her neck to see, a shipyard worker was standing on the scaffolding surrounding the ship currently under construction.

Ignoring the ladders connecting the different levels, he ran across a narrow plank, grabbed hold of a steel pole and swung down to the levels below. As he descended at breakneck speed, Margaret held her breath. If he wasn't careful, he could easily plunge to his death.

But within moments he was on the ground and the crowd parted to let him through.

'Jimmy,' he said, addressing the man who had ordered the others to move the girders, 'we'll not be able to lift those off him without a crane. Get one over here. Toni, fetch the stretcher. And a cart too.'

The new arrival couldn't be much older than her, yet to her surprise the men did his bidding without argument. He shoved dark hair out of his eyes and knelt by the injured man's side. 'How are you holding up, Hamish?'

'I've been better, Alasdair. I've a feeling I'll no' be home for my tea.'

A brief smile crossed the younger man's face as he ran his hands across Hamish's body. 'Aye, well. I'll get someone to let the wife know. In the meantime, let me have a look see.'

Why didn't they lift the girders off Hamish? He needed to get to a hospital as soon as possible. Why were the workers listening to this man? Where was her father? He should be here, telling them what to do.

'Alasdair, lad, we have to get him out from

13

under that weight,' one of the men said. It appeared she wasn't the only one wondering about the delay.

The dark-haired man shook his head. 'He's punctured an artery at the top of his leg. The pressure of the girders is stopping him from bleeding like a pig. If we take them off without putting on a tourniquet first, he'll not last more than a few minutes.' He yanked off his belt and wrapped it around the top of the injured man's thigh. 'Hold on, Hamish. We're going to move you in a bit. I just need to do something first.'

He glanced up, his eyes narrowing as he caught sight of her. 'You. Do you have anything I can use as a bandage?'

Margaret stiffened. He'd spoken to her as if she were a nobody. Anyway, she didn't have a handkerchief and her dress was stained with soot from the yard. 'No. I'm sorry.'

'You're wearing a petticoat, aren't you? Tear a strip off and pass it to me.'

As several pairs of eyes swivelled in her direction, she blushed. 'I can't do that. Not in front of everyone.'

'You're going to have to. There's nothing else. I need something to staunch the bleeding that's not covered in muck.'

'That's Bannatyne's lass,' one of the men said. 'Best leave her out of it.'

'I don't care if she's the Queen of Sheba. She shouldn't be here, but since she is, she can help.'

Her face burning, Margaret lifted the hem of her dress. She tried to rip a piece off her petticoat but couldn't make even the tiniest tear. 'I can't.'

Alasdair gave an exasperated shake of his head. 'Someone help her.' When no one made a move, he rose to his feet. 'Is the crane here?'

'Aye, son. And the stretcher.'

'Right then, secure the poles.' While the men started tying ropes around the girders, Alasdair stepped towards her. Before she could stop him, he lifted her dress and tore a strip from her petticoat with his teeth.

He looked up at her and a smile flitted across his face. 'Sorry, Miss Bannatyne.' He was so close she could see the freckles scattered across his face. Thick, long lashes framed eyes the colour of the sky in winter.

As soon as the ropes were tied, Alasdair knelt once more on the ground beside the injured man. 'Hamish, I know it hurts like buggery now, but it's going to hurt even more when we lift the girders. You can yell as loud as you like. No one here will mind.' He squeezed Hamish's shoulder. 'Right, lads. As slowly and as carefully as you can.'

The ropes tightened, then inch by inch, the lengths of steel began to lift. Hamish screamed, his arms thrashing about in agony. Margaret watched in horror as blood spurted over Alasdair's hands.

'Hold still, Hamish. For the love of God, just hold still.'

If Hamish could hear Alasdair he was in too much pain to pay heed. He continued to flail his arms, trying to push Alasdair away.

'Someone hold him down, for God's sake!' Alasdair shouted, his bloodied fingers slipping on the straps of his makeshift tourniquet.

One of the men pressed down on Hamish's

shoulders and Alasdair tightened the belt until the blood slowed to a trickle. Satisfied, he moved on to the gash in Hamish's lower leg, wrapping the strips of Margaret's torn petticoat tightly over the wound. Within moments his temporary bandage had turned red.

'Pass me some planks,' he ordered.

Eager hands thrust several at him. He discarded a few before selecting four of equal length. He placed one on either side of each of Hamish's legs and tied them quickly with more belts.

'Let's get him onto the stretcher, lads,' he said. 'Go carefully. His legs are likely broken. The planks will help – but only a little.'

As they moved him, Hamish screamed again, then mercifully fell silent. They laid his unconscious body on the stretcher and set it on the back of the cart.

'Take him to the Infirmary. As quickly as you can. Avoid the potholes. I'll let the boss know what's happened, once I find out what went wrong.'

'Is he going to be all right?' Margaret asked, grabbing Alasdair's arm.

'You need to leave, Miss,' he replied curtly. His expression softened. 'There's no more any of us can do here. It's up to the doctors at the hospital now.' He turned back towards the men. 'Right. Those who have nothing to say about what happened, back to work.'

As the cart rolled away she looked up. Her father was standing at his office window, staring down. Doing nothing. Just looking.

'What in God's name were you doing down there?' her father barked when she returned to the office. Mr Ferguson, her father's manager, was standing next to him. Why had neither of them come to help?

'There was an accident. Didn't you see?' Her heart was still beating so fast she felt light-headed.

'It's a shipyard, Margaret. There's always accidents. You had no business to be down there getting in the way. I asked you to stay in my office until I returned. Why can you never do as you're told?'

Tears stung the back of her lids. The day had started with so much promise. When her father had suggested she come with him to the shipyard she'd been thrilled. It was the first time he'd ever invited her to go anywhere with him.

'I brought you here, Margaret,' her father continued, 'so you can see what your sons will inherit one day, not to be showing your undergarments to the men. Look at the state of you!'

She shook her head impatiently. 'I wasn't in the way. I helped. They needed a bit of my petticoat to use as a bandage. They had nothing else.' What did the state of her clothing matter when a man had been badly hurt? 'What do you think will happen to him? Can we go to the hospital to find out?'

'Don't be ridiculous, Margaret. I don't have time to go checking up on the men every time one of them gets injured.'

'But he's really hurt! Don't you want to make sure he's all right?'

'Ferguson will let me know in the morning. Now let's get you home before the men have anything

17

more to talk about,' her father said. 'Really, Margaret. I only left you for a short while. All you had to do was wait for me.'

It hadn't been a short while. It had been over two hours.

He picked up his hat, but before they could leave there was a sharp knock on the door and without waiting for an invitation to enter, Alasdair strode into the office. His arms and hands were still covered with Hamish's blood, the front of his shirt splashed with crimson. Taller than her father by a few inches, and muscular without being stocky, his dark hair was longer than most men wore it and tousled as if he'd just climbed out of bed. Despite Alasdair's dishevelled appearance and workman's clothes that contrasted sharply with her father's hand-made suit and crisp white shirt, the men shared the same undeniable air of authority. And, while Alasdair's manner with Hamish had been gentle and kind, his eyes were now slate-grey cold, and his full mouth set in a grim line.

'What are you doing in here, Morrison?' Mr Ferguson said, with an anxious glance at Margaret's father. 'I'm sorry, sir. The men know they aren't permitted to come up to the office.'

'I wouldn't have had to if you'd come down. The front scaffolding collapsed. I've had to send Hamish McKillop to hospital.'

'Anything you want to tell me can wait,' Mr Ferguson said.

'No it can't. That scaffolding wouldn't have collapsed if it had been erected properly and not in a rush. We've told you before. There's too much cutting corners going on. Mr Bannatyne needs to

18

be aware of that.'

'Mr Ferguson runs the yard,' Margaret's father snapped.

Alasdair turned his wintry eyes to her father. 'He might run the yard but he does it under your orders. That's the third accident this month. The workers have the right to a safe workplace.'

Margaret had never heard anyone speak to her father like that before.

Her father's face suffused with colour. 'And who are you to tell me how to operate my yard? Get the blazes out of my office and back to work.'

Mr Ferguson stepped forward and took Alasdair by the elbow. 'On you go, Morrison.'

Alasdair stared at the hand on his arm until Mr Ferguson released his grip. 'I'll go,' he said quietly. 'But the men won't be working on that ship until the scaffolding has been checked.' With a scathing look at Mr Ferguson, he turned on his heel and left.

'Who is that whippersnapper? What makes him think he has the right to speak to me like that?' her father demanded, his voice shaking with fury.

Mr Ferguson twisted the cap in his hand. 'His name is Alasdair Morrison, sir – one of the time-served riveters and their foreman.'

'Ian Morrison's son?'

'The same.'

'Damn that man. And his son. How the hell did Morrison's lad come to be working in my yard?'

'He's been here since he was fourteen – apart from the time he served in the war. He's a good worker. The men look up to him – as they did his father.'

'Fire him!'

'You can't fire him, Father! He helped. He's only telling you something he thinks you need to know.' Margaret had been listening to the exchange with growing dismay. She didn't know what shocked her more: the way Alasdair had spoken to her father, or the way her father had responded. 'You should have seen what he did! Hamish might have died if he hadn't been there.'

'Stay out of this, Margaret.'

'Your daughter is right, Mr Bannatyne. We can't fire him. The unions will strike if we do. And that ship needs to be finished on time.'

Her father knotted his hands behind his back, returned to the window and looked outside. 'Is Morrison right about the scaffolding?'

Mr Ferguson shifted uneasily. 'It was put up in a bit of a rush, sir. If you recall we're on a tight schedule with the ships. But I told them to make sure it was robust.'

'I pay you, Ferguson, to ensure the yard is run properly. These issues should not be my concern. If you can't do the job I pay you for, I'll find someone else. Do I make myself clear?'

'Yes sir.'

'And as for Morrison. He's a trouble-maker just like his father. I don't care how you do it but get rid of him the first chance you can.'

Margaret stared out of the window as their chauffeur drove them home. So much for her father spending time with her. She'd imagined telling him about her lessons – how her tutor, Miss Fourier, made her practise her Latin and Italian

20

until she could read a little Virgil and Dante in the original, or even what she'd found on her latest walk down at the seashore in Helensburgh. She hadn't really been interested in seeing the shipyard – what girl would be? – and to begin with she'd found it every bit as grey, dirty and as unappealing as she'd anticipated. Stepping out of the car on arrival, the incredible noise of shouting, hammering, the screech of metal on metal, the rumble of horse-pulled carts on the cobbles, had pounded through her head, making it difficult to think, let alone speak. Nearly as bad was the smell of grease and oil, burnt steel, smouldering coal and hot tar. Lined with cranes and warehouses, virtually every inch of space on the quayside had been filled with workers – some no more than boys – almost identical in their flat caps and waistcoats, some loading and unloading carts, while even more swarmed over the steel girders supporting the half-built ships. But she'd soon become aware of a sense of purpose behind the apparent chaos. Her father had told her that the ship, rising high above her, was destined to be part of the Cunard line. It would be beautiful when it was finished and these men had made it from nothing and she'd been curious to see more.

However, to her dismay, her father had taken her straight to his office and instructed her to stay there until he returned.

She shuddered. Well, she had seen more of the shipyard, just not in the way she'd expected.

'You don't really mean to have Alasdair dismissed, do you?' she asked her father now. He hadn't spoken a word since they'd left the office, concentrating instead on the sheaf of papers on his lap.

He looked at her and frowned. 'There's no room for sentimentality in business, Margaret. Especially not these days. We have to stay competitive and that means producing ships as quickly and as cheaply as we can while maintaining quality. Clyde-built ships have the reputation for being the best in the world and I mean to keep it that way.'

'But those workers. They're the ones who build the ships. Don't they matter?'

'It's up to them to take more care so that they don't have accidents and can continue to work.'

'Isn't it also up to you – I mean Mr Ferguson – to make sure they don't get hurt?'

'In that accidents cost the yard time and money. Yes.'

'But–'

'Enough, Margaret! It's bad enough having one of the labourers question me, without my own daughter doing it too.' His expression softened. 'There's a lot to a business, my dear. I can't expect a young girl to understand that.'

If he was right then she was glad she wasn't expected to take over from her father. She wanted to press him further, but the day had already been spoiled.

'When you have a son I'll teach him all he needs to know,' her father continued.

The thought of marrying – let alone having sons – seemed so far in the future she could hardly imagine it.

'You will ask Mr Ferguson to let us know about

Hamish, won't you?'

'Who?'

'Hamish. The man who was injured.'

'Yes. Of course.'

'And you'll tell me?'

Her father patted her knee absent-mindedly. 'I said I would. Now, Margaret, could you be quiet for a while? I need peace to think.'

Back at the house Margaret's father dropped her off, telling her he had business in town. Disappointed they wouldn't be spending the day together after all and shaken by what had happened, she felt a sudden longing for her mother. If only she were here and not in Helensburgh.

As her steps echoed in the large tiled hallway of their Glasgow home, images of the accident at the shipyard spilled through her head: Hamish on the ground; the pain and fear in his eyes; all that blood and no one sure of what to do. Until Alasdair had arrived, that is. Despite his being so much younger than the other men, there had been an almost palpable sense of relief amongst them when he'd taken control. He seemed to know exactly what to do, assuming he'd done the right thing. If Sebastian had been at the shipyard that morning, as a doctor, would he have done anything different than Alasdair had? Would Sebastian have removed Hamish immediately or also waited to tie a belt round Hamish's leg to stop the bleeding? Or had Alasdair just been guessing it was the right thing to do? Perhaps the injured man wouldn't survive because of the delay in getting him to hospital – or perhaps it was the only reason he was still alive.

She ran upstairs and along the corridor to her brother's room. It still smelt of him; the tangy scent of tobacco mixed with the spiced soap he had used. Like Fletcher's room, Sebastian's had been left untouched. Their books, the shoes they once wore, their tailored suits, polo sticks and cricket bats were all where they'd left them, as if one day they would return and life would carry on as before.

She crouched in front of Sebastian's bookshelf. They were still packed with his medical journals, volumes of chemistry, botany and *materia medica* along with medical tomes depicting gruesome illustrations of disease and injury. She'd often sat reading quietly in the chair by the window on the rare occasions Sebastian studied for his surgical exams.

She trailed her fingers along the spines until she found what she was looking for – *Gray's Anatomy* – and heaved the tome of over a thousand pages over to Sebastian's desk. She pulled out the chair and sat down. She couldn't ask her brother's advice, but she could find out for herself. She wanted to know what Alasdair had done and why.

Most of all, she wanted to know if he'd been right.

Chapter 1

Eight years later

Spilling out of the lecture theatre along with the other students, Margaret felt giddy with relief and exhilaration. Although she had no doubt that she would pass her final exams – she had worked too hard over the years not to – it still felt unreal that very soon she would be working as a doctor. Until then she had almost two whole glorious weeks with no studying, no specialist breathing down her neck, no patients to be examined and drilled on, just days and days of sleeping in and catching up on all the unread books she'd had to put aside these last few months.

She hooked arms with Martha and Lillian as they stood on the steps of Glasgow University.

'That wasn't too bad,' Martha said, the glasses perched on the end of her nose glinting in the sunshine.

'Perhaps not for you,' Lillian retorted, 'but I'm sure I got my duodenum mixed up with my ileum.'

Margaret smiled. Typical Lillian – always teasing. It was unlikely that the three of them would even have met if they hadn't been the only female medical students in their year. Small, plump, serious Martha with her long red hair pulled tightly off her face and twisted in a plait was the epitome

25

of a Minister's daughter and the complete opposite of headstrong, aristocratic, beautiful dark-
haired Lillian who, with her sleek bob and daring
knee-skimming skirts, turned heads everywhere
she went – even those of their resentful male
counterparts.

Yet, despite their differences in outlook and
personality, they had become immediate and fast
friends, and Margaret would miss them terribly.
Martha was leaving for India in less than a week
to work as a missionary, while Lillian was going
to London to set up a practice with her fiancé,
Charles.

'Right,' Lillian said. 'What shall we do now? A
little shopping perhaps?'

'I'm saving,' Martha said.

'Of course you are,' Lillian replied with an exasperated sideways glance at Margaret, 'but window
shopping costs nothing and surely you must need
a mosquito net or another Bible to take to India?'

'I have already bought everything I need,'
Martha said stiffly. 'It's all packed.'

'We can't possibly just go home,' Lillian insisted. 'We have to celebrate. Let's have a drink at
least.'

'A cup of tea, you mean,' Martha said, looking
pointedly at her watch. 'It's only just past two.'

'A walk then?' Margaret suggested, stepping
into her familiar role as peacemaker. 'It's such a
beautiful day. We should make the most of it.'

Glasgow, which even in the summer was usually
so smoggy it was difficult to see to put one foot in
front of the other, was uncharacteristically clear.
Today the sky was blue, the sun hot enough for

them to remove their suit jackets and drape them over their shoulders, and there was just enough of a breeze to keep the smog away.

As they headed towards Dumbarton Road, they stopped in respectful silence as a horse-drawn carriage adorned with black feathers passed by. A small, white coffin lay in the back. The carriage was followed by several distraught relatives, their muffled sobs all too audible. A knot of frustration formed in the pit of Margaret's stomach. It was too common a sight in Glasgow. Hardly a day went by without the funeral cortege of a child taken by diphtheria or scarlet fever or any of the several infectious diseases that killed one child in five. During their years as medical students they all had pronounced children dead and mourned along with the parents. No matter how advanced medicine was becoming there was still no cure for many of the illnesses they'd seen during their training.

'Now I definitely need a drink,' Lillian muttered, and before Margaret or Martha could object, she marched across the street ignoring the honk from an oncoming tram and disappeared into the Highlander Public House.

'In there?' Martha shook her head. 'She has to be joking.'

Although women did go into bars it was frowned upon, especially for women of their class and most definitely not in the afternoon.

Margaret gripped Martha by the arm. 'Come on, let's live dangerously for once. We'll just have a sherry or something. No one will even notice us.'

She knew that was unlikely. Three unaccompanied women dressed as they were in neat suits and crisp white blouses would stick out like sore thumbs. But today was a day for doing something daring and different. Martha seemed to realise this too, allowing herself to be pulled inside the low, grimy building.

The few couples in the ladies' bar looked up as they entered, their eyes swivelling towards them before quickly looking away. Lillian had already secured a small table at the rear. 'I've ordered us sherries, Margaret,' she said, taking out her silver cigarette case. 'And a lemonade for you, Martha. I know there is only so far I can go.'

Margaret glanced over at Martha, who looked like she'd swallowed a lemon, and bit down on her lip to stop herself from laughing out loud.

When their drinks arrived, Lillian raised her glass. 'I propose a toast. Here's to your missionary work in India, Martha – may you convert many and heal even more.' She turned towards Margaret. 'And Mags, here's to your success as House Officer Extraordinaire at Redlands – and may the post you so covet soon become available at Rotten Row.'

Margaret laughed. 'That's unlikely to happen – at least not until the powers-that-be stop giving the jobs to men only.' She held up her glass. 'But I'll drink to the hope of it. And let's not forget about your upcoming wedding, Lily.'

'I imagine you and Robert will be setting a date for yours soon, Margaret,' Lillian said, after they'd chinked glasses. 'I have to say, he's a patient man.'

'No more patient than your Charles. He also

agreed to wait until you finished your studies.'

Lillian fitted a cigarette into its holder before lighting it. 'That's because we'll be working together. At least until the sprogs come along.' She hesitated. 'Your Robert has more cause for urgency.'

'What on earth do you mean?' Margaret said sharply.

Lillian placed her cigarette lighter carefully on the table. 'All I meant, my dear, is that the landed gentry are always in need of money. Fortunately for me, Charles has plenty of the stuff.'

'Come off it, Lillian, don't pretend that's why you're marrying Charles,' Margaret protested.

Lillian blew a perfect smoke ring – a skill she was especially proud of – and smiled dreamily. 'I am rather fond of him, I admit. But money always helps. Father needs an injection of cash if he's going to stop the family pile from falling down about his ears. Unfortunately, Charles's family aren't as hideously wealthy as yours, Margaret, but then again few families are.' She was quiet for a moment, fiddling with her cigarette while staring pensively at Margaret. 'I'm not sure I should be telling you this but I've heard the Locksleys have got into a spot of bother. Something about investing in America. I gather they might have to sell off part of their estate if they can't come up with some funds. Lucky for them they are about to be united with the Bannatynes. I can't imagine your father will let his in-laws starve.'

Margaret frowned at her friend. What Lillian was saying couldn't be true, otherwise Robert would have said something. Unless, of course, it was a temporary state of affairs and he didn't want to trouble her. And as for Lillian's insinuation that Robert was marrying her because of her wealth – that was nonsense. Nevertheless, she felt a ripple of unease. She'd often thought that there should be more passion between an engaged couple; Robert rarely tried to kiss her, although until now it had never bothered her. They got on, and that's what mattered most. Robert understood how important medicine was to her. He'd even agreed that they should wait until she had completed her first year as a doctor before they married. If he was so desperate to get his hands on the Bannatyne money surely he would have pressed her to set a date before now? But Lillian and Robert's fathers were friends and Lillian would never have mentioned the Locksleys' financial troubles – not if she wasn't sure of her facts.

'You're not suggesting Robert is marrying me because his family needs money?' Margaret asked Lillian.

'No, of course not,' Lillian replied, studying the end of her cigarette. 'Don't mind me! You know how I open my mouth sometimes and all sorts of nonsense just comes spilling out.' She held up her glass and made a show of studying the amber liquid inside. 'It doesn't help that this sherry's gone straight to my head.'

'Ignore Lillian, Margaret,' Martha interjected. 'She just likes to tease. Robert loves you dearly. Why wouldn't he? You are clever, beautiful and kind.' She took a sip of her lemonade and wrinkled her nose. 'I don't know why you ladies are getting married anyway. Not everyone needs a husband to be happy. Our work is what's important.'

Lillian gave a sly smile. 'Are you certain you're not one of *those* women, Martha? It wouldn't bother me if you were, you know. Might even try it myself one day.'

'Leave her alone, Lily,' Margaret said. She suspected that Lillian often said these outrageous things simply to annoy Martha.

Martha rolled her eyes. 'I can stick up for myself, Margaret. And no, for the record, I'm not one of those sort of women. Just because I haven't had a suitor doesn't mean I'm not interested in the opposite sex. Unfortunately, decent God-fearing men are few and far between.'

They stopped talking as a couple edged past their table, the man's arm resting lightly on the woman's waist.

'Hardly any young men left at all,' Martha continued, eyeing the departing sweethearts.

Lillian and Margaret followed her gaze. 'I daresay there is going to be a generation of single women living together as they grow old, sewing and tending their gardens. What a fate. The war has a lot to answer for,' Lillian said.

'If I hadn't met Robert, I don't think I'd have minded staying single,' Margaret said. 'But I would like to have children one day. What about you girls?'

'I suppose I could manage a couple as long as I have a nanny or two.' Lillian removed her cigarette from its holder and ground it out in the ashtray.

'The children in India will be my children,' Martha said.

Lillian leant over and gave her a shove. 'Oh, get

off your high horse, Martha. You can't tell me you want to live your whole life without sex.'

'I never said I did! And keep your voice down, we don't want the whole bar to hear.' She leant forward and whispered, 'What do you think it would be like?'

When Lillian lifted an eyebrow, Martha gasped. 'You haven't!'

Margaret shook her head. Really, Lillian took it too far sometimes. 'Of course she hasn't, Martha. She's just teasing you.'

'Are you certain about that? For all you both know I'm a regular at those petting parties when I go to London.'

'Because we know you're not stupid. Naughty perhaps and provocative, but not stupid. You'd never do anything to ruin your reputation,' Margaret replied.

Lillian laughed. 'How well you both know me.' She drained her glass. 'Right, whose round is it?'

Martha shook her head. 'I can't stay. I promised my father I'd help him write Sunday's sermon. Perhaps we could go for tea after church?' She looked from one to the other. 'You'll both be at church on Sunday, won't you?'

'Not this Sunday, I'm afraid,' Margaret said. 'I'm going to Helensburgh to see Mother.'

'How is she?' Martha asked.

'Much the same.'

Lillian leant across the table and squeezed Margaret's hand.

'I'll see you before you leave for India,' Margaret told Martha as her friend picked up her handbag.

'You must! I couldn't go without a proper goodbye.'

They were silent, knowing that this might be the last time the three of them were together.

Martha stood and hugged Lillian, then Margaret. 'I'll always be here for the two of you, you do know that, don't you?'

'Of course we do,' Margaret replied, swallowing the lump in her throat. 'And us for you.'

Lillian gave Martha a gentle nudge. 'Off you go before you have us all in tears!'

'Oh help, I hope no one we know sees me leaving this place,' Martha muttered before scurrying out the door.

Margaret handed Lillian a handkerchief. 'I take it you want another sherry, Lily?'

Lillian nodded, surreptitiously dabbing her eyes. 'You take it right.'

While Margaret stood at the counter waiting to be served, she noticed it was possible to see into the public bar next door through a connecting archway. The air in there was thick with cigarette and pipe smoke and she caught a glimpse of men seated round scarred wooden tables, their pints of beer clutched in their work-soiled hands. Amidst the rumble of voices and laughter, she heard the strains of a fiddle being tuned up.

Putting the change in her purse, she carried the drinks back to their table.

'I think there's music starting. Won't be able to hear ourselves think in a minute with the noise,' she said to Lillian, 'Shall we go somewhere else?'

Except, when a fiddle burst into life accompanied by a cacophony of cheering and clapping, she found herself tapping her foot in time to the music.

Lillian leaned forward, her eyes sparkling with mischief. 'Let's go through to the bar.'

Margaret hesitated. 'It's the public bar.'

'So what! Aren't we the public too? Come on, it could be the last chance we have to let our hair down for a while.'

Lillian was right. Once they started work there would be little opportunity for relaxing. Apart from that they would have their professional reputations to uphold. Here, no one knew them. She smiled at her friend. 'Very well. Why not?'

Clutching their drinks and giggling like school-girls, they sneaked through the adjoining swing door into the public bar. The noise and smoke enveloped them as they pushed their way through the throng of workmen to find a table in the corner at the back. A couple of men elbowed their companions and raised their eyebrows, another made a remark about how women, now more of them had the vote, were all wanting to be men and why didn't they just put on a pair of troosers while they were at it, but otherwise they left the two women alone.

Margaret couldn't remember when she last had so much fun. Hidden in the crowd, she and Lillian applauded and whooped along with everyone at the end of each song until suddenly the tempo changed. The bar slowly quietened as soft fiddle chords soared around the room.

The tune wasn't familiar to her but it spoke of loss and longing. She glanced at Lillian to find that she too was spellbound. Suddenly the crowd parted and Margaret could finally see who was playing the fiddle so beautifully.

The mop of unruly dark hair was shorter, although still long enough for a lock to fall over his face as he played, but she recognised him instantly. Her stomach lurched. It was Alasdair, Alasdair Morrison – the man from the shipyard. She'd thought about him a lot in those first months after the accident, wondering if they'd meet again. In her schoolgirl fantasies, they had and she'd been cool and just a little disdainful and he'd been impressed by her sophistication. Over the years he'd faded from her mind until she'd almost forgotten about him.

His eyes were shut as he caressed the strings of the fiddle with his bow, an expression of such deep sadness etched on his face that it made her breath catch in her throat. When the last notes trailed off, he opened his eyes and, as their gaze locked, everything and everyone around her seemed to disappear. Her heart beat a tattoo against her ribs.

'What on earth has got into you?' Lillian asked. 'You've gone bright red.'

Alasdair picked up his jacket, his eyes still on her. Flustered, Margaret stumbled to her feet, almost knocking over her empty glass in her haste. 'We should go.'

'Go? Now? Oh, no, I'd say it's just getting interesting!' her friend said, staring over Margaret's shoulder.

Margaret spun around. Alasdair was making his way towards her, shrugging off the congratulations of well-wishers with a distracted smile and an occasional handshake as he kept his eyes

35

fixed on her. A few feet away, his steps slowed and his forehead knotted.

Her heart still thumping wildly, Margaret turned away, draped her jacket over her shoulders and grabbed her handbag. 'Come on, Lily.'

'Too late,' Lillian drawled.

'Hello.' A soft voice came from behind her and she whirled around to find him standing in front of her. She'd forgotten how tall he was, but she remembered only too well the unusual grey of his eyes. His face was leaner now, his cheekbones sharper, and small lines feathered the corners of his eyes as if he were used to laughing. 'Do we know each other?' he continued with a smile. 'I've a feeling we've met before.'

So he hadn't recognised her. She felt an irrational pang of disappointment.

'Yes, I mean, no. We met at the shipyard. Years ago. You tore a piece off my petticoat.'

Lillian raised her eyebrows. 'Margaret Bannatyne! You're more of a dark horse than I've given you credit for.'

The dawning recognition in his eyes was replaced by something Margaret couldn't quite identify but could have sworn was regret. 'Ah, Miss Bannatyne. Of course. I didn't recognise you at first. You've changed.'

'It has been eight years, Mr Morrison. I was just a schoolgirl.'

Blushing furiously, Margaret turned to Lillian. 'Lillian, may I introduce Mr Morrison? Mr Morrison – Lady Lillian Forsythe.'

'Lady Lillian.' Alasdair acknowledged Lillian with the briefest tip of his head.

'Years ago one of my father's workers was badly injured and Mr Morrison saved his life,' Margaret added.

Alasdair's mouth narrowed into a tight line. 'Well, maybe. Not that it did him any good.'

'What do you mean?' Margaret demanded. 'My father told me Hamish survived the accident.'

Alasdair had already threaded one arm through the sleeve of the jacket he had carried over his shoulder. For a moment he seemed to waver. Then he finished slipping his jacket on, and tugged the collar straight. 'I'm afraid you ladies must excuse me.' He gave Margaret one last long look. 'It's been a pleasure to meet you again, Miss Bannatyne, and to meet you, Lady Lillian, but I have to go.'

'How intriguing!' Lillian murmured, her eyes following him as he pushed his way back through the crowds and towards the door. 'I could have sworn he was entranced by you. Not that he has the remotest chance, but he looks like a man who doesn't give up easily. I wonder what made him turn tail?'

Margaret shook her head. She couldn't let him disappear without finding out what he'd meant about Hamish. 'I have to go after him.'

Lillian cocked an eyebrow. 'This day is getting stranger by the minute. I hope you're planning to tell me all.'

'Later, Lillian.' Margaret dropped a kiss on her friend's cheek and hurried after Alasdair.

Margaret had to weave between the pedestrians thronging the pavement along Dumbarton Road.

She'd almost given up when she caught sight of his broad back and dark hair.

'Mr Morrison! Wait! Please.'

He stopped and turned, barely concealing his look of impatience. 'What can I do for you, Miss Bannatyne?'

'What did you mean about Hamish?' she demanded. 'What happened to him?'

'What could it possibly matter to you? Why should a Bannatyne care?'

She felt a surge of anger. His looks hadn't changed very much but neither had his manner. He was just as rude and arrogant as she remembered.

'Please don't presume that you know what matters to me.'

He frowned down at her. 'If you really wanted to know about Hamish you wouldn't have waited all these years to find out.'

'Of course I asked about him. I was told the doctors set his broken bone and discharged him home after a few days.' It had taken her almost a week of nagging her father to find that out. Not that she was going to tell Alasdair that.

Alasdair frowned at her and carried on walking and she had to almost run to keep up with him. 'Mr Morrison – Alasdair – just tell me what happened to Hamish and I'll let you go on your way.'

He stopped and turned to face her. 'Let me go on my way?' He raised an eyebrow. 'I don't need your permission, Miss Bannatyne.' He studied her for a moment. 'Very well, then. Since you ask, Hamish did survive the accident. It wasn't the injuries that killed him. Not directly anyway.'

'Hamish is dead?' Her throat closed. After everything the poor man had been through that day. 'How did he die? Did his wound become infected?' Back then the possibility had never occurred to her. However, after years of studying medicine she now knew that setting broken bones was the easy part. Wounds, especially those that happened in the workplace, often became infected, the infection raging through the blood until it killed the victim. All these years she'd believed Hamish had survived, and it was a bitter blow to find out he hadn't. Tears burned the back of her lids and she blinked. She wouldn't give this man the pleasure of seeing her cry. Hamish was dead. That was all that mattered. There was no more to be said.

'Good day, Mr Morrison. I wish I could say it was a pleasure meeting you again.' She squared her shoulders and began walking away. She'd only gone a few steps when she felt a hand on her shoulder.

'We could go on all evening like this, you chasing after me and me chasing after you.' She couldn't help noticing how his eyes crinkled up at the corners when he smiled.

'I don't wish to take up any more of your time.'

He looked at her keenly and his expression softened. 'What happened to Hamish really does matter to you, doesn't it?'

She didn't know which she resented more: the earlier derision in his eyes or the sympathy she saw there now. Unable to trust herself to speak, she nodded.

He pulled a fob watch out of his pocket and

glanced down at it. 'Look, I've got a little time before I have to be somewhere. Let me buy you a cup of tea.' Before she had the chance to reply he had taken her by the elbow and had steered her inside a tearoom.

Pulling out a chair for her, he squeezed in opposite, his legs brushing against her knees under the small table. She quickly jerked hers away.

'Tea?' he asked, appearing not to notice, although the small smile twitching the corners of his mouth suggested otherwise.

Margaret nodded again.

'Tell me what happened to Hamish,' she said when the waitress had taken their order and left.

Alasdair leaned back in his chair. 'As I said, Hamish did survive the accident. However, it left both his legs useless, and a man without the use of his legs can't work. Without work, Hamish and his family had no way to feed themselves. We all did what we could to help them out but Hamish was a proud man and would only take what he needed to save his family from starving. He died a few years ago. His wife followed a year later and then two of the children. There's nothing left of that family apart from one lad. He's working at the shipyard now. Unfortunately too late to help his family.'

'I'm truly sorry to hear that. I'm certain my father would have had him and his family taken care of, if he'd known. Hamish was one of his workers, after all.' But even as she said the words she wondered uneasily if they were true. Her father hadn't appeared too concerned about Hamish's welfare that day and she doubted whether he would have made enquiries at all had she not badgered him.

'Miss Bannatyne, I can't imagine you have the slightest idea how your father's businesses work.'

She stiffened again. The man wasn't just rude – he was patronising. 'I know his yard is successful and that he employs thousands of people – people who'd be out of work if it wasn't for him.'

'Bannatyne's is successful because your father spends as little as he can so he can maximise his profits. Most of the other shipyards have some insurance for the workers – not your father. He says it's too expensive. Says there's no reason to pay men who can't work when there are plenty to fill his place.'

'I don't believe you!'

'Aye, well. That's up to you. You asked, I answered.'

She waited until the waitress had placed their teas in front of them before she spoke again. 'You have no business spreading lies about my father.'

'Lies, is it?' He leaned forward and looked at her keenly. 'Are you certain about that?'

'My father is a good and fair man.'

Alasdair laughed harshly. 'Your father is many things but good and fair aren't among them.' He shook his head and gave her a rueful smile. 'Look, Miss Bannatyne, I've said enough. I have no wish to run a father down to his daughter no matter how I feel about that particular man.' He tilted his head. 'Come to think of it, I doubt he'd be happy if he discovered you've been talking to me. I'm not one of his favourite people.'

She wondered if Alasdair was *anyone's* favourite

41

person. He wasn't exactly the friendliest soul. 'I can talk to whoever I please. He wouldn't do anything to you.'

He laughed shortly. 'I didn't mean to me. Your father can't touch me. He'd love to but he can't. No, it's you I'm thinking of. I can't imagine he'd be best pleased with you.'

She stiffened. 'Don't be ridiculous. I'm a grown woman.' Everything about this man – especially what he'd said about her father – annoyed her. However, there was still something she wanted to know. 'How did you know how to help Hamish?'

She'd wondered about that often over the years. Haemorrhage had to be controlled by pressure; if it couldn't – if an artery had been damaged, as she was certain had been the case with Hamish – then applying a tourniquet above the bleeding vessel was the best way of stopping someone from bleeding to death before getting them to hospital where the artery could be ligated. How had Alasdair, a shipyard worker, known exactly what to do?

He studied her for a moment with his cool, grey eyes. 'I was in France during the war. The last year of it anyway. I saw enough bleeding and broken bones to last me a lifetime. Me knowing what to do when there's an accident at the yard is the only good thing that came out of the war.'

'You don't think we should have fought?'

'I didn't say that. But I often wonder what it was all for. It changed nothing for the ordinary man. They told us we were fighting to make this a land fit for heroes when we returned. They lied. This is no land fit for heroes. In fact it's worse than it was before.'

'My brothers both lost their lives in defence of their country,' she said quietly.

His eyes softened. 'I know. And I'm sorry. My dad told me. Too many good men died in the war and your brother Fletcher was one of the best.'

'You knew him?' she whispered.

'Aye. If he'd lived, Bannatyne's might be a different place.'

She blinked away the tears that burned once more behind her lids. So Alasdair didn't despise all Bannatynes, then. 'That day at the shipyard,' she found herself saying, 'I was shocked and horrified. I wanted to be able to help someone the way you helped Hamish.' She smiled. 'Now I can. I just sat my last exam as a medical student. That's why my friend and I were in the bar. We were celebrating.'

Alasdair's eyebrows shot up and he whistled. 'Well, I never. A doctor. Good for you.' For the first time she saw approval in his eyes and despite everything he'd said before, it sent a warm glow all the way through her.

She took a sip of her tea. 'I'm starting as a House Officer at Redlands Hospital in a couple of weeks.' She couldn't quite manage to keep the pride from her voice.

'Never heard of it. What kind of hospital is it?'

'One for women. It's all female doctors that work there.'

'Can anyone go there?'

'As long as they're female – and can afford the fees.'

'Better that you were working for those without

43

money. They need doctors more than the women you'll be caring for, I've no doubt.'

She bristled. Couldn't she say *anything* without incurring his disapproval? Just when she was warming to him he said something clearly intended to provoke her. More unsettling was that he made her feel defensive – and she had no reason to feel that way.

'If it were up to me, I would have taken a House Officer's post at the Western or the Royal, but they give those posts to men. Don't think the poor have the prerogative on unfairness. And, for your information, I have cared for the poor. During my training.'

'I suspect you've never seen poor like those who live in the Gorbals – or Govan.'

Why was she bothering? she thought, exasperated. 'I don't know why you are so ready to judge me – you know nothing about me.'

'Perhaps it has something to do with who you are and the way you are dressed. I'm no expert but I imagine the outfit you are wearing would feed an unemployed man and his family for a year.'

'I doubt that,' Margaret replied, stung. Although her suit was made from the finest tweed, it wasn't even her most expensive outfit – not by a long chalk. She couldn't help noticing earlier that his wool jacket was worn and one of his boots was coming away at the sole.

Alasdair pushed his empty tea cup aside. 'It has been pleasant talking to you, Miss Bannatyne, but I've a shift to get to. At Bannatyne's as it happens.'

'You still work at the shipyard?' So her father hadn't found a way to fire him after all.

'Aye. Night foreman.'

'I'm surprised you continue to work there when you so clearly disapprove of my father and the way he runs his business.'

'I work for your father because, like everyone else, I need the money. Apart from that, I make sure he runs the yard as safely as possible. Unfortunately, there are still too many like Hamish.' He took some change from his pocket and signalled to the waitress to bring the bill.

'Does the nightshift start so early? It's not even four yet.' Although she'd said everything she'd wanted to say, she was unaccountably reluctant to say goodbye.

'It doesn't start until eight, but I have people I need to see before then.'

'Friends?'

Once more he gave her the slow smile that made her feel warm inside. 'You are very inquisitive, Miss Bannatyne.'

'You claim to know all about me. It's only fair I should know more about you.'

'There's nothing about me that would interest you. But seeing as you've asked – I'm going to Govan to see some of the men who used to work for your father before he laid them off. And I should be getting on my way.'

He stood and held out his hand and automatically Margaret shook it. His grip was firm without being too tight, but even through the thin cotton of her gloves she could feel how rough his hands were.

'I'd like to go with you.' When his eyebrows rose, she added hastily, 'To see where the ship-

45

yard workers live.'

'You want to go to Govan?' If anything, his eyebrows rose even higher. He might well look surprised, she had no idea that that was what she was going to say until the words were out of her mouth.

'Why not?' If she went she could see for herself what life was like for her father's workers. It had nothing to do with the fact, she told herself, that she wasn't yet ready to part from this man. 'I'm going to the opera with my fiancé this evening, but until then I'm free.'

His eyes took on the wintry look she remembered so well. 'I read about your engagement in the paper. Somehow I doubt Viscount Locksley would approve of his fiancée gadding about the East End.'

'Robert no more tells me what to do than my father does!'

An expression she couldn't read flickered across his face. 'Nor, for that matter, would my friends be happy for Bannatyne's daughter to drop in on them as if they were exhibits in a zoo,' he continued.

'Really! You are the most infuriating man I have ever met. I am a doctor. I'm used to treating the less fortunate. You seem to think I know nothing about how the poorer residents of Glasgow live, but I can assure you I have been in their homes before. They might have very little but they get by. I can't imagine the people in Govan are less well off than the people in Partick.'

He studied her through narrowed eyes. 'Very well then, Miss Bannatyne. If you wish to see how

46

the people who depend on the shipyards live, I'll take you. As long as you're ready to go now.'

'I can find my own way.'

'You wouldn't last a minute. Not dressed like that. Haven't you heard of the razor gangs? Govan is one of the places they like to hang about and God knows what they'd do to you if you stumbled across their path.' He shook his head. 'They won't touch you as long as you're with me – I've helped too many of them out of a tight spot.'

'Helped them? Why? Aren't they thugs and murderers?'

'They are not always guilty of what they're accused of. Besides, every man has the right to justice.' His mouth turned up at the corners. 'I work nights because during the day I work at Reid's the solicitors. I expect to qualify in a few months and after that, who knows? Perhaps take my bar exams.' His smile grew wider and a dimple appeared in his left cheek. 'You see, Miss Bannatyne, you weren't the only one with a dream.'

Chapter 2

They took the Subway to Govan. Margaret had never used it before – there had never been any call to. Most days she walked to the university or hospital or, if the fog was too thick or if it was raining, the chauffeur took her.

The damp, foul-smelling tunnel was claustrophobic and the tightly packed platform worse.

Once seated, she was acutely aware of Alasdair's thigh pressing against her leg as the carriage rocked from side to side, forcing her against him. When he put his arm round her to steady her, she could smell the soap he used. She stole a glance up at him. Even with the stubble on his face, he was an extraordinarily good-looking man. She pushed herself upright. What on earth was she thinking – and what had possessed her to go with him?

She was relieved when they alighted at Govan station and once more into the daylight. Not that there was too much of that. Thick smoke hung in clouds, obscuring the sun that had shone down on the West End. In contrast to the elegant town-houses in that part of the city, the tenements here were squashed together, most of them looking as if they hadn't been repaired since they'd been built. Towering over them were the cranes of the shipyard silhouetted against the skyline, the smell of soot and coal and the sound of steel rendering steel, reminding her of her visit there eight years ago.

The streets were jam-packed with groups of men and women standing around gossiping while children amused themselves nearby. At first it all seemed little different to Partick but when she looked closer she noticed that most of the children were barefoot, wearing clothes that, judging by the number of holes in them, had clearly been passed down from child to child. And instead of balls and hoops, the children played in the rubbish-strewn streets with whatever they could find, using bits of broken pottery to mark out lines for hopscotch, or pushing metal rims salvaged from old prams with sticks. The games were the same as children played everywhere, but these children looked cold and gaunt-eyed and almost all of them had running noses and, no doubt, lice.

'I'll take you in to meet Toni and his wife Mairi first,' Alasdair said, nodding in the direction of several people as they passed. The men doffed their caps in return and despite their laughing remarks, most of which she couldn't follow but suspected involved her, she could tell they held Alasdair in genuine high regard. 'I worked with Toni at the shipyard,' Alasdair continued, 'but he was laid off three years ago and hasn't worked since – probably because he took part in the strike in twenty-six. Your father has no time for strikers.'

Did everything have to come back to her father? She bit back the retort that rose to her lips.

The tenement where Toni and Mairi lived was up a narrow back street which was even more full of rubbish than the last one and Margaret had to watch where she put her feet. The close had last been painted many years ago judging by the peeling paint and green algae clinging to it. The damp was immediately evident and seemed to seep almost instantaneously into Margaret's bones.

Alasdair, however, seemed not to notice. He took the stairs two at a time, stopping by some doors to call out a greeting. On each landing was a shared lavatory, some of which were cleanish, and outside one a woman holding a pail of strong-smelling urine was waiting her turn. She looked at Margaret and blushed a deep red, doing her best to shield the pail from Margaret's sight.

Toni and his family lived on the fourth floor. As they passed each flat, Alasdair pointed out the little brass plates on the doors, telling her that it was the ticket system. Each floor, he said, had been divided then subdivided into single rooms in order to accommodate the ever-increasing numbers of families that had flooded into Glasgow in search of work. She told Alasdair she already knew about the ticket system. In an attempt to limit overcrowding, Glasgow City Council had sent out sanitary inspectors to decide how many people could safely live in each flat. That number was on the little plaque and the sanitary inspectors would carry out periodic visits, most often at night, in an attempt to ensure that the numbers were being adhered to.

'Of course they aren't,' Alasdair finished. 'It's not as if there is anywhere else for them to go. Except the streets. And they'd be lifted from there by the polis and sent on their way. At least this way they have a home of sorts.'

He knocked on a door. Margaret studied the plaque while they waited for it to be answered. Five. Five in a single end? Surely not?

The door was opened by a pretty woman in a well-worn dress, her blonde wavy hair partly hidden under a scarf. She broke into a smile as soon as she saw Alasdair. 'Well now, it's yourself. Come in, come in. Toni won't be long. He'll be glad to see you.'

She had the same soft Highland accent Margaret had often heard from the nurses in the Western and which she found very easy to listen to.

Alasdair introduced the two women. If Mairi

recognised her name she gave no sign of it.

'I'll no' be shaking your hands at the moment,' she said to Margaret. 'I'm just after changing the baby's nappy and I've yet to wash my hands.' While she was speaking her fingers fluttered nervously. 'Please excuse the mess. Here now, Johnny! Am I not after telling you to get the weans outside so I can get cleared up?'

Johnny, a boy of around six with the same pudding-style haircut she'd seen on all the children in the street, wiped a hand across his mouth and stared at Margaret. 'Who's the posh wummun, Mammy?'

'Ssshhh now. Don't be rude. Go on. Out with you all.' Mam lifted a pile of clean laundry from a chair, looked around wildly and seeing there was nowhere else to put it, placed it back down. Margaret sat down on the vacated chair and as Mairi bustled around buttoning coats and hustling what seemed to be a gaggle of children, one of whom was in nappies and carried by his elder sister who couldn't be much more than three years old herself, out the door, Margaret looked around the room.

There was a large black stove set against one side with a long, wide mantelpiece on top of which jars and tins of all shapes and sizes jostled for space. A sink, with a wooden worktop on either side, was set against a grimy window, a large dresser containing plates, pots and pans took up most of the wall opposite and a double bed was tucked into the recess of the third wall. Apart from the chair she was sitting on there was only one other, a large threadbare armchair next to the stove. A pulley, heavily laden with washing, hung from the ceiling. She'd seen at least five children and with the two parents that made seven. Where did they all sleep? How on earth did they manage in this tiny single room?

'How many children do you have, Mairi?' Margaret asked.

'Seven. The older two are outside somewhere.'

So that made nine of them. Not just illegal to be all crammed into this space, but impossible to imagine.

The door opened and a heavyset man with a thick moustache entered. 'Alasdair! I heard you'd come. And that you'd brought someone with you!' He patted his wife's bottom. 'Have you made tea for them yet, woman?' His accent was an unusual, but not unattractive, mix of Italian and Glaswegian.

'They've just this minute arrived, Toni. I'll get the kettle on.'

'Use fresh leaves now,' Toni said to his wife. He perched on the end of the bed and grinned. 'Now who is this good lady? Aren't you going to introduce us?'

'This is Miss Bannatyne, Toni.'

'Not *the* Miss Bannatyne?'

'Aye the one and the same.'

The smile vanished from Toni's face. 'What have you brought her here for?' He turned to Margaret. 'Forgive my plain speaking. Nothing personal, you understand.'

Why *had* she come? Alasdair had been right. She had no idea people lived like this. She hadn't lied to Alasdair when she'd told him she'd visited

52

homes of the less well-to-do. As part of her obstetric training she'd attended twelve outdoor cases – most of which had been in the Partick tenements. Although she'd thought all the homes she'd visited sparsely furnished and cramped, they had been relative palaces compared to this one.

'Alasdair told me a little of what it's like for you. I wanted to see for myself,' she said, shifting uneasily in her chair. Mairi was bound to be as ill at ease to have Margaret here as she was to be there. It was one thing having a man witness your domestic disorder, quite another having another woman. But she was here now and however much she wanted to leave, she couldn't. It would be unforgivably rude. At least not until she'd had her cup of tea.

'Margaret is a doctor, Toni. She thinks I'm exaggerating about conditions her father's workers live in.'

Toni flushed. 'Not all the workers. The time-served trades do all right.'

Margaret sent Alasdair a triumphant glance.

'Yes, they do all right.' Alasdair returned Margaret's look. 'They can afford to live in decent houses, but how many of the workers have a trade, Toni? And as for the rest? Most are just labourers or – like yourself – unemployed. They live here, crammed cheek by jowl, earning barely enough to put food on the table. Italians, Irish, Scots, Jews, Catholics, Protestants. No wonder there's trouble, sometimes.'

'You must miss Italy, Toni?' Margaret said, thinking it best to change the subject.

53

'Never lived there. My father came here before I was born. He thought we'd make a better life for ourselves in Scotland. He was right. But it all changed after the war. The yards have been going through difficult times since then.'

'What do you do if one of the children is sick?' Margaret asked. She really wanted to know.

'We've been lucky. They've had colds and coughs – everyone has. It's the smog I blame, meself. There's others no' as lucky as us, though. There's not a family on this stair who hasn't lost a child. We nearly lost our Meg a year ago, but the wife pulled her through. Don't know how she did, but she did.'

'What was wrong with her?' Margaret asked.

'I don't know,' Mairi said over her shoulder as she fussed over the stove. 'I think it was whooping cough. She was making this awful sound. I just kept her in my arms and walked her up and down. I can tell you I was terrified out of my wits – said a few prayers that night, that's for sure – but somehow she pulled through.'

'Why didn't you take her to the hospital?'

'They wouldn't have taken us,' Mairi said, placing a cup of dark tea in front of Margaret. 'Toni doesn't have the card, see, since he was let go from his job.'

'The voluntary hospitals won't turn away a sick child whether the parents can pay or not,' Margaret protested.

'Aye, so some people say. They also say as many die in hospital as out of it. I thought it best to keep my child with me. Perhaps if she'd got worse...'

'Did any of the other children get it?'

'Sent them away to their gran in the country. As soon as I saw Meg was unwell.'

'That was a good decision,' Margaret said.

Mairi shrugged. 'I'm no expert. What little I do know I picked up from my Mam. She used to be a nurse.'

'Here?'

'No, on the Outer Hebrides.' Mairi smiled. 'That's where I'm from. Came to Glasgow to do my nurse training but then I met Toni and well ... that was that.'

'Next time one of them gets ill, let Alasdair know and I'll come out to see them,' Margaret said.

This time it was Alasdair's turn to look surprised.

'That's very good of you, er – Margaret – er – Doctor, but my wee ones are all fine at the moment,' Mairi replied. 'Same can't be said for Audrey's. A more sickly bunch you never saw. Mind you, if she kept her place clean they might not be so sickly. Not that there's much she can do with no money and that wastrel of a husband spending what little they do get.'

Margaret glanced around. Apart from being too small this little flat was spotless.

Catching Margaret's look, Mairi squared her shoulders, her eyes defiant and proud. 'Aye, we may be all squashed in together but I keep this place ship-shape. As best I can. It would help if there was running water. I can't tell you how many trips I have to make to the back close to fetch it. Keeps me fit though.' She smoothed her dress over her hips. 'Toni says I'm as trim as the day we married.' The two men had given up on the women's conversation and were conversing quietly, their heads bent close to each other. 'Mind you, my stomach will never be the same after all these children.' She winked at Margaret. 'Doesn't seem to put him off, though, if you get my meaning?'

Margaret laughed. She did indeed.

A short while later, the children, complaining that it was raining cats and dogs 'ootside', filed in bringing with them the scent of wet wool and, if Margaret wasn't mistaken, a baby's full nappy. With them inside it was impossible to think let alone carry on a conversation so she and Alasdair had taken their leave.

Despite the weather there were several children still playing on the streets, but as the rain began to fall in earnest, several windows opened and women leaned out shouting for their offspring to 'get upstairs', or 'get inside or they'd feel the back of a hand'.

They stepped back into the close as they waited for the rain to ease.

'It's not as bad here as you led me to believe, is it?' she said. 'I mean, everyone is poor – I can see that – but they have roofs over their heads and enough to eat.'

Alasdair stared at her in disbelief. 'Toni and Mairi manage well enough, but every day's still a struggle to feed themselves and their family, to buy clothes to put on their backs, even to buy coal for their stoves. But their family is one of the lucky few. I thought you'd realise that. If you really want to see how most people live, then come with me.'

Holding his jacket above her head to shelter her from the rain, he led her through a nearby back close and into the yard behind. Instead of a space for washing, or a small yard for children to play in, crammed in was another tenement block.

'This is the council's solution to lack of space. Over a hundred people live here. No wonder they call it the bad lands.'

Speechless, Margaret followed him into the narrow passage. The smell was indescribable: a nauseating mix of faeces, grease, decaying food, a combination she quickly came to associate with poverty and that would never leave her. There were no lights and the narrow walls seemed to close in around her.

'This way.' Alasdair took her hand and led her down a narrow staircase, the darkness deepening as they descended. He halted in front of a door and rapped.

A few moments later it was opened by a woman of about fifty. It was hard to tell. She was missing all her teeth except one at the front, and both her apron and her headscarf were filthy. It took every ounce of Margaret's willpower not to recoil.

'It's you, Alasdair,' the woman said, her expression shadowed in the semi-light. 'Have you brought something for me?'

'I'll be back with something later, Angela, I promise. Can we come in?'

'Aye. Well. If you want.'

The smell in the almost completely dark cellar – for that's what it was – was almost worse than the stench in the close entry. Margaret wished she could take her handkerchief and press it over her nose to block it out, but she couldn't – not without offending Angela.

The cellar wasn't more than eight foot by eight foot, and light filtered through the one small, narrow window set high above the straw-covered floor. There was no furniture apart from a single chair and no fire, nothing to take the chill from the air. This wasn't a home – it was a living hell.

As her eyes slowly became accustomed to the gloom, she saw there was a tiny figure lying on a bed of straw, covered only by a thin blanket.

'Hello, Lisa,' Alasdair said softly, crouching in front of the small bundle. 'How are you today?'

'I'm all right,' a small voice whispered back. The child's cough shook her tiny frame and ended on a wheeze.

'Is Lisa your daughter?' Margaret whispered to Angela.

'Not mine. My dead sister's – God rest her soul.' Angela crossed herself. 'But I love her as if she were my own, poor mite.'

Alasdair rose to let Margaret take his place. She dropped to her knees in front of the child and, pulling off her gloves, felt her forehead. It was burning. Next, she felt for a pulse. It was difficult to find at first and when she did locate it, it was rapid and weak.

'Has Lisa seen a doctor?' Margaret asked.

'Aye. We've no money but Dr Strong comes to see her when he can.'

'And what does Dr Strong think is wrong?'

'Pneumonia. In both lungs.' Angela lowered her voice. 'Nowt to be done, he says.'

It was as Margaret thought. Dr Strong was

right – there was no cure for pneumonia – but this little girl shouldn't be left to die on nothing but a bed of straw.

A shaft of sunlight lit the room for a few moments and, as it did, Lisa reached out for Margaret's hand, touching her engagement ring with her narrow fingers. 'Pretty,' she murmured. She looked up at Margaret and gave her the ghost of a smile. 'Like you. Are you an angel come to take me to heaven?'

Margaret swallowed the lump in her throat and tugged the ring from her finger. 'No, sweetheart,' she murmured back. She placed the ring in the child's palm and wrapped the small hand around it. 'You can keep it for me if you like.' It was a useless, pathetic gesture but all she could do. As fury and despair threatened to overwhelm her, she stumbled to her feet.

Alasdair left Angela's side and reached out a hand to steady her. 'Are you ready to go?' he asked softly.

Unable to trust her voice, she nodded.

He turned back to Lisa's aunt and touched her on the shoulder. 'I'll be back in a while with some food for you and the bairn.'

Outside, Margaret breathed in deep lungfuls of air. Compared to the fetid atmosphere in the cellar, even the smog that shrouded Govan was a relief.

'Why, you're crying...' Alasdair said. He gently drew the pad of his thumb across her cheeks.

Margaret pulled away as if she'd been stung. 'I'm not! It's this dashed soot-filled air.'

'I shouldn't have taken you there,' he said,

shaking his head.

'Why not? I said I wanted to see how people lived and you showed me. Dear God, it's worse than anything I've read in a Dickens novel. That child should be spending her last days in a clean, warm bed,' she took a shuddering breath, 'not like that. We have to get her out of there.'

'And take her where?' he continued, his voice as gentle as his touch had been. 'The hospitals won't admit hopeless cases, you know that. Besides, there are hundreds like her.'

Margaret dashed the tears from her eyes with a trembling hand. 'Something has to be done.'

'Aye. But what?'

'I don't know. A hospital – right here for hope-less cases. A fund to help those who can't help themselves. Anything!'

He looked down at her, his eyes still warm, and something shifted inside her chest. 'You have a soft heart, Margaret Bannatyne.'

'That child needs more than a woman with a soft heart.'

'I know.' He took her arm. 'I think you've seen enough for one day. Let me take you home.'

Margaret blew her nose and squared her shoulders. 'Didn't I hear you tell Angela you were going back there?'

'It can wait.'

'No, it can't.' She forced a smile. 'I know you think I'm a spoilt rich girl who can barely manage to dress myself in the morning, but I am perfectly capable of finding my own way home. I can't say I care too much for the Subway, but isn't there a passenger ferry I can take across the Clyde?'

'Aye. It's how most of the workers cross the river. I'll walk you to where it picks folk up.'

As they approached the river where a boat was just pulling in from the other side, she turned to him and held out her hand. 'Good day, Mr Morrison.'

'I think you can call me Alasdair, don't you?' He held her hand for a moment longer than was necessary. 'I didn't think you'd last a minute here – I thought you'd turn tail and run. I was wrong. I was too quick to judge you and for that I'm sorry.'

She decided not to tell him that she'd had several moments when that was exactly what she wanted to do.

He looked as if he was about to say something more but, as the ferryman indicated he was ready to take on passengers, Alasdair gave a small shake of his head and released her hand.

Chapter 3

Arriving back at her parents' townhouse in the West End, Margaret couldn't help but see it with new eyes. It was part of a row of grand townhouses as far away from the smoke and noise of the city as her father could manage while remaining within easy reach of the shipyard.

Although smaller than Bannatyne Lodge – their home in Helensburgh – it still had several bedrooms, a drawing room and a morning room, each one furnished with the best money could buy, including handmade silk curtains from India and carpets imported from Turkey.

She'd never really considered her wealth before – she'd never had to. It was true that she'd treated many poor patients during her training, but they'd usually been cleaned up by the nursing staff before she was asked to see them. She had never, ever seen anyone who lived like Lisa and her aunt and, until today, had anyone told her, she wouldn't have believed them.

She looked at her watch. It was well after six. If she wasn't quick she'd keep Robert waiting. They'd arranged to go to the opera followed by a late supper. As she soaped herself in the bath her thoughts kept drifting back to Lisa. There had to be more she could do for the child and others like her. But what? There was nothing she could do about the pneumonia but the child might never have contracted the disease if she'd lived some-where warm and dry. At the very least she shouldn't be left to die in a hovel. As she'd told Alasdair, there should be a hospital for people like Lisa. A place where, even if they couldn't be cured, they could die in comfort and peace.

Her father couldn't know what it was like in Govan. Although Lisa and her aunt weren't em-ployees of the shipyard, as the largest employer in the area, as a man even, he had an obligation to the community to ensure their most basic needs were met. He should be badgering the council leaders, many of whom he knew personally, to take some action. She had to talk to him about what she'd learned. If he knew, he would surely do *something*.

Her thoughts drifted to Alasdair. Despite his disapproval of her and her father, she'd enjoyed sparring with him. In many ways he reminded her of her brothers. He had the same restless energy Sebastian had had, and the same gentle way of talking – at least to those he approved of – as Fletcher. She shook her head and stepped out of the bath. She should be thinking about Robert, not her father's difficult, disapproving employee.

She dried off and changed into the drop-waisted, beaded evening dress the maid had left on the end of her bed, finishing off her outfit with a pair of pearl earrings that matched her dress. She touched her lips with lipstick and dabbed perfume behind her ears. Finally she pulled on evening gloves and was ready.

'You look beautiful, as always, darling,' Robert said, rising to his feet when she entered the drawing room. Tall and slim, elegant in his tails and crisp white shirt, her fiancé looked as handsome as ever.

He crossed the room and kissed her on the cheek. 'I shall be the envy of all the men tonight.' He took up his usual position in front of the fireplace and grinned down at her.

'You are still coming to Bannatyne Lodge this weekend?' she asked, passing him a drink.

'Sorry, old thing. Meant to say. Father wants me in London for a week or two – possibly longer. You don't mind, do you?'

'Of course not.' She suppressed a flash of irritation. Wasn't he going to ask how her day had gone? Did he even remember that today was the last day of her exams? 'If we don't want to miss the overture, we'd best be off.'

Robert sketched a bow. 'In that case, your carriage awaits.'

The carriage was a silver Rolls-Royce, an older model than her father's, but grand enough. Robert didn't drive himself, preferring to leave it to the chauffeur. As Margaret settled into the plush leather seat alongside Robert she couldn't stop thinking about the children she'd seen that afternoon. How many people would the purchase price of this car feed? How many, the tickets to the opera? Yet she didn't even know how much they cost. She had no idea what anything cost – not a loaf of bread or a pint of milk. Not even this dress she was wearing, or her shoes. The outfit had been ordered by her from London and paid for by her father. She was given an allowance but she rarely had to spend it – whenever she shopped, she signed chits which were sent to her father to be paid.

All through the performance of *Madame Butterfly* and at dinner afterwards at Rogano's, she couldn't get the images of the people in Govan, and Lisa in particular, out of her head. More disconcertingly, she couldn't get Alasdair out of her mind either.

'You're very quiet,' Robert said, after the waiter cleared away their dessert plates. 'I thought you'd be in better form. Wasn't today the last day of your exams?'

'Yes, it was.' So he had remembered, he just hadn't thought it sufficiently important to mention before now.

'Didn't it go well?'

'It was fine.' She leaned forward. 'Robert, do you think we do enough for others – I mean people less fortunate than ourselves?'

'What's brought this on?' He steepled his fingers and studied her across the top of them. 'I think we do. Both our families employ hundreds – in your father's case thousands – of people. I would say that's good enough.'

'What do you do about the servants who are no longer able to work?'

'I have no idea. Pension them off, I suspect.'

'How can't you know? Aren't they your responsibility?'

'My father's responsibility. Darling, you know as well as I do that we are born into the place we are meant to be. We can't help it. You do your bit – more than your bit – and I do mine.'

'But what exactly do you do?'

He frowned. 'I'm not sure I care for this line of questioning. You make it sound as if you disapprove of me.'

'No, I don't. Of course not. But it shouldn't be a difficult question to answer. You're almost thirty and, as you say, your father takes most of the responsibility for your estates. As far as I can see you don't do anything except enjoy life.' Now she thought about it, she realised Robert was interested in very little except shooting and polo. Why had that never mattered before? She couldn't help but contrast his languid, couldn't careless attitude with Alasdair's pent-up restless energy, and, to her dismay, Robert didn't come out of the comparison too well.

'Is that so bad? When my father does pass away, I'll have more than enough to do. That's why I need to go to London – to see to his business interests.' He smiled. 'I shall miss you. I trust you'll miss me too.'

'Of course,' she said automatically.

Robert took her hand. 'Now you've finished your exams, we should set a date for the wedding. I was thinking about next summer.'

She did her best to hide her dismay. Yet she'd known this conversation was bound to come up sooner rather than later, and wasn't marriage to Robert what she wanted? He was a good, kind, undemanding man. It just felt too soon. Perhaps because she was over-tired and out of sorts? The visit to Govan had shaken her.

He frowned down at her bare fingers. 'You're not wearing your ring! Should I take that as a bad omen?'

She'd slipped off her gloves before they'd started eating and had completely forgotten about her engagement ring.

As she explained about Lisa, her voice wobbled. But Robert didn't appear to notice her distress. On the contrary his lips had tightened.

'You gave your ring to a child from a slum! Do you have any idea how much it cost?'

'Yes, I mean no. I'm sure it was expensive, but we'll get another one.'

'Get another one? And where do you think I'll find the money?'

A chill crawled along her spine. 'I'll do without then. You can't mind that I gave it away. That child and her aunt had nothing, Robert – nothing.

Between us we have more money than we know what to do with. When we marry I hope we can use some of it to help those less fortunate than ourselves.'

A strange expression crossed Robert's face. 'So you are still intending to marry me, then?'

'Of course.'

'Next summer?'

'I'm sorry, Robert, could this wait until you get back? I have a bit of a headache.' She withdrew her hands from his and rubbed her temples with her fingers.

His face softened. 'You do look tired, darling,' he murmured. 'And I have an early train to catch in the morning. Shall we call it a night?'

As he helped her on with her coat, he bent his head to whisper in her ear. 'I don't really mind about the ring, my love, it's just that I want everyone to know you're mine.' He kissed her ear lobe. 'I can't wait to make you my wife. Promise we'll set a date as soon as I get back.'

Chapter 4

When Betty, the upstairs maid, woke Margaret the next morning, it felt as if she hadn't slept at all. She'd tossed and turned all night thinking of little Lisa. The sooner she spoke to her father, the better.

Telling Betty to leave the tea tray on the table, Margaret dismissed her and sat at her dressing table to brush out her long hair. Dark circles ringed her eyes, making them seem a deeper blue. She didn't look like a bride-to-be who had everything to look forward to: she looked miserable, like a woman who'd been given a death sentence.

She laid her hairbrush down and selected a dress from her wardrobe that she particularly liked for the way it matched her eyes and slipped it on. Then she pinched her cheeks with her fingers and applied some lipstick. Now she looked more like herself. Like a woman who knew what she wanted and how to get it, not the pale version of herself that had stared back at her earlier.

She was pleasantly surprised to find her father still at breakfast when she went downstairs, although it was almost nine o'clock. Normally he left for the office before seven, having breakfasted alone at six. He rose to his feet, smiling broadly. He so rarely smiled that when he did, it was like a gift. Her spirits lifted. He was in a good mood which would make it much easier to broach the subject of Govan.

'Good morning, my dear. Did you sleep well?'

'Yes, Father,' she lied. 'Aren't you going into the office today?'

'In a while, but I wished to speak to you first.'

'And I have something I'd like to discuss with you.'

His smile grew wider. 'I thought you might.' He waited until she'd served herself with some scrambled egg from the side table and the servant had poured her coffee before indicating with an impatient flick of his finger that he should withdraw.

'Robert had a word with me yesterday, as perhaps he told you,' he said, when they were alone. He smiled again. 'He's asked me if I would be happy if you set a date for your wedding for next summer.'

She laid her fork down. 'I think it's something he and I should have discussed before he approached you,' she said quietly.

'The way of the aristocracy, I assume. We shall get used to it. Besides, we had other matters we needed to speak about. It only came up because it was part of that conversation.'

'What matters?' she said, baffled.

'Business, my dear. Nothing to worry your pretty little head about.'

She recalled what Lillian had said yesterday in the public house and a ripple of unease ran up her spine. 'This pretty head, Father, happens to have a good brain in it. What, may I ask, has our wedding to do with business?'

'It has everything to do with it. Connections are everything – especially the right connections.' He beamed again. 'He'll be Lord Locksley one day and you shall be Lady Locksley. That will make everyone sit up, eh?'

'Father, I'm not marrying for a title, I'm marrying for love. Besides I'm not ready to set a date.'

Her father frowned. 'What do you mean? You have been engaged this last year. Long enough by anyone's standards.' Her father threw down his napkin. 'You are twenty-five, Margaret. Many women your age are married with children. I've indulged you. I allowed you to go to university, but always on condition that when the time came you would do your duty.'

'Duty, Father? We don't live in the Victorian age any more. People marry for love, not for duty.'

'Other people, perhaps, but not the Bannatynes. Since Sebastian and Fletcher lost their lives, you and I have both known what is expected of you.' His voice softened. 'Had they lived you could have done as you pleased – my sons would have taken over the business and provided me with an heir to inherit.' He shrugged, his eyes bleak. 'Now you are all I have left and I only want what is best for you. I want you to be happy. Haven't I done everything in my power to do that? Given you everything money can buy – dresses, jewels, furs, trips abroad. All I do, everything I do, is for you – and one day your sons.'

She threaded her hands together and placed them in her lap, so he couldn't see that they were shaking. It was ridiculous to feel so nervous of one's father. 'You've given me everything you thought I wanted, Father, and for that I thank you. But it is not what *I* want.'

'Want? What has want got to do with it?' He placed his hands on the table, and glowered at her. 'It's time you gave all that doctoring nonsense up and settled down.'

'I can't! Not yet! I have a job, Father. I just need to work for a while longer. A year, that's all. What's the point in all the years of training if I can't make myself useful?' She swallowed. 'I visited Gown yesterday. Do you have any idea how people live there? They are without food, without a decent roof over their heads, without access to medical care. Many of them work in your shipyard or have worked there and have been laid off. Do you know what being out of work means for them? I'm sure you couldn't, otherwise–'

'What possessed you to go there?' he interrupted.

'I–' She knew that to tell him about Alasdair would infuriate him further. 'I'm a Bannatyne as you say, I wanted to see for myself how the people we employ – or used to employ – live. Surely that's what a decent employer does?'

He threw his napkin on the table. 'How dare you lecture me? What do you know about running a business? What interest have you ever taken before? Why do you think people pour into this city from all over the world? Because men like me and my father before me have made it wealthy.' He was breathing so hard, Margaret was becoming concerned. 'They had plenty when times were good – you never heard them complain then. But when times were lean – they wanted more. And when they didn't get it they went on strike! And look where that got them. If they don't have money they only have themselves to blame.'

'Father!' Margaret said, shocked. 'You don't mean that. What about the children? How can they be held responsible for their fathers' actions? And the wives – and those who can't work because they are injured – or sick?'

'You haven't a clue what you're talking about. That's why I need you to marry. A man would never think the way you do – a man would understand that a business has to be profitable.'

Margaret took a deep, steadying breath. This was not how she'd imagined their conversation to go.

'Please, Father, let's not argue. I haven't said I'll not marry Robert. I just need more time. He's away for a week or so. By the time he comes back from London, I'll be ready to set a date.'

Her father stalked to the door and flung it open. 'Just make sure you do because, my girl, if you don't, you may find yourself without a home or any way to support yourself.'

Reeling from their argument, Margaret sat stunned. Her father had never spoken to her like that. Then again, she thought ruefully, they'd rarely spoken at all – at least not about anything that mattered. But she wasn't a chattel who he could tell what to do! And as for her father donating money to Govan, clearly she'd been deluding herself. But when she married Robert she'd have control of her fortune and could do with it what she liked. If Robert agreed. Nothing in her conversation with him last night had indicated that he'd felt that they had a duty to others. However, she was certain that eventually she could talk Robert round. He loved her, after all – if only she could be sure how she felt about him.

You were until you met Alasdair Morrison again, a voice inside her whispered. She shook her head. That was ridiculous! She'd only met Alasdair twice, and he was difficult, contrary and disapproving. Yet – yet, Robert had never made her feel as if every cell in her body was alive, the way Alasdair had.

The realisation brought her up short. She was intrigued by Alasdair. He was different and she'd enjoyed sparring with him. But ... attracted to him? She was suffering from pre-wedding jitters, that was all.

She crumpled her napkin and pushed back her chair. Robert would return from London before long and then everything would be as it should be.

She paced the floor as the day stretched in front of her. There were all the books she'd promised herself to read, some embroidery she wanted to finish, or she could telephone Lillian and ask if she wanted to meet for lunch, but none of these options appealed to her.

She made up her mind. Returning to her bedroom, she redressed in a plain suit and the blouse she normally wore when working on the wards. Catching sight of the teddy she'd had since a child, she picked it up and stuffed it into her handbag. Back downstairs she pinned her hat to her hair, took her umbrella from the stand by the door, shrugged into her coat and lifted her medical bag. She was going back to Govan.

Chapter 5

Margaret took a tram to Partick and then the ferry, alighting at the same place she'd boarded the day before. The day was grey and miserable, matching her mood.

She'd only walked a few yards when a man wearing a leather jacket stepped in front of her.

'Now then, darlin',' he said, in a broad Glaswegian accent. 'Where might you be aff tae?'

'You're blocking my way,' Margaret said sharply. She was in no mood to be trifled with.

'Well now, so I am.' He made no move to let her pass and instead reached out and touched the fur collar of her coat. 'Very nice.' He grinned, revealing a mouth full of rotten teeth.

She slapped his hand away. 'Get your hands off me.'

The smile left his face and Margaret felt the first stirring of alarm. But what could he do to her in broad daylight? However, as two men appeared and took up a stance either side of him, her anxiety increased.

'Who do you have here, Billy?' one of them asked. He too was wearing a leather jacket. 'I doubt the missus will be too pleased to find you've got a new girl.'

Glancing around she noticed several people watching but none of them made a move to help. Amongst them was little Johnny – Mairi and Toni's son. The child caught her eye and darted away. She couldn't blame him. What help could a child not much higher than her knee offer?

'I'm not his girl,' Margaret snapped. 'Now if you'll let me get on my way, I'll bid you good day.'

'I'll bid you good day,' the second man mimicked. 'You're going up in the world, Billy. Always knew you liked them posh.'

She lifted her chin and stepped to the side, determined to pass, but Billy moved at the same time, blocking her path. More men had gathered behind him and she could sense several others behind her. Now she was surrounded. Her heart was beating so fast she could feel the blood pumping in her veins.

Billy wrenched her handbag from her hand. 'What's in here then?' He opened it, pulled out the teddy bear and laughed. 'This'll no' buy much.' He tossed it on the ground and grabbed her medical bag from her other hand. 'This looks more promising.'

Margaret tried to snatch it back, but Billy held it above his head and out of her reach.

'Leave her alone,' a voice she recognised came from behind her and she almost sagged with relief.

'She your woman, Morrison?' Billy said. 'Well then. I would never have guessed.'

Alasdair stepped in front of her, shielding her with his body. 'Give her things back to her and get on your way,' he said grimly.

'I don't think I'm going to do that, Morrison,' Billy replied. He placed her bags on the ground and a knife appeared in his hand. 'You shouldn't have got involved.'

In the blink of an eye, Alasdair had grabbed Billy by the arm and shoved him against a nearby wall and placed his forearm across Billy's throat. He twisted the arm holding the knife up Billy's back and the knife clattered to the ground. 'You or any of your gang come within a foot of her again and you'll have me to answer to,' Alasdair snarled. The primitive, savage look in his eyes chilled her to her core.

'You and what bloody army, Morrison?' one of the men who'd been with Billy said, jutting out his chin. He moved his hand towards the wide leather belt he was wearing.

'Us, lad, us.' The group of men who'd been standing behind her stepped forward as one.

'This isn't the last of it, Morrison,' Billy muttered as Alasdair released him. 'You won't always have that lot watching your back.' With one last scowl in her direction, he and his companions disappeared into a nearby street.

'Thanks, Paddy,' Alasdair said to the man who appeared to be the leader of the group that had come to their aid.

'No bother, lad. You're one of us, like it or no. And we take care of our own.'

'I was on top of it.'

'Not much one man can do against three,' Paddy said affably. 'Billy's Boys don't fight fair.'

Alasdair grinned. 'Neither do I. Now you lot better get going before the polis turn up.'

As the crowd dispersed Alasdair took hold of Margaret's elbow and hurried her up the street. 'What the hell are you doing here?' he growled. 'Didn't I warn you about the razor gangs!'

She shook her arm free. 'Didn't you say that they owed you for representing them? Didn't look like it to me.'

'Not the Billy Boys, no. They have no reason to like me. They're dangerous men, not to be messed with. You were damned lucky I was at Toni's when Johnny ran up to tell us what was happening. God knows what they could have done to you!'

'I wanted to see Lisa.'

'You should have let me know you were planning on coming. I would have met you.'

'How was I supposed to let you know?' She glared at him, determined not to let him see how shaken she was.

Alasdair pulled a scrap of paper from his pocket and removed a pencil from behind his ear. 'This is my landlady's neighbour's number. If you ever get it into your head to come back, telephone at seven in the morning. If I'm not there leave a message for me. Now, I'll see you home,' he continued before she could respond, his mouth set in a grim line. 'Don't even think of trying to prevent me. You've had a shock.'

'Home? I haven't the slightest intention of going home. Not until I've seen Lisa and given her this.' She held up the teddy bear, noticing for the first time how sorry her childhood toy was with his missing eye and worn fur. 'I know he doesn't look like much, but—'

Alasdair stared as if he couldn't quite believe what he was seeing. Then he threw back his head and laughed. 'You constantly surprise me, Margaret Bannatyne.'

'Oh, for heaven's sake call me Margaret.'

He looked into her eyes. 'Margaret. Something tells me my life isn't going to be the same with you in it.'

Her already racing heart upped a beat. 'Is that a bad thing?' she asked softly.

His gaze deepened. 'No, I suspect it's a very, very good thing.'

She tore her gaze away from his. 'Can we go and see Lisa now?'

'We'll go in a moment. But first we need to let Mairi know you're all right. Toni is out and she was worried about you.' He smiled at her. 'Seems you've made a conquest there.'

'Just the one?' Her heart was still hammering.

Alasdair laughed again. 'Don't push your luck, Margaret Bannatyne.'

'Dr Bannatyne,' Mairi said, opening the door. 'You're all right, then. Thank the Lord.' She looked over Margaret's shoulder. 'Here's Toni now! But what am I doing leaving the pair of you standing at the door? Come away in. Let me just shoo these scamps from under my feet. Hey, you lot, out with you!'

Margaret stood aside to let several of the children scarper past her.

'I didn't expect you to come back,' Mairi said as soon as Margaret was seated. 'You shouldn't have come by yourself. Alasdair, didn't you warn her?'

Alasdair dragged a hand through his hair. 'I tried, but I think you'll find Dr Bannatyne has a mind of her own.'

Mairi looked her up and down and her lips twitched. 'Aye, well, I gathered as much. You look as if you need a cup of tea, pet, and with plenty of sugar in it.'

'Thank you, but I don't want to put you to any trouble.'

Mairi smiled. 'A cup of tea's no trouble. And if I have one too, it'll give me an excuse to take the weight off my feet for a minute or two. Here, let me take your coat.'

'I heard what happened,' Toni said to Alasdair.

'It was no big deal.'

'You humiliated Billy in front of his friends –

and a woman. He'll not forgive you for that.' Toni glanced at Margaret but his eyes held none of the warmth they had when he'd spoken to Alasdair.

'Forget it, Toni,' Alasdair said with a warning note in his voice. 'Let's go outside. I have something I need to talk to you about. It'll only take a minute.'

After they'd left, Mairi handed Margaret a mug of tea so strong she could have stood a spoon in it. 'Now then, Dr Bannatyne, what brought you back here?' she said.

'I wanted to see a child I saw yesterday and I thought while I was here I could see anyone else who needs a doctor. Audrey's children perhaps?

'Just bring a handkerchief – that's all I can say. And put a big drop of that perfume you're wearing on it while you're at it. Otherwise you'll not be able to suffer a minute.' She looked thoughtful. 'You could see them in here if you like. There's not much space but it's a damn sight cleaner.'

'You wouldn't mind?'

'No. I feel sorry for her and her bairns.'

The toddler crawled over and raised sticky hands towards her. Margaret shuddered inwardly but nevertheless obeyed the unspoken demand and scooped the child into her arms, surreptitiously checking for nits as she did so. Luckily there didn't appear to be any evidence of lice. There was, however, a nauseating odour coming from the cloths covering the baby's bottom.

'Let me take him,' Mairi said. 'I'll change him then put him outside in his pram. While I'm doing that I'll pass word around that there's a doctor in the house.' She grinned. 'My, my, I never thought

'I'd say those words. Imagine! I just wish we had a parlour I could take you into.'

'Here is just fine,' Margaret said. 'All I need is lots of boiling water and some clean towels. I have everything else in my bag.'

As Mairi moved the kettle back onto the stove, Alasdair came back into the room and sat down next to Margaret. 'Toni says to let you know he'll be back in a tick,' he said to Mairi.

Mairi looked as if she were about to say something. Instead she gave a little shake of her head and turned back to Margaret.

'I'll ask one of the children to fetch some water from the tap in the back close while I'm putting the baby outside and put some more on.' She grinned. 'We might not have much, but we can supply you with plenty of hot water.'

'Before I see anyone, I'd like to see the little girl I saw yesterday,' Margaret said, picking up her handbag and medical bag. 'I won't be long.'

Alasdair stood too. She knew there was no point in trying to stop him from coming with her. Neither did she want to. The thought of coming across Billy and his gang again terrified her.

Five minutes later they were back at the cellar door.

When Angela answered it was clear that she'd been crying. Dread crawled along Margaret's spine. 'Is Lisa–?'

'She passed away during the night.'

'I am so sorry, Angela,' Margaret replied, her throat tight. Alasdair's hand reached for hers and gave it a squeeze. 'Is she still here?'

'Aye. They'll be coming for her later.'

'Could I see her?' Margaret held out the teddy bear. 'I brought this for her.'

'It was good of you. She would have liked that.'

Margaret stepped past Angela. It took a few moments to accustom her eyes to the gloom but Lisa was where she'd left her the day before. Still on her bed of straw. But instead of lying curled up on her side she had been straightened, her little arms folded across her chest.

Margaret tucked the teddy in under the crook of her arm. 'I'm sorry, Lisa. I wish I could have done more,' she whispered.

She felt a hand on her shoulder and looked around to find Alasdair. She could almost feel the pity radiating from him.

'She's at peace now,' he said softly.

Angela stretched the palm of her hand towards Margaret. Even in the gloom, the diamond of her engagement ring sparkled. 'You'll be wanting this back,' she said. 'Lisa has no use of it now, but it made her happy for the few hours she had it.'

'You keep it, Angela. Sell it. It'll pay for the funeral and you can use the rest to rent somewhere more comfortable.'

'No. It's yours. We never meant to keep it.' She pressed it into Margaret's hand and smiled ruefully. 'Any road, if I tried to sell it, I'd only get a fraction of its worth. 'Sides, I'd be lifted by the polis before I'd gone more than a few feet. Wummen like me don't come by diamond rings. At least not honestly.'

Reluctantly Margaret took the ring back. She rummaged in her handbag for her cheque book and pen. She wrote the first sum that came into

81

her head, and signed.

'God bless you dear,' Angela said, her eyes widening when she read the amount. Within seconds it had disappeared into the pocket of her apron.

Back in Mairi's, Audrey was waiting for her with one of her children. It only took one look at his little bowed legs for Margaret to know that, like so many children in Glasgow, he had rickets. However, she needed to check whether he also had rheumatic fever – a common life-threatening condition. When she listened to his heart she was relieved to find it sounded normal. She pulled the child's vest down and turned to his mother. 'Give him some cod liver oil. And some fresh fruit and vegetables every day.'

'Now where would I get the money to pay for that!' Audrey blushed. 'Sorry, Doctor, but I canna remember the last time I saw a piece o' fruit that wasn't nicked aff a barra.'

Baffled, Margaret turned to Alasdair to translate. Mairi's accent was easy to understand but Audrey might as well have been speaking a foreign language for all Margaret understood of what she was saying.

'Some of the children help themselves to the odd bit of fruit when the grocer up the street isn't looking.' He sounded amused.

Margaret was horrified. 'They steal!'

Alasdair laughed. 'They don't think of it as stealing – more like borrowing something that they might repay one day.' His expression darkened. 'They shouldn't have to steal just to get something to fill their bellies.'

'Will an orange cure whit's wrong with his legs?' the boy's mother asked.

'No. I'm afraid not, but it might stop it getting worse.'

She didn't really think so, but she couldn't bear to tell Audrey that her child was likely to suffer from the condition for the remainder of his life – however long that might be. 'I know there's a doctor – a surgeon – who is trying a new procedure. He breaks the bones in the legs and resets them. He thinks it makes them straighter.'

'And where will we get money for this, doctor?'

'I don't know,' Margaret said honestly. She dipped into her bag for her cheque book again, but before she could lift her pen, Alasdair bent over and whispered in her ear. 'Don't,' he said. 'They'll never be able to cash it anyway.'

Margaret hesitated before replacing the cheque book in her bag. He was right. She was such an idiot. Of course, where would Audrey – or Lisa's aunt, for that matter – be able to cash a cheque? She opened her purse and removed all her loose change, regretting she carried so little cash. 'Buy him as much fresh fruit as this will pay for.'

When the mother and child had left, Alasdair turned to her. 'For God's sake don't offer them hope just to rip it away.'

'Och, leave the doctor be, Alasdair,' Mairi intervened. 'She's only trying to do her best. But,' she turned back to Margaret, 'Alasdair is right. You shouldn't give them money. Audrey's man will only spend it on drink. I doubt she'll manage to hang on to enough to buy a single apple.'

Alasdair pulled a hand through his thick dark

hair and smiled at Margaret. 'I'm sorry. I know you're only trying to help. Forgive me?'

She couldn't resist his smile. He was right, though – giving money was simply an easy way to salve her conscience.

Alasdair took a mug of tea from Mairi and sat down, closing his eyes. He looked tired, Margaret thought – more than tired, he looked exhausted. His eyes opened and he caught her looking at him and raised an enquiring eyebrow.

'Are you working tonight?' she asked, hoping she didn't look as red as she felt.

'Aye.'

'How do you manage? No one can work during the day and at night as well. It's impossible!'

'I only work mornings at the solicitors'. In the afternoons I study – or sleep.' He grinned. 'Sleep more often than I should.'

'And then you come down here.'

'I like it here.'

'And how do you find time to play in the bar?'

'Now you sound like my mother used to. My life suits me just the way it is. It won't be forever. Once I qualify, I'll give up working at the ship-yard then.'

'Really? And abandon everyone?' She couldn't resist the jibe. It was about time he experienced even a little of the discomfort he made her feel.

'I won't be abandoning them. In fact I'll be able to do more. I'll be able to give them proper legal advice as to their rights. Might even keep one or two of them out of gaol.' He winked at Mairi.

There was a knock on the door and another mother came in followed by several of her children. Margaret saw them all. Three had lice, two coughs, but the last, although undernourished, was otherwise healthy. As soon as she'd seen them, there were others waiting, forming an orderly, if noisy, queue outside Mairi's door.

As the patients continued to flood in, Margaret was acutely aware of Alasdair's eyes resting on her. She would look up and they would share a smile before she'd catch herself and look away, turning back to her patient, glad of a reason to hide her confusion.

He was good with the children. No matter how grubby they were, he'd pick them up and toss them into the air. It wasn't just them that liked him either. When he teased the younger women they would blush and giggle behind their aprons. This was a different Alasdair – a more relaxed Alasdair and she liked this one better.

Every now and then she'd overhear snippets of conversation Alasdair was having with the men who drifted in and out of Mairi and Toni's small home. It was almost always about conditions down at the yards – they didn't all work at Bannatyne's – but sometimes it had to do with rent arrears, threatened evictions, and once, some serious trouble someone had found themselves in with the law.

Eventually there were no more patients to see and Alasdair insisted on walking her to the ferry stop.

'You did well today,' he said.

'How kind of you to say so,' she said, not attempting to keep the sarcasm from her voice.

He stopped and looked down at her. 'Do you

know you are the most surprising woman I have ever met?' He raised his hand and pushed a lock of hair behind her ear. 'And one of the most beautiful.'

Her skin burned where his knuckles had brushed against it.

'I'm engaged to be married, remember.'

'So you say,' he said. 'But you and I both know that the only person you'll marry is me.'

Her heart skipped several beats. 'You mustn't say things like that.'

His eyes searched hers. 'Why not? If it's true?'

'I won't come back if you do,' she said, as the ferryman indicated he was ready to leave.

She clambered aboard, annoyed to find she was disappointed when Alasdair didn't follow her. She opened her purse. Dash. She'd forgotten she'd given all her cash away. She glanced over her shoulder. Alasdair was watching her with amused grey eyes. 'Can I borrow sixpence?' she said.

His smile grew wider. 'A Bannatyne asking me for money. Never thought I'd see the day.' He thrust his hand in his pocket and brought out a handful of change. 'Help yourself.'

She picked out sixpence from his palm. 'You are the most annoying man I have ever met,' she hissed, holding on to the side as the boat drew away. Alasdair ran alongside.

'As for coming back – I've no doubt you will,' he shouted. 'You won't be able to stop yourself.'

Chapter 6

He was right. The next morning at seven, she phoned the number he'd given her and, true to his word, he answered. Neither did he sound surprised when she said she planned to come to Govan that afternoon. Instead, he told her he'd be waiting at the ferry stop for her. She told herself that she was going back because she could make good use of her skills while waiting to start at Redlands, but deep down she suspected that was only part of the truth.

And so their routine was established. Every day at three she took the Subway or a tram and ferry down to Govan, where he would meet her. People were getting to know her and instead of eyeing her with suspicion, they would smile, the men touching their caps, the women raising their hands in greeting, the children abandoning their games of tig to run alongside her, asking for a penny. However, she'd learned her lesson and instead of giving them money she would bring an apple or an orange or a few sweets. Sometimes a woman would stop her and ask if she could see them or one of the children.

Alasdair always came to find her at the end of the afternoon – she saw some patients in their homes – and always insisted on accompanying her back to the West End. By unspoken mutual consent they always parted before they reached

Margaret's home.

She looked forward to their chats. He constantly surprised her – he was far better read than her, could read and speak Latin, and was gentle and funny but quick to condemn what he considered social injustice. To her relief, he never once repeated the remarks he'd made about marriage. She'd decided he'd been teasing her and pushed his comments to the back of her mind.

They discussed books and, more often than not, politics – the latter almost always leading to a furious debate. Alasdair thought the Russians had been correct to get rid of their monarchy but she couldn't agree. He was bitter about the General Strike two years earlier, insisting the TUC had betrayed its members by calling off the strike – leaving the workers in a far worse position than they'd been before. It was only the Communist party, he said, who continued to fight for workers' rights. Despite their differences of opinion, their conversation was easy and often he would make her laugh with his stories about the shipyard, or the things people came to ask him about – one woman insisting he find her cat for her. Sometimes as they talked his hand would brush hers and her skin would tingle.

Despite what she'd told herself, she knew she should keep away from him, but as long as she was needed in Govan she couldn't stop going. Besides, her job at Redlands was due to start the following week and they'd probably never see each other again.

Today, a man in a trilby and a suit stopped her just as she was entering the close where Mairi lived. Alasdair had left her there and gone to meet with some men in the nearby public house.

'Dr Bannatyne,' he said, 'I've been hoping to meet you.' He didn't look very pleased. He held out his hand. 'Dr Forrest.'

She shook his hand. 'How do you do? I've been wondering when I'd meet one of the doctors.'

'Is there somewhere we can talk?'

'I'm a little busy. Is there someone you wish to discuss with me?'

'Very well. We'll talk here. I gather you've been treating patients in this area. Yet you don't have a practice here.'

'I've only recently qualified. I'm about to start work at Redlands as a House Officer. In the meantime I've been coming whenever I can.' She waved her hand vaguely. 'There is so much disease, no wonder you and the other doctors are snowed under.'

'We see as many as we can.'

'But not everyone?'

'It's impossible. Each of us have thousands of patients on our lists.'

'Then I'm glad I've been able to help, even in a small way.'

'That's just it. You are not helping. You are seeing patients who are on our lists and giving them contrary advice. This is most irregular and we want you to stop.'

Margaret stiffened. 'I'm sorry if I have seen anyone who is your patient. But most of the people I see, as far as I'm aware, are not on anyone's list. They are either unemployed or the wives and children of the unemployed, and don't have either insurance or the money to see a doctor.'

'They find the money when they need it. But if you see them for free then there is no reason for them to save.'

'Save? Save what? You must know how they live. Most of them have to sell their furniture, their blankets, even in the winter, just to eat. For them it's a choice between staying fed or seeing a doctor. If I can help in a small way, I shall.'

'If you really wanted to help you'd have a practice here with the rest of us, instead of floating down from your ivory tower whenever it suits you.'

'It costs money to set up a practice.'

'Money *we* have had to find and need to recuperate to feed *ourselves*. We don't have the luxury of seeing patients for free. We have to make a living – if we didn't, we'd have to give up our practices here. You're a Bannatyne – I can't imagine you know what it is like to have to make a living.'

'Dr Forrest, I can see that I might have trodden on your toes and I am sorry. Perhaps I should have come to see you and introduced myself, but I had no idea that I would end up seeing patients.'

'Now that you know, I take it that you'll stop.'

'Stop? No. I intend to carry on as long as I am able.'

'And when you've had enough of ministering to the poor, when you get bored, what then?'

She held out her hand. 'Thank you for your advice, Dr Forrest. I shall think about what you have said. In the meantime I have patients to see.'

As always, Alasdair was waiting for her that afternoon. 'You're unusually quiet,' he said, when, it being less foggy and wet than usual, they were walking from Dumbarton Road towards Margaret's home. 'Did something happen?'

She told him about Dr Forrest and what he'd said. 'He has a point,' she said. 'I didn't think.'

'People needed seeing and you saw them.'

If only it was that simple. She'd been thinking about what Dr Forrest had said all afternoon. 'But he *is* right. I start my hospital job next week and I won't be able to visit Govan any more. They've come to depend on me.' She looked at him. 'You were right too. That first day, you said I shouldn't offer people hope, not if I couldn't follow through on my promises.'

'You've done more than anyone could expect and they love you for it.' The look in his eyes made her pulse race.

'And I like caring for them. I wish I could start a practice here.'

'But you can't?'

'No. Even the simplest practice needs at least three rooms – one for patients to wait in, one for me to see them in and another for a dispensary. And it's not just that. If I did have a practice in Govan, I would have to live close by. I couldn't travel from the West End in the middle of the night if I were needed. Babies have a habit of coming at the most inconvenient times.' She paused. 'Unless, of course, Robert agrees to finance a practice. Although I can't for the life of me see him living in Govan.' The image made her smile.

'You're not still planning to marry him?'

The sudden harshness of his tone took her

91

aback. 'He's my fiancé.'

'I know what he is, Margaret! That's not what I asked you.' He grabbed her hand and pulled her into a doorway. 'You must know how I feel about you. And I think you feel the same.'

Her heart stood still. Before she could speak, Alasdair had taken her face between his hands and lowered his mouth to hers.

The world disappeared as she pressed into him, returning his kisses with a depth of need that almost frightened her. This was how it should be between two people who loved each other. This was how it should be between her and Robert – but wasn't.

She placed her hands against Alasdair's chest and pushed him away. When he released her she stumbled backwards. 'You shouldn't ... we shouldn't ... it's wrong–'

'It's not wrong.' Alasdair was breathing hard. He gripped her arms. 'It's very, very right. Tell me, Margaret, has he ever kissed you like that? Have you ever kissed him back the way you kissed me?'

'You mustn't ask me that. I've promised Robert I'll marry him. He deserves better than this.'

'Then break it off.'

'I can't. I won't.'

'You have to.'

'Why, Alasdair?' She was almost crying. 'So I can marry you? We both know that's not possible.'

'Why not? Because you're a Bannatyne? I thought you had more courage than that.'

'I'm not as strong as you think.' She whirled away, knowing his eyes were on her until she disappeared out of sight.

Chapter 7

The next morning Margaret took the train to Helensburgh, telephoning in advance so the chauffeur would meet her. She prayed her mother would be in one of her better frames of mind – she badly needed her advice.

Only two weeks ago, her life had been happy – or at least content – but now everything felt wrong. If either Martha or Lillian had still been in Glasgow, she might have confided in them. She'd seen them both briefly before they'd left, but she'd not said anything about her trips to Govan – or about Alasdair, and they'd been too excited about their own plans to quiz her. But how she wished they were still here. She could telephone Lily in London, but this wasn't something that could be discussed on the phone.

Even if she never saw Alasdair again, it wasn't right to marry Robert when she didn't love him – and she now knew, with absolute certainty, she didn't. At least not in the way a woman should love the man she was to spend the rest of her life with. Yet they could have a life together. They were similar, they liked the same things. When they were married she would have access to her fortune and would have enough to set up a practice in Govan or endow a hospital there. She might not be blissfully happy with him but she could be content. Somehow, it didn't seem enough any more.

As soon as she stepped off the platform at Helensburgh station and into the bracing sea air she felt a little better. She'd always been happy here. Bannatyne Lodge was at the top of the hill with large gardens and a spectacular view of the sea as well as the harbour where her father still kept his yacht, although as far as she knew he hadn't sailed since her brothers' deaths. Her heart tightened as she felt a sudden pang of pity for her father. Everyone expected her and her mother to grieve, but had anyone thought how much the loss of his only sons had affected him? Within a matter of months he'd lost his two boys and their companionship and also, she now realised, his hopes for the future.

Kate, the housekeeper and the wife of Jim, the chauffeur who had met her at the station, was waiting for her in the hall.

'Oh, it's good to see you, Miss Margaret,' Kate exclaimed. 'We've missed you these last weeks. I'm not chiding you, mind – I know you've been busy with your exams and all. How did they go, anyway?'

'They went well, thank you.'

'You're looking awful skinny and tired, pet. Come away in and I'll get you something to eat.'

To her dismay, Margaret felt tears prick behind her eyelids.

After her brothers had been killed, and she and her mother had returned to live in Helensburgh, Margaret had sought out the company of the servants in the kitchen. Kate had gently, but firmly, removed her, telling her that her father wouldn't approve. Nevertheless, Margaret knew that Kate, and Jim, loved her. She blinked rapidly and swallowed hard. 'That would be lovely, but first I must see Mother. Is she dressed?'

'Aye. As it happens today is one of her better days.' Kate gave her a gentle shove. 'Up you go while I heat up some soup.'

Margaret ran up the flight of stairs pausing for a moment on the first turn to look out of the window. This was where she remembered her darling brothers best: their rapid footsteps on the stairs, the way they took three at a time, especially Sebastian, always so impatient to get where he was going. Here was where she still heard the sound of their laughter, their cheerful voices teasing her and the servants. Here was where she sailed with them and walked with them on the estate, they with their guns, her following after them like a puppy. Here was where they played cricket and kept their horses. Here was where their ghosts, although she knew there was no such thing, would have returned. She wondered if her mother felt the same way, which might explain why she so rarely came to Glasgow.

Composing herself, Margaret knocked on her mother's door.

'Come in,' a tremulous voice answered. Her mother was sitting in her armchair, facing out to sea. As always when she did manage to get dressed, her mother was all in black in a style of gown that had been fashionable during the war. Margaret crossed over to her and dropped a kiss on her mother's parchment-dry cheek. 'Mother! It's so lovely to see you up.'

A brief smile crossed her mother's face. 'Margaret. It's good of you to visit, child. Is your father with you?'

'I understand the yards are keeping him busy, otherwise I'm sure he would have come.'

'There's no need to lie to me, Margaret. Your father no longer has any patience with me.'

'You mustn't say things like that, Mother,' Margaret said, even though she knew it was true. Her father rarely made the time to come to Helensburgh. 'Why don't you, come up to Glasgow sometime? We – *I* – miss you.'

'I will. One day. When I'm feeling better.' She raised a fluttering hand to her brow.

It's what she always said. Her mother had seen countless doctors. They'd listened to her chest, felt her pulse, taken every sort of specimen they could and tested it, but the results always came back the same: negative. Whatever was wrong with her mother didn't have a physical cause.

'Why don't we try a little walk in the gardens. It's a beautiful day,' Margaret suggested.

'Perhaps tomorrow.'

Margaret sat down. 'I've passed my exams, Mother. I am now Dr Bannatyne. What do you think of that?'

'Does that mean you and Robert will be getting married soon? I do hope so. I would so love grandchildren.'

'I need to talk to you about that. Lately...' she trailed off. Her mother wasn't listening. She was gazing out the window and on to the garden.

'My boys should be out there. Sometimes I like to imagine they still are.'

Margaret shuddered, remembering the day the telegram came about Sebastian. It had been bad enough when news of Fletcher's death had reached them, but only three months later her father had come into the drawing room, holding a telegram, his face grey and his eyes moist. When he'd told them Sebastian was dead her mother had screamed – the sound bouncing through the house. Unnoticed, Margaret had pressed herself into a corner, horrified when her mother had launched herself at her father and pounded at his chest with her small fists.

Nothing had been the same after that. Her father had spent more and more time at the shipyard, barely coming home before bedtime, whilst her mother withdrew to her bedroom refusing to come out even for meals. Eventually the doctor was called out and decreed that what her mother required was fresh country air and rest.

Taking Margaret with her, her mother had gone to live in their house in Helensburgh but had continued to spend most of her time in her room, except for increasingly rare trips to their home in Glasgow at the weekend. Those weekends, empty days and cold silent dinners, apart from the clink of cutlery on china, were unbearable. Shortly after her sixteenth birthday Margaret had been sent to live with her father in Glasgow during the week as well as the weekends. She hadn't wanted to leave her mother, but she'd been given no choice in the matter. She kept hoping that one day soon the mother she'd known before her brothers' deaths would resurface. So far that hadn't happened.

'I miss them too.'

'No one can miss a child the way a mother does. No one.' Her mother reached over and clutched Margaret's wrist with her bony, blue-veined hand. 'You'll discover that when you have children.'

And there was the nub. She could no longer imagine having Robert's children. Even the thought made her queasy.

'I don't know what to do, Mother. I don't think I can marry Robert.'

'Why not? Hasn't that all been decided?'

'I know we're engaged but people break off their engagements all the time.'

'Not you. Your father will never allow it. Don't go against him, Margaret. Your father can be ruthless. Nothing must stand in the way of him getting what he wants. And, if he can't get a title for himself, he needs you to get one for him. Apart from a son to inherit his businesses, he has everything else he wants – certainly more money than he can spend in several lifetimes.'

'But Father loves me! He wants me to be happy.' She had to believe that.

'He wants you to be happy, but only if it makes him happy too. He needs an heir, Margaret, and you must provide it.' She laughed harshly. 'Why do you think he took you back to Glasgow when you were sixteen? Because he couldn't bear to be apart from you? No, he took you away from me, knowing you were my only comfort, to punish me for being ill, but more importantly because he wanted to make sure that you would meet only the right sort of men.'

Margaret recoiled. 'No! That can't be true!'

'If your brothers had lived it might have been

different,' her mother continued, as if Margaret hadn't spoken. 'Your father should never have let them go to war.'

'They would have gone whatever Father had said.'

'Fletcher wouldn't have.'

'What do you mean?' Margaret whispered.

'Fletcher didn't believe in the war. He was on the side of the anti-war protestors. He would have joined the Socialist Party if your father hadn't hated them so much.'

'I had no idea Fletcher felt that way. He joined up, after all.'

'He only enlisted because your father made him.'

'Father made him?' Margaret repeated, feeling sick.

'Fletcher could have been excused! Shipbuilding was protected, but your father wouldn't have it. He thought that some time in the army would toughen Fletcher up. Make him more fitting to take over the shipyards. Those damn yards. They cost me my son and your father is to blame!'

The venom in her mother's eyes stunned her anew. 'Mother! You mustn't say things like that.'

'Why not? It's the truth.' Her mother pressed her hands to her eyes. 'I'm tired now, Margaret. I don't wish to think about things that upset me any more. You and your father must do the best you can. I can't help you. I'm sorry. You must manage on your own.'

Chapter 8

That Monday, Margaret started her first official job as a doctor. Redlands hospital was a large red-brick building, set back from Great Western Road and not far from Margaret's home in Great Western Terrace. As the House Officer she was required to live in, and one of the servants had delivered her trunk to her rooms there earlier that day.

Everything about Redlands spoke of money and wealth. Originally the home of a successful Glasgow merchant, it had been bequeathed to the women of Glasgow by his heirs. Over the years, the house had been added to by the purchase of two townhouses on either side. Along with an operating theatre it had fifteen beds and a new, separate maternity annexe. While most women still delivered at home, some chose to follow the new fashion for having their babies in hospital, and the professional well-to-do women the hospital catered for would never agree to be admitted to Rotten Row alongside their poorer sisters. All the specialists, except for one or two of the visiting doctors, were women – Dr Gilchrist, the ophthalmic surgeon, being one of the first women to graduate in medicine from Glasgow.

Whatever Margaret's disappointment at not securing a post at the Rotten Row Maternity Hospital, she knew she was fortunate to be working alongside some of the most formidable and experienced women doctors in Britain.

Inside there was a large reception hall with a marble floor and marble pillars, its walls graced with paintings that wouldn't seem out of place in Kelvingrove Art Gallery. Ten of the families that lived in one of the Govan tenements could live here and still have room to spare. Thinking of Govan immediately led her to think of Alasdair. She hadn't seen him since the day he'd kissed her, but she thought of him all the time.

She was shown into Dr Quigley's office. The head of the hospital was a contemporary of Dr Louise McIlroy and although Dr Quigley hadn't served in the war, she'd gained a great deal of experience at the Royal while the male doctors had been away.

'Welcome, Dr Bannatyne. Please take a seat. Congratulations, by the way. We're always delighted to have another woman join our ranks. We know better than most what it takes. It behoves us to work harder than our male colleagues. Both at medical school and in practice.'

'Thank you, Dr Quigley. I'm looking forward to working with you. And looking forward to working here.'

'I daresay you would have preferred a resident's position at one of the larger voluntary hospitals. Never mind, it will come. In the meantime, the teaching here is second to none. Although you are now qualified we expect our doctors to keep up with the latest innovations. Our continuing reputation depends on it.' She sniffed. 'I can assure you we have no incidences of puerperal fever here. Just

101

as well. One case would be enough to close us down.'

The absence of puerperal fever, something that had plagued the larger hospitals over the years, was in no large part due, Margaret suspected, to the type of patient who was admitted.

'A clean white coat every day is an absolute requirement as is scrupulous cleaning of hands and instruments,' Dr Quigley continued. 'We also have a list of rules and regulations for visiting surgeons.' She passed a piece of paper across to Margaret. 'As you can see we insist that gloves and gowns as well as masks are worn at all times in theatre. Masks must be worn at all times in the labour suite too. If any of the visiting doctors attempt to refuse, you must alert me at once. Is that clear?'

'Perfectly. I have purchased several white coats. I assure you I wouldn't dream of wearing the same one twice.'

'Of course, of course. But we have to be sure. You do see that. As you're aware, your post is as House Officer, which means, at least at first, that you'll be confined to the hospital. I'll have one of the nurses show you to your room when we've finished. I think you'll find it comfortable.

'Now where was I? We plan to employ a House Surgeon after the summer, but until we do you will have sole responsibility for all the wards. You must see every patient twice a day and record their treatment and progress to present to the doctor in charge of their case. Most of us come in to see our own patients as often as is necessary, but of course if you have any concerns you must let me know immediately and I will contact their doctor or come and see them myself. You will be responsible for ordering any special tests that might be required, such as X-rays or other pathological tests, but of course you will test urine samples yourself. You'll have responsibility for all the obstetric cases but must notify the obstetrician or doctor in charge when labour has progressed sufficiently or if there are any circumstances requiring her presence. If necessary you will help with the anaesthetic both in labour ward and in theatre, where you may also be required to assist.' She slipped another sheet of paper across the desk. 'It's all written down. These are the rules for the House Officer. Everything should be clear. We might be a small hospital but we are a busy one. If there is anything you are worried about you may speak to me if I'm here, or the doctor in charge of the patient. Otherwise it will be up to you to make your own decisions. How does that sound?'

'Wonderful! Shall I get started?'

Dr Quigley's expression relaxed. 'I like it that you're keen. But I think we should get you settled into your room first, don't you?'

The work wasn't onerous and the time passed quickly. Every day she had a couple of hours off for supper before final ward rounds. On the third day, not feeling particularly hungry, she decided instead to go for a walk in the Botanic Gardens, which were immediately adjacent to the hospital.

She'd taken only a few steps when she heard a familiar voice call her name. She spun around to find Alasdair standing behind her. Her heart stopped. It had been almost a week since she'd seen him last. Almost a week of sleepless nights as she'd lain in bed thinking of his mouth on hers, his hands on her waist, the feel of his hard chest under her palms. Nights when she'd recalled every word they'd said to each other, her heart shattering into a thousand tiny pieces at the thought she might never see him again.

'What are you doing here?' she whispered.

'Did you really think I would give up so easily? I've been waiting here every day since Monday, knowing that sooner or later you'd appear.' He grinned. 'I tried to get inside to see you, but a fierce-looking woman in a nurse's uniform turfed me out. Something to do with being a man.'

'You should go,' she said.

'Only if you swear you don't love me.'

She couldn't. Of course she couldn't.

He stepped towards her and took her by the shoulders. 'I love you, Margaret Bannatyne, and I believe you love me too. If I'm wrong tell me and you'll never see me again.'

She could only nod. She had no idea what the future held for them, even if there were a future, but she was helpless to do anything to change the way she felt about him.

Alasdair took her by the arm and led her through the gate of the gardens and towards a part enclosed by hedges. He pulled her into his arms and whispered into her hair. 'I've never met anyone like you. I think about you all the time until I think I'll go crazy with wanting you. I never wanted to fall in love with a Bannatyne, but you crept into my heart from the moment I first saw you. You're everything your father isn't – good and kind–' He held her at arm's length, '–and so damned beautiful. No other woman has ever made me feel a fraction of the way you do.'

He pulled her back into his arms and she gave herself up to him, knowing, at last, she was exactly where she was meant to be.

Later, as they sat close on one of the benches, she turned to him.

'That day at the shipyard, my father said your father was trouble. What did he mean?' His eyes took on that wintry look she was coming to know so well.

'Before the unions, my father was always the one to stick up for the workers, and your father didn't like that. Even worse, he hated the fact that my dad didn't believe in the war. Dad thought it was just a ruse by the imperialists to make lots of money. And your father and many like him did just that. More ships were built on the Clyde during the war than at any time before.'

'But we needed ships!'

'Aye, so we did. To carry munitions and to bring more poor souls to their death.'

'The war had to be fought.'

'Did it? Are you sure? My dad wasn't the only one who thought it was wrong. Your brother did too. Many in the Labour and Communist parties thought it was wrong too – including the leaders.'

'Yet you fought,' she said.

'I didn't say I agreed with my father. I was young. I thought there was glory in fighting. I thought that we were fighting to make this a land fit for heroes. That's what we were told and, more fool us, we believed them. If anything our lives were worse when we came back. There weren't enough jobs for all the returning soldiers. Not nearly enough.' He sighed and as his eyes darkened, Margaret buried her head in his shoulder.

'My father,' Alasdair continued after a while, 'was one of those who called the strike in 1919. Do you know they used tanks and soldiers to break up what was a peaceful, legitimate gathering?'

Margaret didn't.

'Dad was arrested that day along with many others. He never worked for your father again. He was a broken man after that. He died less than a year later, my mother six months after him. I'm sure losing him was the reason she didn't fight the pneumonia.'

'I am so sorry.' She sat up so she could see him.

He took his gold fob watch from his pocket and rubbed his fingers across the case. 'My mother gave this to my father as a wedding present. It is all I have of them except,' he looked at Margaret, his eyes dark with remembered pain, 'the belief that the ordinary man, and woman, has a right to a decent life, free from hunger and cold. At the very least he should be allowed his dignity. After Dad died I took up the fight on his behalf, and your father hates me for it.' He turned the timepiece over in his hands. 'If I ever lose faith I look at this and I hear Dad's voice as clearly as if he were still alive.' He returned the watch to his pocket and gave Margaret a sad half-smile.

'But my father never fired you.'

'He couldn't. He would only have had another strike on his hands. Things were bad for the shipyards after the war and a strike might have put your father out of business as it did other yards which, by the way, he was quick to buy up. He couldn't stop us striking alongside the rest in 'twenty-six. Not that it achieved anything. All it did was make our working conditions worse and put more power in the hands of people like your father. He might be ruthless, but he's not stupid.'

It seemed that the father she'd thought she'd known was only a figment of her imagination. 'He won't be happy when I tell him I'm not going to marry Robert and that I'm courting you instead.' She shivered. Although it didn't bear thinking about, he'd have to be told.

Alasdair placed his hands on either side of her face. 'Perhaps if I was a better man I would let you go.'

'Don't you dare even think of letting me go, Alasdair Morrison.' She kissed him long and hard to make sure he understood, and they were both breathing heavily when they broke apart. 'It's my life, Alasdair, and I'll be the one to decide what to do with it.'

She usually had Sundays off, the occasional evening too, and this was when she would meet with Alasdair. She still hadn't told her parents about him and this troubled her. However, in a few months, Alasdair would have sat and passed his law exams. Her father was much more likely to accept a lawyer as a suitable beau for her than someone who, God help her when her father found out, worked in one of his shipyards.

She would tell her parents about him soon, but only after she'd told Robert. It was only fair. He'd had to extend his stay in London and he'd written to her apologising for staying away but telling her he'd be back as soon as he could. To her relief there were no words of love and no mention of setting a wedding date. Perhaps he too had realised that they weren't meant for each other? She hoped so. She wrote back, keeping her letters light and matter of fact. She couldn't break things off by letter. That would be cowardly and Robert deserved better.

Chapter 9

On her first afternoon off, she returned to Govan. As she'd hoped, Alasdair was there visiting Mairi and Toni. When he saw her, his face lit up and her heart tumbled inside her chest.

'Margaret, we've missed you!' Mairi said, turning from the stove. 'And we're not the only ones, I'm thinking,' she added with a mischievous sideways look at Alasdair.

'It's good to see you again,' Alasdair said, his casual greeting belied by the expression in his eyes.

There were one or two patients needing to see a doctor, but mindful of her conversation with Dr Forrest, she made sure they weren't on his or one of his colleagues' list before she examined them. After that she had a cup of tea with Mairi while Alasdair talked to Toni. When she got up to leave, he did too.

Although the sky was heavy with threatening rain, they took the ferry before starting to walk along Dumbarton Road. Her heart hadn't resumed its normal pace ever since she'd stepped inside Mairi and Toni's home and seen him there.

'I missed you,' Alasdair said.

'I missed you too.' At that moment the sky darkened and the heavens opened. Within minutes they were both soaked to the skin. For once there were no trams in sight.

Alasdair pulled her into a doorway. 'I live in the next block. Come on, let's go there. You can dry off.'

Margaret's heart leaped to her throat. She wanted to be alone with him, but to go to his rooms? Yet they couldn't huddle here in the close. Wordlessly, she nodded her agreement.

They crept up the stairs to the first floor, thankfully passing no one on the way.

He had two rooms – one a small sitting room with a door off which she assumed to be his bedroom. The sitting room, which also served as a kitchen, was sparsely furnished but clean. Along the wall with the window ran a worktop on top of which was a two-ringed electric cooker and a couple of pots and pans, a plate and a cup and saucer. In addition to a couple of armchairs on either side of a gas fire, there was a table laden with books on law, many of them half open. Once more she wondered at his energy. To hold down two jobs as well as study for his exams...

Outside, thunder crashed, followed by a flash of lightning. He left her for a moment, returning with two frayed towels, one of which he passed to her. 'It's clean, I promise.' He used the other to rub his hair dry, before bending to light the gas fire. It lit with a pop.

'Come and sit by the warmth,' he said.

Her teeth chattering, she did as he asked. 'I shouldn't be here.'

'You can't leave until the storm is over.'

He took his coat and wrapped it around her. He crouched in front of her and as she looked into his eyes the world seemed to stop turning. Very gently he took her face between his hands. 'I love you, Margaret Bannatyne. I'll never stop loving you.'

Her heart was hammering so hard she could hardly breathe. Her senses had never been so alive. She was acutely aware of the drumming of the rain, the clap of thunder, the rumble of a passing tram, the hiss of the fire and the feel of his palms against her skin. He smelt of grease and wood smoke.

He brought his mouth down on hers and everything receded until all she was aware of was the sound of their ragged breathing, the heat in her abdomen, the liquidness of her limbs.

When he pulled her to her feet, she pressed against him. She should stop this, she knew that, but she was powerless to do anything except return his kisses. He tipped her chin so she was looking directly into his eyes.

'I think you love me too.'

All she could do was nod.

'You can't marry your lord, you know that,' he said softly. 'There's only one person you're going to marry and that's me.'

She felt as if she were at the edge of a precipice, that the tiniest step would either take her to safety or plunge her into something strange and wonderful, but knowing that whatever she did or said next would change her life forever.

She sighed, wrapped her arms around his neck and pulled his mouth back down to hers.

Later, they lay in his bed, the sheets tangled about their limbs. She should have been shocked by what they'd just done, but instead she felt a wild, surging joy. All the restlessness and anxiety she hadn't even known she'd been feeling was replaced with a deep peace. It was as if her soul had been missing a part for a very long time. For once she wasn't worried about the future or the past. All she wanted was here, beside her in this room.

She ran a fingertip across his hard muscled chest. 'My hair must be all over the place,' she murmured.

'You have never looked more beautiful to me than you do now.' He propped himself on his elbow and looked down at her. 'All my life I'll remember this moment.'

'And I have never felt happier.' Sooner or later she would have to face the consequences of what she'd done. Dear God – Robert! She sat up, holding the sheets to cover her breasts. 'What time is it?'

Alasdair jumped out of bed and without the least bit of self-consciousness of his nakedness walked across the room, picked up his waistcoat and retrieved his fob watch from its pocket. 'Six.'

She scrambled out of bed, grabbing her clothes. 'I must go. Robert is coming back tonight and I have to see him. To tell him I can't marry him.'

'I'll come with you,' Alasdair said.

She shook her head. 'This is something I have to do on my own.'

Chapter 10

Margaret's heart was pounding as Robert pulled out a chair for her. It had been the wrong decision to agree to dinner. She should have suggested a walk or that they go somewhere else more private.

'So, did you miss me, darling?' Robert said, as the waiter laid a napkin across his lap. 'I'm sorry I was away longer than I said I would be, but matters were more complicated to sort out than either my father or I thought.'

Margaret took a deep breath. 'I–'

Robert glanced across the room and towards the couple who had just entered. 'Look, darling, it's Cynthia and Percy. We haven't seen them for ages. Do you mind if I ask them to join us? I know my timing isn't very good, but we'll have all the time in the world to talk, after all.'

'Robert–' She reached across the table for his hand but it was too late. He'd already beckoned the couple over.

Dinner seemed to go forever. At any other time

she might have enjoyed Cynthia and Percy's company – indeed she had enjoyed it in the past – but now, their anecdotes of hunting and trips to the country, the ostentatious talk of their wealth along with the way they treated the waiter made her cringe.

She managed to make a show of eating, while fielding questions about her work, until the restaurant was almost empty and Cynthia and Percy rose to their feet.

'Have to be off. Oh, sorry, never asked, when's the wedding?'

'Robert and I were just about to discuss that when you two appeared,' Margaret said, forcing a smile. 'We'll let you know.'

Then with final kisses and *let's catch up soon,* they were gone.

'Did you mean that, old thing? Were we going to fix a date over dinner? I'm sorry, I didn't think. I wouldn't have asked them over if I'd known.' He gave her a smile that once made her feel warm inside but now only made her want to cry.

'I can't marry you, Robert,' she blurted. She'd meant to lead gently into this conversation but there was no time. They were the last people left in the restaurant and the waiters were already setting up for the next day.

His brow furrowed. 'What do you mean you can't marry me?'

'I've met someone else.'

He leaned back in his chair. 'That's impossible. I've only been gone a few weeks. Unless, for God's sake, Margaret, don't tell me you've been carrying on behind my back.'

'I only met him since you've been gone.'

He covered her hand with his. 'It's because you were lonely. It's my fault. I'll make it up to you.'

She tugged her hand away. 'I wasn't lonely. I love him.'

A look of disbelief crossed Robert's face. 'Don't be ridiculous, Margaret. Besides, it's too late to back out now.'

'I know I should never have agreed to become engaged when I wasn't sure of my feelings for you,' she hurried on. 'But I'm sure now. I do care for you, Robert, but not the way a woman should for the man she intends to marry. You are a dear friend and I hope you will stay one.'

'A friend! Do you have any idea how far this has gone? Your father has loaned mine a considerable amount of money to pay off some of my father's debts – the rest to be paid off when we marry. Your father only loaned the money to mine because he understood that we were getting married and that the Locksley estates will eventually belong to our children. That's what I was doing in London. Meeting with lawyers and making sure everything went the way our fathers intended.'

A chill swept across her skin. 'Was that the business you were discussing with my father? Before you left for London?'

'What if it was? Margaret, we were – are – engaged. It was only natural your father wished to discuss finances with me.'

'And what did my father get in return?' she asked bitterly.

'A promise that my father would do what he could to secure him a baronetcy. Now don't you see why you can't back out?'

The chill was replaced by a hot wave of anger. 'So all I've been is a bartering tool. I marry you, your father's debts are cleared, and my father gets a baronetcy. Robert – how could you!'

'Why do you think I agreed to marry you,' he spat, taking her aback with his vehemence. 'You can't imagine there was another reason. Your father may be extremely wealthy but he's still a tradesman at heart and you a tradesman's daughter.'

'Robert, please!' His pride was wounded – that's why he was saying these things. 'I know I've hurt you, but...' She swallowed. 'Didn't you ever love me?'

'That's exactly what I mean about you being a tradesman's daughter. People like me don't expect to marry for love. We marry because it is advantageous to both parties. People in my class understand that. It is our responsibility. Our duty.'

'Oh, Robert,' she said sadly. 'I thought I loved you when I agreed to marry you. How could you have contemplated spending the rest of your life with me when you didn't love me?'

'Because, you little idiot, there would have been compensations. Business wasn't the only thing that kept me in London. I have a mistress there. If we had married I would have kept her from you, but I would never have given her up.'

Margaret folded her shaking hands in her lap. That Robert might have a mistress had never occurred to her. How could he? Yet, she wasn't much better. She had a lover too. At least she had the decency to do the right thing. 'Do you love

115

her?' she asked quietly.

'Why do you keep going on about that? Love has nothing to do with it. Your own father has kept a mistress these last years. You can't be so naïve that you didn't know!'

Margaret stumbled to her feet. The waiter appeared behind her with her stole. She huddled into it, trying to stop the shaking that had taken over her whole body. 'I'd rather live on bread and water than be wealthy and live how you describe.'

'You only say that because you don't know what it is like not to have money. I hope for your sake your new lover has enough to keep you in the style you are accustomed to, otherwise God help him.'

She slid the large diamond ring from her finger and held out her hand, pleased to note it was steady. 'Goodbye, Robert. I'm sorry things have ended this way. I hope my father doesn't expect the money he loaned your father returned, as I hope your father will keep his side of the bargain. Then we can all be happy without making monstrous lies of our lives.'

Chapter 11

Knowing she had to tell her father next, she went to the house on Great Western Terrace the following evening. To her relief her mother was there, having made one of her rare excursions to Glasgow. Her father hadn't yet returned from work.

116

'Are you staying for supper?' her mother asked when they were seated in the drawing room.

'I can't. I have to get back to the hospital in time for evening rounds.' She doubted if she could eat a thing anyway.

Her mother plucked at the neckline of her dress. 'I understand from your father that you may have news for us. He insisted I come to Glasgow to hear it.'

Margaret ran her tongue over her dry lips. 'Mother, I...'

Just then there was the sound of a door slamming and her father's voice rang through the house. Margaret leaped to her feet.

She waited until her father came into the drawing room. He'd always been a handsome man, but tonight he looked almost haggard. Her heart gave a painful thump.

'Margaret! To what do we owe this unexpected pleasure?' he said, his expression lightening. He poured himself a large whisky from the side table. 'Would you like a sherry?'

'No. Thank you. I would like some water, however.'

He filled a glass and handed it to her. 'How is work? Are you ready to give it up yet?'

'No, Father. There is something I have to tell you...'

'And what is that? I gather Robert is back. Have you come to let us know you have set a date for the wedding?' He sat down, crossed his legs and studied her. 'I must say, I'm delighted. The sooner we get him involved with the firm, the better.'

So that explained his welcome. 'I have broken it

off with Robert. We shan't be getting married after all.'

Only the ticking of the clock disturbed the deathly silence that followed her announcement.

'You can't be serious!' her father said eventually.

'I am, Father, perfectly.'

'Have you completely lost your mind? Everyone is expecting you to marry this summer. Robert's father and I–'

'I know about your arrangement, Father. Robert told me.'

'Your feelings are hurt – is that it?'

'I dislike the notion of being used, Father, yes. But that's not the reason I broke it off.' She took a deep breath. 'The thing is, I've met someone else.'

Her father narrowed his eyes. 'Who? Who the hell have you met? Someone we know?'

Margaret took a sip of water in an attempt to moisten her dry mouth. It was ridiculous to be so nervous. But the truth was, she finally admitted to herself, although he rarely raised his voice her father frightened her.

'Yes. In a way.'

'Who then? Out with it, girl.'

'He's working as a solicitor's apprentice at the moment.' She named the firm. 'He's only there part time but he expects to qualify soon and is seeking a permanent post.'

'Only part time? What kind of man only works part time?'

She forced herself to look him directly in the eye. 'It's Alasdair Morrison. He's night foreman in one of your yards.'

Her father stared at her as if he couldn't quite believe his ears. 'You are courting Alasdair Morrison! Then you are truly out of your mind.'

'Oh, Margaret,' her mother whispered. 'What have you done?'

'Just how long has this been going on?' her father barked.

'A few weeks.'

'A few weeks! You've been sneaking around behind our backs for weeks–'

'I should have told you before, I know that, but I had to tell Robert first. I knew you wouldn't approve.'

'And you were right. I would have put a stop to it immediately.'

'But you couldn't have put a stop to it,' Margaret said quietly.

Her father banged his glass down on the table. 'I thought I'd made it clear what was expected of you.'

Margaret looked over at her mother who refused to meet her eyes.

'Alasdair is only working in the shipyard until he qualifies. You should be glad that he's a man who isn't scared of hard work.'

'He's still a navvy! My daughter carrying on with one of my workers – you'll make us the laughing stock of Glasgow! And Alasdair Morrison of all people! That man has been a thorn in my side for years. I should have fired him years ago.' He swung back to his wife and glared at her. 'I told you, Elspeth, something like this was bound to happen when you persuaded me to let her go to medical school. I knew she would end up mixing with the wrong sort.'

Her mother shrank back in her chair.

'This has nothing to do with my going to medical school.' Margaret lifted her chin. 'Alasdair is a good man, otherwise why would I be seeing him? If you met him properly you'd see for yourself.'

'There is no possibility of your mother and I ever meeting him socially. But we'll say no more about it,' her father said, striding to the door. 'Tell him you're unable to see him again. I'm sure Robert will agree to forget all this nonsense.'

Margaret stumbled to her feet. 'I won't break it off with Alasdair!'

Her father stopped with his hand on the doorknob. He kept his back to her. 'Oh, but I think you will, my girl. I think you will.'

'That's where you're wrong. I will never marry a man I don't love. Look at you and mother. You can hardly bear to be in the same room together.'

Her father whirled around. 'How dare you speak to me like that!'

She and her father glared at each other. 'I dare because someone has to stand up to you!'

For a split second she thought her father was going to stride across the room and hit her, such was the fury in his eyes. But then he seemed to get hold of himself and, no longer able to support herself on legs that had turned to jelly, Margaret held on to the back of the chair for support. Was this really the man who must have once loved her mother? Who most certainly loved his sons. Who'd taught Margaret to drive when she was eighteen? Now she wondered if he even liked her.

120

Perhaps he'd wished she'd been the one who'd died instead of Sebastian and Fletcher. The thought chilled her to her very core. 'What do you have against him, Father?' she murmured. 'You don't even know him. Not really.'

'I know everything I need to about him. That man will never be permitted to come near you again.'

'May I remind you, Father,' Margaret continued, striving to keep her voice level, 'I am almost twenty-six. You can't treat me as if I were a child.'

'So be it. But as long as you continue to defy me you are no longer welcome in my home. As far as I am concerned you are dead to us!'

She glanced over at her mother, but despite the despair she could see in her eyes, she knew she was not going to get any support from that quarter. It would take more effort than her mother had to give.

Margaret looked her father in the eye. 'I won't stop seeing him.'

'In that case,' her father said, turning back towards the door, 'you have made your choice. There is nothing more to say. Furthermore, I shall be stopping your allowance. It won't take long, I imagine, before you discover that life without the comforts you are used to isn't the life you want to lead.'

'Then you don't know me, Father. You don't know me at all.'

But before she could add anything else there was only an empty space where he had stood.

Chapter 12

Every day after that awful meeting Margaret expected to hear from her parents, if not her father then at least her mother. But every day she was disappointed. She'd written apologising once again for keeping her relationship with Alasdair from them and imploring them to meet him, but so far, neither of her parents had replied.

She hoped, given time, they would come round.

This evening was the first time she'd been able to see Alasdair since the fall-out with her parents. However, one look at his face and she knew that he had bad news for her too. Her stomach churned as they walked slowly through the park.

Alasdair guided her towards their favourite bench. 'I've been let go from the shipyard,' he said as soon as they were seated. 'I assume it's because you told your parents about me.'

Margaret nodded, feeling sick to the pit of her stomach. 'They were asking about Robert. I had to tell them I'd broken off my engagement.'

'You broke it off?'

'Of course. I said I would.'

'Was it very bad?' His eyes glinted. 'I should have been with you when you told your parents. It would have been the right thing to do.'

'I meant you to be there, but perhaps it was better you weren't.' She shuddered, imagining how much worse the scene if he had been.

'The solicitors' office have told me they won't be keeping me on when I qualify after all – I suspect your father got to them as well.'

She knew immediately Alasdair was right. 'He says he will stop my allowance. I don't care about that, but he says he and my mother will have nothing more to do with me unless I give you up.'

Alasdair crouched down in front of her and cupped her face. 'My poor darling. I never wanted this. I know you care for me, Margaret, but do you care enough? Are you prepared to be with a man who, right now, has no way to support himself? Perhaps your parents are right? Perhaps we should part?'

'You don't believe that, do you?' she asked quietly. 'If being with you means my parents won't have anything to do with me, then so be it. I don't want a life that doesn't have you in it. I'd rather not know where the next meal is coming from than give you up.'

'You don't know what it's like to be poor and I'll not be the man to show you.'

'I have a job. I'm able to support myself.'

'I want to be the one to support you.'

'You'll find something else. I know you will.' She hesitated. 'The workers would strike if you asked them to.'

He shook his head. 'They would. But strikes are last resorts, Margaret. I'll not bring the men out, have them suffer weeks without pay, because of something that is between your father and me.'

And then she was in his arms, the warmth of his breath on her neck as he drew her tight against

123

him, holding her as if he couldn't bear to let her go.

'What will you do now?' she murmured into his chest.

He pressed his lips against her hair before pushing her gently away from him so that he could look at her. 'I've got two arms and two legs, haven't I?' He laughed. 'I'll find another job and another firm to take me on. Your father doesn't own the whole of Glasgow, you know.'

However, it seemed her father wasn't content with destroying Alasdair and his future, but hers too. When she returned to the hospital that evening she was summoned into Dr Quigley's office. The older doctor was unusually sombre – even for her.

'Please take a seat, Dr Bannatyne.'

There was no offer of tea, no friendly *how are you getting on?*

'I'm afraid that the board of governors are to meet to discuss terminating your employment at the hospital.'

Margaret's stomach knotted. 'There's nothing wrong with my work, is there?'

'On the contrary, you have the makings of a fine doctor.'

'Then why?' she asked, although in her heart she already knew.

'Your father is a major contributor to the hospital. He says unless the hospital dispense with your services, he'll withdraw his subscription. I understand one of the committee – Mrs Waterstone – is a close friend of his. It is she who raised the motion.'

Margaret's heart sank. 'Mrs Waterstone and my father have been friends for years, that's true.'

'Why on earth would your father exert pressure on the board to have you removed from the staff?'

'He and I have had a disagreement.'

'It must have been a serious one for him to take the line he has. Do you feel able to tell me what it is about?'

'Nothing more than my courting someone he doesn't approve of.'

'Is that all? Are you quite certain? Has there been any other impropriety I should know about? As you'll appreciate, we have every right to insist that the doctors working here have the highest moral standards.'

'I can assure you – apart from seeing someone my parents don't approve of and perhaps the sin of keeping it from them longer than I should have, I have done nothing wrong.' She was mortified and furious in equal measure. How could Father do this to her? It was unforgivable of him. If he thought she would capitulate and give up Alasdair then he didn't know her at all. Her mind ran on. She would have to find another post. The Asylum was the obvious choice. They were always looking for doctors and as far as she knew her father wasn't a subscriber. She could apply for a resident position which would mean she could live in. Mental illness wasn't the area of medicine she wanted to pursue but if it came to a choice between that and giving up medicine altogether, she would take whatever she could get.

'I don't wish to leave, but I see you have no

125

choice but to let me go,' Margaret continued, rising to her feet. 'I have patients I need to pass on to someone before I leave but I shall see to that immediately.'

'Please, sit down, Margaret,' Dr Quigley said, using her Christian name for the first time. 'I haven't agreed to let you go. I have no liking to be told what I may or may not do in my hospital, no matter how powerful or how rich the man.'

'What about the hospital committee? Won't they have the final say?'

'Yes. They will. But the committee is made up of thirty determined women, the majority of whom are either doctors at this hospital or who refer patients here. They, like me, are tired of being told what they can and cannot do. Many of them served during the war and proved themselves to be excellent doctors – at least as good as any man. Yet when the war was over, and even now, posts that they once held have been taken from them and given to their male colleagues. Not everyone feels this is unjust, but there are many who do. I believe that when it's put to the vote, common sense and justice will prevail.'

Margaret felt a tiny flicker of hope. 'But what about the loss of his subscription? Knowing my father, it will be substantial.'

'Do you remember Mrs Little?'

Margaret was unlikely to forget the lady with the uterine prolapse she'd seen near the beginning of her time at Redlands. The wife of a landowner, she'd been too embarrassed to visit her usual physician and had been suffering for years unnecessarily. Margaret had sorted her problem easily and

126

saw her at home every few weeks to check her pessary was still holding things in place.

When Margaret nodded, Dr Quigley continued. 'She's a good friend of mine. I took the liberty of speaking to her about you. I don't know what you did for her,' she held up her hand although Margaret had no intention of breaking her patient's confidence, 'and I don't want to know, but whatever it was she certainly took a shine to you. She's like me. She doesn't care to be bullied. She has offered to compensate for any funds your father might withdraw and to add some more besides. Don't worry, she's rich enough not to notice.'

Margaret swallowed the hard lump she had in her throat. The kindness of the women was unexpected. They might be doing it partly to stand up to her father, but for them to even think of it was so much more than anyone could have asked.

'I don't know how to thank you and the committee – or Mrs Little.'

'My dear, carry on working as hard as you have been. That's all the thanks any of us want.'

Chapter 13

Although she still had a job, despite his confidence Alasdair didn't find a solicitors' firm prepared to take him on when he qualified. Margaret was certain her father had something to do with that too. Neither was Alasdair able to find another shipyard to hire him as a riveter; instead he was forced to take a job down at the docks as a labourer. Unfortunately an ordinary labourer earned far less than a time-served tradesman, so Alasdair had to work double shifts just to pay his board and lodgings. On top of everything he still had to find the time to study for his law exams.

It made the little time they were able to spend together doubly precious. They spent most of it in his flat, her reading while he pored over his books, until inevitably he would look up, grin and pull her into his arms as they tumbled onto his bed. When the weather was fine, they walked in their usual haunt, the Botanic Gardens. Whenever she tried to treat him to even a cup of tea he would shake his head. Sometimes they visited Mairi and Toni. Unlikely as it had seemed only a few months ago, she and Mairi had become friends. Mairi knew Margaret and Alasdair were together but if she also suspected they were lovers, she never said. Occasionally Alasdair would bring his fiddle with him, and she always knew by the way he held her eyes when he was playing just for her. She would return his gaze, letting the haunting music envelop her, her heart lifting and falling depending on what he played.

Except the last time they were there, she noticed that he played a borrowed fiddle instead of his own. She waited until he was walking her back to the hospital before she asked about it.

'I lent mine to a friend,' he'd replied, not meeting her eyes.

She felt a pulse of anger. 'Don't lie to me, Alasdair. If you start lying to me, then what we have together means nothing.'

'Ssshhh! Keep your voice down! We don't want the whole of the West End to hear, do we?'

'I don't give a fig about anyone else!' She stopped and put her hands on her hips. 'I'm not moving another inch until you tell me where it is.'

He gave her that slow smile that always made her heart melt. 'I always knew you were a stubborn woman, Margaret Bannatyne. Very well, then. If you must know, I sold it.'

Her chest tightened. She should have known. It had been her birthday the week before and he'd treated her to dinner in a smart café, explaining that his sudden rise in means was from working some extra shifts on a building site.

She knew he had his pride, she just never realised how much. 'Oh, Alasdair! It was your father's fiddle, your most treasured possession.'

Fire burned in his eyes. 'No,' he said softly, 'you're the most precious thing in my life and nothing and no one matters more to me.' He stepped towards her and cupped her face in his hands. 'One day, I promise you, I'll be making enough money to afford to buy a dozen fiddles just like it.'

'But what of your dream of becoming a lawyer? What if you can't find a firm to take you on?'

The light in his eyes burned brighter. 'Don't give up on me, Margaret.'

'That will never happen – not in a thousand years.' She grabbed his shirt and pulled him towards her. 'As long as you promise that you'll never give up on me.'

'I could no more do that than cut off my arm.'

'In that case, you idiot, kiss me.'

They agreed to wait to get married until after he'd passed his law exams and secured a permanent position as a solicitor's assistant. Even though her time at Redlands was almost at an end, Margaret had gone to see Dr Quigley to tell her of her impending nuptials and to ask whether the board would see fit to keep her on until that time. To her surprise Dr Quigley had been warm in her congratulations. 'This country needs couples to marry and have children,' she'd said, clasping Margaret's hands. 'We lost so many young men during the war that it's important to bring new life into this world again.' The second surprise was when the board of directors agreed to extend her contract for a few more months. At least she'd be able to put aside some money for her and Alasdair's future together.

When Alasdair passed his exams and with marks so exceptionally high that he found a firm of solicitors who were delighted to take him on, they happily set a date for their wedding. It was a small affair. Margaret had written to her parents informing them that Alasdair was now a qualified solicitor and that they were marrying. She added that she hoped they would attend their wedding. When there was no reply, Margaret had to accept that they would not come. In the end there was only Lillian and Charles, now her husband, Dr Quigley and one or two of the nurses from Redlands as well as Toni and Mairi and a couple of Alasdair's friends from the shipyard. Despite the small number of guests, Alasdair had insisted they marry in church. 'It won't feel right,' he'd said, 'unless we marry in God's house.'

Her dress was a simple cream gown embellished with lace round the neckline. Lillian had insisted she borrow her diamanté tiara and she'd worn it with a small veil and the necklace her parents had given her on her eighteenth birthday. Alasdair wore the new suit he'd bought to celebrate securing a position as a fully qualified solicitor. She thought he'd never looked more handsome.

As she walked down the aisle on Charles's arm she wished it could have been her father giving her away. It should have been her father.

However, she refused to let her parents' absence spoil her happiness. When she stood next to Alasdair at the front of the church, it was with absolute certainty that she would give up anything and everyone to be with this man.

After the service was over, they went to an inexpensive hotel restaurant to have lunch. Alasdair had booked a cottage on the west coast for a few days but they'd be spending their first night as man and wife in the flat they'd found together in Garnethill and where they were to start their married life. It was more than they could really afford – with two bedrooms as well as a large kitchen, a separate sitting room, and an indoor bathroom with hot and cold running water. He'd also insisted they employ a daily and Margaret had quickly hired the services of Peggy, an older woman who had a kindly face and who had once worked as a maid at Redlands.

'My earnings can only improve with time,' Alasdair had said, when she'd queried whether they could afford it all. 'Might as well start how we

131

mean to go on. In a few years I expect to have enough saved to buy our own place.'

They were going to try for a baby immediately (Alasdair wanted five, she thought two was enough, so they settled on three) and with this in mind, Margaret hadn't taken on any new patients over the last few weeks. She would continue to look after the women who were already booked under her to have their babies but as they delivered, her case load would naturally dwindle to nothing. She had every intention, however, of returning to work as soon as the children were old enough and while she was at home she planned to keep up to date with medical advances.

After their wedding breakfast they took a taxi cab to their new home, which was on the top floor of a red sandstone tenement in Garnethill. At the foot of the stairs, Alasdair scooped her into his arms.

'You can't carry me all the way up!' Margaret protested.

'I can – and will – carry you to the ends of the earth if I need to.'

However, he was breathing deeply by the time he reached their front door. He put her down so he could retrieve the front door key from the pocket of his waistcoat, and once it was unlocked, he'd picked her up again and carried her over the threshold, kissing her thoroughly before placing her back on her feet. 'Whew, Mrs Morrison, I think you might have to lose a few pounds.'

She laughed and looked around their new home. Peggy had laid a fire in the grate and it still burned brightly. There were flowers in the vase on the

132

table and another small bunch on the mantel-piece. Her trunk had been sent on to the flat a week earlier and Peggy had unpacked all her belongings. Very little of her old life was in that trunk; only the things she'd taken with her to Redlands: some clothes, her coat with its fur-trimmed collar, three hats and her silk underwear. Everything else, apart from what she was wearing, had been left behind at her parents' homes with only the tiniest frisson of regret. Where would she wear her evening frocks and furs anyway?

She took him by the hand and led him into the bedroom. She'd asked Peggy to leave her pur-chase in the bottom drawer of the bureau and now she bent down to retrieve it. When she held the fiddle out to Alasdair a slow, disbelieving smile crossed his face.

'I promised myself I'd get it back for you,' she whispered.

'The same one?' He looked incredulous.

'It took me a while to find it, but I did eventually. The pawn shop had sold it on already and the new owner wasn't keen to part with it. Luckily I per-suaded him.' She didn't say he'd only agreed to sell it back to her at twice what he'd originally paid. Although it had cost her almost the equivalent of a month's salary, it was worth every penny to see the look in her husband's eyes.

He took the fiddle from her and caressed the wooden instrument with gentle fingers. Then he picked up the bow and, holding her gaze, played the same tune he had the day they'd met again in the bar. After the last notes died away he placed the fiddle back in its case, turned to Margaret

133

and looked at her with soft grey eyes. 'I still can't believe that God blessed me with you. You could have had anyone and everything you ever wanted yet you chose me.'

'You are all I ever wanted. I would live on bread and water for the rest of my life as long as I could be with you.'

He gripped her by the shoulders. 'It will take time and I doubt I'll ever be as rich as your father, but I promise I'll do everything in my power to make you happy.'

'Oh, my darling, I'm already the happiest woman on earth,' she said, stepping into his arms.

Elizabeth Elspeth Morrison was born one cold and wintry January morning in Redlands Hospital. Dr Quigley insisted on it. As soon as her daughter wrapped her tiny hand around Margaret's finger, she knew she had fallen in love for the second time in her life. It made it all the harder to understand how her parents, her mother especially, could continue to stay away from their only child. There was nothing Elizabeth could ever do that would make Margaret turn from her. She'd written to her parents again, telling them about the birth of their grandchild, but once more there was only silence in return.

But she had a new family now and it was to them she owed her time and energy. She threw herself into motherhood, putting all thoughts of her parents firmly behind her, and after a longer wait than she and Alasdair had expected, James Fletcher Sebastian was born almost three years after Elizabeth.

134

Margaret loved being a mother. Sometimes, as her children slept, she would sit and watch them, willing them to wake up soon so that she could hold them in her arms again. At times, however, when the children were sleeping and Alasdair was at work, she felt restless, as if something was missing. She adored her small family, knew she was the luckiest woman in the world, but deep down she still wanted to be more than Alasdair Morrison's wife and Elizabeth and James's mother. She wanted to be Margaret again. Dr Morrison. That, however, would have to wait until the children were older and attending school. In the meantime she kept up to date with the latest medical journals, paying a shilling or two to attend lectures at the Western Infirmary and sometimes leaving the children in Peggy's care so she could go to Govan and see as many as she could of those who were sick and didn't have the money for a doctor.

Three months after James's birth there was a knock on the door. Peggy opened the door and to Margaret's astonishment – and delight – her parents were standing there.

'Mother – Father! Please come in.'

Her father looked around her small, but cosy, home as if it were a hovel, but her mother came over to Margaret, took her hand and squeezed it hard.

Elizabeth hid behind Margaret's legs and peeped up shyly at the grandly dressed woman who was her grandmother.

'Mother, Father. This is my daughter Elizabeth Elspeth. Elizabeth, say how do you do to your grandparents.'

'You named her after me?' Margaret's mother whispered, her eyes glistening.

Elizabeth detached herself from Margaret and held out her hand to her grandmother. 'How do you do?'

Margaret bent down to pick up James from the pram where he'd been napping until the sound of strange voices had woken him. 'And this is James Sebastian Fletcher.' She placed her son in his grandfather's arms.

Her father held the tiny bundle as if he were holding precious china. 'He's a fine-looking lad.'

'He has his father's determination,' she replied quietly, 'as well as his eyes.'

'Where is he?'

'Alasdair? My husband does have a name, you know, Father. He's at work but I expect him back at any moment.'

'I have a proposition for you both. It's time to let bygones be bygones.'

Her heart gave a small leap.

'I'd like nothing better than for all of us to be friends.'

'I doubt we will all ever be friends,' her father replied, his gaze once more resting on James in a way she couldn't remember him ever looking at her. 'But we shall do our best. I – we – want you to come and live at home.'

'All of us?'

'All of you.'

'Alasdair too?' She had to be sure.

'Him, too. I want to spend less time down at the yards and I think it's time my son-in-law became involved.'

'You want Alasdair to come back to work for you?' She could hardly believe what she was hearing.

'Not *for* me, Margaret. With me. He needs to learn how to run the business and that will take a few years.'

A warm glow took hold in her chest and blossomed. This was the day she'd been waiting for. With her parents back in her life everything would be perfect.

A few moments later Alasdair burst through the door, his look of delighted anticipation vanishing as soon as he saw their visitors. He pulled off his scarf and handed it to Peggy. 'Mr and Mrs Bannatyne. To what do we owe the pleasure?'

'I was telling Margaret that her mother and I wish you and your family to come and live with us.'

'Do you indeed? What has brought on this change of heart?'

From behind her parents Margaret sent him a warning glance. 'Alasdair, please. Let Father have his say.'

Alasdair folded his arms and leaned against the bureau. 'Go on. I'm listening.'

Her father repeated his offer. 'Naturally James, as my heir, will take over when he reaches his majority.'

Instead of looking pleased Alasdair shook his head. 'My son will make his own way in the world – like his father and my father before me.'

'Are you saying no?' Her father barked. 'What kind of man denies his son his rightful heritage? Because that is what you are doing.'

Disappointment washed over her. So that was the real reason he wanted to heal the rift. He didn't want her – or Alasdair – or even Elizabeth for that matter. He wanted his grandson.

James, no doubt sensing the tension in the room, began to wail and Margaret took him from his grandfather.

'I've said all I'm going to say on the matter,' Alasdair said steadily. 'You and Mrs Bannatyne are welcome to visit us and the children any time you please, but we will be staying where we are.'

Her father picked up his hat. 'You are even more of a fool than I gave you credit for. Come, Elspeth, it's time to leave.'

'You shouldn't have been so quick to refuse him,' Margaret said when they were alone again and Peggy had taken the children to their bedrooms.

'You don't agree?'

'If you worked for my father you could change things. You could change everything! Don't you see? You could ensure the men have good working conditions. You could persuade him to put some of his profit into Govan to support the families of the men who aren't working. We could even build a hospital there.' It was still her dream.

'You believe that? After all he's done to you?'

'I know he's really only interested in James but you could have made conditions.' She gave an exasperated click of her tongue. 'You're so pigheaded sometimes, Alasdair. So protective of your pride.'

'If I worked for your father I'd be selling my soul, can't you see that? Day by day he'd have a

138

bit more of me until there was nothing left of the man who went to work for him – nothing of the man you married.'

'It doesn't have to be that way!'

'But it would be.' He shook his head. 'What about the men? They would see it as a betrayal. They would never trust me again.' He was still in almost daily touch with the shipyard workers, using his skills as a qualified lawyer to help them with their grievances.

'There's no point in arguing with you, is there? Not when you've clearly made up your mind.'

He reached over and pulled her into his arms. 'No, my love, there isn't.'

She sighed and laid her head against his chest. 'Despite everything, Alasdair, I miss my parents, especially my mother. And the children should know their grandparents.'

He threaded his fingers through her hair. 'I wouldn't stop them seeing the children, you know that. But not if it means giving up our lives to live the way your father wants us to. I promised you before and I promise you again, one day you and our children will have everything you could ever wish for.'

She shifted her head so she could look up at him. He was still the stubborn, proud man she had first fallen in love with, and would always be. And she wouldn't change a single thing about him.

'Oh, my love. Don't you know? We have everything we could ever want, right here.'

Chapter 14

If money was tight in the early years of their marriage, it became tighter still. The flat they rented absorbed most of Alasdair's salary and Peggy had to be paid. Then there were the occasional trips to the seaside, new clothes for their growing children, and a dozen other expenses such as the cost of coal, which Margaret had never had to consider before. Discovering how much everything cost had been an enormous shock. Until the falling-out with her father she'd never had to pay for anything, always ordering whatever she wanted without even asking the price, the bills sent to her father. She hadn't seen either of her parents since they'd called, her letters unanswered once more.

Money was tight for everyone. The crash of the stock market in America and then in Great Britain had almost destroyed the economy; ship building in particular. She'd read in the *Glasgow Herald* that almost a third of the workforce was now unemployed.

It was money that caused their first real argument. And it was a bitter one.

A few months after her parents' surprise visit Alasdair had taken on some pro bono work with the Scottish Transport and General Workers' Union. It would add at least another few hours onto his already busy week and was bound to bring him face to face with her father at some point. However, she knew how important the work was to Alasdair and supported his decision, even though it meant he'd have even less time to spend at home with her and the children.

On the whole she left their finances to Alasdair. After he'd paid their monthly expenses, he put a sum aside in a tin box tucked away at the back of a kitchen cupboard. That was their savings towards the house they hoped to buy one day. The rest of his wage he gave to her towards housekeeping and Margaret kept that in a different jar on top of the mantelpiece. She never counted it as Peggy was a shrewd haggler when it came to shopping for groceries, so there was always plenty left over. Occasionally she dipped into it to pay for her lectures and today was such a day. There was a Dr Hamilton over from America and Margaret planned to leave the children in Peggy's care for a couple of hours so she could attend his talk. But when she looked in the jar it was almost empty, with barely enough to cover the entrance fee. Puzzled, she went to the savings tin but there was nothing at all in it.

She wasn't unduly alarmed. No doubt Alasdair would have an explanation. When they'd finished supper that evening, and the children were in bed, Margaret brought the subject up. 'I know it wouldn't be Peggy – she's as honest as the day is long.' She refilled his tea cup and passed it across to him. 'Did you put our savings in the bank, sweetheart? It's just so I know.'

Alasdair looked up from his paper and frowned. 'Damn.' He brushed his hand through his hair. 'I should have told you. I'm sorry, I meant to, but

I've been busy. I knew you wouldn't mind so I gave some of it to the men who are out of work. They're pretty desperate, you know.'

'Of course I don't mind you making a contribution.' After all, they had food on their table, unlike those families.

Alasdair wiped his mouth with his napkin. 'Many of these families would have starved – or frozen to death – without the money those who could paid into the relief fund. I was better off than most so it stood to reason I put in the most. Even then there wasn't enough to go around.' His face darkened. 'I couldn't stand by and do nothing. You don't know what it's like to go hungry, but I do. I see these families most days. I see their pinched faces, their lips blue with cold, their children wasting away in front of their parents' eyes. Sometimes I can't sleep for thinking of them. When we advised them to take action against their employers, how can we stand back and let them face the consequences of that advice?'

She bristled. 'And that advice, Alasdair? Are you sure you didn't encourage them to strike because you have a deep resentment against my father and others like him?'

'You think I do what I do to get back at your father?' His mouth flattened into a straight line. 'You know me better than that, Margaret.'

'I thought I did.'

'I had to help. I only wish I could have done more.'

It wasn't just about the money – although Alasdair should have kept some aside for emergencies – it was the fact he hadn't discussed it with her beforehand. He was well aware of how she felt about sharing decisions. Women had so recently been given equal franchise with men and Alasdair knew how she felt about their hard-won rights. At the very least she expected the same equality within her marriage. However, he had been working long hours, so perhaps it wasn't surprising he'd forgotten to mention it. This time she would let it pass.

'I'll go there. Bring some food and whatever else we can spare.'

'That would be a great help.'

Her alarm deepened as she realised he was avoiding her gaze.

'It would mean asking Peggy to look after the children for a couple more hours each day, but I'm sure she wouldn't mind. Which reminds me, I need to buy our daughter a new coat. Her sleeves are almost up to her elbows on her current one and she could do with new shoes as well. We'll just have to use some more of our savings, but a pound should cover it. Did you deposit what was left in the bank?'

Alasdair scraped his chair back and thrust his hands deep in his pockets. She knew her husband well enough to realise he was deeply uncomfortable about something.

'The thing is,' he said, 'there's no bank account. I invested what was left.'

Margaret laughed. 'You are joking, aren't you?'

'It was an opportunity too good to miss. Someone I know – a client – is a chemist. He needed money for a patent on a new medicine he's discovered. It's a sure-fire bet.'

Margaret felt herself grow cold. 'A sure-fire bet? You've gambled with our savings?'

'Not gambled, Margaret – invested. I don't want us to be poor for the rest of our lives. I've already done our children out of their inheritance. I owe it to them to make sure they have a secure future. If this client comes good, we could make a very good return. Enough for me to buy my own practice and set you up in one in Glasgow.'

A wave of anger washed over her. 'Don't you think you should have talked it over with me first? I'm a doctor, remember. I would have been able to read the papers this client of yours has written. I might not have been able to understand all the chemistry but I would have been able to make a reasonable judgement about this drug he is patenting.' Was this how he really saw their marriage? With him making the financial decisions without her having any say? She had no doubt that they would never see the money Alasdair had invested ever again. 'And I do mind. Not about the money that you gave to the people who needed it. You're right there. If you'd have told me about the fund I would have agreed with you that we should make a donation. What upsets me is that you didn't discuss the other matter with me. I thought it was understood we would share that kind of decision.'

'I'm telling you now. My love, don't be angry. We'll save it up again.'

When he reached for her, she stepped back, shaking her head. 'No, Alasdair. It's not all right. You're more like my father than you think. This

144

is just the kind of thing he would have done.'

The ensuing argument had been fierce and had ended with them lying in bed, both staring silently at the ceiling.

Then a hand reached out for hers and squeezed it. 'I'm sorry, I should have discussed it with you first. I was wrong. But he was leaving for America and had other investors interested. I had to make a quick decision or lose out.'

'You could have told me afterwards.'

'I meant to, but there never seemed to be a good time. We hardly see each other.' Alasdair turned and raised himself on his elbow. 'Forgive me?'

'As long as you understand that it wasn't the money that made me angry, but the fact you didn't talk to me about it. I'm a grown, intelligent woman. Don't you see? By shutting me out, by keeping all this from me, you're treating me no better than my father treats my mother. Worse, even. I'm your wife, not your child. You have done me a great disservice.'

He traced the line of her jaw with the tip of his finger. 'I know how much you have given up for me. You hold my heart in your hands, you do know that?'

She felt herself soften towards him. 'As you hold mine in yours.'

'Now say you forgive your idiot fool of a husband who truly respects and admires you more than anyone.' He grinned down at her. 'And who misses you every moment you are not with him, who adores you...' – he punctuated each phrase with a kiss on her eyes, then her mouth, moving

145

to the base of her throat, his hand moving to the curve of her hip, '…who lusts for you.'

As always his touch set her body on fire, and her body arched towards him. She still had something she needed to say. 'You have to promise me, Alasdair, that you will never keep things like this from me again.'

'I promise.' He bent his head and kissed her deeply and then, inevitably, hungrily, they made love.

Chapter 15

Margaret was sitting in the front room embroidering the collar of a dress for Elizabeth's fifth birthday in two days' time, when there was a loud banging on the front door.

Hoping the noise hadn't woken the children, she hurried to answer it, wondering who could be calling at this late hour. Most likely someone looking for Alasdair. His reputation among the Glasgow East Enders as a man to turn to for advice and help had continued to spread wide and far.

She opened the door to find a young man on the doorstep. 'If you're looking for my husband, he's down at the union offices,' she said, 'although I am expecting him home any moment.'

Such was their routine these days. Alasdair would spend the day at his office, only popping home to have tea with her and the children, before heading straight back out again on union business.

This evening had been no different. There was a meeting with some men down at the shipyard – her father's, as it happened – about strike action they were planning over pay and working conditions. They'd had supper, then he'd read to Elizabeth before changing out of his good suit and into his older one from the days when he'd worked as a solicitor's apprentice. He said the men were more likely to relax around him when they forgot he was no longer one of them. He'd set off at seven. It was wet and windy but as always Alasdair was walking the couple of miles to the union offices. She'd kissed him, distracted, as James was calling her, and Alasdair had left, the door blowing closed behind him.

'Are you Missus Morrison? Alasdair Morrison's wife?' The lad had removed his cap and was twisting it nervously between his hands.

Something in his troubled expression sent a chill up her spine. 'Yes. But as I said, he's not at home. Is there something wrong?'

He shuffled his feet. 'I came to tell you that the polis have got your man. They're saying he killed someone.'

Icy tendrils wrapped themselves around Margaret's heart, drawing the feeling from her body. She clutched the doorframe for support. 'Alasdair? My husband? You must be mistaken–'

'There's no mistake. I was sent to tell you.' He took a step backwards and turned away. 'Your man's been taken to Partick Police Station,' he called out over his shoulder before hurrying back down the stairs.

'Wait!' she shouted but it was no use. He'd

gone. Closing the door, she leant back against it. This didn't make any sense! Was it someone's idea of a sick joke? But Alasdair *should* have been home by now. Grabbing her coat and scarf, she hurried across the landing to the flat opposite.

'Can you look after Elizabeth and James for me?' Margaret said when Grace answered. 'I can't explain just now – but I have to go out.'

Grace raised her eyebrows but, to Margaret's relief, didn't ask any questions. 'I'll come right over. They'll be fine with me, pet, don't you worry. Take as long as you like.'

'Thank you. Thank you. They're both asleep but should either of them wake up, tell them I'll be back soon.' A wretched, twisting fear still in the pit of her stomach, she hurried out into the street and flagged down a black cab. During the seemingly interminable drive to the police station, for the first time in years, she prayed. When the taxi pulled up she shoved a few coins at the driver and ran up the front steps.

'I'm Mrs Morrison,' she told the constable at the front desk. She was out of breath and panting. 'I've been told my husband's here. His name is Alasdair – Alasdair Morrison.'

The policeman made a show of looking in the large ledger in front of him, his stubby finger tracing down a list of names. Margaret resisted the urge to reach over and turn the book round so she could look herself.

'Ah, yes,' he said, just when she was ready to scream with frustration, 'Alasdair Morrison. Arrested two hours ago.'

Shock jolted through her. 'There has to have

been some mistake. Check again. It's Alasdair *James* Morrison...'

The policeman lifted his head and stared at her with eyes that looked as if they'd seen it all. 'Aye. The very man. The sergeant's with him now.'

'Take me to him.'

'I'm afraid that won't be possible.'

'I'm his wife. I insist I see him.'

'I don't care if you're Queen Mary, Madam, this man is under suspicion of murder. You can make arrangements to see him once he's transferred to Duke Street.'

Under suspicion of murder! The lad hadn't been mistaken. There had to be some explanation and the sooner she saw Alasdair the sooner she would find out what it was.

Margaret drew herself up to her full height. 'I'm Dr Morrison – William Bannatyne's daughter. He is a personal friend of the Procurator Fiscal and unless you wish to find yourself in very deep water I suggest you take me to see my husband.'

'Aye, I've heard that one a few times as well. Everyone seems to be friends with someone in high places.' He sighed. 'I don't make the rules, Madam, I just follow orders. But wait here and I'll get the Duty Sergeant for you.'

While she waited, Margaret paced the small waiting area, jumping every time a door opened. After what seemed like an eternity the constable finally returned in the wake of an older, stern-looking police sergeant.

'Mrs Morrison,' the sergeant said looking at her curiously, 'your husband is in the holding cell but you can see him for a few minutes. Constable Barrows here will escort you.'

Relief flooded through her. 'Thank you.'

'Don't thank me.' The sergeant's look was cold. 'I'm not doing it because of your threats, Mrs Morrison, which I don't take kindly to, but because I hope you can speak some sense into your husband. The sooner he tells us the truth of what happened this evening, the better for him. Would save us all a lot of time and trouble if he does.'

'What is my husband saying? Whatever it is will be the truth. My husband is a lawyer, not a criminal.'

But the sergeant had already turned away, as if she no longer existed. The constable lifted the lid of the hatch and motioned her through.

Their footsteps echoed on the grey concrete floor, and the stench of damp and unwashed bodies, even urine, flooded her nostrils as she followed him down a dark staircase to the cells below. Constable Barrows banged his truncheon against the steel bars. 'Morrison! Visitor!' He looked at his pocket watch. 'You've got five minutes – no more. I'll be right here.'

When Alasdair stepped forward from the shadows Margaret bit back a cry. His cheek was bruised and there was a large cut on his forehead. His shirt was covered in blood, the cuffs of his sleeves saturated with it. Altogether far more blood than would have been caused by any injuries she could see. He clutched the bars of the cell with manacled hands.

'Margaret! Thank God! How did you know I was here?'

150

She laid her hand on his. 'You're hurt!'

'It's not my blood. At least not all of it.' He smiled sourly. 'I've a bit of a bash on the back of my head, though. Bloody policeman.'

'What's this all about? Why have you been arrested? Who hit you? Whose blood is it?'

Even in the dim light she could see how shaken he was. 'I was walking back home from the union offices when I heard some commotion up ahead. Two men came running out from one of the back lanes.'

'Who?'

'The police asked me that already. Several times.' He shook his head in frustration. 'I don't know who they were. I couldn't see them properly. It was dark and they were too far away. I knew something wasn't right, so I went to look.' He frowned. 'I couldn't see anything at first, then I heard a moan. A young lad was lying on the ground. It was obvious he'd been set upon. There was blood everywhere.' Alasdair paused.

'Go on,' Margaret urged.

'There was a knife sticking out of the top of his leg and he was trying to pull it out. I told him to leave it, but he wasn't hearing me.' Alasdair shook his head again. 'I remembered that from my time in the army when men got pieces of metal or wood stuck in them from the explosions. In the beginning we pulled them out but one of the doctors told us that sometimes it was better to leave them in until we got the men to the field hospital. I put my hands round the knife to hold it still lest he do more damage.'

Margaret nodded. It was what he'd done when

151

he'd stopped the men from lifting the girders from Hamish until he'd applied a tourniquet. She was certain Alasdair's actions had saved Hamish's life. However, although she'd heard a surgeon give a talk on just this recently, not everyone in the audience had agreed with him.

'Someone must have called the polis,' Alasdair continued, 'because the next second they were there. I tried to tell them the lad needed to get to hospital and they were to leave the knife in him until he got there but they wouldn't listen. The next thing I know I've been hit over the head. When I came to, the policemen had slapped cuffs on me and were hauling me to my feet.' A look of anguish crossed his face. 'The lad was dead, I could see that. They'd pulled the knife out and he'd bled to death.'

Margaret tightened her grip. 'Oh, my love, he might have died anyway. But if you've told all this to the police, why are they detaining you? Surely they could see you were trying to help!'

Alasdair's eyes filled with confusion. 'They think I killed him.'

'But they can't!' She couldn't take it all in.

The constable who had been hovering nearby came and stood beside her, gripping her by the elbow. 'Time's up, Madam.'

Margaret shrugged him away and grabbed Alasdair's hand again, desperate to hold on to him for as long as she could. 'What do I do?'

'Go see Mr Mortram in the morning,' Alasdair said, referring to his employer. 'Tell him what I've told you. He'll help me get out of here.'

The sun was making a weak appearance through the smog by the time Margaret turned the handle of her front door. The children were still in bed, Grace asleep in the chair, snoring softly. Margaret touched her on the shoulder to wake her. The older woman stretched, belched and rubbed sleepy eyes. 'Everything all right?' she asked.

'A mix-up,' Margaret said, not wishing to lie but not wishing to be drawn into conversation either. Surely Alasdair would be home to have supper with them this evening. If he wasn't, then everyone would find out he'd been arrested soon enough.

Knowing there was no chance she would sleep, she removed her soiled clothes and wrapped herself in her dressing gown and made a cup of cocoa. Alasdair being arrested was nonsense. Someone somewhere would know who the real attackers were and come forward. Someone would have seen or heard something. She wondered who the lad who'd come to her door was and how he'd found out. Perhaps *he* had been there. Perhaps he had witnessed everything? If so, why hadn't he told the police? Unless he still planned to.

She felt some of the tension ease from her shoulders. It would all be sorted out soon. But Alasdair had asked her to go and see Mr Mortram, so that's what she'd do.

She washed and changed into the suit she kept for the times she attended lectures at the university. She wanted to create the right impression when she met with Mr Mortram, and the tailored dark blue skirt and jacket gave her a necessary boost of confidence.

153

Peggy arrived just as Margaret was finishing getting ready and Margaret told her what had happened.

'They think he killed a man.' She couldn't believe she was saying those words.

Peggy's eyes widened. 'Mr Morrison would never harm a fly.'

Margaret covered her face with her hands. The night had taken its toll. 'It feels like I'm in the middle of a nightmare but I'm not going to wake up, am I?'

Peggy placed an arm around her shoulder and squeezed. 'You have a good cry, lass. Just let it all out.'

Margaret shook her head. Now was not the time for her to fall apart. 'I have to go to his office. They'll know what to do.'

'What are you going to tell the bairns?'

'I don't know, Peggy. Perhaps they don't need to be told anything just yet. Not when their father could be home any moment. Just tell them Mummy's had to go out for a while.'

She kissed her sleeping children goodbye, pinned on her wide-brimmed hat and took the tram to the office where Alasdair worked.

Margaret had never met the partners of Alasdair's firm, but her husband had always spoken highly of them. Mr Mortram, the senior partner, was alone in his office when the receptionist ushered her in. He came towards her, hands outstretched, his expression puzzled. He was in his late forties with thinning blond hair and intelligent eyes.

'Mr Mortram, I'm Margaret Morrison,' she said,

taking his proffered hand. 'Thank you for seeing me.'

'Not at all. Not at all.' He indicated towards a pair of armchairs on either side of the fireplace. 'Please, Mrs Morrison. Do take a seat.' No doubt he was wondering what had brought her here.

Margaret did as he asked although she would much rather have remained on her feet and been allowed to pace.

'Is something wrong? Is your husband ill?' Mr Mortram asked.

'Not exactly.' As concisely as she could she explained what had happened.

His hitherto benign expression had changed while she was talking, his face becoming a mask of disapproval. 'Alasdair arrested for murder! But this is—' he stopped and shook his head. 'Mrs Morrison, I'm shocked and yes, to be perfectly honest, dismayed by what you've told me but I don't see how we can help. We're not criminal lawyers.'

'But you *are* lawyers,' she said stiffly. 'And Alasdair's employers – colleagues – friends – there must be something you can do?'

'It's a criminal lawyer he needs. I can give you a name, of course.' Mr Mortram pursed his lips. 'I warned your husband that his union activities would get him into trouble sooner or later. The movements he's involved with have a reputation—'

'This has nothing to do with his union activities or his political party,' Margaret protested. 'This is simply a mistake. He went to help that lad. If you knew anything about my husband you would know he's not a killer!'

155

'Of course not, of course not. I must speak to my partners and let them know. You must see that we can't keep Alasdair on. If he is acquitted–'

If Alasdair was acquitted! 'You are going to let him go?'

'You must appreciate our position. We have a reputation to protect. Your husband will understand that.'

Alasdair had thought she'd get help here. How wrong he'd been.

Margaret stood and held out her hand. 'If you'd be so kind as to give me that name, I'll be on my way.'

Chapter 16

The lawyer that Mr Mortram recommended had an office in West George Street and Margaret went there immediately, still determined that by that afternoon Alasdair would be released from custody and home with her.

Behind a typewriter in the marble-floored foyer of the grand office building sat a woman in her late fifties with frizzy grey hair and spectacles. Although she must have heard the door open and close behind Margaret, she looked up only when Margaret cleared her throat.

'I'd like to see Mr Johnston,' Margaret said.

The woman peered at Margaret over the top of her spectacles while continuing to type. 'Do you have an appointment?'

'No. But I need to see him as soon as possible.'

'Mr Johnston is a busy man.' She moistened the tip of her finger with a flick of her tongue and leafed through a leather-bound book on her desk. 'He'd be able to fit you in on the twentieth.'

'But that's more than two weeks away. I need to see him at once!'

The woman shook her head. 'Impossible, I'm afraid.'

Her attitude reminded Margaret of the more obstructive nursing sisters she'd come across when she'd been on the wards. The worst of them had protected the consultants as if they were demigods, not just from the training doctors but, even more determinedly, from the patients and their relatives. Margaret had no intention of leaving without seeing the lawyer. She knew how to deal with women like the one in front of her.

'I'm sorry, I didn't quite catch your name,' she said evenly.

'Miss Donaldson,' was the reluctant reply.

Margaret picked up the telephone receiver and handed it to her. 'Please tell Mr Johnston that Dr Margaret Morrison, daughter of William Bannatyne, wishes to see him. Immediately.' She hated that once again she was forced to resort to using her father's name but it was the easiest and fastest way to get what she needed.

Miss Donaldson's eyes widened and she made a show of consulting her diary again. 'Mr Johnston just happens to have a spare thirty minutes right now if that would suit?'

'It would suit very well indeed.'

After a brief call to her employer, Miss Donald-

157

son showed Margaret into Mr Johnston's office. The lawyer's room was reassuringly well furnished with a large mahogany desk and two deep arm-chairs. A Turkish carpet in reds and blues covered most of the floorboards and a large gilded mirror hung over an engraved marble fireplace.

The man behind the desk rose to his feet and, as he came towards her, Margaret took a moment to study him. He looked to be in his late forties and his deeply pouched eyes were kind and intelligent. Margaret was irreverently reminded of a St Bernard.

He held out his hand. 'How do you do, Miss Bannatyne.' He indicated to the chair on the other side of the desk with a sweep of his large hands. 'Please take a seat. Would you like some tea?'

Margaret shook her head. She had no wish to waste a moment of her precious half hour waiting for Mr Johnston to summon Miss Donaldson and then another agonising wait while tea was served.

Mr Johnston surveyed her over the top of steepled fingers. 'Now what can I do for you?'

'I'm here because my husband has been ar-rested. They say he's murdered someone. It's not true! I need you to get him out of gaol. Immedi-ately!' To her dismay her voice cracked on the last word.

Mr Johnston's bushy eyebrows crawled up his forehead. 'Take your time, my dear. Compose yourself.' He waited a few moments. 'Start at the beginning and don't leave anything out.'

She took a deep, steadying breath and repeated what Alasdair had told her, emphasising that they hadn't had much time to speak to each other. The lawyer listened carefully, but instead of leaping to his feet and insisting that they march down to the gaol to secure Alasdair's immediate release, he sighed, stood, and held out his hand. 'Thank you for coming to see me. I shall look into it.'

Margaret stared at him in dismay. 'Look into it? But surely we can get Alasdair released? Even if on bail?' Although how she would find the money for that she had no idea.

'My dear Mrs Morrison, I'm afraid the law doesn't work that quickly. It is more of the tortoise than the hare. I shall have to speak to the Procurator Fiscal and the police, establish what charges they intend to make, what evidence they have to support these charges and so forth. I also have to meet with your husband and confirm with him that he wishes me to represent him. All of this will take time.'

Margaret felt herself deflate like a pricked balloon. 'How much time?'

'I have other cases, as you can imagine. Let's say a week – no more than ten days.'

'Ten days! I want him home now! His work – we have children...' Her voice caught again and she dug her fingernails into her palms. She had to stay calm. 'At the very least can't you get him released while the police complete their investigations?'

'Mrs Morrison, you say your husband has been accused of murder. In which case, no judge will give him bail, never mind allow him home.' He slipped some papers into a buff-coloured file and looked at his fob watch. 'I'm afraid I need to leave for a meeting. Now if your husband agrees

159

and I am to represent him there are my fees to discuss. Miss Donaldson will let you know what they are.' His eyes softened. 'Try not to worry too much at this stage, Mrs Morrison. We may well discover that the evidence the police think they have is insufficient to make a charge of murder stick. In the meantime I suggest you go home and leave everything up to me.' He waggled the bushy eyebrows at her. 'As soon as matters are clearer I shall be in touch.' His mournful face broke into a smile, making him seem younger. 'With a spot of luck your husband will be home with you and your children before you know it.'

Whether it was the Bannatyne name that caused Miss Donaldson to mention an eye-watering sum for this first appointment or whether that was what leading criminal solicitors charged, Margaret wasn't sure. As she gave her address for the bill to be sent she wondered how on earth she was going to pay it.

And that was only the start of it. Miss Donaldson explained an advance fee would be required, payable as soon as Mr Johnston agreed to take the case, and more for an advocate should it go to trial. Although there was no way on earth she could afford the amounts mentioned, Margaret did her best to hide the fact from Miss Donaldson. She wasn't going to give the odious woman any cause to alert her boss that he might be taking on a client who couldn't pay him.

Instead she smiled, wished her good day, and walked out of the door as if she were used to agreeing similarly large sums of expenditure

160

every day.

Back on the street, her head spinning, Margaret thought about what to do next. She'd been hopelessly naïve to think that everything was going to be all right when it clearly wasn't. She pushed away the exhaustion that swept over her. Whatever Mr Johnston said, she had no intention of waiting to be summoned before she met with him again. In the meantime there was his fee to find. She rubbed her aching neck. 'Think, woman, think!' Her fingers brushed against the necklace around her throat.

It was all she had left of her old life, the only reminder her mother and father had once cared for her, and she'd clung to it even when times were at their hardest.

She walked down to Argyle Street and stepped into the arcade where most of the jewellers had their shops. She went into the first on her left and, knowing her face was bright red, asked the man behind the counter whether he'd like to buy the necklace.

He took it from her, examined the diamond with an eyepiece and offered her a sum which was a fraction of what she knew it had to be worth.

'Four times that amount and you'd be still getting a bargain,' she protested.

'Times are hard, as I'm sure you know,' he replied. 'There's more people selling than there are buying at the moment. It's the best I can do.'

She tried two other jewellers but had the same offers – a little less in fact – so retraced her steps and sold it to the man in the first shop. It was still only enough to pay the first part of Mr Johnston's time. She had to find more.

There was one obvious place she could go – her father. The money she needed would be a drop in the ocean to him. Surely, despite everything that had happened between them, he'd help her now?

Blow her father! She'd managed without him so far and she would manage without him now. Who else then could she ask? With Martha still in India there was really only one other person. Lillian.

Although they'd kept in touch over the years, they'd not seen each other since Margaret's wedding day. Lillian had only worked as a doctor for a short while as she'd fallen pregnant soon after her marriage and was now the surprisingly proud mother of three children – two boys and a girl. Her letters were full of them and their antics and it was hard to believe how disparaging she'd once been of women who gave up everything to look after their children.

Margaret hated the thought of going to her best friend, begging bowl in hand but, she told herself, she would find a way to repay her as soon as Alasdair was free and back at work. This was just another hurdle in her and Alasdair's married life. Justice would prevail, Alasdair would be released and they could carry on as before.

Feeling marginally better, she stopped at the post office and asked to be put through to Lillian's residence in London.

The sound of her friend's voice on the other end of the phone undid her and she burst into tears. She hadn't realised until that moment how she'd been holding in all her terror, her grief and her shock. She sobbed for several minutes, wasting more of her precious money and causing Lillian to demand whether she was all right, what about the children? Where was she? Was anyone with her? And for heaven's sake just tell her!

By the time Margaret could speak again, the first set of three-minute pips had been and gone. She dabbed at her cheeks with the sleeve of her blouse and composed herself before explaining what had happened, right up to the point where she'd seen Mr Johnston. Then she swallowed, the words sticking in her throat, and asked if there was any way Lillian could loan her a hundred pounds? She would, of course, pay it back as soon as she was able.

She expected Lillian to interrupt to tell her that she need say no more, but instead there was a long silence at the end of the phone and, for a moment, Margaret thought they'd been cut off.

'I am so sorry, darling, how awful for you all! But the trouble is I don't have any spare cash to send. This bloody awful Depression has hit us all.' Through the crackling line came the sound of a deep sigh. 'I would ask Charles, but there would be no point. He's a stuffy old thing and I know he would never agree. He'd be too worried people would find out. Our patients,' she gave an embarrassed laugh, '–his patients really – you know I haven't practised for years – would never tolerate it. I am so sorry, my dear, but you do see, don't you, why I can't do more?'

Margaret was too stunned to reply. Where had her once fiercely independent friend gone? The woman who would never have allowed her life to be dictated to by any man – not even her husband.

'I do have to say, it's quite the most thrilling thing that's happened to me in years,' Lillian said. 'I would come to you in a flash if I could.' There was a long pause. 'Forgive me, darling, that was a crass and thoughtless thing to say.'

It *had* been a tactless comment, but it was also the most Lillian had sounded like Margaret's once headstrong and daring friend.

'If I had money of my own it would be a different matter, of course,' Lillian continued. 'All I can manage is ten pounds. I wish it could be more. I shall wire you it immediately. And if you need to get away, you and the children are welcome to stay in my cottage in Perth. There's no one in the main house – but I think you'd be cosier in the Gatehouse – and it is larger than one might think. You'd be perfectly happy there, darling, and it would get you away from Glasgow. Charles can have nothing to say about that.'

'I'm not leaving Alasdair,' Margaret murmured. She was so embarrassed she could barely speak.

'Of course not. I do wish I could be there to hold your hand and lend an ear. You know I'd come like a shot if I wasn't due to give birth again in a few weeks and Charles – as my doctor – has absolutely forbidden me to travel.'

Good for Charles. When had he turned into the epitome of a Victorian husband?

'Please, Lillian, don't even think of wiring me money.' Ten pounds wasn't nearly enough to cover Mr Johnston's fees and now she was too embarrassed, too humiliated to take it. So she thanked her friend again, told her not to worry and that

164

she'd manage.

Margaret replaced the receiver. The postmistress was looking at her curiously, no doubt wondering about her tear-stained face and drawing her own conclusions. Margaret doubted she'd even begin to guess. She lifted her chin and returned her look, forcing the other woman to drop her gaze.

What now? What on earth was she going to do?

When she got home that afternoon, Peggy was giving the children their tea at the kitchen table.

Elizabeth got down from her chair and ran towards her. 'Where have you been, Mummy? You weren't here when we woke up and you've been gone for ages!'

Margaret picked her daughter up and hugged her. 'I had to go out for a while but I'm here now.'

'Where's Daddy?'

Peggy and Margaret shared a glance over the top of her head.

'Let's go into the sitting room.' She placed Elizabeth on the floor and gathered James into her arms, breathing in the baby scent that still clung to him.

She sat on the chair with James on her lap. Wrapping her free arm around Elizabeth, she pulled her close.

'Daddy's had to go away for a little while.' She hated lying but the truth was too complicated to explain to a child of five.

'But he never said goodbye.' Elizabeth's mouth trembled. 'He always says goodbye.'

'And he would have but he had to go during the

night and he didn't want to wake you. I said I would kiss you for him.'

'When is he coming back? Tomorrow?'

'I don't know, my darling. Perhaps a bit longer. He'll come home as soon as he can. He won't want to be away from us a moment longer than he has to.'

Elizabeth's eyes were wide and round as if she were giving her mother's words some thought. Then she popped a thumb in her mouth, a habit she'd given up a long time ago. Margaret didn't have the heart to chide her.

'Please don't be sad, Mummy. It makes me sad,' Elizabeth mumbled around her thumb, pressing her body into Margaret.

Margaret bit down on her bottom lip so hard it hurt. 'I'm only sad because I miss Daddy.' She forced a smile. 'But he'll be home soon. In the meantime you'll help me look after James, won't you?'

Elizabeth removed the thumb from her mouth and scrambled down from Margaret's lap. 'We'll look after him together.'

But Alasdair wasn't home soon. Not the next day or the days after that. Every afternoon Margaret telephoned Mr Johnston from the post office asking whether he had news for her, but the answer was always the same. He was making progress with his enquiries but had no firm news for her as yet. The moment he did he would arrange to see her.

Inevitably the story had made the *Glasgow Herald*. To Margaret's immense relief there hadn't

166

been a photograph of her or Alasdair accompanying the article and she wondered if her father had used his influence with the newspaper's owners to keep their photographs out. If so, she fervently hoped he'd continue to do so.

The dead lad – he was only nineteen – was called Tommy and her heart ached for him and his family. Margaret scanned the article, the hairs on her neck prickling as she read the name in full. Tommy Barr, youngest son of Billy and Betty Barr. Billy Barr's son! The son of the man who'd threatened her back in Govan. Had Alasdair known? He couldn't have. He would have told her.

Every day Elizabeth asked when her father was coming home and when Margaret told her she still didn't know, her daughter became increasingly subdued. James, her sweet, contented little boy, on the other hand, was almost oblivious.

While Margaret waited to hear from the lawyer, she methodically went through every item in her and Alasdair's small flat, placing anything she thought could be sold into a pile. She sent Peggy to the pawnbroker's with the whole lot – furniture, linen, even, heartbreakingly, Alasdair's fiddle. But, as the jeweller had said, there were far more people selling than people buying. There was no point attempting to sell Alasdair's fob watch, she reasoned to herself. It wouldn't fetch much. Margaret rubbed her fingers against the gold plating. No, it wasn't just the money; selling the fiddle had been painful enough but this would be like parting with the final bit of Alasdair himself and that she just couldn't do.

Even having sold everything she could, she still

hadn't been able to gather a fraction of what she needed to cover Mr Johnston's fees.

When she'd told Peggy that she had to dispense with her services, the older woman had placed her hands on her hips and pursed her lips.

'Do you think I'm going to leave you and those bairns now? When you're like a bunch of lost souls?'

'You have to, Peggy. I can't afford to pay you any longer. I need every spare penny for the lawyer.'

Peggy's lips twitched. 'Aye well it's no' as if you pay me that much to begin with. If money wus important to me I would've got a job at one of the Big Hooses in Kelvinside or Queen's Park. The wummen are always asking aboot for domestic help.'

'Why didn't you take one of the posts before now?'

'Because it suited me only to work half a day for you – what with my Mam needing my help and you kindly keeping an eye on her.'

Margaret had attended on Peggy's mother, a formidable matriarch of seven children, at least once a month over the years Peggy had been with her. The old lady wasn't in the best of health, bringing up a large family in a damp house with very little money for food and fuel had taken its toll, but her children, now grown up and with the exception of Peggy, married, had pooled together and rented a warm comfortable home for her and Peggy in Maryhill. Sadly too late for Mrs McQuarrie's health. Mrs McQuarrie's chronic bronchitis had affected her breathing to the point where she could hardly walk a few steps without having to stop to catch her breath and Margaret thought it was unlikely the old lady would see many more months.

'It's not as if I need the money, pet.' Peggy wiped her hands on her apron and slid a cup of tea in front of Margaret. 'My brothers and sisters are happy to give a bob or two for Mam as long as I look after her.'

'You could get part time work with another family – at least they'll be able to pay you.'

'No, if I take a job with them it won't be long before they're asking me to stay to help oot with their bairns – or to dae mair hours because they haven't been able to find a cook and they are having people over. I like it here. You don't mind when I come or when I leave as long as I do me hours. And if you didn't look after Mam I would have had to pay another doctor. So it seems to me you have more than a few hours in the bank.' She glanced over to where Elizabeth was sitting with James in the crook of her arm as she read to him. 'I cannae leave those poor bairns the noo.'

Margaret's throat ached with the effort needed to hold back tears. God knew she needed all the help she could get. The children alternated between wide-eyed silence and fractious, clinging behaviour. No matter how much Margaret tried to give the impression that everything was normal, they sensed something was badly wrong. Right now they needed the stability Peggy could give them.

'You can always give me the pay you owe me later,' Peggy continued. 'When Mr Morrison is

169

back at work and the pair o' you are on your feet again. In the meantime my family will no' let me starve.'

The next afternoon, Toni and Mairi called to see her. After her friends had fussed over the children, Margaret asked Peggy to take Elizabeth and James out for some fresh air. She didn't want to risk them overhearing.

As soon as they were on their own, her friends voiced their dismay at the turn of events. 'Everyone in Govan knows Alasdair didn't do it!' Toni proclaimed angrily. 'What the hell are the polis doing to find out what really happened, that's what I want to know. Even Billy Barr doesn't believe your husband did it. God help the real murderer when Billy gets his hands on him.'

'Doesn't anyone know who it was? Someone must have seen something!'

'We've been asking but if anyone knows anything then they're not saying.'

'How's Alasdair bearing up?' Mairi asked, with a warning glance at her husband. 'How are *you* bearing up?'

'I'm all right, but I don't know how he is. I've only been able to see him once – the night he was arrested.' Margaret rubbed her forehead wearily. 'Our lawyer is going to arrange another visit but I don't know when yet. That's what's so hard about all this.'

Toni reached into the inside pocket of his jacket and pulled out an envelope. 'This is for you and the bairns.'

Margaret opened it to find thirty pounds. It was

almost twice as much as she'd been able to make from the sale of her belongings.

She placed the money back inside the envelope and passed it back to Toni. 'I can't take this. It's a small fortune. It must be your entire savings.'

'Hah! I wish it *was* our savings,' Toni said. 'No, this is from the folk in Govan. When we heard Alasdair was arrested we put a hat around.' He grinned. 'People were generous. Don't even think of not keeping it. Folk would be offended. Your husband helped them out when times were hard so now it's their turn to help.'

Tears stung Margaret's eyes. 'Please tell them how grateful Alasdair and I are. I know how much every penny counts in the households in Govan. It should be Bannatyne's giving them money not the other way around.'

But thanks to the kindness of the people of Govan she was almost halfway to gathering the money she needed for Mr Johnston and perhaps it would be enough. Alasdair was bound to be released soon and then the remainder of Mr Johnston's fees wouldn't need to be found.

Chapter 17

Despite her optimism, Alasdair remained in police custody. Each time she spoke to Mr Johnston he told her not to worry, that it was only a matter of time before Alasdair was freed, but so far it hadn't happened and Margaret was more and more at a loss to fathom why not. Johnston was supposed to be one of the best criminal lawyers in Scotland, if not *the* best, yet to her he seemed to be dragging his heels.

To make matters worse she still hadn't been allowed to visit Alasdair in prison.

Finally Mr Johnston sent a telegram asking to see her and she'd rushed over to his office fully expecting that at last he had the news she longed to hear: Alasdair was to be freed and she should arrange to collect him.

She sat in impatient silence while Mr Johnston leafed through the papers he had in a file on his desk.

The lawyer sighed then linked his fingers together and cracked each knuckle in turn, each snap sending a tiny shock through Margaret. When he eventually raised his eyes, he looked more woebegone than ever. He cleared his throat. 'I have completed my enquiries and I have to tell you matters look very bleak indeed. I'd go as far as to say that in my view there is every likelihood that your husband will be found guilty of murder.'

It was as if someone had tipped ice cold water down her neck. 'But he's innocent!'

Mr Johnston shook his head. 'I'm afraid that what matters is whether the other side can make a good enough case to convince the majority of the jurors that your husband did indeed do what he is accused of. The prosecution has the statements of the two constables who found your husband at the scene of the crime and with the murder weapon in his hand, and all we have is your husband's version but no witnesses to verify it. Indeed, the only witnesses I have been able to locate strengthen the prosecution's case rather than ours.'

'What do you mean?' Her voice seemed to be coming from a long distance away.

'Almost everyone I have spoken to says that there has been trouble between your husband and Billy Barr, the victim's father, for many years. It's well known that Billy Barr has long terrorised the streets of Glasgow. I gather that your husband was one of the few who repeatedly stood up to him. He was even seen to assault him on one occasion.'

She bit her lip so hard it hurt. However, the pain helped focus her mind. 'But I was there! Alasdair only took Mr Barr's knife from him because he threatened me. He didn't hurt him. There were witnesses to that!'

'Yes. Men whom your husband has helped. People who owe your husband – members of opposing gangs – so not altogether convincing witnesses, at least not as far as the Crown's concerned. And I'm afraid that as you are Mr Morrison's wife, your version of events won't be much use either.'

'But why would Alasdair kill Tommy Barr? What possible motive could he have had? If his argument was with anyone it was with the father.'

'Many of the witnesses say your husband swore to put Barr behind bars and his gang out of business. I gather the son was second in position only to his father.'

'Which is all the more reason for people to know Alasdair wouldn't have murdered anyone. My husband believes in the law! If he thought someone had committed a crime he would want them

173

charged in a court of law – not stabbed in a back lane!'

'It's not me that requires to be convinced, Mrs Morrison.'

When Margaret started to speak again he held up his hand. 'Let us consider first the policemen's evidence. Apparently they heard shouts and sounds of a scuffle coming from the lane. They were no more than a few minutes away. When they got there they saw your husband bending over the victim, knife in hand. The constables have both signed statements and will testify that your husband was alone and that no one else passed them coming from the lane.'

'The real murderers ran away before the policemen arrived! They passed Alasdair!'

'Yet he can't identify them – he can't even describe them beyond saying they were of average height.'

'It was dark! And I explained the first time I came to see you about the knife. My husband learned things when he was in the army. That sometimes it's safer not to withdraw a knife from a wound. Sometimes it's only the pressure of the knife on major blood vessels that stops the victim from bleeding to death. Perhaps if the constables had listened to Alasdair that boy might have lived!'

'That, I'm afraid, is a matter of some disagreement in the medical world. The doctors I have spoken to say it is not what is done. On the contrary they say they have never heard of such an approach when it comes to knife wounds.'

'Speak to Dr Bruce Marshall, then. He was in

the war. They learned all sorts of things in the field.'

As Mr Johnston made a note, she threaded her fingers together and forced herself to speak calmly. 'Furthermore, there must be other people's fingerprints on the knife. The real murderer, for a start!'

'I'm afraid the only prints on the knife – apart from those of the victim – belong to your husband.'

'Then whoever it was must have been wearing gloves!' She took another steadying breath. 'I know it looks bad for Alasdair, but why can't people accept his version could be as true as the version the prosecution are presenting? Isn't it up to them to prove Alasdair guilty, not for him to prove his innocence?'

'In theory, not so much in practice. All the jurors will have to go on is the evidence they are presented with and as yet, we have nothing to contradict the prosecution's case. Our case rests on two other men being in that lane – men no one else saw – and on your husband's fingerprints being on the knife because he was trying to stop the victim pulling it out. The prosecution on the other hand have two utterly reliable witnesses, men trained to remember exactly what they saw. Moreover, the prosecution claim that the motive is the bad feeling between Mr Barr and your husband. That is weak – I will give you that – but it is a motive of sorts. Indeed, the fact that Mr Morrison came to your aid in the past, even if it was because Mr Barr was threatening you, only adds to the Crown's case that he had a longstanding grudge against Mr Barr and his family.'

'But we weren't married then. We'd only just met.'

Mr Johnston cracked his knuckles again. 'That wasn't the only incident. Apparently Mr Barr and your husband have been seen arguing on several occasions. Even with all that against us, we might have been able to take our chances in court. However, two more things are going against us. Firstly, your husband has been in trouble before.'

The anxiety that had coiled like a snake in the pit of her stomach slithered upwards, squeezing her chest. 'What trouble? I know he's taken part in strikes but...'

'I'm not talking about his union business – if only I were. According to the police, your husband has been arrested before – when he was in the army – for striking a sergeant without provocation. If the war hadn't come to an end when it did he probably would have been court-martialled. As it was he spent a few days in a military gaol.' He frowned, glancing down at his notes. 'It doesn't help our case.'

Why hadn't Alasdair told her this? What else didn't she know about her husband?

'But if it happened when he was in the army that was years ago! He wasn't more than a boy himself then.'

'A man who like the rest was trained to kill.' As the grandfather clock ticked into silence, he gave a small shake of his head, his eyes looking more mournful than ever. 'The second thing going against us is that we have a new Chief Constable in Glasgow who is determined to rid the city of the scourge – as the press call it – of the Glasgow gangs and the associated murder rate. Indeed, that is the main reason he was appointed to the post. When he was Chief Constable in Sheffield he managed to put the fear of God into the gangs there and is determined to do the same here. And the fact that your husband is prominent – not just through his association with you, or rather your father, but through his work with the unions – makes the Chief Constable even keener to make an example of him. He has pledged to show the world that Glasgow will not tolerate crime – whether the perpetrator is a solicitor or a member of one of the gangs.'

'But Alasdair isn't, nor has ever been, a member of any gang. The very idea is ridiculous!'

'No one is claiming he is a member of a gang – only that he is involved with them, however tangentially.'

'What can we do?' Margaret whispered. 'We can't just give up.'

'What we need is a witness of our own. Someone – preferably more than one – who is utterly reliable, along with some solid evidence pointing to another perpetrator. Then we might be able to put doubt in the jury's mind. We have searched for anyone or anything to substantiate your husband's version of events, but have drawn a blank so far. Yet someone, somewhere, must have seen something or – at the very least – know what really happened. But so far – nothing. That makes the prosecution even more certain there is nothing to be found. Your husband is due in court a week on Friday to enter his plea. He has authorised me to instruct Mr Williams, the advocate I have found to represent him, that he wishes to enter a not-guilty plea. If he persists in going with a not-guilty plea, the Crown is keen to go ahead with a trial as soon as possible. They see no reason to delay and, unless I can come up with new evidence, we can't refuse. So you see why I said the situation is bleak?'

'But not hopeless. Surely?'

He studied her for a while. 'Without new information coming to light, there are really only two options open to us if we want to be certain to avoid the death penalty.'

The room seemed to tilt and sway. She'd come here expecting to hear that Mr Johnston was on the verge of having the charges against Alasdair dropped. Instead he was talking about avoiding the death penalty! 'You can't think they will really hang him?' The words came out as a whisper.

'I'm very much afraid that is the penalty for murder.'

Margaret swallowed hard. 'What are you saying?'

Mr Johnston cleared his throat. 'Either your husband pleads guilty but with a plea of self-defence – and I am not at all sure that will wash–'

She clenched her hands together so tightly her nails dug into her palms. 'Or?' Her mouth was so dry she could barely speak.

'Or he pleads guilty and we plea bargain his sentence. That way it won't have to go to trial and with a bit of luck we may be able to get his sentence reduced to life.'

'Life!' Margaret echoed.

'He's still in his thirties. With good behaviour he might only have to serve fifteen years.'

'Alasdair will never plead guilty to something

he didn't do – and certainly not murder.'

'Then he must take his chances in court.' Mr Johnston gathered the papers together and replaced them in the file. 'There you have it. I truly wish I could have given you more reason for optimism. One way or another, Mrs Morrison, it appears as if your husband is going down for the murder of Tommy Barr. The best we can hope for is to save his life.' He placed his interlinked hands on the desk and leaned forward. 'I've arranged for you to visit Mr Morrison tomorrow at Duke Street. For his sake and yours, warn him that unless we can find new evidence in the next couple of days, he should think long and hard about pleading guilty.'

That night Margaret brought James and Libby into bed with her, knowing they needed to be close to her.

James had started talking – just a few words here and there but enough, for short spells anyway, to divert Elizabeth who James, unable to get his tongue around her name, called Libby.

Alasdair should be here to witness it all. Everything happened so fast at this age, and once missed could never be re-experienced. She couldn't bear to think of a future where Alasdair would not be around to see his children grow up.

Even with the comfort of their hot bodies next to her, she'd never felt more alone. She tossed and turned all night. Everything that had been said in the meeting with Mr Johnston kept going around and around in her head. It was no longer just a case of continuing to find money for Alasdair's defence. If Johnston were to be believed, and she saw no reason to doubt him, there was every chance Alasdair would be convicted of murder and no amount of money or lawyers was going to change that. They needed to find witnesses of their own – or even better, new evidence – or Alasdair would hang. Even thinking it was possible made her want to be sick.

When she did eventually fall asleep it was to dream that she was alone in a field so foggy she could barely see her hands when she held them in front of her. She sensed something hidden in the murky depths she didn't want to see. At that moment the fog cleared and in front of her was a body hanging from gallows, swinging in the wind. Time slowed until it felt as if there were minutes between each of her heartbeats. A sudden gust of wind turned the swaying body in her direction. The face was blue, the eyes bulging, but she saw immediately it was Alasdair. He raised his hands towards her and she cried out. Suddenly she was awake, her heart racing, her nightie damp with perspiration.

Fear kept her pinned to the bed for a long time. *It was only a nightmare,* she told herself over and over. Alasdair was still alive.

But for how long?

Knowing she'd be unable to get back to sleep, she eased herself out from between her children, careful not to wake them.

She couldn't let him hang! Not if there was any way to stop it.

Chapter 18

By the time she'd bathed, Peggy had arrived and the children were up. Peggy set her newly washed hair for her while the children watched in wide-eyed silence. Then Margaret dressed in her favourite frock, adding a touch of lipstick, before finishing off her outfit with a blue felt hat that matched her dress.

The children clung to her when she told them she was going out and Peggy had to prise them away with the promise of cocoa followed by a trip to the park.

Although there was a new prison in Glasgow – Barlinnie – some prisoners, Alasdair amongst them, were still held at the old one in Duke Street near the town centre. Duke Street prison was notorious for its living conditions, but it had the single advantage of being closer for Margaret to get to.

She stood at the gates and suppressed a shudder. This was where the flotsam of Glasgow life ended up. Worse still, this was where those found guilty of murder were hanged.

She couldn't help but think of the last person to have been hanged here – a woman charged and found guilty of murdering her paperboy. How terrified she must have been when she'd learned she was to die. How terrified she must have been going to the gallows. And she'd been guilty!

Margaret pushed the morbid thoughts away and clasped her hands together to stop them shaking.

Inside, the small, cramped waiting room with its bare, peeling walls was crowded – almost exclusively with women. Some sat in tight-lipped silence but most gossiped and knitted as if coming to visit their husbands in gaol was no different to a trip to the wash house.

The woman next to Margaret unwrapped a piece of greasy brown paper revealing a piece of bread and dripping covered with a thin coat of sugar. She took a bite with evident relish.

'So what's yours in for, hen?' she said, turning to Margaret. As she spoke, small bits of bread flew from her mouth, several landing on Margaret's lap, others only narrowly falling short of hitting her face. She wanted nothing more than to put a foot or two of distance between them, but she was hemmed in on the other side by a large woman who was snoring gently, her arms folded across her ample bosom.

'My husband is innocent,' Margaret said shortly.

'Of course he is, of course. Aren't they all?' She winked at Margaret.

'But my husband really is,' Margaret insisted. She hated to think anyone, whether they knew Alasdair or not, would think for one moment he was guilty. Or, a small voice whispered, that you are associated with someone accused of murder. She pushed the traitorous thought away. If Alasdair could bear this, so could she. She averted her eyes and stared straight ahead.

The woman folded her now empty piece of brown paper before placing it in her pocket. She peered closer at Margaret. 'We don't get many of your sort in here. What did he do, then? Rob his clients? Steal money from his business?' Her smile grew wider. 'Break into a bank? If he did I hope he bought you something pretty.'

Thankfully at that moment the police guard came in to announce that visiting hour had started. He led them through to another larger, but equally sparse and bleak, room and told them to take a seat at one of the tables.

As she waited for Alasdair, Margaret smoothed down her dress and surreptitiously pinched her cheeks to put some colour in them.

When eventually she saw him, she had to stifle a cry behind her hand. His face was gaunt and pale and covered in stubble, his hands handcuffed in front of him. But his eyes still burned fiercely, his shoulders were back and he wore his prison garb as if it were a suit of the highest quality.

Alasdair's eyes locked onto hers when he saw her and the world slowed and stopped until it was just the two of them. In that look she saw all his love for her. Even now, dressed as he was, and in danger of his life, he still made her pulse race. Alasdair stepped towards her but as she rose to meet him, her hands outstretched, a policeman put his hand on her arm. 'No touching,' he said, not unkindly.

As Alasdair took his seat opposite her, lowering his handcuffed wrists below the table and out of her sight, the fire in his eyes dimmed and his mouth formed into a thin line. 'You shouldn't have come. I don't want you to see me like this.'

'I would have come sooner if I could. You're my

husband and I love you. Nothing would keep me away.' Tears burned behind her eyelids and she blinked them away. She mustn't cry. 'Are they treating you all right?'

Alasdair gave a small, dismissive shake of his head. 'Never mind me, what about you and the children? Are you all right? Are they all right? What have you told them?' For a moment she glimpsed despair, shame, humiliation in his eyes, but almost as quickly the look was gone.

'I told the children you had to go away for a while. They both ask for you all the time. They want to know when you're coming home. James is too young to take much in, but Elizabeth suspects something is badly wrong.'

His shoulders slumped. 'I missed her birthday.'

Margaret managed a small smile. 'There'll be more birthdays. She knows you would have been there if you could have been. But we need to talk about your case, Alasdair,' Margaret hurried on. There was so little time. 'I understand Mr Johnston has been to see you?'

'Yes. Two or three times. But how can we afford him and the advocate he's instructed?'

'Don't worry about that – we'll manage.'

'I'm still your husband, Margaret,' he said quietly. 'I know how little money we have saved and I know how much all this must be costing.'

'I sold a couple of things – nothing I'll miss. And the shipyard workers took a collection.'

His expression darkened. She knew how much he would hate hearing that. 'You shouldn't have had to sell a thing. And the Govan folk need every penny for themselves. We'll give it all back as soon as I'm out of here.' He dragged a hand through his hair. 'Although I gather Mr Johnston doesn't think much of my chances. He thinks I should plead self-defence – or even guilty. Don't you think a man should have a lawyer who believes in his innocence?'

'He does believe in your innocence!' she cried, although she wondered if that were true. 'He just doesn't think Mr Williams will be able to prove it.'

Alasdair leaned forward, pinning her with his blue eyes. 'You believe I am innocent, don't you, Margaret?'

'Of course I do! How can you even ask such a thing? But Alasdair, they say you were almost court-martialled for striking an officer during the war. Why didn't you tell me?'

'Because it was in the past. Because I had no wish to think about those times any more than I had to.'

'Tell me what happened.'

His expression was shuttered as he looked into the distance. It was as if he'd gone somewhere she couldn't follow.

'It was a fool of a sergeant major. He took against one of the lads in our company. The lad, Fergus, was only just sixteen – he'd lied about his age so he could enlist. I imagine he had no idea what he was letting himself in for. It was near the end – we were ordered over the top – to attack an enemy outpost. Everyone knew it was suicide but what could we do? Orders were orders. Half of us didn't make it past the first wave, but I did – God knows how. I was with the sergeant when we stumbled across Fergus taking shelter in a foxhole. He was terrified, and who could blame him? The sergeant ordered us to attack again but Fergus wouldn't. I don't think he was capable of movement. I had to go. That night I learned that the sergeant had reported Fergus for cowardice and he was to be shot the next morning. For God's sake, we all knew the war was all but over! I argued with the sergeant but he was the filthiest sort. He wouldn't listen to reason.' Alasdair shrugged. 'I punched him – I think I might even have killed him if my mates hadn't pulled me off.' His eyes were wintry, his expression closed. 'Didn't make a difference. They shot poor Fergus anyway and flung me in solitary. I would have been court-martialled, but as I said the war was coming to an end and up until then I had had a decent record.'

'I wish you had told me.'

'There was nothing I wanted to remember about those times. The whole bloody war was a farce.'

'Oh, Alasdair! Can't you see how they can use it against you?'

A faint smile crossed his lips. 'Perhaps if I'd known then I was going to be charged with murder I wouldn't have intervened.' His expression clouded over again. 'But, dear God, Margaret, how could I have done otherwise? And as for what got me here – what sort of man would I be if I stood by and let someone die without lifting a finger to help? Sometimes a man has to do what is right regardless of the consequences! I had my fill of killing when I was in the army. I'll not stand by again. No matter what the cost. I could no more not have punched that sergeant than I could have walked away from that lad. And if I had to, I would do it again.'

Margaret felt a tinge of exasperation, but quickly suppressed it. But oh, did Alasdair have to be everyone else's knight in shining armour?

'They are going to bring all that up at the trial. They are going to say it proves you have a violent streak. They intend to use what happened with Billy that day in Govan too.' She leaned across the table. 'You must see how it makes you look!'

'What happened in the past doesn't make me guilty now.'

'I know that. But–'

'Don't, Margaret! Don't say what I think you're going to,' Alasdair interrupted, disappointment shadowing his eyes. 'I will never plead guilty to something I didn't do. What man would? And what kind of wife would ask it of her husband?'

'A man who has no choice. And a wife who doesn't want the man she loves to die! Please, Alasdair, I couldn't bear it.' She could no longer hold back the tears. 'If you won't do it for yourself – do it for me and the children. Mr Johnston wouldn't have suggested it if he didn't think it was the only way.'

'I wonder if Johnston would be so quick to plead guilty if he were the one facing a lifetime in prison.'

'A lifetime in prison is better than no life at all.'

'To some, perhaps. Not to me. I'm not ready to give up, Margaret. I still have friends – powerful friends. Friends who know I'm innocent.'

'So where are they? These people who believe

187

in your innocence? What are they doing to ensure your release? Please. Listen. Think of me and the children–'

'That's all I think about.' A muscle twitched in his cheek. 'But to say to the world that I killed a man! Do you want Elizabeth and James to be known as the offspring of a murderer? You the wife of a murderer? You'd be forever tainted. How could I do that to you? How could I do that to our children?'

'At least you'd live and as long as you were alive there would be hope. New evidence might be found – the real killer might confess – anything could happen.'

They stared at each other for a long moment, both breathing deeply.

'Have you given up on me, Margaret?' he said eventually, his eyes searching hers.

'I will never give up on you – never. Do you hear me? Remember the promise I made you before we were married? I said I would never give up on you as long as there was breath in my body and I meant every word! As long as the sun comes up in the morning, as long as there are stars in the sky, I will continue to love you and be proud to bear your name.' Tears were streaming down her cheeks but she made no attempt to brush them away.

At that moment the bell signalling the end of visiting rang and one of the police guards stepped forward. As he took Alasdair by the arm, Alasdair shook him off. 'Not in front of my wife,' he growled. He held Margaret's gaze, his eyes anguished. 'God, if I could only hold you. But now it's your turn to listen to me, my love. If I lose the case – and I still have faith I won't – you must take a different name. Move somewhere with Elizabeth and James where no one will know you. Start somewhere fresh. Your friends will help.'

She dried her face with her handkerchief, blew her nose and looked her love in the eyes. 'I won't abandon you. You will be found not guilty. I'll make sure of it. One way or another, I will get you out of here.'

Chapter 19

Margaret stood on the corner of Duke Street as people bustled past her, their lives seemingly carrying on as normal whilst hers was falling apart. Although it was mid-summer, the rain had been falling for almost two weeks now and there was no sign of it letting up. The wet weather, however, hadn't kept people indoors and, as usual, the streets were thronged, many using umbrellas almost as a weapon to push their way along the streets, keeping as close to the buildings as possible to avoid getting splashed.

She longed to go home and hold her children in her arms, even for a few moments, but knew if she put off doing what she had to do, her courage would fail her. She'd made a promise to Alasdair to do everything in her power to get him out of prison and back home where he belonged – and she'd meant it. She'd been almost certain that

189

Alasdair wouldn't agree to plead guilty, so the previous night, as she'd lain sleepless and terrified, she'd come up with an alternative solution, and there was only one man left who could help her with that.

Knowing at this time of day her father was most likely to be at the shipyard, that's where she headed. Too agitated to take a tram, she walked down to the riverside, thinking of what she would say, and wondering how far she was prepared to go to get Alasdair released. Whatever it took was the answer.

It was lunch time for the day shift when she arrived at the yard and she had to fight her way through the streams of men pouring from the gates, collars turned up against the rain and caps pulled low over their foreheads.

She envied them. Their lives might be hard but at least they knew what the days and weeks to come held for them and tonight most of them would be sitting around the table with their families. Stepping between carts and barrels while trying to avoid the puddles as best she could, she marched along the front of the shipyard and into the management building. Ferguson was in the office on the ground floor and when he saw her a look of astonishment crossed his face.

'Miss Ban – I mean Mrs Morrison – I didn't realise your father was expecting you.'

'He's not. Is he here?'

'He's on site.'

She shook the water from her umbrella. 'Would you let him know I'm here? I shall wait for him in his office.'

Ferguson grunted something to a passing boy who took off as fast as his legs could carry him, and Margaret, with memories of the last time she was here rushing back, climbed the stairs to her father's office and let herself in.

She crossed to the window and looked out over the yard. Was it really almost fourteen years since she'd last stood here in this very spot? Fourteen years since she'd first set eyes on Alasdair and the course of her life had changed forever.

Little here had changed. The shipyard was still as it had always been, busier even. There was a new ship on the slip due to be launched in a few weeks' time. No doubt about it, it was a thing of beauty and the men who had worked on her using the skills passed on from father to son had every reason to be proud of what they'd built. Other shipyards might have suffered and even closed during these last lean years, but Bannatyne's had gone from strength to strength. Despite the Depression her father had become even wealthier. According to Alasdair he'd bought up the smaller yards and bought into the shipping lines themselves, taking a share of their profits, whether of cargo or of passengers. He'd also invested heavily in shares in steelworks both in Scotland and America. Yet little of the additional wealth had found its way into the pockets of the shipyard workers and their families.

If only her father had used some of that money to create better living and working conditions for the men who gave their sweat to make him rich. Unlike the other shipbuilders, or to be more precise, their widows, who had created parks, built libraries and public baths, her father had done little to ease the lot of the working man. He had, she knew, endowed libraries and even a ward at the Royal Infirmary but that wasn't because he cared – it was because that's what rich men did if they wanted a title.

There was so much that still needed to be done. The poor needed more sanatoria, more hospitals for the chronically ill and most of all new homes; homes that had running water and proper sanitation.

Perhaps if her husband hadn't been so proud, so determined to oppose everything her father stood for, it could all have been so different. She and Alasdair could have used the Bannatyne fortune to change hundreds, if not thousands, of lives. Now they stood on the brink of losing everything including Alasdair's freedom and possibly even his life.

She shook her head, appalled at the direction her thoughts were going in.

No. Despite all that had happened she wouldn't exchange a day, not even a minute, of her life with Alasdair – the joy, the laughter, the music, the way her breath still caught in her throat whenever she saw him, the way pride blossomed in her chest when she saw how he commanded love and respect from the people he helped. Just being in the same room as him made her heart sing. She wouldn't change a moment of that for a lifetime of ease and comfort. With all its joys and sorrows, it was the life she'd chosen and she couldn't regret it.

So there was no point in thinking about what might have been.

The sound of the office door opening broke her

reverie and she whirled around to find her father looking at her, his expression unreadable.

'I suspected you'd come crawling back here sooner or later.'

He'd aged in the months since she'd last seen him. There were more lines round his eyes than she remembered and his expensive suit didn't quite hide the fact that he'd lost weight. An unexpected wave of regret washed over her. Everything might have been so different had Sebastian and Fletcher lived.

She waited until he sat down at his desk before approaching and standing before him, her hands clasped tightly.

'I need your help, Father,' she said quietly.

'You have some nerve, I give you that. Do you have any idea what you and that man have done to me? My business depends on contacts – the right sort of contacts. Do you know how many of the men I once called my acquaintances won't look me in the eye now? And as for any chance of a baronetcy–' He shook his head, his face turning more puce by the minute. 'You have shamed and embarrassed this family. I will never forgive you for that.'

'I am sorry, truly sorry, to have caused you and Mother pain, but Alasdair is innocent.'

'Are you certain he didn't kill that man? He was there. The knife that was used had his fingerprints on it. There has been trouble between him and this particular gang before – or so I'm told.'

How did her father come to be so well informed? By the police? The newspapers? His friend the Procurator Fiscal?

'Of course Alasdair is innocent. I would swear it on my life. I know my husband. If he had a quarrel with someone he would fight with words and the law – not with his fists – and certainly not with a knife in some dark lane. My husband is an honourable man. Even your acquaintances would agree.'

'Your husband has a history of violence, Margaret. I can't believe you are not aware of that. His Bolshevik cohorts, elevated though some of them might be, have no more use for his sort than I do. Look at the mess the common man is making of this once great country! Look at what is happening in Germany and Italy! They are nothing but anarchists! That's what happens when you give the common man power above his station.'

Alasdair always said that change had to come from the people themselves, the ordinary man and woman. That, as long as the power remained with the lucky select few, a country could never really change and she agreed with him. Promises had been made and broken countless times by people like her father. But now was not the time to argue.

'I didn't come here to debate politics with you, Father,' she said wearily.

'Then why did you come?'

She hesitated, wondering whether she'd made a mistake coming here. Nothing in her father's manner suggested a softening towards her. But she was his only surviving child. Whatever had happened between them, surely he wouldn't refuse to help her now? She placed her hands palm up on his desk.

'Please, Father, I'm begging you. I'll go down on my knees if you want me to. If you have any love left for me – help me – help Alasdair. If not for our sakes, then for your grandchildren.'

'You should have thought about your children when I gave you the chance! They – you – could have had the world at their feet. But you and your husband threw my offer back in my face.'

'Alasdair is a proud man. He wants to be the one to provide for his children.'

'And look where he is now!'

Margaret bit back the words that bubbled up inside her. She couldn't afford to antagonise her father any further than she had already. If he refused to help them she didn't know what she'd do.

He narrowed his eyes. 'Does your husband know you are here?'

'No,' she admitted. 'As I said, he is a proud man. He'd hate it if he knew I'd come to you.' There was nothing for it but to plough on. 'The lawyers I engaged – Mr Johnston and Mr Williams, the advocate Mr Johnston instructed – think there is a good chance Alasdair will be found guilty.'

Her father shrugged, as if it were of no consequence to him that her husband could be hanged. 'And what do you imagine I can do about that?'

'I need money to pay the lawyers and more to offer a reward to encourage any witnesses to come forward with new information. It's the only way to find the person who really killed Tommy Barr.'

'And what do I get in return?'

Margaret frowned. 'Surely it's in your interest

too for my husband to be found innocent? Didn't you say that your association with a criminal was damaging your name and your business?'

Her father laughed harshly. 'I think the damage has already been done.' He paused. 'Witnesses could be found – of that I have no doubt. Pay people enough and they'll say anything. But how could we – or more importantly the police – be sure that these witnesses,' he signalled quotation marks in the air, 'weren't perjuring themselves?'

'Alasdair is innocent. They'd only be confirming what must have really happened.'

'Even if it meant them lying in a court of law?'

She swallowed hard, knowing that in the next few moments she was about to cross a line that she'd have to live with for the rest of her life – a line her husband would never forgive her for crossing if he ever found out. 'If that's what it'll take to get him out of gaol and his name cleared, then I wouldn't care.' She looked directly at him. 'You have the means to ensure Alasdair is found innocent.'

He reached across his desk and opened a walnut box inlaid with mother-of-pearl. Taking a cigar, he lifted it to his nose, sniffed it appreciatively before taking his time to light it. Margaret felt her nerves stretching to breaking point.

'Let us be quite clear,' he said, when the cigar was lit to his satisfaction. 'You want me to use my money to find witnesses who will swear that they saw things even if they didn't see anything. And if that's not sufficient for your husband to be found not guilty, you wish me to persuade people I know, people who owe me favours, to use their influence to alter the verdict?'

A knot twisted deep down inside of her. He wanted her to say it out loud, knowing what it would cost her. 'If it is the only way to get Alasdair his freedom, then yes.'

Her father leaned back in his chair and expelled a cloud of smoke. 'Well, I never. Maybe you're more like me than you care to admit, Margaret.' For the first time she saw in his eyes a glimmer of admiration. He stood and walked across to the window. He was quiet for so long, Margaret wondered if he had forgotten she was there. When he turned to face her, his face was grey but his eyes held a steely coldness that made her shudder. 'You could have had everything. Wealth, power, your family around you, but for that man.' The muscles in his jaw clenched and unclenched. 'Much better that he'd been the one who had died...'

'You can't mean that! I know you and Alasdair have had your differences but–'

'I do mean it, God help me. But Lord knows I have no desire to have my grandson branded the child of a murderer!'

'Then you'll help?'

He walked back to his desk and sat down. 'Very well. Forget the reward, it will only muddy the waters. I'll pay your lawyers' fees. You continue to meet with Johnston as you've been doing, but leave the rest to me.'

Margaret closed her eyes. 'Thank you–'

'But I have conditions.'

'I'll do anything–'

'You haven't heard what they are yet. You will give up your children into my care. You will agree never to see them again.'

'No!' She couldn't believe what she was hearing.

Her father raised his eyebrows. 'Don't you want your son to grow up to be someone? He could have all this!' He made a sweeping gesture with his hand. 'He could be one of the most powerful men in Scotland and beyond. I have interests abroad – there is another war coming – and more ships will be required and more ships means a greater demand for steel. America is growing and it needs more steel than can be supplied. Your son could be richer than I one day. He may even be knighted! Would you deny him his heritage – his natural right?'

'My son and my daughter *will* grow up to be somebodies, Father, you can be sure of that. They will grow up to be kind and just, to know that privilege brings responsibility, that they must care for and help those less fortunate. That's what matters – not money and not power. Not unless it can be used for the common good.'

'You will never have anything to do with your children again,' he continued, as if she hadn't spoken. 'No letters, no contact. Ever. I shall tell them in a few months that you both died.'

Margaret gripped the chair as his words sliced into her.

'I will never give up my children! And Mother would never agree.'

'Your mother will do as she is asked.' He stood in front of her. 'Think carefully before you refuse me. As much as I can use my power to prove your husband's innocence, so too can I use that same influence to ensure that he hangs. And if he hangs, how do you think you'll support the children and yourself?'

The thought of Alasdair hanging was still impossible to contemplate. 'I'll find work. I'll go back to being a doctor.'

'And who do you think will employ a woman with two children – the widow of a convicted murderer? Even if you do find work I imagine I'll find it easy enough to persuade a judge to declare you unfit to be a mother and to remove the children from you.'

'You must hate me very much, Father,' she whispered through frozen lips.

'Hate you?' he said, appearing genuinely surprised. 'This has nothing to do with my feelings for you. I only wish to have Alasdair Morrison out of my life once and for all and to gain custody of my grandson. Whether your husband hangs or whether he leaves the country a free man is up to you. A simple choice, Margaret. Your husband's life for your children. It shouldn't be difficult. They'll want for nothing and you'll have your husband. I'll even give you money to start again. Not in this country, of course. But you're both young enough to be able to start a new life somewhere else. You could even have more children.'

'I'd rather die before I agree to any of this!'

'Ah, Margaret. It isn't that simple. If you don't sign custody of your children over to me your husband will hang – have no doubt about that. Furthermore, I shall take the children anyway. If I can't get them through the courts, it should be easy enough to have you admitted to an asylum.

199

Then the courts would have no choice but to place the children with me.'

Her heart was knocking so hard against her ribs, Margaret could barely breathe. She knew only too well about the women locked up in asylums – not because they were insane but because they were an embarrassment to their families. All that was needed was two doctors willing to sign a form along with the next of kin. And with Alasdair in gaol her father would fulfil that role.

'One way or another I will get those children,' her father continued. 'The only question for you is whether you save your husband's life in the process.'

'You're the one who is insane!'

'As I said, it is up to you. I shall have papers drawn up giving me custody. You have until a week on Monday to tell me your decision. If you agree to my terms you can sign the papers then.'

Margaret stumbled outside. She'd made everything worse by going to her father. Something was broken in him.

To threaten to have the children removed from her, to have her committed! It was absurd! He would never get away with it. She had powerful friends too. Or at least she'd had once. Dr Quigley had long since retired and gone to live near the sea in Fife with a niece and her family, and she hadn't seen Mrs Little since she'd last treated her several years ago. But there was Lillian – she would know it was nonsense. Why then didn't she feel re-assured? She might be able to find people to say that she was sane – but all her father needed was two to say she wasn't.

Even if he failed in his attempt to certify her as insane, it would be a simple matter for him to persuade the courts she wasn't a fit mother. He knew people and if he could manipulate the law for or against Alasdair, he could certainly find someone who would sign whatever he wanted him to.

Of course she could argue, defend herself, but what if she lost? The thought of being permanently separated from her children sent waves of terror through her.

Blindly, she hurried from the yard and onto the street, bumping into pedestrians and only narrowly avoiding being hit by a tram, a ship-worker pulling her out of the way just in time.

She took a seat on a park bench, ignoring the strange looks from the passers-by and the rain that drenched her. Thoughts whirled around her head. Had it been a set-up all along? Was Mr Johnston in cahoots with her father? Was that why he was so ready to give in?

She no longer knew what to think – who to trust.

What to do now? There had to be something. She'd promised Alasdair she wouldn't give up. There had to be a way to save him and keep her children.

Chapter 20

Mairi took one look at Margaret's face when she opened the door to her and ushered her in, telling her not to say anything until she'd dried off and had something hot to put some colour in her cheeks.

As soon as Margaret's hands were wrapped around the cup, Mairi sent the children outside and told them to get their father as fast as their legs would carry them. She wouldn't let Margaret speak until she had drunk all of the scalding sweet tea. The baby was sitting on a pile of blankets gnawing on his fist and studying them with big brown eyes.

'Now tell us what's happened,' Mairi said, after Toni had hurried through the door and exchanged a few anxious words with his wife.

Still reeling from the meeting with her father, Margaret told them what the lawyer had said, Alasdair's response, and her father's ultimatum. Her cheeks burned as she related the conversation. Although she knew Toni had no love for her father, it was still humiliating to admit the lengths he was prepared to go to, to get his way.

Mairi looked at Margaret in horror. 'What man would threaten to do that to his only child?'

'A man like Bannatyne,' Toni muttered, shaking his head.

'What are you going to do?' Mairi asked, turning back to Margaret.

'I don't know. I go round and round ... one minute I think I have to do what my father wants, and fight to get the children back when Alasdair is released – the next I know it's impossible. How can I give up my children? How can I be sure I'd get them back if I did? But if I don't!

'I even thought of running, hiding somewhere with the children where my father can never find me, but I can't leave Alasdair! My father will see him hang for certain then!' She dropped her head in her hands and cried, only dimly aware of Mairi crouching by her side and rubbing her back as if she were a child. She'd tried to be strong, she'd tried to believe everything would be all right, but she had no more strength left. Even as the words rang in her head she knew she had to find more from somewhere. She'd fought her father before and won and she'd promised Alasdair she wouldn't give up. She wiped her eyes, blew her nose and took a shaky breath. 'There has to be another way to save Alasdair.' She was pleased to hear that her voice sounded, if not quite as firm and determined as she wanted, at least halfway normal.

'We'll no' let him hang!' Toni banged his fist on the table. 'Not as long as we live will that man hang!'

A surge of hope made Margaret light-headed. 'You know something that will save him?'

Toni removed his pipe from his pocket and took his time filling it. 'There's men who will do any-thing to help your husband; men who owe Alasdair their own freedom, men who have no reason to love your father and a few besides who owe *you* their lives.'

'I don't see...'

'Hear him out, Margaret,' Mairi murmured, covering Margaret's hands with hers. 'Go on, Toni.'

'We work in a shipyard. The men who built these ships know every inch of them. And the rest know where those ships are going and when. If we could get Alasdair out of gaol we could hide him on one.'

The hope drained away almost as quickly as it had risen. For the second time in as many hours she could hardly believe what she was hearing. It was as if she'd stepped into a nightmare where nothing and no one were as she expected, where the world had different rules, or none at all. She gave her head a little shake to clear it. 'You mean help him escape?'

'Aye. Why not?'

'Because it's dangerous! People could get hurt – or killed. We'd all be breaking the law then. All face imprisonment. And what if it didn't work? Even attempting to escape would convince everyone that Alasdair murdered Billy Barr's son. It would be the same as if he stood in the dock and admitted it–' Yet – yet. Even as she protested, part of her was already considering the ins and outs of it, the pros and cons.

Toni placed his elbows on his knees and leaned forward. 'As I said, most of us have no love for your father or the polls. We'd take our chances.'

'How would you do it?' She should, at the very least, listen to what Toni had in mind.

'Anything's possible if you know the right people. There's many from here who have brothers or sons who work in the prison. We'd have to think more on it. Plan it properly. But it can be done, I'm sure of it.'

'Alasdair would never agree. He'd never break the law or let anyone break it on his behalf.'

Toni and Mairi exchanged a look. 'We wouldn't need his agreement,' Toni growled. 'We'd take him – knock him out if we have to – and put him on board one of those ships. He'd be out of the country before he knew what was happening.'

'And the children and I would go with him?' She couldn't believe she was even giving this plan serious consideration. Toni was almost as crazy as her father. Yet hadn't she been prepared to break the law when she'd told her father to find a 'witness'?

Her friends shared another look. 'No, least not straight away. Hiding one man on board is one thing, a whole family, especially when two of them are children, is another.'

'We wouldn't need to hide. We could buy tickets just like any other passenger.'

Mairi shook her head regretfully. 'Oh, Margaret, if you and the children booked berths then it would soon come to your father's ears. Even if it didn't, as soon as Alasdair was on the run they'd be looking for you and the children. They'd search every nook and cranny of every ship leaving the docks. You'd lead the police to him – and to us.'

'You and the bairns could follow later,' Toni added. 'Once things had died down.'

She stood and started to pace, thinking furiously.

205

The smallness of the room meant she could only take a few steps in one direction before she had to turn around again. 'Supposing all that works. Supposing you do manage to free him, supposing you do manage to get him on board, and supposing I can convince him to go without us, that still leaves the problem of the children and my father. If Alasdair does manage to escape Father will be even more determined to take the children from me. And he'd have greater cause to claim I was an unfit mother. I might even be charged for helping Alasdair escape. I could go to prison and the children would be without their mother and father then. And even if the police don't suspect me, my father is perfectly capable of getting me put away in an asylum.' She shuddered. 'If he succeeds that will be even worse than prison. At least in gaol I'd have some certainty of getting out eventually.' She shook her head. 'No, I can see you mean well and I thank you. But it will never work.'

'Then Alasdair hangs,' Toni said bluntly.

'There is a way Alasdair can be saved and you keep your children,' Mairi interrupted. She'd been sitting quietly over the last few minutes, a small frown between her brows. 'You know my family comes from the Outer Hebrides? Well, my sister Flora still lives there with her husband and three children. I got a letter from her the other day. She was complaining that one of the children was sick and when she took him to the doctor's she had to wait hours to be seen. Flora knows one of the practice nurses, who told her that the doctor on North Uist – Dr MacLean – has been looking for a winter assistant for the last few weeks but so far he's had no applicants to his advert – not even a single enquiry. He's worried he won't manage to get anyone. Not many people want to live in what they think of as the edge of the world. You could apply for the post. Your father would never think to look for you there.'

Margaret's heart began to race as hope flared once more. 'How can I be sure this doctor would take me on?'

'Flora says Dr MacLean's pretty desperate. There's far too much work there for one man on his own. You could write to him and ask if the position is still open.'

The flicker of hope died as quickly as it had ignited. 'He'd never employ someone whose husband was accused of murder, let alone someone accused of murder who'd escaped from prison. No matter how desperate he might be.'

'Then take a different name!' Mairi said, making no attempt to hide her exasperation. 'You'd have to any road if your father is not to find you.'

'Practising under a name that's not my own could get me in nearly as much trouble as conspiring to help Alasdair escape.' But it was worth considering – perhaps her only chance. If she and the children couldn't go with Alasdair, and it seemed they couldn't, at least not at first, then they had to go somewhere her father couldn't find them. There was of course the Gatehouse in Perth that Lillian had offered but it would be one of the first places her father would search for her. And there was the further necessity of having to earn money. She'd very little left and no prospect of finding more. She and the children had to eat.

207

'Even if he did agree to take me on, what about Libby and James? I wouldn't be much use to Dr MacLean without someone to care for the children.'

'They could stay with Flora until you find someone you could rely on closer to the surgery – it's a good bit from where my sister and her family live. We'd have to tell Flora and her husband the truth, but they know how to keep secrets. The islanders do like a wee gossip but they have no fondness for outsiders knowing their business. If I told her she couldn't breathe a word of who you were, nothing and nobody would get it out of her.'

'I don't know, Mairi. If Alasdair escapes he'll never be able to come back here. He'll always be on the run. And wherever he landed he'd need to work.'

'Getting him a new name and identity wouldn't be too difficult. There's people here who can pretty much do anything if you know who to ask – and if you have a pound or two to give them.'

The plan was risky but it could work. And what other option did they have? Her father was perfectly capable of carrying out his threats. It was the only certain way for her to keep her children and save Alasdair's life.

She squared her shoulders. 'Very well. Let's do it. I'll write to Dr MacLean tonight. How long do you think you'll need to plan everything?'

'Has a trial date been set?'

'I only know it's going to be soon.'

'And when is your father expecting an answer?'

'In ten days.' She felt another surge of hopelessness. Surely that wasn't enough time to arrange everything? 'I could probably stall him for a few more but...'

'It's long enough if we move quickly. I've already sounded the men out. Hold on, wait just a minute, I've remembered something.' He jumped up and snatched the newspaper from the table. He turned back to the two women, pointing to the front page headline. 'The King and Queen will be visiting the Clyde to launch the new ship for the Cunard line exactly eight days from now. Couldn't be better timing!'

'What do you mean, Toni? The whole of Glasgow will be teeming with police,' Mairi retorted.

Toni smacked his hand on his thigh. 'Exactly! They'll be too busy keeping an eye on the royal visitors and not on Duke Street, won't they? So that's decided. Eight days it is, then. I'll find out what ships are leaving that night and speak to the men I need to. There's a lot to do so I'd better get going.'

'What will I tell Alasdair?'

'Whatever you need to get him on that boat.'

Back home, Margaret got the children ready for bed. As soon as they were tucked up and drifting off to sleep, fuelled with a renewed sense of purpose, she started making plans. Whatever the risks in Mairi and Toni's scheme – and there were many – at least this way, her and Alasdair's fate was in their own hands.

First of all, she needed to find out whether Dr MacLean was still looking for a winter assistant.

She kept all the back issues of the medical journals in the small cupboard in the sitting room alongside her medical books. Although she read them from cover to cover as soon as they arrived, she never threw any of them away, in case she needed to refer to an article at a later date.

She lifted the latest copies from the shelf and sat on the floor and started going through them. She found the advert in the May edition. It was simple and to the point. *Winter Assistant required for island in the Outer Hebrides until the end of February. Monthly stipend and small house. Hours long. Would suit bachelor and keen fisherman.*

This last made her heart sink. She wasn't a bachelor and she certainly wasn't interested in fishing. Would Dr MacLean accept a woman? A married woman with two small children at that. Unlikely. No matter how desperate he was. In which case she would have to pretend to be a widow. A cold shiver ran up her spine and she prayed she wasn't tempting fate. Thanks to Mairi, she could assure him that suitable arrangements had been made for the children to be looked after so he need not worry that they would interfere with her duties.

She eased herself from the floor and crossed over to the small gate-leg table she used in lieu of a writing desk. She unscrewed the top of her fountain pen and started to write. She wrote that she was a widow (again that shiver of disquiet) and, although she hadn't practised for a number of years, she'd done everything to keep up to date with medical advances. She told him she'd two small children, but would arrange for them to stay with relatives of a friend. Finally she wrote that she was eager to take up the position as soon as possible and if he decided she was acceptable, she could come immediately.

When she was finished there was still the matter of how to sign herself. She couldn't take the job as Dr Margaret Morrison or even Dr Bannatyne. She'd be too conspicuous and too easy to trace. She needed another name. The name of a woman doctor on the medical register in case Dr Mac-Lean checked. And it had to be someone who wasn't already working in this country. She tapped the end of the pen against her teeth. There was one obvious choice. Martha. She was still in India and had no plans to return to Britain in the foreseeable future.

Margaret hesitated, her pen poised over the paper. She should ask Martha's permission, but if she did, time would be wasted while letters went back and forth. And, she suspected that Martha, no matter how sympathetic she might be, would refuse. Martha hated dishonesty in any form. As did Margaret, but she only had to think of what would happen if she didn't manage to get a job that would remove her from her father's reach to know she had no choice. It would only be for a few months. What Margaret would do after that she couldn't imagine.

'Forgive me, my friend,' Margaret whispered and signed the letter *Dr Martha Murdoch*.

Chapter 21

The days rushed past in a flurry of preparations. Although there was still time before she was due to sign the papers handing over custody of her children, Margaret was terrified that her father would take action to remove them without waiting for her decision. In the meantime she telephoned Mr Johnston every day, still hoping against hope that she'd been mistaken about him and that he'd have found a witness. But the news was always the same. No new witnesses. No new evidence.

Mairi had called at the flat, whispering out of earshot of the children that the plans had been laid. There was a boat leaving for Canada the same day as the new ship's launch and that was the one they planned to stow Alasdair away on. A policeman they knew had arranged to be on duty the day of the planned escape. They would make sure it would appear as if he'd been overpowered.

She'd also received a telegram back from Dr MacLean. To her relief, it stated that the post was still vacant. She should come for a month's trial and if she suited, the position would be extended to the end of February. A letter would follow but in the meantime could she arrange to come immediately?

The day after she received the telegram was her scheduled visit with Alasdair. There were only three days left before her father expected an answer, two before the planned escape. If Alasdair was going to flee, he had to be convinced today.

The hope in her husband's eyes when he entered the room almost undid her. He thought she'd come because she had good news for him. She wanted nothing more than to put her head in her hands and sob. But there was no time for histrionics. She had to find a way of telling Alasdair about their plans and getting his agreement.

She started speaking almost before he was seated. 'We haven't found new evidence or new witnesses yet. We need to accept it's unlikely we'll find anyone before your trial.' She hated putting it so baldly but he had to be convinced there was no hope.

His shoulders slumped, but just for a moment. He looked up at her, worry etching his eyes. 'And the children? Are they all right?'

Margaret looked down at her hands. 'Yes. For the moment.'

The guard sat on a chair by the door, holding his newspaper up close to his face and making a show of reading it.

'What do you mean "for the moment"?' He made to move his shackled hands towards her. 'What is it? Tell me. Is one of them ill?'

'No, it's not that. They are both well. But there is something...' She glanced nervously at the policeman. 'Something I need to discuss with you.' How on earth was she going to tell him when they could so easily be overheard?

Alasdair caught her look. 'Any chance you could make yourself scarce for a bit, Dougie?' he said over his shoulder.

Dougie put down his paper and winked. 'Come to think of it, I do need the lav – excuse the language, Miss. I can give you ten minutes – no longer.'

When he'd left, Alasdair stood. 'Dougie owes me for a favour I did his uncle. He's a good man.' He held out his shackled wrists. 'Let me hold you.'

She slipped under the circle of his arms and he pulled her close. She felt the beating of his heart as he held her against him and for a moment she just let her head rest there as she had done so many times during their married life.

'Now tell me,' Alasdair murmured into her hair.

Tripping over her words she told him about the meeting with her father. His muscles tensed when she got to the part about signing the children over.

'If I don't, he'll see you hang, Alasdair. If you were in danger before, you're in worse danger now. I'm so sorry. I only went to him because I thought that even if he had no love left for me, his pride would never let you be convicted. When you refused to plead guilty I thought it was the only way to keep you safe.'

'And how did you imagine he was going to help?' His eyes were as cold as a December morning.

'I didn't care.' She turned her face away. 'Whatever way he could.'

'You must have known he would have to bend the law.'

She met his eyes. 'You are innocent. How can it be right that you get convicted?' She took a deep breath, trying to ease the tightness in her chest.

'But yes, Alasdair, even if it meant breaking the law, agreeing to others committing perjury, offering bribes, whatever it took, whatever it takes – I would agree to it if it meant you were free or safe.'

'Does he really think for one minute that either of us would agree to sign our children over to him?'

'Don't you understand? He will take the children anyway! Whether you're convicted or not.'

She burrowed her head in his shoulder. 'I've gone over and over it until I thought I was going mad. I even considered signing over the children – at least you would be free and we could fight to get the children back then. But I can't take the chance. I can't!'

'I won't trade my children for my life.' He was quiet for a very long time. 'I'll plead guilty,' he whispered into her hair. 'Johnston told me that the Crown wouldn't go for the death penalty if I did. I'll get a long sentence but they won't hang me.'

She raised her head and gripped his arms. 'Don't you see, Alasdair? It's too late for that now. It's too risky. Changing your plea to guilty will make no difference. Father can still use his influence to make sure you hang! Then you'll be dead and he'll take the children anyway.' Her voice caught on a sob and he tightened his arms around her. 'We can't trust him. He's crazy. He's only telling me that he can make sure you'll be found innocent to make me sign over the children. It would be easier for him rather than having to go through the courts or have me committed. Even if he made good on his promise and later we said we handed the children over under duress, we couldn't be sure the courts would believe us.'

'Then you and the children must go. Forget about me! Hide somewhere – make a new life for yourselves...'

Although taking the children and hiding was part of her plan, it was one thing fleeing Glasgow when she knew Alasdair was safe, quite another thing when he was still in danger of losing his life. 'There is a way to save you and for us to keep the children. Toni has a plan. With help he can get you out of gaol and on a ship.'

Alasdair frowned down at her. 'You want me to escape? Dear God, Margaret. Do you have any idea what you're suggesting?'

'Just listen to me–'

'And what about you and the children? They'd never be able to smuggle the four of us on board a ship, that much I do know.'

'No, no, of course not. We know that.' Margaret knew she was running out of time. Dougie could return any minute. She *had* to convince Alasdair that their plan was the right one. 'I've managed to get a job as a doctor in the Outer Hebrides. That's where Mam's family come from. Remember? Mairi's sister Flora will look after the children. My father will never think to look for us there.' She searched his face, praying he would see it was their only way. 'I'm going to assume my friend Martha's name. We can stay there until all the fuss has died down, then myself and the children can join you – wherever that may be.'

'I'm not leaving without you. Not when I know what your father intends.' He studied her through

216

his thick, long lashes. 'But you must go – get away as far as you can from your father. Today. Tomorrow at the latest. Take the post. Make a new life for yourself and our children. Whatever the future has in store for me I can accept as long as you and the children are together, safe and happy.'

'We'll never be happy without you! I told you before I would never give up on you. How can I leave you when I don't know what is going to happen to you?' She closed her eyes in exasperation. 'Will you just listen to me for once, Alasdair Morrison!' she hissed. 'This plan of Toni's is the only way.'

'My love, they'll come looking for you as soon as it's discovered I've escaped!'

Margaret glanced over to the door, expecting Dougie to come walking back in at any moment. 'They would be looking for four people, a family. Not a single man and a woman on her own with two children.'

Alasdair's eyes glinted. 'You've got it all worked out, haven't you? Is there no end to the surprises you keep throwing at me, Mrs Morrison?' He bent his head to kiss her hair. 'It could all go wrong, my love, terribly wrong. People could get hurt, or caught. They'd be charged with aiding and abetting a crime and I'd be responsible for that. And by escaping I will look as guilty as they believe me to be.'

'You are not responsible for everyone's actions, Alasdair! If they weren't willing to take the risk they wouldn't have offered. It's up to them if they want to help you. After all, you have helped so many in the past – why can't you let them do the same for you?'

'It's not right. The law is the law, Margaret. It's what I believe in.'

'I know. But we have no other way. There *is* no other way.' Margaret pressed her body into Alasdair's and wrapped her arms around his neck. 'Will you do it?' she whispered. 'For my sake, and our children's, will you do it?'

'You know what you are asking of me?'

'I do.' Her voice caught on a sob. How could she let him go when she might never see him again? 'I wouldn't ask if it wasn't the only way. If you love me–'

'If I love you! There isn't a man in the world who loves a woman more than I love you.'

'Then say you'll go. For the love of God, Alasdair, say you'll go.'

Her heart banging against her ribs, she looked up at him, willing him to agree.

Alasdair took her face between his palms, the handcuffs only allowing him enough room to cup her chin. 'I'll not change my plea. This is what we are going to do. You take the children to the Hebrides.' When she made to protest he stopped her words with his fingertip. 'Before you leave, go and see Simon Firth. I've worked with him in the past. He's not experienced,' he gave her a wry smile, 'in fact I doubt he's ever been involved with a murder case, but he's bright and he's hungry for success. If he were more experienced I would have suggested him before but it seems to me he can't do worse than Johnston. Most importantly, he knows me. He'll know I'm innocent. Unlike Johnston.'

'But—'

'Hear me out. From the time I enter my plea, the Crown has a hundred and ten days before it moves to sentence. That law exists to stop prisoners from languishing in gaol indefinitely but it can work in our favour. Firth can use the time to find witnesses. Real witnesses. Not bought ones. You see, I still have faith.'

'I can't leave you when you are in prison! Don't ask me to.'

'You have to, Margaret. You have to protect our children. I can't do that from in here.'

'But what if you are found guilty? My father — you know what he's capable of.'

'I've taken on your father before and won and I'll do it again.' He searched her face. 'You said you wouldn't give up on me. I need you to trust me. I need you to have faith that I can do this. And I need to know you and the children are out of harm's way. Please, Margaret, do that for me.'

How could she leave him now? Did he know what he was asking? Did he truly appreciate the risk he was taking? When she didn't reply he continued, 'All I have left is you and the children and my dignity. Don't take that away from me. If I escape I'll be telling the world I am guilty. I'll be telling the men I helped not to believe in justice — that they shouldn't trust in the law. I'll be telling my children the same.'

'But if you hang—'

'Then I'll hang telling the world I am innocent.'

She clutched him tighter. 'I couldn't bear it! I couldn't go on living in a world without you in it.'

A glimmer of a smile crossed his face. 'I have no

intention of having my neck stretched for something I didn't do. But it won't come to that.'

She knew his mind was made up and she would never change it.

'If you are found guilty, I'll come back. Even if I have to walk across the ocean, I'll come.' She clung to him, pressing her body into his, wanting to imprint the smell and feel of his body against her into her memory. How could she bear to let him go when she might never see him again?

'We *will* be together again. You are my heart, my soul, my life, and God will not keep us apart.'

Just then Dougie came back into the room. 'Your time's up, son,' he said to Alasdair. 'If I don't return you to your cell, they'll be wondering what's up. It won't help anyone, least of all you, if they know I've been treating you softly.'

'Tell the children that I love them.' Alasdair lowered his voice and she could see her anguish reflected in his eyes. 'Tell them that their father tried to be a good man.'

'It's time, son,' Dougie repeated gruffly.

'One minute, Dougie.' Alasdair tipped her chin with his forefinger. 'I love you, Margaret Morrison. I love everything about you and every inch of you. I'll love you for as long as there is breath in my body.' He smiled a little. 'And after that too.'

He bent his head and her mouth found his. She put all of her love into that kiss, wishing that she could stop the world from turning. Only when Dougie took Alasdair by the shoulder did they pull apart. 'Have faith, my love,' Alasdair repeated, his eyes never leaving hers.

'I'll love you till my dying breath, Alasdair Morrison.' She waited until he'd left the room. As her heart shattered into a thousand pieces she put her head in her hands and sobbed.

Chapter 22

Simon Firth's office was the antithesis of Johnston's. It was in a rundown part of Scotstoun, close to Fairfield's shipyard and, rather than a purpose-built office, it was a converted flat at the top of a red-stone tenement. Needless to say there was no secretary and it was Firth himself who answered the door to Margaret's knock.

The lawyer was red-haired, thin-faced and pale, and there was a patch of eczema above his right brow. He was wearing a threadbare suit, the lapels of which were flecked with cigarette ash, and a shirt with a worn collar. His shoes were scuffed and the room littered with files, books and papers. Margaret's heart sank. If Johnston couldn't help them, what chance this man?

Nevertheless, Alasdair was putting his faith in him so she had to too. She explained why she'd come and the progress, or rather lack of it, with Alasdair's case so far.

'I read about it, of course.' A piece of ash from his cigarette fell on the floor but Firth didn't seem to notice. 'Knew it was rubbish straight away. Alasdair Morrison is the last man to murder someone. Wondered a bit when I heard Johnston had taken on the case.'

'He's the best. Or so I was told.' Yet he had done so very little.

'Most expensive, anyway. Not the same thing.'

She reached into her bag and removed some notes from her purse, holding them out to him. 'I have only a few pounds.' It was the best part of what remained of the collection Toni had given her.

'Put that away. Your husband sent work my way when I was just starting off. I owe him a favour.'

'He'll insist.'

'He may do, but he's not here, is he?' Firth smiled, revealing yellow, discoloured teeth. He lit another cigarette although the first one was still burning in the ashtray. 'He can pay me when I get him off.'

'You think you can?'

'Do my bloody best. Pardon the French. You say that there's a Dr Marshall who believes that what Alasdair did with the knife – trying to stop the lad from pulling it out – was the right thing to do?'

'Yes.'

'Wonder why Johnston didn't take a statement from him then. Of course, he may have done. I'll need him to send me Alasdair's file.' He grinned wolfishly. 'Can't wait to see his face when he learns he's been fired.'

'Alasdair said that he'd tell him.'

'Good. Now you say Alasdair has to enter his plea on Friday?'

She nodded.

'Right, then. As he told you, once he does, we

have a maximum of one hundred and ten days before he has to be sentenced. Say the prosecution believe they need five days for the trial – on the safe side ten – to present their case before sentencing, then we have a hundred days from Friday to find the evidence we need – a hundred has a nice round feel to it, doesn't it?'

'Do you think that's long enough?'

'Will bloody well have to be. Excuse my French again. Can't understand why Johnston hasn't done more in the time he's had. Sign of a lazy lawyer – at best.' He picked up a fountain pen and tapped it against his teeth. 'Will find that out too, no doubt. Now where will I get in touch with you?'

'I have to leave Glasgow.' She reached across his desk and rummaged through the piles of papers until she found a scrap to write on. 'This is our friends Toni and Mairi's address. You can reach me through them.'

'Forgive me, Mrs Morrison, but why are you going away? It seems a strange time to leave.'

Reluctantly she explained about her father and his threats.

'I see. What do you think his chances are of influencing the case?'

'He knows people. Powerful people. People who will sign whatever he asks them to.'

His expression sharpened. 'So I have Bannatyne's might to contend with too.'

'Does that worry you?'

'Not at all. Ask Alasdair. He knows I like a fight. We both do.'

Alarmed, she leaned forward. 'Don't underesti-

223

mate my father. You'll be making a mistake if you do.'

'I never underestimate anyone, Mrs Morrison, but people have a habit of underestimating me. And that suits me just fine. To be perfectly honest it works to my advantage. For what it's worth, I think you are doing the right thing by going into hiding. I could represent you if your father tried to carry out his threats but that would take my time, and attention, away from your husband. Once I have him out it will be a different matter.' He glanced at the calendar on his desk, stood and held out his hand. 'A hundred days, Mrs Morrison. No time to waste. The clock is ticking.'

Chapter 23

Uist

As the boat drew alongside Lochmaddy pier, Margaret exhaled. It had been a long, arduous and nerve-racking two days of travel. She'd expected at any moment to be stopped, her father to emerge, the children to be snatched from her, while she was carted off to one of the mental institutions. But what was worse was not knowing what had happened to Alasdair. She couldn't even attend his committal hearing and let the world know she was standing by her husband. He had pleaded not guilty and the trial date had been set for the twenty-third of December. Ninety-nine days away.

Please God, enough time for Firth to find something that would help Alasdair's case.

During the journey from Glasgow, she'd been as careful as she could be not to attract attention. She and the children had taken a bus in the early hours of the morning along with several other sleepy travellers. No one had paid them more than a passing look on the long and bumpy journey. They'd had to wait at Mallaig for several anxious hours before the steamer was due to leave and, determined to avoid the ever-garrulous and friendly questions of her fellow Glaswegians, Margaret had taken the children off to a café for bowls of soup and a sandwich, ensuring that they arrived back at the pier just before the ship departed. On board, she'd found seats as far away from her fellow passengers as she could manage and tried her best to keep Libby and James occupied with colouring pencils and paper.

The children's excitement at their first-ever ferry trip had soon waned as they'd sailed further west. Tossed about on the ocean as the clouds grew heavy with rain and the wind picked up, it had felt as if the sailing would never end. The boat had lurched and bucketed its way through the waves, even more as they'd crossed the Minch, and inevitably Elizabeth had been sick although thankfully James had slept most of the way. He'd woken now and was in her arms, looking around with his usual curious stare. The only good thing about the rough sea voyage was that most of the other passengers were too queasy themselves to want to engage her in conversation. But, finally, they were here.

Although it wouldn't be dark for another couple of hours the landscape looked flat and bleak – drained of all colour. As bleak as the way she felt.

She felt a small hand slip into hers and looked down at her daughter.

'I still feel sick, Mummy.'

'You'll feel better as soon as you get on dry land,' Margaret reassured her. 'We'll be going ashore any minute.'

'Are *you* all right, Mummy?' Elizabeth asked.

Elizabeth had been asking the same thing for days now. Margaret had tried to hide her grief, fear, dismay and sometimes downright fury at the turn their lives had taken, but her daughter had clearly picked up on her mother's wildly fluctuating emotions.

'I am perfectly fine,' Margaret answered, putting as much bravado into her voice as she could manage. Balancing James in one arm, she crouched down and pulled the lapels of Elizabeth's coat close. *'Everything's* going to be fine. We are going to have such fun. You'll see.'

'I don't want to live with Aunty Flora. And neither does James. We want to live with you, Mummy. Else how will Daddy know where to find us?'

Not knowing what else to say, she'd told Elizabeth that her father was having a long sleep, just like Sleeping Beauty, but one day they'd be together again. She couldn't tell her daughter Alasdair was in gaol and she couldn't bring herself to say he was dead – even if that would have been safer for all of them. She prayed that she wouldn't one day have to tell her child that Daddy was asleep forever.

'We've talked about this, Libby. You and James can't live with me. Not to begin with.' She squeezed Libby's hand. 'And Daddy will always be able to find us. In the meantime he is keeping us all in his heart as we are keeping him.' She sucked in a breath to steady her voice. 'You will get used to being at Aunty Flora's after a while and in the meantime we still have tonight and most of tomorrow.'

They were to stay with Dr MacLean that night and make the onward journey to Grimsay, where Flora and her family lived, the next afternoon. However much Elizabeth didn't want to be separated from her mother, Margaret knew she'd find it just as difficult to be without them. When her daughter still looked doubtful, Margaret pulled her close. 'You are going to have to be brave. We are *all* going to have to be brave. We'll be homesick for a while, but that will go. You'll see. Aunty Flora and Uncle Peter will take good care of you. They have children around your age so you'll always have someone to play with. And once you start school, you'll make lots of new friends.'

Elizabeth wriggled away and regarded her with solemn grey-blue eyes, so like her father's it made Margaret's throat tighten. 'I'll be brave for a little while,' she said finally.

The boat shuddered to a halt and the crew leaped to tie it to its moorings. Laughter drifted up from the pier where several people stood chattering excitedly in Gaelic, craning their necks as they searched for loved ones on board. They were a motley crowd. The men wore flat caps, wellington boots and thick serge shirts, those whose trousers were not held up by braces, held up by string. The women either wore wellingtons, incongruous with their skirts, or boots and ankle socks, their hair covered by scarves. There were several children waiting too, many of whom were barefoot. Margaret knew only too well this wasn't a wealthy community but it was one that desperately needed doctors – possibly even more than the people of Govan. Until the Scottish Board of Health had introduced salaries for rural doctors, the people here had been without.

But what really took her by surprise was how crystal clear and sweet smelling the air was. She could see as far as the horizon. She'd become so used to the smog of Glasgow it was like inhaling sea-scented perfume.

As the gangway was lowered, Margaret swallowed. This was it. This was either where she took her first step in her planned deception, or it was where the police would be waiting for her and everything would be over before it had begun. Had she done the right thing abandoning Alasdair? Because despite everything they had agreed, it still felt as if that was what she was doing. And as for the running and hiding – the deceit – the lies she still had to tell! She fingered the watch inside her pocket and straightened her shoulders. As long as Alasdair had a chance to prove his innocence and the children were safe, then the answer had to be yes. Besides, it was too late now for regrets.

Margaret told Elizabeth to stay close to her

while she carried the suitcases. Not that they were very heavy, or full. She'd been able to take very little with her. A few books, a couple of favourite toys and enough clothes to last them over the coming winter, supposing Dr MacLean kept her on.

He must. If he didn't she had no idea what they would do or where they would go. She had almost no money left, barely enough to last until her first pay and certainly not enough to travel anywhere else. The flat she'd shared with Alasdair in Glasgow had been rented, the furniture second hand and past its best, and she couldn't risk selling what little remained of their possessions that might have fetched a few more pounds in case she attracted attention. Instead she'd left them for Peggy to do with as she wanted. Apart from their two children, all she had left of her life with Alasdair was her wedding ring, their wedding photograph and the fob watch that she'd been unable to bring herself to sell.

One of the crew waiting on the pier hurried up the gangway, pushed back his cap and reached for their suitcases. 'I'll take those,' he said. At the sound of his voice, his accent so similar to Mairi's, she felt her throat tighten. She would give anything to be back in the small flat in Garnethill, their two friends singing along as Alasdair played his fiddle, the children sleeping soundly and their biggest worry being how to make ends meet.

'Thank you.' She tightened her grip on a wriggling James, took Elizabeth by the hand and picked her way down the gangway, noting the fishing boats tied up alongside the pier and the neat piles of creels that lay close by. Mairi had told her that most of the islanders depended on the unpredictable and seasonal occupations of fishing and crofting to eke out a meagre existence.

A car, precariously balanced in a large net, was being unloaded by a crane while a group of men who had disembarked in front of her watched with folded arms. They looked as out of place as she felt. They weren't crofters or lobster fishermen, that was clear from their expensive tweed jackets and plus-fours and even more so from their sense of entitlement, the same sense of entitlement her father possessed. Another wave of anxiety washed over her. These were the sort of people most likely to recognise her. She hadn't noticed them on the ship – no doubt they'd spent the crossing in the saloon or in the first-class lounge. She ducked her head to avoid catching their eyes.

The crew member placed their bags on the ground. She tried to pass him a penny, but he shook his head and backed away. 'No need, Miss,' he said.

Realising she'd offended him, she quickly slipped the coin back inside her purse and looked around. 'I'm expecting Dr MacLean to meet me. Is he here?'

'So you're the new doctor? Well, well – they did say it was a woman. Didn't believe it myself at first, but everyone told me it was true.'

Margaret forced a smile. 'I'm Dr Murdoch.' It was the first time she'd called herself by her assumed name and when she tripped over it, she hoped the man wouldn't notice. 'This is my daughter, Libby and my son James.' If he'd noticed her small hesitation he gave no indication of it. Instead he held out a large hand and shook Libby's gravely. *'Failte.* That means welcome in Gaelic.'

Margaret became aware that everyone – except for the men in the plus-fours who had marched off in the direction of a nearby hotel – had stopped whatever they were doing and were watching them with unabashed curiosity.

'Now then, you'll be looking for your hire car. That'll be Johnny Ban. He's over there.' He pointed to a man standing by the only vehicle in sight. He was holding a shepherd's crook in one hand and a parcel wrapped in brown paper and tied with string in the other. 'Johnny only has the Gaelic, but he knows where to take you.'

She'd expected Dr MacLean to meet her. A hired car was an expense she could ill afford.

'Isn't Dr MacLean here?'

'No. Johnny Ban was just now after telling me that the doctor's out on a call, otherwise I'm sure he'd have come himself.'

As she walked towards the vehicle the crowd parted to make way for her, the men removing their hats and the women nodding, she heard the word *doctor* being whispered.

She nodded self-consciously in return. She'd hoped to avoid drawing attention to herself, but it appeared that the arrival of the new doctor – and a woman at that – was considered something of an occasion.

Johnny unpeeled himself from the car and tipped a finger to his cap. He held out his hand and she went to shake it before realising that he

231

was reaching for their suitcases. He placed their bags inside the boot along with the parcels and shepherd's crook. Aware that all eyes were still on her, Margaret ushered her wide-eyed children into the car and took a seat beside them. As Johnny closed the door behind them she breathed a sigh of relief.

The car crept along at a snail's pace along the untarred road and when she glanced behind her she saw that most of the children waiting on the pier were now scampering behind, laughing and pointing. A few of the older locals appeared to be following too. Were they planning to accompany them all the way?

As they made their majestic progress, the car blowing its horn to move people from the road, they passed several houses, a couple of general merchant stores, a post office, another hotel and a large, imposing court house. A few minutes later, Johnny drew up outside a house that was far more substantial than any of the others they had passed. It was a two-storey building set back from the road and shielded by the only trees Margaret had seen so far. Johnny jumped out and opened the door for them with a flourish.

It seemed they'd arrived. They could have easily walked and saved a few pennies.

Conscious of several pairs of eyes still on her, Margaret raised her hand to knock on the front door. But before she could, the door was flung open by a tall woman with grey hair scraped back into a bun, accentuating her thin, angular face and protuberant front teeth. She glowered at Margaret.

'You're here then.'

Clearly. Given they were standing on the door-step. Margaret held out her hand. 'I'm Dr Murdoch and this is my daughter Libby and my son James.'

'I know who you are.' The woman swivelled her eyes towards the children. James simply stared back but Elizabeth, who had crept round behind Margaret, was peering at the stranger with large, bewildered eyes. The woman's expression softened and a glimmer of a smile stretched her thin lips. 'My, aren't you bonnie?' She lifted her eyes back to Margaret and the smile, small as it had been, vanished. 'I'm Miss Dolina MacGregor, Dr Alan's housekeeper. He's out on a call and I have no idea when he'll return but he's instructed me to see to you until he gets in. Leave your suitcases in the hall. I'll take them up later.'

'Oh, I nearly forgot. I haven't paid Mr Ban,' Margaret said.

'Mr Ban?' Miss MacGregor frowned. She shook her head and muttered something in Gaelic under her breath. 'There's no need for you to pay *Mr Ban* anything – he'll send the practice a bill. Now, come through to the sitting room.' She led the way down a wood-panelled corridor, still talking as they followed her ramrod back.

'Dr Alan insisted I light a fire and the summer not done yet. Waste of good peats if you ask me, but what do I know?' She picked up a cushion from the chair next to the fire, patted it and indicated with her head that Margaret should sit.

Elizabeth, who hadn't let go of Margaret's hand, pressed herself against her mother's legs, her eyes fixated on Miss MacGregor. James reached up small hands to be lifted and Margaret took him onto her lap. He buried his head in her shoulder.

The housekeeper bent down in front of Elizabeth, placing her red hands on her knees. 'Now child, would you like some supper? Of course you would. A boiled egg with a scone – and some nice milk straight from the cow to go with it – how does that sound?'

Elizabeth pressed herself more firmly into Margaret's legs.

'I don't wish to put you to any trouble,' Margaret protested politely.

The woman straightened up, placed her hands on her skinny hips and glared at Margaret. 'The wee ones must be hungry. They need something to eat before bed. I expect you would like something too,' she added, almost as an afterthought.

'Thank you. That would be lovely.' Margaret realised she was starving. Now they were here and no one had challenged them, the tension that had kept her stomach in knots over the last few days had eased a little.

'Right, then. The kettle's on. I've set places for you at the table so sit yourselves up. This is where Dr Alan has his meals – no fancy city ways here – the dining room is used as a waiting room for the surgery.'

She bustled out of the room and Libby and Margaret, still holding James, each took a seat at the one of the places that had been laid for them at a gate-leg table in front of the window.

'You all right, sweetheart?' Margaret asked Elizabeth.

'That lady scares me, Mummy,' she whispered. 'She looks like a witch – a mean and nasty witch.'

Although Margaret was inclined to agree with her daughter, she held her finger up to her lips and glanced nervously at the door. 'Ssshhh! That's not kind! I'm sure she's very nice once we get to know her.' However, she was bemused by the house-keeper's reaction. She'd expected a warm welcome, not this frosty reception.

Miss MacGregor reappeared and plonked down a large teapot and a plate of scones on the table. 'We don't get bread here so this is what we make instead. They're like ordinary scones but not as sweet. There's butter too. Home-made, of course – and jam. Wait now and I'll get the eggs.'

She hurried out again and Margaret poured Elizabeth and James a glass of milk from the jug. James took his between his two small hands and drank thirstily. Elizabeth just sat with her hands in her lap, looking pale and unhappy.

'Drink up, Libby.'

'Not hungry.'

'Try a little. We don't want to offend Miss Mac-Gregor.' Somehow, however, it seemed that they had already.

Elizabeth took a small sip of milk. 'Yuck. It's warm. And tastes funny.'

'Give it to me.'

The housekeeper returned with a tray of boiled eggs and added them to the table. 'I think that's everything. I'll leave you to it.'

'Oh, Miss MacGregor, before you go could you tell me how to contact Mr Ban again? I want to make sure he's able to take us to Carinish tomorrow. Mr MacDonald, whose wife is going to look after the children, is going to pick us up there tomorrow afternoon.'

'Aye, I'd heard that your children were going to stay with–' she pursed her lips, 'folk in Grimsay.' Her mouth turned down at the corners. 'Well, you needn't worry, all the arrangements have already been made.'

'I want to stay with you, Mummy,' Elizabeth mumbled.

'I know, Libby.'

'Small children living apart from their mothers. Would never have happened in my day. Not if it could be helped.'

Margaret stared at the housekeeper. For Miss MacGregor to make such a remark in front of the children almost beggared belief. If she only knew how it was tearing Margaret up inside knowing that all too soon she was to be separated from them for the first time ever, surely the housekeeper would never have thought such a thing, let alone said it. And Margaret's domestic arrangements were none of her business anyway. She bit back the response that rose to her lips. Now was not the time to take her to task.

'The children know how much I wish they could stay with me and how much I'm going to miss them,' she said calmly. She smiled at Elizabeth and smoothed a lock of James's hair from his eyes, before dropping a kiss on his forehead.

Thankfully the sound of dogs barking and the front door banging prevented any further discussion. A draught rattled through the sitting room and a shiver of unease rippled up her spine. She was about to face her first real hurdle. What if Dr MacLean somehow guessed she wasn't who she said she was?

'That'll be Dr Alan now,' Miss MacGregor said.

Heavy footsteps clumped past the door and there was the sound of thumps and crashes coming from somewhere within the house. A moment later, the sitting-room door was flung open.

Margaret had imagined an older man but Dr MacLean, she guessed, was in his mid-forties, a little thick around the waist, but with a lovely smile. His hair was sticking up from where he'd removed his hat.

Margaret laid down her napkin, set James on his feet and stood up. She smoothed down her skirt and tucked her hair behind her ears.

'Apologies, Dr Murdoch! But may I call you Martha? Yes, of course I may!' His voice boomed around the sitting room as he shook her hand.

'Would you mind calling me Margaret? It's my middle name and the one I have always preferred.'

'Martha – Margaret – makes no difference to me. Would have liked to have been here to meet you, but had a delivery in Sollas. Nurse called me to help. Breech. You done much maternity?' He waved his hand in the direction of the chair Margaret had just vacated. 'Sit, girl. Sit.'

'Some, during my training and–' She caught herself just in time, about to add that she'd seen many cases when she worked in Redlands, but the less said about where she worked the better, 'and some in the district. But that was a while ago, Dr MacLean.' She sat back down, realising for the first time just how difficult pretending to

237

be someone else was going to be.

'None of this Dr MacLean falderal – everyone calls me Dr Alan and you'll be Dr Margaret.'

She felt a tinge of relief. To be referred to by her first name would make life a little easier.

'Now where were we?' her employer continued, 'Oh yes. Maternity. You'll soon pick it up again. The nurses know what to do. Done it plenty of times. They'll keep an eye on you. I'd be surprised if you couldn't do it in your sleep when you've been here for a while. If you stay, that is. Last assistant didn't.' He glared at Margaret as if it were her fault.

'I have no intention of leaving,' Margaret said firmly. At least not until either Alasdair was released or, God forbid, in order to attend his trial. 'As long as I suit,' she added, fervently hoping she would.

'Teeth!'

Margaret was stunned. She ran her tongue around her mouth.

'My teeth are fine,' she said. 'Why do you ask?'

'Not your teeth. I can see that there's nothing wrong with them. I meant how are you at pulling teeth?'

'Dr Alan,' Miss MacGregor interrupted, 'Why don't I show the children where they'll be sleeping tonight and leave you to talk to Dr Margaret?'

'There's a lobster in the sink,' Dr Alan said. 'Perhaps the children would like to see it?'

'You didn't put it in the sink, did you? How many times have I told you to put them in the pail by the door?'

'What pail?'

The housekeeper folded her arms and tutted. 'The same one that's always there.'

Once again, Margaret was taken aback. The way Miss MacGregor chastised Dr Alan seemed far too familiar. Who was the housekeeper to the doctor? A relative? A maiden aunt perhaps? That would explain the casual, almost scolding, attitude she took with her employer, if not her disapproval of Margaret.

Miss MacGregor picked James up from the floor where he'd been tapping a spoon against a bucket and held out her hand to Elizabeth. 'Come on, child, let's go see your room. You can help me make up a hot water bottle if you like and there's some kittens in the barn we can go and see.'

Surprisingly James accepted being lifted by a stranger and, albeit reluctantly, Elizabeth took the proffered hand. Margaret blew a kiss to her daughter and waited until the door closed behind them, before turning back to Dr Alan. 'I've never pulled teeth before. Why do you ask?'

'Because you'll have to pull them here. No dentist.' He looked at her sceptically. 'You don't look very strong.'

Margaret decided to let that pass. 'Miss Mac-Gregor mentioned you use the dining room as a waiting room. Is the surgery also in the house?'

'Yes. I'll show you. If you've finished your supper?'

'I'm quite finished, thank you.'

He took her down a dim passageway, past a collie and a Labrador lying in the hall, who wagged their tails hopefully, and opened a door at the end. 'This is the waiting room.'

Margaret glanced inside, taking in the jumble of mismatched chairs. A well-worn rug covered the wooden floor and a few still-life pictures adorned the walls. It smelt strongly of beeswax and the bevelled mirror above the unlit fireplace gleamed. It might be sparsely furnished but it was spotless. Whatever Miss MacGregor's other faults there was nothing wrong with her housekeeping skills.

Dr Alan opened the door next to it. This room was much smaller, with a cracked leather examination couch and a stainless steel table and a sink. It also had, she noticed with dismay, a fishing rod, a pair of waders in the corner and a shotgun propped up against the wall.

'I—' he smiled broadly, 'we now, hold outpatient surgeries in community halls across the island as well as here.'

'Are they as well equipped as this one?' Margaret tried to keep the irony from her voice but if Dr Alan noticed he didn't let on.

'I carry most of what I need in my bag. The nurses set the rooms up in advance. We have two district nurses here in North Uist – Effie here in Lochmaddy and Anne McAllister in Carinish. Could do with more, but we're glad to have them. They cover the island between them. See those who don't need to see the doctor. Pregnant women and so on. Not that we manage to see the women more than once before they deliver and sometimes not at all. We try and get them to come more often, but travel, and expense, are issues for most of the people here.'

Only one antenatal visit? Sometimes none? In Glasgow they encouraged women to come to antenatal clinics regularly throughout their pregnancy. It was known to reduce the infant mortality rate substantially. At least one thing was the same here – she'd have the support of experienced nurses.

Dr Alan pointed to a book lying open on the desk. 'You must write down every patient you go to see in there. No exceptions. We need to keep our accounts straight. The minister's wife, Sophie, comes in once a week to do them and she'll have your guts for garters if you don't enter every visit and every time you dispense medicine.'

'I'll remember,' Margaret promised.

'Sophie used to be one of the district nurses, but gave it up when she married. A minister's wife has too much to do.' His face relaxed and he smiled. 'But Dolina – Miss MacGregor – helps out. Lets us know who's in and who can be seen by a nurse instead of the doctor. That sort of thing. She knows most of the families. Keeps us all in line.' He dragged a hand through his hair, making it stick up more than ever. 'Right, then. The treatment room.' He turned and Margaret followed him in to another room across the hall. 'This is where we do dressings, minor procedures and so forth.'

'What about the more serious surgical cases?'

'If there's time we send them to Glasgow, or Stornoway. We are hoping to have an air ambulance for emergencies soon. Assuming the weather's good enough for it to land and take off.'

'An air ambulance? Really. But that would be wonderful.' Nothing she'd seen so far had led her to think there might be such a thing.

'Won't be this winter, I'm afraid. We'll have to make do with the ferries in the meantime, or manage ourselves. Many's an operation I've had to carry out on a kitchen table and by the light of an oil lamp.'

She assumed he was teasing. 'What kind of emergencies do you get?'

'Same as in the big city of Glasgow, I should think. Perforated ulcers, haemorrhage, accidents, you'll soon get to know what's what.'

'What about the cases that can't be sent to Glasgow?'

'Then we have to do the best we can. Hope you remember how to wield a scalpel.'

Wield a scalpel? She hadn't anticipated doing surgery. She hoped her surgical skills weren't too rusty.

'Religion?'

'Excuse me?'

'Religion, girl, religion. What church do you attend?'

'Church of Scotland.' She'd never been much of a church goer, but Church of Scotland was what she always said when asked to state her faith.

Dr Alan looked relieved. 'Two services on a Sunday. You need to attend at least one. People expect it.' He took his pipe from his pocket and proceeded to pack it. 'Now, what else do you need to know?'

'Whatever you can tell me.'

'Infectious diseases are our biggest problem. TB, measles, scarlet fever and so on.' His smile faded. 'Trouble is the patients often don't call me out until they are very ill. We lose far too many. Young and old.'

In that respect it wasn't too different from the mainland. Infectious diseases were the biggest killer there too.

'What else?' Dr Alan continued. 'We have a small hospital near the surgery. Not a hospital exactly. It's where those who can no longer afford to keep themselves come – and those who have lost their marbles. We do have two or three beds in a small annexe for anyone we need to keep a close eye on while we're waiting to transfer them to Glasgow or Stornoway.

'None of the houses – except this one – has electricity and that comes from a generator and is rationed. We're lucky here in that we have running water and an inside bathroom. Most of the locals still have an outside lavatory. I'm afraid the cottage you'll be staying in is the same. Still, you'll get used to it, I'm sure. At least it has running cold water. Many of the people here still have to fetch their water from the well when they need it. Another difficulty is that there are no telephones.'

'Not even at the surgery?' Yet wasn't that a good thing? The more cut off the island was, especially from the mainland, the better.

'I'm afraid not.' He stopped and gave her a keen look. 'You must find us very primitive.'

'No. Of course not.' She could hardly tell him she did. 'But how do the patients let you know when they need you?'

'They go to the post office and send a telegram. The telegram boy brings it here and waits for a reply. I also have a regular schedule for visiting on the island. I stop at the shop, or the post office

243

if there is one, in each area and ask if any of the locals have left a request for me to come and see them. It works well enough.'

'What about at night? The post offices will be closed.'

'The locals rarely call the doctor out at night. Although medical care here is subsidised by the government, you'll find many people still think they have to pay the doctor. Most keep aside half a crown for that purpose. But in an emergency they'll send someone to the surgery or come themselves if they can. Of course sometimes I'm out on a visit. If I'm on one part of the island it can take several days before I can get to the patient.' He smiled tiredly. 'It is one of the reasons I'm glad to have you here. At least now, if I'm away, you'll be able to attend when I can't.'

'May I use your car, if that happens?'

'Of course. But the car isn't always suitable. The roads only go so far. I make many of my visits on horseback, as will you.'

'I'm afraid I've never been on a horse. And I didn't think to bring jodhpurs.'

'Good grief, woman – then you'll have to learn. Don't worry, Dobbin knows what he's doing. You just point him in the right direction and off he goes. And Dolina can cut down a pair of my breeches for you easily enough. She's a fine needlewoman. Now then where was I? Don't keep interrupting me, girl. Sometimes it's just as easy to walk – at other times you'll have to get a boat over to the house you need to visit. Most of them don't have roads up to their front door. Dolina will keep you right.' He lit his pipe and puffed for a few moments. 'I'm going to start you off in the surgery on Monday and give you the local visits in the afternoon. We'll wait a few days before I send you further afield. You'll soon get the hang of things.'

Margaret was feeling more anxious by the minute. She couldn't ride, hadn't practised surgery since graduating, and had never removed a tooth. But she could learn. She *would* learn. She had to.

'Thank you for taking a chance on me. I won't let you down.'

'No other applicants. Either you or no one. But,' he added hastily, 'I'm sure you'll do very well.'

So if Dr Alan hadn't been desperate he probably wouldn't have taken her on. As it was, he was probably regretting doing so. And if she had had any other choice but this job, she might have turned tail and run. Going on horseback to see patients in homes without electricity or running water would be a challenge she hadn't considered. On the other hand, it couldn't be any worse than the conditions in Govan. And most of all, here, at least so far, she and the children were safe.

Dr Alan pulled his fob watch out of his pocket and looked at it. 'Time for a dram. Dolina will be down shortly to pour us one.'

She never drank whisky. Having tried it once, the amber liquid had burned her throat and brought tears to her eyes. She'd much rather check up on the children. But Dr Alan was already heading back towards the sitting room and she had no option but to trot after him.

'Dolina!' he bellowed, finding the sitting room

245

empty. 'That woman is never around when I need her.'

'I think she's upstairs with my children.'

'Your children. Oh yes. I'd forgotten about them.' He filled two tumblers from a decanter on a small table next to the fireplace and handed one to Margaret. 'You do understand why you can't stay in this house, I'm sure.' He cleared his throat. 'Single man, and a single woman, even a widow, would cause no end of gossip. And even if the cottage we have for you was large enough for you all, it would be impossible for you to have the children with you. Our hours are unpredictable and long.'

'I do understand. Completely.'

Just then there was a knock on the door. 'That'll be someone looking for the doctor if I'm not mistaken,' Dr Alan said. He thumped his glass down on the table and gave it a long, regretful glance. 'I was looking forward to that.'

'Would you like me to go in your place?' she asked.

He gave Margaret a tired smile. 'No. Absolutely not. I don't expect you to take the on-call until you've been here a couple of weeks. Wouldn't be right. Plenty of work to keep you busy during the day. You enjoy your dram and I'll see you in the morning.'

Margaret waited until he was out of the room, before tipping her untouched whisky back into the decanter. Then she gathered up her bag and went in search of her children.

Chapter 24

Margaret tossed and turned all night, only sleeping in fitful bursts and when she did it was to dream of Alasdair. The dream wasn't a happy one. In it she'd been walking towards him but he'd shaken his head and turned away from her. She'd started to run after him but no matter how hard she tried she couldn't catch him up. She'd woken to find her pillow wet with tears and she'd lain in the ink-black darkness wondering if she'd ever see him again.

Finally, in the small hours she had fallen back asleep, only waking what felt like minutes later when Elizabeth tapped her face. Her daughter was dressed and hopping from foot to foot.

'Wake up, Mummy,' she said.

Margaret bolted upright. She'd been so deeply asleep she hadn't heard them get up from beside her. 'Where's James?' What if her ever-curious child had wandered outside and into the sea?

'Dolina just brought him down to the kitchen. But I've been up for ages. I've been to see the kittens again and been with Dolina to milk the cow. She told me to tell you she's left hot water for you in a jug in the bathroom. But hurry, Mummy.'

Margaret threw back the covers, her heart resuming its normal rhythm. 'You mustn't refer to Miss MacGregor by her first name, sweetheart.'

Elizabeth frowned, obviously puzzled. 'She told me to, Mummy. She's really nice. Not a witch at all. I like her. Come on, hurry up!'

It was clearly a different Miss MacGregor to the one Margaret had met.

While Elizabeth waited impatiently for her in the bedroom, Margaret used the bathroom and dressed as quickly as she could in a clean blouse and the same suit she'd been wearing the day before. They tiptoed downstairs, passing a grandfather clock in the hall, which to Margaret's horror showed the time to be well after eight. What kind of mother would the already disapproving Dolina think she was?

They followed the smell of frying bacon into the kitchen. It was a large, bright room with a scrubbed wooden table in the centre and a stove on top of which a kettle whistled. Frilled curtains hung from the windows and a large dresser displayed a collection of china. It was much warmer in here than the chilly upstairs bedroom. James grinned, showing off his baby teeth when he saw her, but immediately went back to studying something on the floor that was clearly fascinating him.

The housekeeper was standing at the sink, peeling potatoes.

'You should have woken me,' Margaret said guiltily, reaching down to ruffle her son's silky hair.

Dolina sniffed. 'Not my place to do so, Dr Margaret.'

'Is Dr Alan still sleeping?'

'Goodness me, no. He's out on his rounds. Been out since six.' She looked pointedly at the clock and then, even more pointedly, at the children.

Margaret ignored her. She was dashed if she was going to apologise to this taciturn, unfriendly woman.

Dolina placed two plates of bacon and eggs on the table. 'Sit yourselves down. I've already given the lad his porridge.'

Margaret fluffed out her napkin and placed it over her knees. 'You've gone to a great deal of trouble, Miss MacGregor.'

'Just doing what I'm paid for.'

Margaret suppressed a sigh. For whatever reason the housekeeper had taken against her, it appeared nothing she could do, or say, was going to make her unbend.

Dolina buttered a scone for Elizabeth and passed it across to her with a smile. Then she turned back to Margaret and studied her with a glint in her eye. 'There's someone in the waiting room. I told him Dr Alan was out and I didn't know when he'd be back.'

'You should have said! Shall I see him?' Margaret put her knife and fork down.

'You could. But finish your breakfast first. He's not going anywhere.'

Feeling uncomfortable leaving a patient waiting, Margaret hurried through her eggs and bacon. As soon as she was finished, she stood up and kissed the top of Elizabeth's head. 'You stay here with James and Miss MacGregor and don't get under her feet. I won't be far away.'

'Can't I come with you, Mummy? I'll be good. I won't make a sound.'

Margaret exchanged a glance with Dolina over

the top of her daughter's head. If this move was difficult for her, how much worse was it for her five-year-old?

'But Elizabeth – I don't care for Libby as a name, it sounds like something made up if you ask me – I need your help!' Dolina said, indicating with a tilt of her head that it was okay for Margaret to go. At least the housekeeper was being kind to the children and that was all that really mattered.

Margaret crouched down beside Elizabeth and touched her cheek. 'You help Miss MacGregor. I'll be back before you know it.'

Margaret hesitated outside the waiting room. As soon as she treated a patient she was breaking, if not the law, definitely the code of practice to which she was bound. But she had no choice. It was only the next in a series of hurdles she'd already had to confront and, no doubt, would continue to face in the months to come.

An elderly man with a collie by his feet looked up when she entered.

'I'm Dr Margaret Murdoch,' she said. 'I'm helping Dr Alan. He's on another call. Would you like to come through to the consulting room?'

'But you're a lass!'

'Yes, well. But I'm also a doctor.'

He looked at her suspiciously. 'I'll wait for Dr Alan.'

'He might be some time.'

He considered her for a long moment. 'Do you know about legs?' he said finally.

'A little. What seems to be the problem?'

'Can't walk. Not without limping.'

'Come through to the consulting room so I can have a look.'

'Can do it as easily here. No point in wasting time. Need to get back to work.'

'If I'm going to help I need to have a proper look. And that's best done in the consulting room,' she said firmly.

Reluctantly he got to his feet. He didn't appear to be favouring one leg over another as far as she could tell. His dog followed behind them, his paws slipping on the polished wooden floor.

'Is the sore leg something that comes and goes?' she asked as they made their way along the hall.

'No. It's there all the time. Can't you see it yourself?' He muttered something in Gaelic she couldn't understand, but was pretty sure wasn't complimentary.

Inside the consulting room she pulled the screen around the examination couch. 'Could you slip your trousers off, please?'

'My trousers! What the devil do you want me to do that for?'

'It makes it easier for me to examine you.'

'Examine me? There's nothing the matter with me!'

'I thought you had a sore leg? Isn't that why you're here?'

He gave a throaty chuckle. 'You thought it's me that wanted to see you. Well, well. Never been to the doctor in my life. There's nothing wrong with me.'

Perhaps he had a problem with his short-term memory?

251

'Mr – um–'

'Willie.'

'Willie. Do you know what day it is today?'

His eyes creased. 'Why? Can't you remember?'

Margaret felt the situation slipping away from her. 'It's not me we're talking about. Please answer the question.'

'Well now. Church is tomorrow. So it must be Saturday.'

'That's right. Now, what year are we in?'

'I think I should wait for Dr Alan. He never asks me these fool questions. Not when I'm bringing Scotty to see him. Mind you, I usually see the doctor when he comes to Loch Portain, but I needed some messages from the shop so I thought I'd just pop in here.'

'Scotty? And who is Scotty?'

'My dog, lass. That one there.'

She glanced over to the collie, who wagged his tail before placing his head back down on his paws.

She gaped at Willie. 'You brought your dog to see the doctor?'

'Aye. No one else here to look at him. Dr Alan never minds. Gives him some pills usually. Keeps Scotty going for a few weeks.' He whistled and the collie jumped up and did a circle of the room. Right enough, the dog was limping.

Willie looked at her expectantly. 'If we can just have some more of those pills, we'll be on our way.'

When the man and the dog had left, Margaret felt a giggle rise in her throat. Soon she was bent over the consultation table, laughing so hard, she could hardly draw breath. It was a long time since she'd found anything amusing and she wished she could tell Alasdair. The realisation she couldn't ripped the laughter from her body like a plaster from an open wound. But, she told herself firmly, she could tell him in her letter. It wasn't the same, but it would be better than nothing. They'd agreed the safest way would be to correspond via Mairi and Flora. That way there was less chance of her father discovering where she was.

She considered whether to log the case in the accounts book, before deciding against writing anything down. Seeing as she hadn't actually seen a patient, she wasn't sure whether the incident even fell into the category of consultation. She also decided not to say anything about it to Dolina, who she suspected knew all about Willie and Scotty but had elected not to tell her.

Back in the kitchen, Dolina gave her a sly smile, confirming Margaret's suspicions. The house-keeper had tidied away and Elizabeth was wiping the dishes, her little tongue poking out the way it always did when she was concentrating.

Leaving James, who was contentedly bashing away at some saucepans, Margaret slipped up to the bedroom where they'd spent the night. She quickly repacked their suitcases and took them downstairs.

'Miss MacGregor, could you give me directions to the cottage I'll be staying in?'

Removing her apron, Dolina took their coats down from the hook behind the back door. 'I'll take you there myself,' she replied stiffly. 'It's not far.'

'Thank you. And can you tell me what time the driver will be picking us up to take us to the pier in Carinish?'

'I told him three o'clock. No doubt he'll come when he's ready and not before,' Dolina replied, ushering them out the door.

The rain had eased up to a soft drizzle as they accompanied Dolina along the narrow, single-track road. With James balanced on her hip and holding tightly to Libby's hand, Margaret kept her head down and her coat collar turned up in an attempt to keep droplets from slithering down her neck. Her feathered hat was totally inadequate for this weather, the gusts of wind threatening to whip it free from its pins.

The housekeeper nodded to the few people, mostly women, they encountered, but didn't stop to exchange pleasantries or to introduce the new doctor and her children. She veered off the road and along a path and up a slight hill. Facing the sea was a small white-washed cottage surrounded by clumps of nettles for a garden.

'This is your house. It was built for the nurse but Effie married a crofter here in Lochmaddy and doesn't need it,' Dolina said, opening the un-locked door. 'You'll find it has everything you require.'

'Is there a key?'

The housekeeper raised her eyebrow. 'There's no need for keys here! Never has been, never will be. An islander would rather starve to death than take anything that didn't belong to them.'

It appeared that even the most innocent com-ment from Margaret caused offence.

The front door led straight into the kitchen. Margaret looked around her new home. 'Having everything' wasn't quite how she would have put it. There were three sparsely furnished rooms – a kitchen, with a monstrous black stove on which she'd have to heat any water she needed, a small sitting room with an open fire, and a bedroom with two single beds, as well as a wardrobe and a night stand. As Dr Alan had warned, there was no electricity or inside bathroom, only a wooden privy at the end of a small path at the back of the house. A wave of longing for her home in Garnet-hill, so intense it took her breath away, washed over her.

There were wall-mounted gas lamps in the kitchen and sitting room, although only oil lamps for the bedroom. Margaret noticed a storm lantern by the back door, which she guessed was for going to the privy outside or for when she was called out at night.

'Probably not as grand as what you're used to, but it's plenty adequate for most folks,' Dolina said.

Margaret met the older woman's eyes. 'This will be just fine.'

'There's a peat stack by the door and some kindling in the byre out the back. Seonag from next door will bring you milk from the cow in the mornings, if you ask her. Payment is between yourselves, otherwise there's the shop just down the road.' Dolina wiped an imaginary speck of dust from the mantelpiece. 'I made up the bed yesterday, but you should put hot water bottles in to keep it aired. The linen will get damp if you

255

don't. There's also some scones, eggs, cheese and so on in the larder as well as some flour and other things you might need. I lit the stove last night.' She lifted one of the rings on top and peered inside. 'You'll need to fill it up with peat before you go out again. It's best if you try to keep it going and not let it go out.'

'Thank you. You've taken a lot of trouble.'

'Don't thank me, thank Dr Alan. It was on his instructions that everything has been laid out for you. Well then, I best get back to my work. I've a lot to do and can't stand all day here chatting.'

Left alone, Margaret and the children surveyed her new home. Without the housekeeper's grim presence it didn't seem as bad as it had on first inspection. The patchwork quilt she'd sewn herself, the Royal Albert vase her grandmother had given her on her twenty-first birthday and the gilt-edged tea set Alasdair had won at a fair would have gone a long way to make it more homely, but although they'd been the last things to go, they'd had to be sold too. However, she would find something to cheer it up – even if it was only a bunch of wild flowers in a jar.

'Look, there's a bed for you and James when you come to stay,' Margaret said, pointing to one of the single beds.

'I don't want to go, Mummy. Why can't we stay at the big house like last night? Please say we can. I'll be good. I can look after James and the kittens and help milk the cow again. I'll be as quiet as a mouse. No one will even know I'm there.'

Margaret's heart ached for her daughter. She pulled her little girl into her arms. 'We can't,

Libby. Dr Alan only let us stay as we'd just arrived. Miss MacGregor has a lot of chores to do, so who would look after you when I was at work? Besides, Aunty Flora's girls will be looking forward to having you to stay with them, I'm sure. I bet they have a cow too, and chickens. And remember you and James will come to stay with me here as often as we can arrange it.'

'I don't like it here. It's dark and it smells funny.'

'It's dark because it's cloudy outside. And it smells funny because no one has lived here for a while. You wait until we have all the lights on and the fires going. I'll sew some covers for the sofa. You'll see, we'll soon make this house cosy.'

Elizabeth remained quiet while Margaret put James down for a nap before unpacking her few belongings. Seeing her daughter's crestfallen face was almost too much to bear. Sitting on the edge of the bed, she wrapped an arm around her daughter and pulled her close. She picked up the photo of her and Alasdair on their wedding day. Elizabeth peered at it from under Margaret's arm. 'I want Daddy,' she sniffed.

'If Daddy could be here with us he would be. He loves you both so very much. But Daddy would want you to be a big girl. He'd want you to take care of James.'

'I'm still a little girl,' Elizabeth whispered.

'I know you are.' She pulled her daughter closer. 'Just think, Libby, Aunt Mairi lived on these islands when she was little. She told me often about what she and her sister used to get up to, all the fun they had.'

Elizabeth turned her big eyes towards her. 'Like what? What did Aunt Mairi do? Did she live with Uncle Peter and Aunt Flora too, like me and James are going to?'

Margaret managed a smile. 'Aunty Flora and Uncle Peter live in the family home where Mairi and her sister grew up. They fished for crabs and dug cockles out the sand. Wouldn't you like to do that too?'

Elizabeth nodded. 'Can I paddle in the sea too?'

'Only when Uncle Peter or Aunt Flora is with you, never on your own. Promise me that.'

Elizabeth jumped up, her eyes alight. 'I promise. Can we go there now, Mummy? Come on, let's go now.'

Margaret hugged her child. It was a relief to see the excitement in Elizabeth's face. 'Not right now, my angel, it's still too early. But as soon as James wakes from his nap, we'll explore the village instead.'

Chapter 25

The journey over the single-track, untarred roads was almost as bad as the sea crossing. Every bump – and there were several – threw them into the air. To Margaret's surprise Johnny Ban arrived only a few minutes after three. Before leaving Lochmaddy, she and the children had lunched on the scones and cheese the housekeeper had left for them.

Margaret's stomach was churning. She had never been parted from her children for more than a few hours and never overnight, but in a while she'd be handing them over to a stranger. The irony that she'd run in order to keep her children only to pass them over to someone else didn't escape her.

Thumb in mouth, Elizabeth stared out of the window, pressing her body against Margaret's. Happily James had fallen asleep.

After an hour or so, Johnny stopped the car near a verge close to the shore. It seemed that here was as far as he went. There was no pier as far as Margaret could see, only a few boulders stretching out into the sea. Johnny hopped out and took Elizabeth's bag from the boot before opening the door for them. As she stepped out of the car, the smell of seaweed pinched her nostrils. Mairi's brother-in-law, Peter, had written to say that he would meet them with his boat to take them the rest of the way. As yet there was no sign of him.

Johnny rummaged in his pockets and brought out a pipe which he proceeded to pack from a pouch of tobacco. Once it was filled to his satisfaction he leaned against the side of the car and placed the unlit pipe in his mouth.

'This is the right place?' Margaret asked.

Johnny nodded. He might not speak English but she hoped that meant he understood her. Just then a boat appeared from around the corner. Johnny removed the pipe from his mouth and jabbed the stem in its direction. 'Peter Beag.'

A sliver of sun peeped out from behind the

clouds, making the sea sparkle. Margaret watched as the boat drew closer.

All she knew of Mairi's brother-in-law was that he was married to Mairi's older sister, Flora, was a fisherman as well as a crofter and that he and his wife had three children. While Mairi had gone to Glasgow in search of work, Flora had stayed behind to care for their widowed mother, marrying Peter some time before her mother had died. Peter had moved into the family home with his wife, as was the tradition when there were only women left in the house. He was also from North Uist and had fished with his father before taking over the boat when his father had become too unwell to continue.

Peter jumped out of the boat and waded ashore, holding on to a rope attached to the bow. Margaret's heart leaped to her throat. With his broad shoulders and dark, tousled hair, it could have been Alasdair striding towards her.

'I'm sorry you've been kept waiting,' Peter said. He tied the boat to a rock and said a few words to Johnny in Gaelic.

'Could you ask him how much I owe him?' It was easier to think of the small details than to think about the forthcoming separation.

Peter turned back to Johnny. The driver replied with a few words in Gaelic, tipped his cap once more and left.

'He says he'll put it on your account. You can settle it at the end of the month.'

Margaret hoped she'd managed to hide her relief from Peter. She didn't want him to know how strapped for money she was.

Peter shook Margaret's hand before crouching down in front of Elizabeth. 'You must be Libby. My goodness you're a strong-looking girl.'

Elizabeth smiled shyly and stepped behind Margaret.

'And this must be James.' James picked up a small stone and held it out, snatching it back as soon as Peter went to take it.

'Thanks for coming out to get us,' Margaret said, sharing a smile about the contrariness of small children with Peter.

'And what would you have done if I hadn't. Swam?' He grinned. 'Come on, Flora has a meal waiting for you. She's looking forward to meeting you and Libby and James. So are the children. We've not been able to get them to sit still or to do their chores.' He lowered his voice. 'We've told them that they are the children of a friend of Mairi's.' He pulled a flask from his pocket and held it out to Margaret. 'Would you take a sip of something warming? Flora made some tea in case you were thirsty.'

'No. Thank you.'

'Right, then. Let me take that bag. You perch yourself in the stern with little James here. Libby, you can sit at the front and be my lookout. If you see any sharks, yell.'

'Sharks!' Margaret exclaimed.

Peter winked. 'Only joking. You'll see them further out sometimes, whales too, but they don't come in – not unless they're ill or made a mistake.' Even the way Peter tipped his head to the side when he spoke reminded her of Alasdair. 'Mostly they stay out in the deep waters. This bit is only

261

covered by the sea twice a day when the tide's in. The rest of the time you can walk from the house easily enough. As long as you're careful not to step in the sinking sands.' Margaret must have looked alarmed as he added quickly, 'Don't worry, the children will keep an eye on James and show Libby where they are. She'll be perfectly safe as long as she knows where not to go.'

When they were all settled, he took the oars, one in each hand, and pulled away from the shore. He pointed his chin in the direction of a building on his right. 'That's the school you'll be going to, Libby. It's not far from the house. Half an hour at the most if you walk quickly.'

'Libby won't be walking alone, will she?' Margaret didn't want the children left on their own for any length of time. She still feared that her father would find out where they were and would spirit the children away.

'She'll be safe enough. There's nothing here that can harm her.'

Except for sharks and sinking sand and the possibility of her father finding them, Margaret thought grimly.

'And of course she'll have my lot to walk with her,' Peter added. 'They'll keep watch over James too when Flora can't.'

The small boat glided effortlessly through the translucent water. Peering over the side, Margaret could clearly see the sand and rocks below. Perhaps if the weather was fine she might teach Elizabeth and, in time, James, to swim.

But, she told herself firmly, they weren't going to be here in the spring. They would be back home with Alasdair.

Sandbank, Flora and Peter's home, was larger than Margaret had expected, rising to two storeys and with several outbuildings. Surrounded on all sides by water, it appeared to be an island of its own.

'It's only because the tide's in,' Peter said as if reading her mind. 'The rest of the time you can cross the *fidean* – that's the bit of grass at the front – to the croft where we keep the cow and hens, unless the tide is very high. And when it's all the way out you can walk across the sands to where I picked you up from.'

'How will I know where and when it's safe to walk?' Margaret asked.

'You'll get to know the tides. They come in twice a day, half an hour later than the day before each time. The tides are at their highest and lowest when the moon is new or full. Don't worry, Dr Alan, or one of the locals will always be able to tell you. But don't start crossing the sands when the tide is coming in. It can come in behind you as well as in front and to the sides of you, although most of the time it will just mean taking your shoes off and wading to a bit where it's higher. If you find yourself trapped, well then the only option is to swim like the blazes. You can swim, can't you?'

She wasn't sure if he was joking or not.

'I have no intention of swimming across,' she said.

'Aye well, we're not great swimmers ourselves. Can't, if the truth be known.'

263

'Don't you need to be able to? What happens if something goes wrong when you're out at sea, fishing?

'If we have to get in the water the cold will kill us within minutes.' He shrugged. 'No point in being able to swim. I was only joking when I suggested it. If the tide's in and you want to come and see the wee ones and I'm not here to fetch you, then you can row. I'll make sure the coble is always left on the far side for you.'

'Coble?'

'This wee boat. You can manage it easily enough. The children do.'

If the children could row it, then so could she.

A woman and three children came out of the house to meet them. Peter helped them ashore as the boy ran down to help his father pull in the boat. The two girls remained with their mother.

'You must be Margaret,' the woman said, walking towards them. Her fair hair was swept up into a bun, with wisps softening her face. She had the most beautiful clear skin that Margaret had ever seen and a warm, welcoming smile. She crouched down in front of the children. 'I'm your Aunty Flora. The girls are Mary and Annie, the lad, Lachie. We are all so happy to have you here.' She looked up at Margaret, her eyes soft. 'You poor things. You've been through so much.'

Margaret's throat closed, making it difficult to speak. Happily Flora didn't appear to expect a reply.

'Come away in,' Mairi's sister said. 'I have a meal ready for you. You must be hungry and tired. I've set the table in the kitchen. Girls, leave Libby and

264

James in peace. Let them get used to their surroundings. You crowd must seem like a pack of
wolves to the poor wee mites.'

What seemed to be the front door – but as Margaret learned later was actually the back – led
through a small scullery and into a kitchen which
was more like a sitting-cum-dining room, furnished as it was with a small sofa, a couple of
armchairs, and a large table set for seven, making
it a tight squeeze. An assortment of chairs and
stools had been placed in front of each place setting. The warmth of a Rayburn stove filled the
room.

'Peter will take the children's case up to the bedroom in just a minute. I've put them in with
Annie. They'll have to share a bed but all the more
cosy, I say. Mary will sleep in alongside Peter and
I. Lachie has the small room. He's getting too old
to be in with the girls.'

'I hope we're not putting anyone out.'

'Put us out? After what you've done for Mairi
and her friends? No indeed! It's no problem for us
to be in together. There's plenty of space as you
can see. There's many a family on these islands
who sleep five or six to a bed. Annie, why don't
you take the children upstairs and show them
where they'll be sleeping?'

Elizabeth sent Margaret an uncertain glance, but
when Annie took her by the hand she went with
her. Mary put James on her hip and followed.

Waiting until they were out of sight, Margaret
closed the door and laid a hand on Flora's arm.
'Any news? A letter?'

'No. Not yet. You've barely arrived and the mail

will take a wee bit longer to catch up. But I'll send a telegram to Mairi to say you,' she smiled briefly, 'or rather the parcels, have arrived safely. Toni will find a way to let Alasdair know.'

Margaret smiled at this woman whose heart was so big that she'd protect a virtual stranger and her children, although she had to be aware that even her small, tangential part in Margaret's impersonation could get her and her family into difficulty with the police. And to take in two extra mouths to feed when, like everyone else on the island, they had little enough for themselves, was an act of kindness Margaret wondered how she could ever repay. When she said as much, Flora shook her head and smiled. 'We all have to help each other while on this earth.'

Any lingering reservations Margaret might have had about leaving her children with Flora disappeared at that moment.

The clatter of footsteps on stairs prevented further discussion and as soon as they were all assembled they sat down to eat. Peter started the meal with a prayer and he'd only just uttered 'Amen' when the children reached across each other and heaped food onto their plates. Margaret glanced over at Libby at the opposite end of the table and was pleased to see her chattering with Annie in between mouthfuls. James was on Mary's lap looking content and unperturbed to find himself amongst strangers. Her younger child had always been happy to go to anyone as long as they smiled at him.

'So what do you think of Uist so far?' Flora asked. 'Mind you, you haven't had much time yet

266

to settle in, but you will.'

Margaret smiled. 'It's very different to what I imagined.'

'Oh? In what way?'

'Mairi talked about her homeland so often I'd built up this picture in my head that was rather romanticised, but now I think about it, that's more my fault than hers.'

Peter laughed and shook his head. 'Oh no now, don't you go blaming yourself on that score. I can just hear Mairi describing the islands to you.' He took his wife's hand. 'I know she misses it here, just as we miss her. How was she and the family when you last saw them?'

'They were all in good health. She has a lovely family.'

'They should come home,' Flora said. 'I don't think the smog in Glasgow can be very good for them.'

'There's barely enough work for those of us here, Flora,' Peter remonstrated gently.

'It's not much better in Glasgow,' Flora said bitterly. 'All these men laid off so the ship owners can keep their profit.' She broke off, looked across at Margaret and flushed.

Peter patted Flora's hand, before turning his gaze back to Margaret. 'You see, it's like this. We islanders are attached to this land and each other by an unbreakable silken thread – no matter how far we travel. It's spun and woven with years of our history and culture, songs and traditions, and the further away you go the stronger the thread becomes.'

Flora laid her hand over her husband's. 'Listen

to you, and you always saying you're not roman-
tic.'

The couple shared a look of such love and
affection Margaret had to turn away. She let her
gaze travel around the room. She, Alasdair, Toni
and Mairi had often sat around the kitchen table
in Garnethill as Mairi had talked longingly about
Uist. Back then, she and Alasdair had discussed
coming here on holiday one day. Neither of them
could ever have imagined the circumstances that
would bring her and the children here on their
own.

She blinked away the tears that burned behind
her eyes. She had to hold on to the belief that one
day they would be together again. Her little family,
sitting down to a meal, laughing and happy.

But right now she was here, without him, with
a terrible gnawing pain in her heart and about to
say goodbye to Libby and James.

All too soon it was time for Margaret to leave and
the family gathered to see her off, turning away to
give her privacy to say her goodbyes to James and
Elizabeth. As if sensing he wouldn't see her for a
while, James wrapped his arms around her neck
and had to be prised from her by Flora, who told
Mary to take him to see the new baby chickens.

Mary tucked him on her hip with the fami-
liarity of a child who had done the same for her
younger siblings several times before and, chatting all the while, carried him away. Margaret
watched them go, feeling as if her heart would
break before turning to her older child.

'It's time for me to go, Libby,' she said softly.

When her daughter's face crumpled and she entwined her hand in Margaret's skirt, she faltered. How could she possibly leave her children? But, and it always came back to this, what other option did she have? Margaret knelt down and gently unpeeled her daughter's fingers. 'I'll see you the weekend after next.'

Fat tears rolled down Elizabeth's cheeks. Heavens, this was even harder than she'd imagined. In desperation Margaret rummaged in her handbag, looking for a long-forgotten sweet left in a crevice somewhere. Her fingers brushed against Alasdair's gold fob watch, which she always kept with her. She took her daughter's hand, placed the watch in her palm and closed Elizabeth's fingers over it.

'This belonged to Daddy. If you ever need me, rub the watch and I'll come. Not come actually, sweetheart, but into your head. You can talk to me and ask me what you should do – and if you listen hard you'll hear me telling you. Or if you're sad, put it close to your ear and listen to the tick-tock. Imagine we're in bed together all cuddled up and that it's my heart you can hear and you won't be sad any more.'

Elizabeth placed her hand to the side of her head. 'I can hear it. It *does* sound like your heart.'

'Put it in your pocket where it will be safe. Now, remember I'll see you in a couple of weeks,' Margaret said, striving to keep her voice from wobbling.

'Promise?'

'I promise.'

'All right then, Mummy.' Elizabeth lifted her

small, determined chin and straightened her shoulders. 'You mustn't worry 'bout me or James. I'll look after him for you. And I won't worry about you. We'll both be brave.'

But before she turned away, Margaret saw her daughter take out her daddy's fob watch and hold it to her ear.

How was it possible to love someone so much and yet leave them?

Chapter 26

By the evening of her first day at work, Margaret was ready to drop. Dr Alan had been keen to put her to work and she'd been equally happy to get stuck in. In the morning she'd seen a full list of patients, at least half of whom had either TB or scarlet fever. She'd taken her time over every patient and consequently morning surgery had overrun badly. With no time for lunch, she'd done a couple of visits on foot that had taken the rest of the afternoon – one to a family whose child had whooping cough, and another to a family whose child had scarlet fever. Both children were poorly, the child with whooping cough in particular, but apart from keeping them in bed and dosing them with aspirin, there was little else that could be done for them.

Before she could return home she still had her notes to write up and she should really share her concerns about the number of scarlet fever cases she was seeing with Dr Alan so he could notify the authorities. She hoped an epidemic wasn't in the offing. Disappointingly, he was still out and Dolina couldn't say when he'd be back.

'It's always like this,' the housekeeper complained. 'He goes out to see four or five patients, but then he hears about others who need to see him, so he just carries on making visits.'

'Hopefully I'll be able to do more soon and he can take time off.'

'Time off?' Dolina smiled wryly. 'Well, we'll have to see about that. Depends on how you do, doesn't it?'

'Miss MacGregor,' Margaret said, exasperated. 'I don't know what I've done to upset you, but I think how I do as a doctor is up to Dr Alan to judge, don't you?'

The housekeeper pursed her lips. 'Aye, that may be right. Or it may not. I don't hold with women doctors. It's not natural. I know how Dr Alan likes things done and he needs a proper doctor to help him out. Someone who has more experience and knows what they're doing.'

'A man, you mean?'

'Aye. A man. You have no idea what it's like here in the winter. Sometimes the doctor has to go out in the dead of night when it's blowing a gale. Many's a time he's had to pull the small boat behind him so he can cross all the lochs. Once, he even had to take shelter behind a rock until the gale blew out. Look at you! You're only a slip of a thing. You'll never be able to pull your weight. I know Dr Alan! He'll take all the hard cases himself rather than let a woman like you go

271

out in all weathers. He might as well have saved himself the trouble of taking you on!'

Margaret gritted her teeth. The woman was insufferable. Although the description Dolina painted of a doctor's life on the islands in winter appalled her, she was damned if she was going to let her see that. Whatever it took to be a doctor on this island, Margaret would do it. 'But he's got me, Miss MacGregor, and like it or not, I plan to stay.'

Having written up her notes, Margaret trudged home. Her shoes and stockings were still damp and she longed for a hot bath in front of a fire. Instead she dried herself as best she could, shivering as she exchanged her wet stockings for dry ones.

After leaving the children, the remainder of the weekend had dragged. The little house, which at first had seemed so small, had felt almost too large without Libby and James. The fire in the stove had long gone out and the house was bone-chillingly cold.

Margaret had scrunched up newspapers and added bits of the dried earth the islanders used for fuel, before poking, prodding and coaxing the fire along until finally it had lit. Catching sight of her soot-covered reflection in the mirror, she'd had to smile. Who, of her former acquaintance, would recognise Miss Bannatyne now?

On Sunday, she'd debated long and hard about going to church, worried that someone, perhaps one of the visitors who'd been on the ferry, might recognise her. But it was clear that Dr Alan expected her to go and, as the doctor, she couldn't hide away forever. Moreover, while she was here it was important that she went about her business as if she had nothing to hide and nothing to be frightened of. So she had gone to church and sat through an overly long morning service, acutely aware of everyone's eyes on her. When the service was over, Dr Alan had invited her to lunch, a collation of cold chicken and rabbit. However, the incessant rain had meant that afterwards she'd had no option but to sit out the remainder of the day in her lonely cottage, thinking and worrying about Alasdair and her children, wondering how they were, what they were doing and whether they were missing her as much as she was missing them. It was as if a large chunk of her soul had been ripped out of her.

The nights were the worst. Alone in her single bed she tossed and turned, guilt and anxiety eating away at her. How were the children? Would James recognise her when he saw her again? Was Elizabeth pining for her? Did the children cry themselves to sleep at night, not really understanding why both Mummy and Daddy had abandoned them?

Lying sleepless, she imagined Alasdair holding her, his arms around her, her head against his chest as she listened to the beating of his heart. And then the tears would come – harsh, painful sobs as she cursed the hand they'd been dealt. But she gave into them only for a while. Self-pity achieved nothing. She had to stay strong if there was any chance of her small family being together again. She made up her mind that she wouldn't cry again. She would have faith.

Nevertheless, she'd been relieved when Monday morning had finally arrived. At least she was back doing a job she'd always loved and work would help keep her mind off Alasdair and the children.

After her supper she poured herself a glass of milk and took it outside. The relentless rain had finally stopped, the wind had dropped away completely and the sun had come out. Bathed in a golden light everything looked quite beautiful. The moors were covered in a carpet of red, blue and orange wildflowers and, just beyond, the sands were a dazzling white. In the distance she could hear the sound of voices floating across the water.

She sat on a rock and hugged her knees to her chest. She had made it through her first working day. Before bed she would write to Elizabeth and James and tell them all about it. Flora, she was sure, would read it to them. She'd written to Alasdair yesterday, told him about Dolina, about Willie and his dog, knowing it would make him smile. She'd told him that she was sure the children would be happy where they were. Just in case, she hadn't mentioned any names. She'd enclosed her letter in an envelope addressed to Flora, who would forward it on to Mairi, and had posted it this morning. She had no idea how long the letter would take to get to Alasdair or when one from him, or the lawyer, would arrive.

The sound of a violin drifted from a nearby house and her chest tightened. The last time she'd heard that particular piece of music was when Alasdair had played it to her, shortly before his arrest. God, she longed for him. Her whole body and soul ached with missing him.

There were ninety-six days until sentencing. Ninety-six days.

The days quickly settled into a routine. After a breakfast of porridge and bread, Margaret would walk over for morning surgery. Visits were in the afternoon and after that she had notes to write up and specimens to test. At the end of the day, if she and Dr Alan were both free, they would discuss the day's patients over a cup of tea and it was consequently usually late by the time she made it home to her little cottage.

Happily, Dobbin, the Clydesdale she rode to make some of the visits, turned out to be as placid and as willing a horse as even the most anxious rider could wish. Dolina had altered a pair of Dr Alan's plus-fours for her so she could ride him while maintaining her dignity, and while they could never be called fashionable, the housekeeper had made a surprisingly neat job of them. The little free time Margaret did have was spent reading medical text books, and writing to the children and to Alasdair. She didn't mind being busy – quite the opposite, she loved the work and it helped fill the empty hours. Finally, she received the letter she'd been waiting for. It had been placed on her kitchen table, presumably by the postman, who turned out to be the same Johnny who chauffeured the hire car. The sun was shining so she took it to her little rock to read, ripping open the envelope with fingers that shook with excitement.

My love,

It feels like years rather than weeks since I saw you last. When I look at the sky I like to imagine that you are looking at it too and thinking of me. I live for the day when I can hold you and our children again. I know that you are safe and that and the knowledge that one day we will be together again is what keeps me going. I keep myself busy by helping my fellow inmates with their legal problems. I may be in prison but I am still a lawyer.

Simon Firth has already made progress. He found Dr Marshall, the doctor you told him about who served on the front lines during the Great War. He is happy to testify that what I tried to do for Tommy Barr was the correct thing. He will go as far as to say that Tommy Barr's life might have been saved but for the actions of the police officers. I wish them no harm. They were only doing what they thought best. Simon was surprised that Johnston hadn't approached Dr Marshall himself and challenged him. Johnston claimed there was little point as there were too many doctors willing to testify the opposite. But I wonder. He wasn't happy that Simon has taken over my case, but that is of little import.

My heart, I count the minutes until I can hold you again. This time I will never let you go.

Yours, always
Alasdair

Only a few days and Firth was already making more progress than Johnston had in weeks. She read Alasdair's letter again before slipping it into the bodice of her dress. She knew she would read it several times more before she went to bed that night.

The next morning, unusually, Dr Alan called her into his consulting room before the start of surgery. Immediately she felt a flare of anxiety. Had he discovered she wasn't who she said she was? He waited until she was seated before leaning forward and pinning her with his bright blue eyes.

'You saw Angus Nicholson yesterday,' he said.

'Yes. Is everything all right? Did his asthma get worse?' She'd visited Mr Nicholson at his home and made a diagnosis of asthma. She'd advised staying away from cutting the hay, advice he'd treated with amazement and scorn. If he didn't do it, he said, then who would?

Dr Alan leaned back in his chair and started to pack his pipe. She was learning that he did this whenever he was thinking. 'His wife called me out last night. Angus's breathing had become much worse and he was having pains in his chest.'

Margaret's heart thumped. 'He didn't complain of chest pain when I saw him.'

'You listened to his chest? Specifically to his heart?'

Margaret nodded. But how much time had she spent looking for cardiac symptoms? Mr Nicholson was young and she'd been so certain that asthma was the cause of his breathlessness.

'Did he have a heart attack?' she asked.

'Yes. I'm afraid so.'

'Is he all right?' She twisted her fingers together so Dr Alan wouldn't see her hands were shaking.

'He will be.'

'Thank God. I'm so sorry...'

Dr Alan leaned back in his chair. 'We all make mistakes, Margaret. Especially when we're starting off. He's going to be all right. I've prescribed diuretics and his breathing is already easier. I've arranged for him to go to Glasgow for further tests as soon as it can be arranged. I didn't call you in to berate you. Only to let you know. Use this as a lesson. You should have taken blood and come to talk to me about him. At the very least, checked his notes when you returned to the surgery. That would have led you to consider alternatives.' He stood, making it clear that the interview was over. 'No harm done, eh?'

Fighting back tears, Margaret escaped to the bathroom to compose herself. Dr Alan had been nice about it but he was right. She had jumped to conclusions. Preoccupied with worries about Alasdair, she hadn't taken enough care.

It didn't bode well for her immediate future here. If she was dismissed, where would she and the children go? She'd only been working for Dr Alan for a short period of time and already she'd made a mistake that could have been fatal for her patient. It was only luck that had saved him. She blew her nose and took a deep breath. She would make sure she never made a mistake again.

Chapter 27

Margaret had only just come to the end of after-noon surgery when Dolina stopped her in the passageway.

'The telegram boy has just brought a message from Locheport. From Nurse McAllister. She has Mrs MacPhee in labour and it isn't progress-ing the way it should. She's asked me to send for the doctor. Dr Alan's gone out to see a child who pulled hot water over himself. I'm not expecting him back for a good few hours.'

'Of course I'll go. What's the best way to get there?'

'Dr Alan's got Dobbin, so you'll need to take the car. Drive as far as Clachan shop and park up. You'll have to walk the rest of the way across the moors. I expect Chrissie MacPhee's husband will meet you along the way.'

'I'd better get going then.'

Happily, the Morris started after only a few turns. The last time she'd driven a motor vehicle had been before her marriage to Alasdair and only a handful of times at that. The car jerked and bucked out of the driveway as she struggled to get it into the correct gear. Deciding that it was safest to keep it in third all the way rather than stall, that's what she did. She had to hold herself un-comfortably upright in the seat in order to see over the steering wheel and the high curved bonnet,

279

but at least she was driving it, and more or less in a straight line. She was just beginning to relax, keeping to a steady twenty miles per hour, when a sheep wandered lazily in front of her. Margaret slammed on the brakes, propelling herself forward and almost into the dashboard. She spent the rest of the journey gripping the wheel tightly while she negotiated the rutted track, keeping her eyes peeled for careless livestock and skittish deer.

She was driving so slowly that it would have been almost impossible to miss the sign for Clachan Stores. Sighing with relief, she pulled off to the side of the road and parked.

The wind had picked up and the clouds overhead were heavy with rain. The weather here was never the same two days running – sometimes it even changed completely over the course of the day. A morning that started out sunny and calm could be windy and wet by evening and vice versa.

In the distance she could see a cluster of houses, smoke rising from their chimneys. It didn't look too far to walk. Balancing against the vehicle, she untied her shoes and slipped on wellington boots. She'd been warned that the moors could be boggy in places.

She'd only gone a quarter of a mile or so when the heavens opened. She turned up the collar of her coat, wishing she had worn a bigger hat, one that would keep her hair from blowing into her eyes and becoming plastered to her head. She'd cut it short before she'd left Glasgow in an attempt to disguise her appearance, but the hat she was wearing wasn't large enough to cover it all. She grimaced as a gust of wind threatened to sweep her off her feet. A bigger hat would only have blown away anyway.

Too small a hat and wet hair turned out to be the least of her worries. As the wind increased in strength, it drove the rain straight at her, blinding her. She had to keep her head ducked down, peering up now and then to get her bearings.

Her muscles were beginning to burn with the effort of negotiating the uneven and rabbit-holed moor and several times she stumbled. Rain snaked down the back of her coat and her hands were numb with cold. A few hundred yards on and she almost walked straight into a loch that was hidden by clumps of heather and reeds. She squinted through the rain, trying desperately to get her bearings. Except now she couldn't even see the houses she'd spotted earlier.

She battled on, squelching through mud and grass until, to her relief, she looked up and saw a man in an oilskin striding towards her.

'You're the doctor?' he called out.

'Yes. Dr Margaret!' she called back, the wind snatching at her words.

By this time he'd reached her side. 'I'm Charlie MacPhee. It's this way.' Taking her medical bag from her, he turned round and strode back the way he came, leaving her stumbling along in his wake.

'How long has your wife been in labour?' Margaret asked, hurrying to keep up with his long strides.

'I can't say exactly.' They both had to shout to make themselves heard above the wind. 'Since the early hours, anyway. The baby doesn't seem to be wanting to be born. The nurse came this morning. She didn't appear too worried at first but then she told me to send for the doctor. I didn't like the look on her face when she said that. I hope everything's going to be all right.'

'Try not to worry, Mr MacPhee.'

'It's Charlie. And I can't help worrying. It's been going on too long. Even I know that! You've got to do something!'

The MacPhees' cottage was situated near to the sea, where a small fishing boat thrashed around in the waves. Stacks of wooden creels and coils of rope were piled along one side of the house. Charlie flung open the door.

'In you go, Doctor.'

Grateful to be inside, Margaret removed her sodden coat and Wellington boots. Charlie handed her a small, clean hand towel. 'Just carry on down to the bedroom – it's to your right there.' A cry of anguish could be heard coming from the direction he was pointing in. 'Please help her, Doctor. I'll be outside in the byre if you need me,' he said and, with a stricken look, hurried away.

Nurse McAllister turned round when she entered, her forehead creased with anxiety. Her face fell further when she saw it was Margaret and not Dr Alan. 'I really think we need someone with experience,' she whispered, walking towards Margaret.

Margaret hadn't met Anne McAllister before. The nurse was tall and thin, around the same age as Effie, but without the other nurse's reassuring smile.

'Well, you have me, Nurse McAllister. Could you tell me what's been happening?' Margaret rubbed her hair and face with the towel and glanced over at the patient.

Mrs MacPhee was propped up in a large, high bed, her eyes squeezed shut, her face contorted with pain. As was normal when delivering a baby on one's own, the nurse had wrapped the strap around Mrs MacPhee's neck and used the ends as stirrups. This was the easiest way to keep a woman's legs raised in the lithotomy position. A fire burned in the grate, casting the cramped room with shadows and flickers of orange. Even in the dim light, Margaret could see her patient was exhausted. In one corner, barely visible, was a hand-made wooden crib.

'Chrissie is twenty-three and a primigravida,' Anne said, meaning that this was the patient's first pregnancy.

Nurse McAllister looked over at the bed before moving closer to Margaret. 'Chrissie didn't come to see us – not once – during her pregnancy! Silly woman. First I knew about it was when they sent for me. Everything seemed to be going well to begin with.'

Margaret set her bag down on the table. 'What stage of labour is she in?'

'Second stage. She's been stuck there for the last few hours.'

'How many hours?'

'Six.'

Margaret's stomach knotted. It was far too long. 'You should have called me earlier.'

'None of us like to call for the doctor unless we

have to. He has enough to do.'

Couldn't she see that this was one of the have-to cases? 'Which is why I'm here. What's the presentation?'

'Normal as far as I can tell.'

Nurse McAllister didn't seem to know what she was doing. If Chrissie had been in the second stage of labour since this morning and was fully dilated, then something was definitely wrong.

'Right. I'll examine her. I presume you have hot water standing by?'

The nurse stiffened. 'Of course. And plenty of it. There's a neighbour on hand – she's in the sitting room. She'll bring us more as we need it.'

Margaret approached the bed. 'I'm Dr Margaret, Chrissie. I'm just going to examine you to see where we are. I know you're scared and tired, but try to relax.'

Chrissie moaned as another contraction ripped through her body.

Margaret scrubbed her hands before inserting two fingers into the woman's vagina. As Nurse McAllister had said, Chrissie was fully dilated. The baby's head should be well down and engaged by now. Turning back to the metal basin perched on the bedside table, she quickly washed her hands again and palpated her patient's stomach. She could easily feel the baby's head. It was engaged but still too high. The nurse should have noted that and raised the alarm sooner.

'When did her waters break?'

'A few hours ago.'

That wasn't good either. The longer a labouring patient's waters were broken, the higher the

284

chance of infection. Margaret suppressed a flutter of anxiety and thought back to her midwifery training, thinking through her options.

There were three. Firstly, she could try a high forceps delivery. If the baby came out, well and good. But if that didn't work there would be only two options left, both of which chilled her to the marrow. If the baby couldn't be delivered by forceps it could die. If the baby died in utero the mother could die too, so the second option and the safest, as far as the mother was concerned, was for Margaret to crush the baby's head and deliver it with forceps. It was the best way of ensuring the mother's survival, but meant certain death for the baby. The last option would be to perform a Caesarean section but given she had no fresh blood with her or an anaesthetic assistant, the surgery could well result in the death of mother *and* baby.

She wasn't going to let that happen. Come hell or high water, she was going to save them both.

'I'm going to do a high forceps delivery,' Margaret said with as much confidence in her voice as she could muster. She leant over the bed and squeezed her patient's hand. 'It will be uncomfortable, really uncomfortable, but your baby isn't going to come out without help. I think you know that.' Margaret looked over her shoulder. 'Nurse McAllister, would it be possible to send a telegram to the surgery and ask whether Dr Alan is back from his visits?'

'Do you think that's necessary?'

Margaret wasn't about to be challenged at every turn. With a curt nod of her head, she motioned for the nurse to follow her to the other side of the room, out of earshot of Chrissie. 'If I have to do a section to get this baby out then I will need Dr Alan to help with the anaesthetic. I hope it won't come to that, but one thing is clear. This baby is not going to deliver itself. The mother is exhausted and the baby in distress. I should have been called much earlier.'

'Calling for the doctor is the nurse's decision,' Anne replied with a mutinous line to her mouth. 'I sent for assistance as soon as I thought it was required.'

'Well, this doctor will be making the decisions now. Please go and send a message to Dr Alan then come back here and help me deliver this baby. Have you given Chrissie an enema?'

'Yes. Of course.'

'Catheterised her?'

'No.'

'I'll do it. You send that message.'

By the time Nurse McAllister returned, Margaret had catheterised her patient and had all the instruments she might need set out on top of the clean towel she had brought with her.

'Right, Nurse. I'm going to use the forceps so I need you to keep Chrissie as calm as possible. I'll give her some ether to help with the pain, but I can't give her too much.'

The nurse nodded sullenly but took her position at the top of the bed and stroked the labouring woman's forehead. 'Now, Chrissie,' she said, 'the doctor's going to help get your baby out. You just try to relax as much as you can.' She looked over at Margaret and nodded.

Margaret repeated her examination now that Chrissie's bladder was empty. After giving her some ether, she inserted the forceps, one blade at a time, ignoring the cry of pain from her patient as she did, and slid them in place on either side of the baby's head. The next bit was tricky. Could she get the blades to line up and lock? They seemed so high in the pelvis, almost too high. Sweat trickled down the back of her neck. But at last she had the baby's head in the grip of the forceps. This was the most difficult part. Her heart was pounding so hard, it felt as if everyone in the room could hear it.

As Chrissie was so drowsy with the ether she couldn't say when her contractions were coming, so Margaret instructed the nurse to put her hand on Chrissie's abdomen and tell her when the next contraction came.

'Now,' Anne said.

Margaret placed one foot on the edge of the bed, leaned back and pulled firmly but steadily downwards on the forceps. The forceps' blades moved a few inches but came to a stop.

'Could you check the baby's heartbeat?' she asked the nurse. She couldn't do it herself as she had to keep pressure on the forceps.

Anne waited until Chrissie wasn't contracting before bending over her with the Pinard stethoscope.

'Heartbeat is fifty,' she mouthed at Margaret.

That wasn't good. The baby's heart was failing. Margaret probably only had a few more minutes at the most. Then she would have to make a decision. Risk the baby dying in utero, which would almost certainly result in the death of the mother, or crush its skull and deliver a dead baby. She was damned if she was going to do that.

She gritted her teeth and pulled again. Perspiration continued to roll down her forehead and into her eyes. There was a chance that she might injure the baby or worse but, given the alternative, it was a risk she had to take.

She lowered herself on her knees almost to the floor. She clutched her elbow tight to her side and leaned down harder than she had before, harder than she wanted. A second pull and then a third. Just when she thought she had no more strength left to keep pulling she felt the baby move and a slight give as the baby's head appeared under the pubic bone. Lifting herself slowly, she made a cut to the right of the vaginal opening, then let the forceps slide upwards with the curve of the mother's pelvis as the baby's head slipped out. Margaret didn't wait for another contraction but quickly delivered the shoulders and body, placing the baby gently on the bed between his mother's legs. Anne had left the top of the bed to come around to where Margaret was standing and clamped and cut the cord. The newborn was limp and blue and wasn't breathing.

'Go on, baby, breathe for me,' Margaret whispered. The nurse folded the baby in a fresh towel and began to rub his limbs and chest vigorously.

'Is my baby all right?' Chrissie asked, her voice trembling.

'You have a son, Chrissie. I'm just going to have a look at him while Nurse McAllister delivers the afterbirth.' Margaret exchanged places with the nurse, who handed over the baby with a grateful look. The rubbing had done nothing to prompt the boy into taking a breath. Margaret bent over him and placed her mouth over the tiny lips and nose and blew gently and regularly, watching the small chest as it rose in response. Between each few breaths she checked the baby's pulse with her fingers across his chest. Slow, very slow. *He had to breathe.*

Then at last, just as she was giving up hope, the baby gasped, coughed and began to whimper gently. Within moments he was a healthy pink colour and the house was filled with his cries. The child was going to live. *Thank you, God.* Now she had to see to Chrissie.

Nurse McAllister checked the baby's observations while Margaret stitched up the cut she'd made in Chrissie's perineum. When she'd done that she gave Chrissie some ergot.

'How is baby?' Margaret asked Anne, who was still bending over the infant.

'Perfect. Everything's how it should be.' Anne looked over at her as she said it and Margaret knew that she was also telling her that the baby's pulse and respirations were normal. The nurse turned to her patient. 'I'm just going to give you – and him – a wee wash, Chrissie, then you can feed him.'

Chrissie propped herself onto her elbows. 'Let me see him, please.' Although she still looked exhausted her child's arrival seemed to have given her a burst of energy.

Anne carried the child over to Chrissie and handed him to her.

289

'He's so beautiful,' Chrissie breathed. When she looked back up at Margaret her eyes were wet. 'I don't know how I'll ever be able to thank you, Doctor.'

Margaret smiled back. 'I was only doing my job.'

'I'm not stupid, Doctor. I know I was in trouble. I know my baby could have died. We owe you our lives and I'm never going to forget that.'

While Anne bathed mother and child, Margaret went to tell Charlie that he had a son who he could see in a little while. In the meantime, she asked him to send a message to the surgery to let Dr Alan know he was no longer required.

The elation she felt was something she hadn't experienced in a long time. She'd saved the child and the mother. Her medical skills had been there when she'd needed them.

Nurse McAllister had other visits to make so Margaret excused her, well aware she had probably made her first enemy. But if pulling the nurse up ensured she would call out the doctor sooner, it was worth it. However, Margaret didn't want to leave; not until she was sure there wouldn't be any abnormal bleeding. She settled herself in the armchair. Chrissie was sleeping, her baby wrapped in her arms. The bedroom door opened quietly and the husband peered in.

'Is it all right if I come in, Doctor?'

'Yes, of course,' Margaret replied softly.

Charlie tiptoed across the room and eased himself down onto the edge of the bed. His gaze rested on his wife and newborn son, his eyes alight with amazement. 'He's perfect, a bonny wee lad, isn't he?'

'Yes, he's a beautiful baby. Congratulations.'

He turned towards her, his eyes shining. 'Thank you, Doctor. For doing your best for both of them. If you hadn't been here I hate to think what could have happened.'

'Well, don't. It all turned out fine in the end. So there's no need to think of might-have-beens.'

'Aye, you're right.' Charlie leant forward and with a gentleness that belied his size, stroked his son's cheek. 'Just you get some shut-eye while you can, wee man, as there'll be a right old ceilidh tonight to wet your head. Oh aye, all your grand-parents, aunts, uncles, cousins, nephews and half the blooming village will be squeezing into this room to gawp at you.'

This is how a family should be, Margaret thought with a pang. A child should be born into the world knowing that he, or she, had not only the parents' love, but the love of the grandparents too. She wished it could have been like that for her. Most of all she wished it could have been like that for Elizabeth and James.

The loud cry of a baby demanding to be fed shook Margaret from her reverie. She helped Chrissie put him to the breast and, confident both mother and infant were doing well and were now in the capable hands of several neighbours, she took her leave of the MacPhees.

The rain hadn't let up and she trudged wearily over the moors, the elation from the delivery slowly evaporating. She thought of the day Eliza-beth had been born, Alasdair's delight and relief

291

mirroring Charlie's. Then three years later, James's birth.

She remembered how she'd felt on both occasions. Tired, delighted, relieved, but most of all overwhelmed with love and gratitude for her new family. Back then, she could never have imagined that she'd be living apart from her husband and her children.

But as she thought back to the image of the little boy in his mother's arms, her spirits lifted. Although she would have given anything to change the circumstances that had brought her here, she couldn't help but be happy she was practising medicine again. She had done something amazing today. She had saved a mother and baby. More than that, she'd saved this little family.

The knowledge warmed her soul.

Chapter 28

Despite being kept busy it felt as if the weekend she was to see the children would never come. The only dampener to her happiness was the discovery that she couldn't spend the night with them. The islanders, Dolina had snapped, did not travel on the Sabbath. The Sabbath was for attending church, reading the Bible and resting. No one, except for the doctor in emergencies, worked, and that included Johnny Ban. But not even Dolina's quoted passages from the scriptures and caustic tongue could diminish Margaret's joy at the thought that soon she would see Libby and James, even if it were only for a day.

Given that she couldn't travel on the Sunday there was no option but for her to arrange to return to Lochmaddy on Saturday evening. She knew the children would be distraught, and if she could have done anything to stay the night with them she would have – even walked. But it was simply too far. When Saturday finally arrived she was up before it was light. She boiled some water in pans on the stove and washed her hair, grateful that since she'd cut it short it no longer required more than a quick brush. When it was dry she pulled on the pair of trousers she wore to ride Dobbin and a warm sweater. She wrote to Alasdair and dawdled over her breakfast but she was still ready long before Johnny appeared at the house.

This time the tide was out so she was able to walk across the sands. She was almost at Sandbank when she heard a shout and she looked up to find Elizabeth running towards her, hair flying, small feet kicking up clods of sand in her wake.

Margaret scooped her into her arms and Elizabeth clung to her, wrapping her arms tightly round her mother's neck.

'Oh, Libby,' Margaret breathed, 'I've missed you so much.'

'I've been watching for you all morning,' Elizabeth replied. 'Watching and watching and waiting. Annie and Mary have as well.'

Margaret's heart ached for her child. She could just imagine her daughter's face, pressed up against the window, her brow furrowed in the way it did when she was concentrating.

'And James? How is he? Have you been helping Aunt Flora look after him?'

'Everyone makes such a fuss over him he doesn't care about me any more,' Elizabeth complained. 'I told him you were coming today and he didn't even want to come and meet you.'

Margaret's heart tightened further. She was happy her little boy was settling in and didn't appear to miss her too much, but she hated the thought that he might be beginning to forget her.

'Can we go and get our bag now? How are we getting to your house?' Elizabeth demanded.

Margaret had hoped that she'd have some time with her daughter before she gave her the news that she couldn't take her back with her and that she was only here for the day.

She placed Elizabeth back on her feet and stood there for a few minutes just drinking her in. Her child had changed in the couple of weeks since she'd last seen her. Her hair was tangled, her feet covered in sand like short socks, but she had colour in her face and a sparkle in her eyes that hadn't been there after Alasdair's arrest. And now she was to be the one to remove the light from her eyes. 'I'm sorry, Libby, but I can't take you and James home with me tonight. There's no way of bringing you back here before school starts on Monday.'

'But you promised, Mummy.'

'I know I did. And I wish that I didn't have to break my promise. But,' she gently squeezed her daughter's shoulders, 'I promise that it is the last promise I shall ever break. Now, let's go and say hello to James and Aunty Flora and the children.'

Margaret strongly suspected that Flora had held her brood back from running out to meet her so she and Elizabeth could have the first few moments together. Now unleashed, they ran outside, shouting with excitement. Flora had James on her hip and when he saw his mother his face lit up and he leaned towards her, holding out his arms. It seemed he hadn't totally forgotten her after all.

'I've news,' Flora murmured as they walked back to the house, the girls alongside them, Flora's two each holding one of James's hands. 'Don't get your hopes up, but I think it's good.'

Margaret's pulse skipped a beat. 'Alasdair? Has he written?'

'No. The letter was from Mairi. I'll tell you everything when we're alone.'

The next hour or so sped by in a happy whirlwind. They had tea in the cosy kitchen with Flora's children. As soon as the children had finished and were excused from the table they tumbled out of the house. Elizabeth looked after them longingly, clearly torn between staying with her mother and going out to play. James, on the other hand, had refused to be put down and was ensconced on his mother's lap.

'Why don't you go with them, Libby?' Margaret said. 'So I can have a chat with Aunty Flora. I'll come and look for you in a few minutes so you can tell me everything you've been up to while you've been here.'

Elizabeth needed no second bidding. 'But don't

be too long, Mummy.'

'What did Mairi say?' Margaret asked Flora as soon as her daughter had scampered off. She'd been burning to know.

'I got a letter from her yesterday.'

'And?'

'I'm to tell you that Toni and his friends haven't been sitting twiddling their thumbs while Alasdair's been in prison. The union have been making noises to get the case looked at again and they've got some important people on their side. Toni has been asking around. You do know they never stopped trying to find the real murderer, don't you?'

Margaret nodded impatiently. Toni had taken the news that Alasdair couldn't be persuaded to escape hard. He had little faith in the justice system and she knew without him having to say it that he thought Alasdair had made a mistake. However, he'd promised to double his efforts to find who had really killed Tommy Barr.

'Well, Toni has found someone who saw something that night. Someone who says she knows who really killed Billy Barr's son.'

Margaret's heart started beating light and fast. 'Who? Why didn't they go to the police?'

'Wait now and I'll tell you exactly what Mairi said.' Flora took out the letter and, agonisingly slowly, unfolded it.

'She says the woman – Mary Murphy she's called – heard a racket coming from her back lane the night Tommy was killed. She looked out of the window and saw two men – one of whom she thought she recognised – running away. A minute or so later she saw a different man hurrying into the lane. He knelt down by something she thought was a bundle of clothes. Almost straight after, she saw two policemen go into the lane and cross over to the man. She didn't want to get involved – the police were there, after all – so she shut her window and went to bed. The next day she went to stay with her sister in Dunoon for a month. She never thought anything more about it until she happened to overhear Toni asking her neighbour if he'd heard anything the night the lad was killed. She hadn't even known about the murder. Says she never reads the papers. It was the second time Toni and the lads had been to all the houses asking, but of course she wasn't there the first time.' She looked up at Margaret and smiled. 'So there is another witness, after all.'

It was as if a light had been lit inside Margaret's chest. 'Does Mr Firth know? Does Alasdair?'

Flora laughed. 'Now hold on. One question at a time. Toni has been meeting with the new lawyer. He'll tell him about this woman. I'm sure they will go together to see her.' She squeezed Margaret's hand. 'This is the news we've been praying for.'

'Alasdair could be released! I should go back...'

'Toni says you're to stay where you are. Your father has sent people in to Govan to ask about you. I doubt he'll find out anything but you never know. Toni says you are to have patience and that you are not to get your hopes up. It could all still turn out to be a dead end.'

'But it can't be! I always knew somebody had to have seen what really happened.' Margaret gripped Flora's hand. 'It *is* good news. Alasdair was right when he told me to have faith!' She didn't know whether she was laughing or crying.

James placed chubby hands on either side of her face and gave her a resounding kiss. 'Not cry, Mummy!'

Margaret kissed him back. 'Mummy's not crying any longer. And it's only because she's happy.'

'Now, tell me. How have the children been?' Margaret asked after she'd dried her tears and blown her nose.

'James is such a contented child. Libby was a little tearful her first night, but since then she's been fine – except at bedtime. I think that's when she misses you the most. She lies in bed with that fob watch you gave her pressed up to her ear, looking a little lost and forlorn.'

Some of the joy went out of the day.

'But the girls have found a way to distract her – they make up stories to tell her at night. I've been listening outside the door. I think there's a few about her hen. According to Annie and Mary that hen has more adventures than Oedipus.'

'I can't tell you how much I appreciate you having her. Having them both. I don't know what I would have done otherwise.'

'Och, a couple more children in the house is nothing to us. The girls and Lachie enjoy having James to fuss over and Libby to show off to.'

Margaret pressed a few pound notes, almost all of what she had left, into Flora's hands. 'I'll give you more at the end of the month.'

Flora took the money reluctantly. 'You'll do no such thing! This is more than enough. Those little mites hardly eat us out of house and home. Libby might need a new dress or two for the winter, though. I can easily knit her a cardigan and she can have the dresses Mary has grown out of if you like, but I imagine you'll want her to have her own things. You can get what you need from either the J.D. Williams or the Oxendales catalogue. Just write to them and they'll send you one, but you can borrow mine in the meantime. They let you pay Cash on Demand or by instalments.'

'Then that's what I'll do. How is Peter?'

'He's been out fishing since Monday. I'm expecting him back tonight, God willing.'

'You must worry about him when he's at sea.'

'What would be the point in that? I trust in the Lord to look after him. Now, how have you been getting on? Are you settling in over by? Have the locals got over the fact that their new doctor is not only young, but a beautiful woman to boot?'

'Not so much of the young or pretty, I'm afraid. The wind plays havoc with my hair.'

They smiled at each other in mutual sympathy. Odd, how even when times were hard, women still cared about their appearance.

'You're looking better than when I last saw you. You don't seem so lost as you did when you arrived,' Flora continued.

'Now I know there is progress with Alasdair's case, I feel so much better. And I have my work to keep me busy. That helps too. As does knowing you are caring for the children. If they can't be with me then I'm glad they're with you. But I miss them... I miss Alasdair.' Her voice cracked a little.

Flora patted her hand. 'Of course you do. As well as your old life. My dear, I can only imagine what you're going through.'

'I owe so much to you and your family. How I'm ever going to repay all your kindness I have no idea.'

'Och, away with you. We like having the children here. You're in a spot of trouble and we've all been in that place at one time or another and if we haven't, then it's likely a day will come when we will be. That's the way we island folk see it anyway. You and Alasdair helped others when they needed it, so it's only right that we should be here to offer you a hand now.'

'Whatever you say, I will always be grateful to you.' She stood and shifted James on to her hip and kissed his cheek. 'Shall we go find your sister?'

After Margaret had seen everything Elizabeth wanted to show her, they returned to the house. Flora was wrapping some scones and cheese in a cloth.

'I'm afraid we are going to leave you and Libby and James to your own devices for the remainder of the afternoon. I don't know if you noticed the people lifting peats on the croft up by on your way in?'

'Yes. Matter of fact I did.'

'Well, that's the Coopers' peat bank. It's a tradition here that we all help each other with the peats and the hay. We'll do one croft and move on to the next. It means that the elderly who have no youngsters at home can get theirs in. The men are usually out fishing so most often it's the women and children who do it.'

'And you're planning to go there this afternoon?'

'It wouldn't be right if I didn't. You do understand, don't you? If you were able to stay the night we'd have all evening to blether.'

'The children and I could come too. Libby and I could help, perhaps? I'm sure we'll find enough up there to keep James out of mischief.'

Flora looked at Margaret and laughed. 'I don't mean to be unkind but those hands don't look as if they are used to rough work. No, it's good of you to offer, but people would only feel uncomfortable with the doctor there. Certain things just aren't done and the doctor working the peats is one of them. Besides, it will give you time to spend with your wee ones on your own. The girls will be coming too and Lachie is already up there so you'll have the house to yourselves.'

Shortly before it was time for Margaret to leave, she and the children went upstairs and laid out the dress, shoes and socks Elizabeth was to wear to her first day of school on Monday.

'Are you looking forward to starting school?' Margaret asked, holding James in her arms. She wished that she could have been the one to take her daughter to school, or at the very least be there to hear all about it when she returned.

'I'm going to learn to read and write. Then I'll be able to read the letters you send by myself and I can write back to you.'

Margaret ruffled Libby's hair. 'I would like that. Very much.'

It was almost as bad saying goodbye to Elizabeth and James as it had been the last time, except that today she would be leaving them with hope in her heart that soon they'd be together again. James was falling asleep in her arms. Holding him close to her, and hand in hand with her daughter, they walked across the sands to where the others were helping with the peats. Flora took the now sleeping James from Margaret and laid him down on a little bed she had made from sacks on top of springy heather. Margaret kissed his plump flushed cheek, inhaling the scent of him and trying not to cry. When she bent to kiss Elizabeth goodbye, her daughter clung to her with a ferocity that took Margaret's breath away. 'Don't go, Mummy.'

'I have to, sweetheart.'

'Then take me with you.'

'I thought you liked it with Aunty Flora and the children,' Margaret whispered.

'I do. But it's not the same as living with you.'

'I know. But it won't be forever.'

'How long?'

'Libby, come and see this,' Annie called over. 'It's the biggest butterfly you've ever seen.'

Elizabeth looked across at Annie then back to her mother. Margaret gave her a gentle push. 'Go on. Before it flies away.'

'Goodbye, Mummy,' Elizabeth said and set off as fast as her little legs could carry her.

'Goodbye, Libby. I'll see you soon.'

But her daughter was already out of earshot.

When Margaret, tired and dispirited at being parted from her children once more, let herself into her cottage that night, it was to find that her little house had been transformed. It had been clean before but now it shone. The stove was lit and giving off a good heat, a pot of soup simmered on the side and a mound of scones, savoury and treacle, had been set on the kitchen table as well as a jam jar of wild flowers.

Tears pricked behind Margaret's eyes. Seonag, the woman who left the milk for her each day, must have done all this while she was away. It was unexpected and thoughtful.

She heard a creaking coming from her bedroom and a few moments later, to her astonishment, Dolina appeared in the kitchen. Margaret almost leaped two feet in the air.

'Good grief, you gave me a start.'

What was Dolina doing here? It was one thing for people to just walk in when she was at home, but to be wandering around her house when she wasn't was too much.

Her heart still thudding, she wondered if she'd left anything incriminating lying around. There was their wedding photograph, but Dolina would think it strange if it wasn't on display, and her letters from Alasdair. But those she kept hidden away at the bottom of a drawer.

'You're back then,' Dolina said, removing her apron.

She didn't appear the least bit perturbed to be caught in Margaret's house. 'Yes. As you can see.'

'I've just put a hot bottle in your bed.' Dolina looked around the room. 'There's some soup and fresh scones for your supper.'

'*You* brought them?'

'Aye, well, I saw the smoke coming from the kitchen the other day. Can't have you setting the place alight, can we?'

So it had been Dolina, not Seonag, who had done all this!

'I'll be back in the morning to stoke up your fire,' Dolina said. 'That's a piddling wee thing you had going. I'll need to see to Dr Alan's breakfast after that.' Her forehead furrowed. 'Not sure how I'll manage you both but I'll find a way.'

It appeared that Dolina was intent on becoming her housekeeper too. But Margaret didn't need or could afford to pay for one. Besides, Dolina was Dr Alan's housekeeper and Margaret couldn't imagine him being pleased at having to share.

'This is all very kind of you, but don't you think you should check with Dr Alan?'

Dolina sniffed. 'I have already spoken to him and he said he was happy for me to help out here when I'm not seeing to the folk waiting for the doctor. It's only a five-minute walk from the surgery and it won't take me long to see to you. I can cook for you the same time I'm cooking for him. He never eats everything I make anyway. Claims I make far too much.'

'But–' Margaret didn't want to admit she couldn't afford to pay her – not when she was trying to save every penny. Neither was she sure she wanted Dolina in and out of her house.

'You'll be out and about at all hours same as him. And if you are like himself you'll be missing meals and not tending to your fire. We can't have the new doctor getting sick now, can we?' She folded her arms and studied Margaret. 'I heard you saved that mother in Locheport. And the baby too. They're saying if you hadn't been there, things might not have turned out the way they did.'

So it seemed as if Dolina was coming to accept a female doctor could be as good as a male one. Nevertheless, Margaret was touched.

'I was only doing my job,' she murmured.

Dolina sniffed. 'Aye, well. So you say. But if you don't do your job in future it won't be because you're hungry or out of sorts. Not if I have anything to do with it.' She picked up an armful of Margaret's laundry. 'Now, I can't stay here chatting all day. I have things to be getting on with.'

Chapter 29

Margaret first noticed Caroline MacIntosh when she'd looked into the waiting room on her way into the surgery. She'd been sitting quietly, a little apart from the others and not participating in the general, almost festive, atmosphere in the room. There were seven patients waiting to be seen, an old man with a jam jar filled to the top with straw-coloured liquid she knew must be urine, two women in their best skirts and jackets, three children who looked as if they'd had their faces scrubbed to within an inch of their lives, and Caroline, who was first on the list Dolina had given Margaret.

Caroline was dressed neatly in a tan skirt, navy blue jumper and a Peter Pan-collared yellow blouse. Her brogues, although they had clearly seen better days, were polished to a high shine, and her auburn hair had been neatly brushed and gathered off her face with a yellow ribbon. But despite the care she'd taken with her appearance there was no disguising her undernourished frame. She was thin to the point of scrawniness.

'Now, Mrs MacIntosh, what can I do for you?' Margaret asked when Caroline was seated in her consulting room.

'I wouldn't have come – I didn't want to bother you, but my Donald insisted.'

'You aren't bothering me, I promise. It's my job to see people. Why don't you just tell me what's wrong?'

'It's my leg. It won't heal. I bumped my shin a few weeks ago and I didn't think anything more about it. But since then the place where I bashed it has turned into a sore. I've put poultices on it and everything but it's not getting better. In fact it's getting worse.'

'Could you take off your stockings and pop up on the examination couch so I can have a look?'

Margaret washed her hands while Caroline did as she was asked.

'How have you been feeling otherwise?' Margaret continued, moving towards her patient. There was an open wound on her leg about an inch in diameter and the skin was red and inflamed around the edges.

'Och, a little tired. But that's not surprising. It's a busy time of the year.'

'Anything else. Any other aches and pains. Fever?'

'No.' She glanced at Margaret from under her lids and blushed. 'I think I might be pregnant, though. I've been needing the toilet a lot. My breasts are tender and I can't remember the last time I had my monthlies.'

'That might account for your tiredness. I notice we don't have a record for you. You haven't been to see us before?'

'There's been no need. I've only stayed down this end of the island since my Donald and I got married a few months ago. I'm from the other end.' There was a wry twist to her lips as she said the words.

'The other end of the island? You mean Grimsay?'

'No. South Uist.'

'Lie back and relax. I'd like to feel your tummy. You don't need to take your dress off. Just pull it up.'

She washed her hands again and waited until Caroline was settled and comfortable. 'So your husband is from here?' Margaret asked, moving her hands over the younger woman's abdomen. As she did, she thought she caught a faint, fruity smell on her breath. 'I mean from North Uist.'

'Oh yes. And his family. They've lived here for centuries. Not that they have anything to do with us.'

Margaret was surprised. Everything she'd learned so far about the islanders suggested they were a close-knit community, as close-knit as the people in Govan had been; mothers looking after daughters, fathers after sons and neighbours helping one another without being asked. Without close cooperation like this, the islanders couldn't survive.

'Why is that?' she asked.

307

'They can't forgive him for marrying from the wrong side. Like most of the folk on South Uist, I'm Catholic, you see. And they are staunch Wee Free. They're worried I'll convert him.'

'I see.' She remembered what Dr Alan had said the night she'd arrived. About which church she was going to attend. It hadn't occurred to her that one side of the island would be Protestant and the other Catholic and that this would be a source of conflict.

'It's the same with my family,' Caroline said. 'They won't have anything to do with us either. They think anyone not born into the faith will burn in hell.' She grimaced. 'We were lucky to find a priest in South Uist who agreed to marry us in the chapel in Daliburgh. Most people closed their curtains so they wouldn't have to see us pass.'

'I'm sorry,' Margaret said. Once it would have been incomprehensible to her that a mother could turn from her daughter for any reason. Not now. Would parents ever realise that they couldn't live their children's lives for them? She couldn't imagine ever treating Elizabeth the way her mother had treated her, or Caroline's mother, her daughter.

She palpated Caroline's stomach. She thought she could feel the edges of a uterus distended by pregnancy, but it was too early to tell.

'If you remove your drawers I'll do a quick internal examination.'

But that was inconclusive too. Margaret thought the uterus was soft – and the edges of the cervix were bluish – both possible signs of pregnancy, but neither was sufficiently so for her to be sure.

'I can't be certain you are pregnant. We'll need to wait a week or two to find out.'

Caroline looked crestfallen. 'Oh Doctor, I was really hoping you'd be able to tell straight away. About me having a baby, I mean.' She sat up and adjusted her clothes. 'I was so looking forward to telling Donald. I know he'd be over the moon. And our parents – if they knew they were going to have a grandchild, how could they continue to stay away?'

Margaret didn't have the heart to tell her young patient that having a child didn't always bring families closer together. 'We'll know one way or another soon enough. Come back and see me in a couple of weeks and I might be able to tell you. In the meantime, do you think you can pass some water into this container for me? And when you've done that I'd like to take some blood – just to make certain everything's as it should be. I'd like you to wait, however, until I've tested your urine. Now, let me see your leg again so I can clean your wound and redress it.'

But everything wasn't going to be all right for Caroline. Recalling the sweet smell on Caroline's breath, Margaret asked the nurse to check for sugar in the urine while she was testing for albumin. Effie was in her late thirties or early forties, with dark wavy hair and a ready smile. They stood together and watched as the urine turned orange.

'Diabetes,' Effie murmured. 'Poor thing.'

It was just as Margaret had suspected. It explained how thin Caroline was and that faint sweet smell she'd noticed on her breath. Until recently, a diagnosis of diabetes, especially in the young, had been pretty much a death sentence. Happily, a way of treating the illness with insulin from the livers of cows and pig had been discovered. However, pregnancy for diabetics was still dangerous – very much so – indeed, often fatal.

She hoped for Caroline's sake that she wasn't pregnant.

'We do have insulin?' Margaret asked.

'I'm not sure. I'll have to have a look. If needs be we can get some from Stornoway.'

Margaret returned to the consulting room. Caroline was sitting in the chair, hands calmly folded in her lap, waiting.

'I'm afraid, Caroline, that you have diabetes. That's probably why you've been tired and feeling thirsty and getting up in the night to pass water. It also explains why the cut on your leg is slow to heal.'

'Oh I know that! The doctor in Lochboisdale told me that a while ago.'

'So you're on insulin already? You should have said. We might need to fiddle around with your dosage.'

'Oh, I'm not on that stuff. Dr Sinclair did give it to me but I swelled up like a balloon and came out in spots. Had to go to my bed for a few days. Soon as he stopped it I was fine.'

'He stopped it?'

'Said it would kill me. So he put me on a strict diet – not to lose weight, obviously. Donald says there's nothing of me as it is. Wasn't much of a diet really. No sugar – that was about it – not that that was a problem. There's no' much of it to be had here and when there is, it's much too expensive.'

Margaret had heard of people being allergic to insulin. It was rare, but happened enough to cause problems. The only way to manage diabetes without it was by diet. However, this was a poor way of treating the illness. Sooner or later most of the patients developed severe health problems which, in turn, eventually led to an early death. And as for getting pregnant! Surely Dr Sinclair must have warned Caroline of the implications for her and the baby? Caroline was certain to lose the baby and likely her own life.

'Did the doctor say anything about not getting pregnant?' Margaret asked gently.

Caroline laughed. 'Imagine anyone telling a Catholic she shouldn't have children! It's like telling the tide it can't come in.'

'Caroline, he should have warned you about getting pregnant because it's very dangerous for someone with your condition.'

'Me a married woman without children? No.' She clutched Margaret's hand. 'You've no idea what having a baby means to me.' Her eyes were shining. 'Don't you see? It will be the best thing that's ever happened to me.' She smiled shyly. 'Except for marrying Donald, that is.'

Margaret kept her expression non-committal. She wasn't sure what the options for Caroline were. She needed to speak to Dr Alan before she alarmed Caroline any more. Perhaps there were innovations that had been made since she last practised although, as she'd told Dr Alan, she had kept up with the medical journals. However, it was entirely possible she'd missed something.

311

In the meantime, should she arrange for Caroline to go to Glasgow? Or admit her to the hospital in Stornoway? She couldn't do either without consulting with Dr Alan first.

She realised Caroline was still looking at her, waiting for her reply. There was little point in continuing the conversation until Margaret knew for sure that Caroline was pregnant.

'I'll need to have a word with Dr Alan. You get off home and either he or I will come and see you.'

'Come and see me? Why?'

'Because we'll need to keep a close eye on your wound to check that it's started to heal. And then, once we find out for definite if you are pregnant, we'll have to decide what to do about that too.'

Caroline frowned. 'I don't know what you mean.'

Margaret leaned forward. 'Caroline, if you are expecting, you, and very likely your baby, will be at risk. Very serious risk.'

'But you'll see us all right, Doctor? You and Dr Alan?' Caroline fingered the cross around her neck.

If Caroline was pregnant as well as being allergic to insulin, then Margaret very much doubted she would be all right.

'We'll do our very best. In the meantime, try and rest as much as you can.'

The clinic went on longer than she anticipated but eventually Margaret finished writing up her notes whilst Effie tidied away. She wasn't expecting to see Dr Alan but to her surprise and relief she found him sitting in the kitchen, sipping tea from a delicate china cup and looking contented and relaxed. Most of the time he was in too much of a hurry, standing to drink his tea and draining his cup in three mouthfuls.

'More in the pot.' He gestured to the stove. 'Help yourself.' He sighed with pleasure. 'Can't remember the last time I enjoyed a cup of tea without being interrupted.'

'Oh, sorry. I'll leave you in peace then.'

'Sit, girl, sit. I can see you have something on your mind. Spit it out. Let's see if I can help, eh?'

She pulled out a chair opposite him and told him about Caroline.

'So what do you think?' Margaret leaned forward, anxious to hear his view. 'Should we send her to Glasgow?'

Dr Alan pushed back his chair and stretched his legs out. He looked up at the ceiling as if seeking inspiration. 'No, there's no point in doing that. If she's allergic to insulin there's not much the doctors there can do except treat her diabetes by diet which, from what you say, the young woman is already doing.'

'At least I should send a telegram to her doctor in South Uist, confirm her allergic reaction to insulin.'

'You could. Aye, you could do that.' He shook his head. 'But I suspect he'll just confirm what this Caroline told you.' He drained his cup and reached over to the stove for the teapot. 'All you can really do, Margaret, is arrange to have one of the nurses dress the patient's wound every other day and report on any significant changes.'

'And if she is pregnant?'

'Then it is in God's hands.'

There *was* something they could do that, if Caroline was pregnant, might save her life. But Margaret didn't want to mention it to Dr Alan. Not yet. And she hoped she would never have to.

She rubbed her face, suddenly feeling drained. 'I'll go back and see her in a week or two. I'll probably be able to tell for sure whether she is pregnant by then. In the meantime, I'm going to get in touch with her doctor in South Uist. Perhaps Caroline is confused about the insulin? Maybe she had an allergic reaction to something else and misunderstood her doctor. Either way I need to be clear what we're dealing with.'

'Of course you do. Once you know for certain, we'll talk again.'

Before she set out on her visits, Margaret walked over to the post office to send the telegram to the doctor in South Uist. She would have much preferred to have spoken to him in person, but that wasn't an option. Although South Uist was one of the islands that made up the Uists, coming after Benbecula which came after Grimsay in the long string that made up the Outer Hebrides, it might as well have been the other side of the world. She thought carefully about what to say. She trusted the postmistress would be discreet, but just in case she wasn't, Margaret didn't want to use Caroline's name. She'd already discovered that what Mairi had told her was true, the islanders knew who everyone was on the island and liked nothing better than to discuss every snippet of each other's lives with one another.

In the end she'd decided upon: *Need information on a young woman seen by you – perhaps last
year – with a diagnosis of diabetes. The patient in
question apparently suffered severe allergic reaction to
insulin. Need to confirm soonest.* She signed it with
her assumed name and qualification and hoped
that Dr Sinclair would get back to her by return.

Chapter 30

Margaret was reading a Somerset Maugham
novel by the light of an oil lamp a few evenings
later, trying not to worry about the children and
Alasdair but failing, when there was a loud rap at
the door. She put her book aside. If Dr Alan was
out on a call, she was next in line for any emergencies.

A man in tweed had raised his hand to knock
again just as she opened the door.

'Dr Murdoch?'

He didn't look like a local. A spider of dread
crawled up her spine. Was he someone her father
had hired to find her? Had she finally been discovered? Her heart gave a sickening thump.

'Yes. Does someone need a doctor?' Her mouth
was dry.

He laughed. 'They might do. But hopefully not
me.' He stuck out a hand. 'I'm Dr Sinclair. I was
in the vicinity so I thought I'd call on you.' He
peered over her shoulder. 'May I come in, or do

you keep all your guests standing on the door-step?'

She stepped back and held the door open. 'I beg your pardon. Do come in.' So this was Caroline's previous doctor. He was a little older than Margaret, with short, sandy-coloured hair. He was wearing plus-fours, a waistcoat and a tweed jacket. He would have fitted in perfectly with the men who had come over on the ferry with her.

He looked around her kitchen. 'They don't exactly spoil you in terms of accommodation, do they?'

Despite her relief that he wasn't someone her father had sent to find her, the look of amused contempt in his eyes made her bristle. Her accommodation was none of his business. 'Please sit down, Dr Sinclair. I'm assuming you're here because of the telegram?'

To her chagrin he flicked his handkerchief over the already spotless chair before taking a seat. 'I gathered you need more information about a previous patient of mine. You could have been clearer in your message.'

'As you must know, very little on this island is secret. I had no wish to broadcast my patient's medical history. There is little enough privacy for patients as it is.'

'You'll get over your mainland sensibilities soon enough. Things are done differently around these parts and the sooner you accept that the better.'

She stiffened. 'I'm assuming you didn't come here to lecture me, Dr Sinclair.' She'd rarely taken such an immediate dislike to someone before. She tried to put her feelings aside and concentrate on getting the information she needed from him. 'You could easily have telegraphed me with the information I requested.'

'I thought I would save us both the tedious business of cryptic messages going back and forth.'

'That's very kind of you. I'm sure you must be as busy in the south as we are here.'

He grinned. 'Don't paint me with a saintly brush, Dr Murdoch. I have a weekend's fishing planned down here with some pals from the mainland.' So she was partly right in one respect. 'I've left my assistant in charge for the weekend and when I heard Dr MacLean's winter assistant was prettier than mine, I thought I'd come and see for myself.'

Although she didn't care for his manner, or his remarks, she decided the best way to deal with Dr Sinclair was not to react. She'd come across many like him before both as a medical student and as a House Officer – the type of male doctor who either liked to show off to the women medical students and doctors or patronise them. Which essentially was the same thing.

'The patient I wanted to know about is Caroline MacIntosh. I understand you diagnosed her diabetes.'

'Did I?'

'Perhaps you will check her notes? I presume you've not discarded record-keeping along with your manners?'

'Ouch.' He leaned back in his chair and locked his arms behind his neck.

Although she was damned if she was going to kowtow to him, she really had to try and keep the sarcasm from her voice. Right now he had information she needed and she wouldn't put it past him to withhold it just to make a point. 'I apologise,' she said stiffly. 'I'm sure you keep records. Would you mind having a look when you get back to your surgery?'

'As a matter of fact I looked through my records yesterday. Happened to find one that I thought fitted the bill. A Caroline McKinnon? Address Yellowpoint, Daliburgh. Diabetic. Allergic to insulin.'

'That sounds like her. But she's Caroline MacIntosh now.'

'I take it she got married then. I have noted all the details down.' He reached inside his jacket pocket and brought out a folded piece of paper. 'Now, are you going to tell me what this is about?' He took out a packet of cigarettes from his pocket, offered them to her, and when she shook her head, lit one for himself.

'Caroline came to see me with a non-healing sore. I tested her urine and discovered she has diabetes – which you correctly diagnosed when exactly?'

He consulted his note. 'Just over six months ago.'

'I gather you tried her on insulin?'

'Most certainly. Whatever you think of us in this backwater, Dr Murdoch,' she bristled again, 'most of us do keep up with latest developments – at least we try.'

'I'm sure you do. And she reacted badly to the insulin?'

'Yes. She suffered a severe anaphylactic reaction.

It's rare, but it happens. Happily, she survived, down to the quick thinking of my nurse who was with her at the time.' He flicked the ash from his cigarette into the pail by the stove. 'The new wonder treatment has kept a lot of people alive, or at least given them a few more years than they might have had without it, but it doesn't suit everyone.'

'I understand they're working on a synthetic substitute which may mean it is less expensive as well as less likely to cause an allergic reaction.'

He looked surprised. However, after his recent assertion that he kept up to date with medical developments, he clearly wasn't going to mention that he hadn't known.

'They're a bit away from having it ready for the general public,' she continued after a pause. At least he knew she kept up. Perhaps he'd pay more attention now.

'What else would you like to know?'

'As I'm sure you're aware, becoming pregnant when one has diabetes is very dangerous. Yet you didn't warn Caroline.'

He narrowed his eyes and surveyed her through a cloud of smoke 'My dear woman, of course I did.' He ground out his cigarette and threw the extinguished butt into the fire. 'I'm not sure I care for the conclusion you've clearly come to that I don't know my medicine well enough to warn patients against doing something that may well kill them.'

'You did warn her against getting pregnant, then?'

He leaned back in his chair and crossed his legs. 'Naturally. I'm assuming since she lived in South

Uist originally that she's Catholic?'

'Yes.'

'Well, there's your answer then.'

Margaret was mortified. She'd charged in with both feet. It hadn't occurred to her that Caroline would have lied to her, but then come to think of it, she hadn't actually said that Dr Sinclair hadn't told her not to get pregnant.

'I apologise. Of course you told her.'

'I gather she's pregnant then.'

'I'm not certain, but I think she is.'

'The fool! I couldn't have been clearer. She does know that if she is, it's likely she and the baby will both die?'

'I didn't want to spell it out quite so badly until I confirmed she was pregnant.'

Dr Sinclair shook his head. 'What a waste. Foolish, foolish woman. But there's always those who won't listen to reason. She's made her bed, so to speak, now she'll have to lie on it.'

'I haven't given up on her. If she's pregnant there is still something I could do–'

His eyebrows shot up. 'You're not thinking of terminating the pregnancy, are you? If so, you're just as foolish as her. It's against the law as I'm sure you're aware. You could get struck off – never mind what the priests and their congregations would have to say if they ever found out.'

She realised she'd made a mistake by telling him what had been on her mind, but it was too late to take her words back now.

'It's immaterial. I suspect she won't even consider it.'

He studied the glowing tip of his cigarette.

'There is a chance if she is pregnant the baby won't survive until term. You might yet be able to save the mother, though I doubt it. Anyway why does it matter so much? She's just another woman producing another baby. These people breed like rabbits as it is! Some might say one less mouth to feed is a blessing.'

'That's a disgusting thing to say!'

'It's only the truth. Why do you care so much, anyway?'

'Don't you care about your patients?'

'In as much as they afford me a living.'

He really was an obnoxious individual. She wanted nothing more than to have him out of her house, but she had one more question for him.

'I'm assuming Caroline's parents still live at the same address?'

He nodded and passed her the note he'd been holding. 'As far as I know. It's on there.' To her relief he got to his feet. 'If you'll excuse me, my friends are waiting for me at the bar.' He straightened his tie. 'Unless, of course, you'd care to join us?'

'No, thank you.' He was the last man on earth she would share a drink with. She opened the door for him.

He studied her for a moment as if something were niggling him. 'You know I have the strangest feeling you and I have met before.'

Her stomach lurched. 'I don't believe so.' She'd never even seen him before today, of that she was sure.

'Where did you study?'

Her mind raced. Should she stick to the truth or

make something up? If only she'd asked him where he'd trained. But when she'd come here under someone else's name she'd decided to keep as close as possible to the truth in every other way.

'Glasgow.'

He was still staring speculatively at her. 'So did I! When did you graduate?'

'1928.'

'I was 1924. Oh well, I suppose we might have met at some medical meeting, although I would have remembered you, I'm sure.'

She handed him his hat, wishing he would hurry up and go. But it appeared he wasn't quite finished yet.

'I have to say, Dr Murdoch, you intrigue me. I am certain I've seen you somewhere before – I have a good memory for faces. Perhaps our paths crossed at university? There's not that many women doctors and pretty ones stick out most of all.' He jammed his hat on. 'Never mind. I'm sure it will come to me.'

When the door closed behind him, Margaret leaned against it as if by doing so she could keep him from ever coming back. Could they have met before? It was entirely possible they hadn't actually been introduced but if they'd been at the university around the same time, he might have noticed her then. And he was right – the few women students did tend to stick out. In which case, she told herself, he would have known straight away she wasn't who she said she was.

Where else might he have seen her? It didn't even have to be at university. In Glasgow she'd been a well-known figure. But then, similarly, he would have known who she was.

But he *had* recognised her, if not yet by name. There was every chance it would come to him, a bit like a word one searches for pops up in one's head as soon as one has stopped searching for it. What would he do then? Confront her?

She rubbed her aching temples.

Should she go now? Take the children and run? There was still Lillian's offer of the Gatehouse in Perthshire. It would be the sensible – the safe – thing to do.

If she did, how would she survive? The little she had left of the money she'd brought with her would barely feed them all for a week once bills had been settled and fares paid. She could of course appeal to Lillian for another loan, but everything inside her shrank from that. Moreover, the thought of uprooting the children when they were only just beginning to settle appalled her. Neither did *she* want to leave. Until now, she'd felt safe here. The work was fascinating, the people warm, she had a friend in Flora. And this was where Toni and Mairi, and through them, Alasdair, knew where to reach her.

Hopefully, Dr Sinclair would forget about her. Perhaps he already had. He might have forgotten about her the minute she'd closed the door.

It was a chance she was going to have to take.

Chapter 31

The following week Margaret put Caroline on her list of visits. Effie had reported that while the sore on the young woman's leg wasn't healing, it wasn't getting any worse.

After surgery that afternoon, Margaret asked for Dobbin to be brought round. Although she was still a little wary of using the Clydesdale as a form of transport, so far he'd looked after her.

It was a perfect autumnal day. There was no wind and the lochs were still enough to reflect mirror images of the hills, clouds and even the flying birds. The island in the sunshine was one of the most beautiful places Margaret had ever visited. It never looked the same two days running. Depending on the weather the light would change, painting the landscape in different colours, illuminating the powder-white beaches stretching for miles, lapped by a sea that was forever changing colour, sometimes turquoise, at other times an indigo blue.

Caroline's home was one of the smaller traditional, single-storey croft houses on the north end of the island. Like many of the other houses outwith the village it was set apart, the nearest house to it only just visible on the horizon. Caroline came to the door, wiping her hands on her apron. She paled when she saw Margaret.

'It's not bad news about my Donald, is it?' she

asked. 'He's not been drowned and you've come to tell me because no one else will.'

'No. Oh, no. It's you I've come to see.'

The worry disappeared from Caroline's face and she smiled. 'Silly me. Fretting for nothing. It's just that I've had a bad feeling all day. Let me tie your horse up for you.'

Although Caroline's house was small and dark, it was clean, tidy and homely. There were a few shells on the mantelpiece as well as a bunch of heather stuck in a small drinking glass. In one corner, a crucifix hung over a picture of the Madonna and Child.

Caroline saw Margaret looking at it. 'My husband and I both worship in our own way, he sticks to his and me to mine. He converted so we could get married in the chapel, but he prefers to speak to God the way he's always done. They won't let him cross the door of his church any more anyway and I don't get to the chapel very often so we have to make do with what we have.' She smiled sadly. 'I don't think the Lord minds too much where we pray as long as we do.'

'Wouldn't it have been easier on you both to have stayed in South Uist?'

'No, not really. There's many in the south side who won't forgive me for marrying out of my faith. Anyway this is the place Donald knows best. He's fished the shores alongside his father since he was a small lad. His dad won't go out with him any more but that hasn't stopped Donald from going by himself. My husband can be stubborn. I'd rather he didn't have to fish on his own, especially not when the weather's bad, but what choice do we have? For better or for worse, this is where we'll stay. Oh, excuse my manners. I haven't asked you to sit. I'll put the kettle on, if you'll stay for a cup of tea?'

'That would be kind.' Margaret noticed she hadn't asked why she was there after confirming it wasn't to do with her husband. She sensed that despite being reassured about Donald, Caroline instinctively still knew that she wouldn't want to hear what Margaret had to tell her.

Caroline set a cup and saucer in front of Margaret along with a sugar bowl and a side plate. 'Nothing to eat for me,' Margaret said quickly.

'Och, you'll take a wee scone and home-made jam. Freshly made this morning.'

Margaret knew there was no point in arguing. The islanders always insisted she take something along with her tea – a *strupak,* they called it. But if things carried on this way, if she were to be given something to eat at each house she called at, soon she'd be too big to fit into any of the clothes she'd brought with her. Nevertheless, she accepted the scone and jam with a smile. 'This is lovely,' she said after taking a bite.

'I'll give you some to take home with you,' Caroline replied, looking pleased.

Margaret noticed a tiny half-knitted yellow cardigan lying on top of a basket. Caroline followed her gaze.

'I don't need you to tell me whether I'm pregnant or not. I just know I am. Since I don't know whether I'm having a boy or girl yet I thought I would use yellow. There's some who say it's bad luck to make clothes for the baby before it's born, but I couldn't help myself. I think I might hedge my bets though, and not finish them until later.'

Margaret's heart tightened. It was unlikely that Caroline would ever hold her child. They sat in silence for a while, drinking their tea, but when she'd been offered and refused another cup, she knew there was no putting off the conversation.

'Now, Caroline, I'd like to look at your leg. I understand the nurse has been coming in and dressing it for you, but that it's not showing much sign of improvement. Perhaps you could fill a small basin with hot water so I can wash my hands? And I'd like to confirm your pregnancy if I may?'

'Surely. There's plenty water left in the kettle.' Caroline took a bowl from the cupboard and filled it with steaming water, adding a little cold from the pail beside the stove. Like many of the houses Margaret had been in, this one had no running water.

'Is the well far from you?' Margaret asked.

'About a mile.'

'That's some distance to walk with a sore leg.'

'I'm used to it. Donald does it for me when he's at home.' Her eyes twinkled. 'He doesn't think it's women's work and beneath him.'

Margaret rather liked the sound of Caroline's husband.

'Shall we go into the bedroom?' she suggested.

When she'd finished washing her hands, Margaret followed her patient into the small bedroom. There was only room for a bed and a chest for clothes, but like the other room it was spotless, with small touches to cheer it up.

She examined the sore on Caroline's leg first. It wasn't better, but at least it wasn't worse. One of the problems for people with diabetes was that often sores didn't heal. In time they'd turn gangrenous, eventually resulting in amputation. That Caroline had managed so far without insulin was surprising. The mortality rate before the drug had come along was high enough – pregnancy made it worse. Even though Margaret knew Caroline would be bitterly disappointed if she wasn't pregnant, it was better than the alternative.

'You get up on the bed and I'll feel your abdomen.' After washing her hands again, she palpated Caroline's stomach. 'No bleeding? Discomfort?'

'No. I feel a little sick in the morning, but that passes soon enough.'

This time there was no mistaking the hard ridge of the uterus under Margaret's fingers. Just to be certain, she did a quick internal examination. The uterus was soft enough for the fingers of her hands to meet. There was no longer even the slightest doubt. Caroline was pregnant.

Margaret eased Caroline's dress over her tummy. 'You can get up now. Why don't we go into the kitchen and have a chat.'

Caroline joined her a few moments later. 'I can tell there's something up. You'd better tell me,' she said.

Margaret would have to get better at hiding her feelings.

'You were quite right, you are pregnant.' Margaret held up her hand as Caroline beamed. 'Please, let me finish,' she said gently. 'The problem is, Caroline, that because you are allergic to insulin, we have no way of controlling your diabetes. That's why the sore on your leg won't heal.'

'I'm afraid I don't understand.'

Normally a patient just accepted what the doctor said, but it was clear Caroline wanted to know more. Perhaps if Dr Sinclair had taken the time to explain her condition better, she might have taken steps not to fall pregnant. However, as a Catholic there were few reliable options open to her. Not having sex at all would have been the only certain way.

'It's very difficult to look after diabetes without insulin, even keeping to a strict diet. And the appetite and eating patterns change when a woman gets pregnant. Vomiting in pregnancy makes everything worse and it's possible you could go into a coma. Furthermore, as the mother's condition gets worse, so does the baby's health.'

'So what are you telling me, Doctor? I'm afraid you are going to have to spell it out.'

'I'm so sorry, Caroline, but this baby is unlikely to go to term. That means it's unlikely to survive long enough to be born alive.'

Caroline ran a tongue around her lips. 'But it might?'

'I don't think so. I'm so sorry.'

Caroline clutched the crucifix around her neck and murmured something in Gaelic. 'I still don't understand what you are trying to tell me. I am pregnant. God gave me this baby. He wouldn't do that just to let it die before it could be born.'

Margaret wished she could find the words to comfort her.

'I'm all right now. Apart from my leg and feeling a bit tired, but that's normal,' Caroline continued, with a defiant look at Margaret.

'You may feel all right now. But that could change. No, let me be clear, it *will* change. It's not just that the baby is likely to die, Caroline. As I said, your being pregnant is making your diabetes worse. That sore on your leg might never heal. And if it doesn't, there is a possibility we will have to remove your leg. And that's the least of it. As I explained, continuing with this pregnancy could be fatal for you as well as the baby.'

'You are saying I might die?'

Margaret hesitated. She shouldn't be giving news like this to a woman on her own. Her mother, or her husband, should be with her. 'There's a chance. A very good chance. Then your husband will be left without a wife or a child.'

'Don't you see, I have to trust in God. He gave me this baby for a reason. I'll put my faith in him.'

'There is one thing we could do.' Margaret's mouth had dried. What she was about to suggest was illegal and by doing so, Margaret was risking everything. Caroline could report her to the police or to the General Medical Council, in which case everything could come crashing down around Margaret's ears. But, if it could save her patient's life, Caroline had a right to know that she had the option no matter the consequences for Margaret. She ran her tongue around her lips. 'We could terminate your pregnancy.'

'What! Kill my baby! No!'

'It's the only way, Caroline. If we do it soon, it won't hurt the child. At the moment it's only a cluster of cells. It doesn't have lungs. It couldn't survive outside your body.'

'My baby *is* alive! My baby has a soul already.'

She stood up and looked at Margaret in disgust. 'How can you – a doctor – who has sworn to protect life, not take it – even suggest such a thing? May God have mercy on your soul for even thinking it.'

'Naturally you'll need time to think about it. At least discuss it with your husband.'

Caroline looked at Margaret with cold, distant eyes. 'I'll do no such thing and neither will you. Now if you'll excuse me, Doctor, I have things I need to be getting on with. Oh, and one last thing, please don't come and see me again. From now on it'll be Dr Alan.'

But Margaret's horrible day wasn't quite over. When she returned home that evening it was to find a letter from Simon Firth, inside which was one from Alasdair. Thinking to savour Alasdair's, she opened Firth's letter first. He had disappointing news about Mrs Murphy. He had accompanied her to the police so she could make a statement but the police had been less than impressed. Indeed, they had gone as far as to say that they found it suspicious that she hadn't come forward before – and was she sure that money or other influences hadn't been brought to bear? The long and the short of it was that her statement alone was not enough to convince the Crown to drop the charges. Simon assured Margaret that he still intended to have Mrs Murphy called as a witness, and that her statement would at the very least put some doubt in the jury's mind. In the meantime he was still making enquiries. Along with Toni and his friends they were trying to find McCulloch, the man Mrs Murphy claimed to have recognised. Unfortunately, it seemed as if he had gone to ground and they would have to consider the possibility that he and his accomplice had left Glasgow – possibly even the country. However, they would continue to search for him until the last possible minute.

Margaret scrunched the letter up and threw it on the fire in disgust. Time was running out. Firth had to find this man. And soon.

She opened the letter from Alasdair, hoping for better news.

My darling,

I hope this finds you well. The days pass slowly without you and the children.

I know Firth would have told you that matters look bleak at the moment, but it is only a temporary setback so we mustn't lose faith. I know it is easy to lose – I lost mine for a while after Fergus was shot.

I know I have been guilty of caring more about my pride than I should have – I sometimes think I should have swallowed it and gone back to work for your father. Together we might have been able to achieve so much.

At night I lie in bed and conjure you up. I see each individual freckle on your face – your blue eyes that sparkle when you smile, I hear the sound of your laughter, like a stream running over the rocks. I see the way your eyes flash when you are angry – I remember the softness of your skin under my fingertips. Most of all

I remember how it feels to have you in my life. That with you I am stronger and a better man. Forgive these clumsy sentiments. You know I find it easier to address a thousand men than to express my love for you.

I miss our children too, my love. I hope that one day they will understand why I did what I did.

Now listen to me, Margaret. Your father came to see me. He demanded to know where you and the children had gone, said that he would set a detective to find you, and it was far better for all concerned that I tell him. He repeated his threats and included poor Firth in his rants. Firth is impervious. He claims he has nothing to lose but everything to gain by helping to win my case. But, my love, be careful. Your father is more dangerous to you than ever. He is not a man who cares to be thwarted.

Yours

A

The letter was unusually pensive. A shiver of unease ran up her spine. It was almost as if Alasdair had given up hope – as if he were saying goodbye. She scrambled in the drawer and finding her pen, started to write.

My darling

Every minute of happiness I have given you has been returned ten-fold. I think of that day when, as a girl on the cusp of becoming a woman, I met you for the first time. Even then I knew you were someone exceptional and I know we were meant to find each other again. You make me the proudest woman on earth. Peter tells me that the islanders are bound to their home by a silken thread – that is how I feel about you. We are forever bound and neither time nor place will ever break us apart. My love for you has no end, no beginning, no limitations.

She hiccupped and stopped to wipe her eyes. She hadn't even realised she was crying. She had to send him the force of her love – make him feel it. Make him have faith in it.

I believe we will be together again and you must too. When I die I want it to be in your arms, your voice the last thing I hear, your breath on my face the last thing I feel. But that won't be for a very long time. We will grow old together, my love. You in your chair, me in mine. Our grandchildren at our feet.
My father hasn't found me yet and I trust he never will.

She didn't tell him about Sinclair. There was no point in worrying him, not when it appeared Sinclair had lost interest in remembering where he'd seen her and definitely not when Alasdair seemed so unsure.

Do not lose faith, Alasdair
Yours forever
Margaret

As she folded the letter inside its double envelope she wondered, once again, if she'd made the right decision leaving Glasgow. Should she have done what her father asked and taken the chance on regaining custody of the children when Alasdair was free?

But she'd known then her father couldn't be trusted and she had no reason to change her mind now.

There were only just over ten weeks to the trial.

Firth and Toni simply had to find the man Mrs Murphy had seen.

It was two days after she'd been to see Caroline before Margaret was able to get Dr Alan on his own. They kept on missing each other. She was either out on calls when he was seeing patients at the surgery or vice versa. Just when she was wondering if she'd ever manage to see him, she found him in his consulting room. He was staring into space, his normally cheerful expression muted.

'May I speak to you for a moment?'

He looked up as if surprised to find her there. 'Yes. Yes. Of course. Sit.'

She told him she'd confirmed that Caroline was indeed pregnant.

'Ah, yes. I was planning to talk to you about that. Donald MacIntosh came to see me in high dudgeon. Said you'd suggested that his wife abort her baby. Is that correct?'

Her heart jumped to her throat. If Caroline's husband had made a complaint about her, it was only a matter of time before the police became involved. 'I suggested it because it's the only way to save Caroline!'

He frowned at her. 'The last I heard it is against the law.'

'Not even if it might save the mother's life? That baby will almost inevitably die anyway – if the mother doesn't die first. They terminate preg-

335

nancies in the cities. They just call it something different.'

'That may well be, but you should have discussed it with me first. I could have told you, you'd be wasting your breath.'

'I'm sorry. But if Caroline had agreed to a termination then the sooner it was done the better.'

'But if there is a chance, however small, that the baby might survive, who are we to take away a life?' He folded his hands on the table and leaned forward. 'We like to think of ourselves as the patients do: that we are gods. But we are not. Caroline and her child are in the hands of a higher power than either you or I. It is out of our hands. You have to accept that.'

'I don't know that I can.'

Dr Alan looked at her keenly. 'When you've been a doctor as long as I have, you'll come to realise you can't save everyone. In many ways it's easier in a city. Especially when you work in a hospital. You see them, treat them, they either get better or they don't. But whatever the outcome, your part is over then. In a community like this it's harder. We get to know the families, we're forced to confront their pain when a loved one dies, sometimes several times over. We know their hopes and their dreams, we keep their secrets and while it is a privilege, it is a burden too. We have to find a way of separating the doctor from the friend. We can be both but not at the same time.'

Margaret thought she saw tears in his eyes. 'Are you all right?' she asked.

He smiled wryly. 'Perhaps I'm not as good at taking my own advice as I should be. A wee girl died from pneumonia last night.'

'I am so sorry!'

'Aye, well. Death. Birth. It's all part of a doctor's life.' He took his pipe from his pocket. 'Not always easy, though.'

They were silent as Dr Alan packed his pipe. He lit it and sat back.

'Is Caroline's husband going to make a formal complaint?' Margaret asked, her stomach churning. She wouldn't blame him, but if he did...

'I don't think so. It took a while but when he understood you were only trying to save his wife's life, he calmed down. He is a reasonable man who just happens to love his wife very much. There will be no formal complaints made.'

Margaret's racing heart began to resume its normal pace. She suspected she had this man to thank that she'd escaped unscathed. The patients trusted him completely.

'He hadn't understood quite how serious her situation was,' Dr Alan continued, 'but he did say that his wife will never agree to a termination – that she thinks if she does, both she, and even worse as far as she is concerned, her child, will burn in hell.'

'What will we do about Caroline? Should we send her to Glasgow?'

'We could. But what will they do there? And that's supposing Caroline and her husband could afford the cost of the journey.'

'They might be able to keep her alive long enough to deliver her baby.'

Dr Alan shook his head. 'When you first told me about her I immediately got in touch with a colleague on the mainland – in case new advances in treatment had come about that I had not heard of. But sadly that wasn't the case. Anything that can be done can be done here just as easily.'

'And what's that?' She felt a flicker of hope. Perhaps there was something she hadn't thought about? Or a new development. Medical science was always advancing.

'Keep an eye on her. Give her fluids if she needs them. Let me be clear. Sending her to Glasgow will make no difference. All we'll be doing is passing on the burden of caring for Caroline on to someone else. It's unlikely her husband will be able to stay with her there. Caroline will still die, but alone. However, if you want me to send her away, that's what I'll do.'

Margaret felt her shoulders sag. 'No. Of course not. Unless that's what she wants.'

'Donald said she'd like you to continue to see her. She said when she calmed down, she realised you were only trying to help. But there is to be no more mention of terminations.'

She couldn't pass on all the difficult and tricky patients to Dr Alan. She had to bear her fair share of those – especially if the islanders were to accept her. And what were the easier cases? The ones where whole families had TB? The ones where children died from scarlet fever or one of the other infectious diseases? The easier cases didn't need a doctor, the nurses were well able to look after them. In a population of this size and with only two doctors it was inevitable that all the cases she saw brought their own difficulties.

'No. Caroline is my patient and I'll see her

through whatever she has to face.' She hesitated. 'There is something else. We agreed that I would come here on a month's trial so see how we suited each other.'

He looked startled. 'Did we? What the hell for?'

She was as taken aback as he appeared to be. 'That was the arrangement. To give us both an out clause should we need it.'

'Good God, woman, this isn't your way of telling me that you've had enough, is it? Missing the bright lights of the city, are you?' He puffed on his pipe with more vigour than usual. 'Can't say I blame you. Uist isn't everyone's cup of tea.'

'No. No! I like it here. Truly.' And not just because she felt safe. She liked the work, the people, the place. If it wasn't for the fact she was separated from Alasdair and her children, she would have gone as far to say she loved it. 'I just wanted to check that you didn't want me to go.'

'Want you to go? Why?'

Margaret was getting that parallel-universe feeling back again. 'Because that's what we agreed. When you wrote to me. But if you're satisfied with my work, I'd very much like to stay.'

'Odd girl. Can't say I understand half of what you're going on about. Of course I want you to stay. What would I do without you?'

'That's settled then?'

'Didn't know there was anything to settle. But yes. You're here until the end of February.' He chewed on his pipe stem and mumbled something that Margaret couldn't quite make out but sounded like 'Sure to have had enough of us by then.'

Chapter 32

There was no further news from Alasdair or Firth, and time marched on relentlessly, ticking off the days when Alasdair would have to fight for his life in court. She'd seen the children twice since the first visit – once when she'd visited them and once when Flora had brought them to visit her.

As autumn came to an end the days shortened markedly and the weather became increasingly unpredictable, giving a foretaste of the winter to come. Sometimes the rain would lash down, driven almost horizontal by a razor-sharp wind. At other times the wind would drop away completely and the sun would shine, bathing the island in gold. On days like that, when night fell, the moon and stars would be bright enough to guide Margaret's steps without the need of a torch.

When she went out on visits, more often than not she was soaked through by the time she reached her patients and she'd come to look forward to the hot cup of tea and warm scone that always greeted her. The islanders were unfailingly and touchingly grateful to her for coming out and any small thing she did for them or their loved ones. Sadly, too often, especially for those who had tuberculosis, there was little she could do. At least her work kept her from brooding.

In the meantime, something happened that

almost pushed Caroline and her worry about Alasdair from Margaret's mind. One evening, she was woken by a loud banging on her front door. Thinking it might be someone needing the doctor, and that Dr Alan was already out on a call, she slipped on her dressing gown and lit her paraffin lamp. But by the time she got to the door there was no one there. She looked outside, hoping to catch a glimpse of whoever had chosen to call at this early hour. The moon was full, casting a light bright enough to see for miles. Yet there was no one in sight.

Who had been knocking? And why hadn't they waited? It had only taken a minute or two for Margaret to come to the door. It was possible they had been knocking for a while and, too impatient to wait, had gone in search of the surgery. She was so tired these days that she fell into a deep sleep almost as soon as her head hit the pillow.

Then she saw it. A basket. The type that the women used to take the fish from the boats. At first she thought someone had left her a gift, but when she bent down to pick it up, something moved inside. Taken by surprise, she reared back. Then she peered closer. Lit by the moon, a tiny hand waved out from a bundle of cloth. It was a baby! Quickly she picked the child up and carried it inside. She laid it on the kitchen table and opened the shawl coverings. It was a newborn, no more than a few hours old and still smeared with blood and vernix. The cord had been cut – there was a little piece of string attached to the stump. The mother, if she'd delivered it on her own, had known enough to do that, but she might need urgent medical help. Certainly she should be reunited with her child and as soon as possible.

'Hello you,' she whispered. 'Now why did your mummy leave you here?'

The baby blinked up at her and she wrapped him up again, worried he would get cold, although judging by the warmth of his skin he'd only been on her step for a minute or two.

But who had left him? And why?

In her arms the baby mewed pitifully, turning his neck into Margaret with the reflex search for sustenance all newborns have. 'You hungry, little one?' She popped her finger into his mouth as she'd done with Libby and James when they were babies and his small jaws sucked with surprising strength. When he realised there was nothing to be gained from his efforts he gave a cry of rage. He needed feeding.

She carried the child into her bedroom and laid him on her bed as she dressed quickly. She would take the infant to Dr Alan – maybe he would have an idea who the baby belonged to, and if he wasn't there, Dolina was bound to know. At the very least they might have an idea where to find some breast milk for him. She wrapped the child in another layer and set off for the surgery, her crunching steps the only sound in the chilly night air. She knocked on the door of the surgery and let herself in, praying that Dr Alan wasn't out on a call.

'Dr Alan!' she called up the stairs. 'Are you awake?'

She waited a few moments. Then she heard creaking as if feet were hitting the floor as someone got out of bed. Moments later a flickering light appeared at the top of the stairs. Dr Alan held the lamp high and peered down at her. 'Margaret? Is that you?'

'I'm sorry to have woken you, but I need your help.'

It was only when the baby let out a feeble cry that he noticed she was carrying something. He hurried down the stairs. 'Who's that you have with you? A sick baby? Come, let's go into the surgery.'

Margaret followed behind him, waiting until he'd closed the door before speaking. 'I found him on my doorstep. He couldn't have been there for long. Whoever left him made sure I was awake before running away. I don't think he could be more than a few hours old.'

'A baby! On the doorstep!' Dr Alan shook his head. 'I've never heard of such a thing. Not here! Let's have a look.'

'Someone tied off the cord as you can see.'

'We should clean the stump. I hope to God the scissors or whatever they used were clean.'

Margaret did as he suggested. As she swabbed the baby's cord, the child started to wail.

'He's hungry. He needs a feed,' she said, wrapping him up again.

'Boiled water will have to do for now. Let's take him through to the kitchen. It's warmer there.'

The baby's cries must have woken Dolina. She appeared in the kitchen and looked around sleepily. 'What's going on here? What's that child doing here? Where's the mother?'

'How could any mother just abandon her child like that?' Dolina muttered, after Margaret explained what had happened. 'It's not right.'

'We need to find her. Do you have any idea who it could be?'

Dolina placed the kettle over the heat to boil. 'Now then. There's Mrs White but she would never abandon her child and then there's...' She thought a bit longer before shaking her head. 'No, none of the women I'm aware of. But as you know, they don't all come to see us when they're pregnant.'

'So how do we find the mother?' Margaret asked.

'We'll find her soon enough,' Dr Alan said. 'As soon as word gets out about the baby – and it will – someone will come forward. It's only a matter of time before someone notices that a woman who was pregnant isn't any longer.'

'We might not have time,' Margaret said. 'What if she has post-partum bleeding? What if she gets an infection? What if...'

'If she's ill someone will call us,' Dr Alan replied calmly.

'Unless she's thrown herself off the pier,' Dolina said, her mouth set in a grim line.

Margaret shuddered. She hadn't thought of that. It was a possibility.

'Or fallen in a bog,' Dolina added. 'Even with a moon you can't always see where to put your feet.'

'Dolina, I think we could do with less of your gloomy predictions,' Dr Alan interrupted. 'Could you fetch Effie please? Tell her to come as quickly as she can. When you've done that, go and fetch Mrs Linklater. Then knock up Constable Watt.

344

Tell him he's needed but don't tell him why.'

'I'll go as soon as I've got something to put this wee mite in.' She returned a few minutes later with an empty drawer. When the baby was settled in his makeshift bed she hurried out, muttering under her breath.

Dr Alan rubbed his chin, looking thoughtful. 'Right, later on we'll have to decide what to do with him. In the meantime, there's still the matter of getting him fed. Someone who has just had a baby might help us out with some milk. Effie will know who all the nursing mothers are.'

Needing something to do, Margaret made a pot of tea. She'd only just poured herself and Dr Alan each a cup when Effie arrived.

'What's going on? Dolina said something about a baby.' She looked at the drawer with the sleeping child inside. 'Good grief. Where's the mother? Is the baby all right?'

'Seems to be. But when he wakes he's going to be hungry. Is there a woman nearby who's still nursing?' Margaret asked.

'Donalda has just had her fifth. She's not far from here.'

'Would you mind asking her if she has milk to spare for the baby. If she agrees she can express some.'

'I think I have some spare bottles in the treatment room. I'll make sure they're sterilised.' Effie bustled out just as Dolina reappeared.

'That policeman sleeps like the dead. Had to give his windows a good rattle to wake him. He's on his way.'

'Good.' Dr Alan got to his feet and stretched. 'I

might as well get shaved and dressed in the meantime. It's going to be another busy day.'

While he was upstairs, Sophie Linklater arrived. Margaret had met the minister's wife several times, and anyone less likely to 'have her guts for garters' as Dr Alan had put it the day Margaret had arrived on the islands, she couldn't imagine. Sophie was short and plump with twinkling eyes, almost the polar opposite to her husband, the minister, who was tall and gaunt and had the largest pair of hands Margaret had ever seen on a man.

It was dawn by the time everyone, with the exception of the policeman, had gathered again. Effie had acquired enough breast milk from Donalda for the first feed and had arranged to return later to collect more. With no refrigerator to store the milk it was the only way to be safe.

Once the bottle was prepared, Sophie took the baby with the confidence of a woman used to handling infants.

They watched in silence as the baby sucked contentedly on the bottle.

'Any ideas as to whom he might belong?' Margaret asked.

'Donalda didn't seem to know,' Effie replied. She slid a glance at Dr Alan. 'Obviously I had to tell her, Dr Alan, why I needed her to express her milk.'

Sophie looked up from the feeding child. 'It's probably a good thing that news gets out sooner rather than later. We have a better chance of finding out who the mother is that way.'

'Surely someone will know? It's not that easy to

disguise a full-term pregnancy,' Margaret said.

'But not impossible. Not if the woman was plump or if she covered up in big jumpers. And not all of the croft houses are close to others. Some are fairly isolated,' Effie said.

'But even the most isolated crofters have to come in for supplies–'

Effie nodded. 'And if the mother's mother is alive, then it would be hard to deceive her. You don't go and have several children without recognising the symptoms of pregnancy in your own child.'

While the others had been away, Margaret had been thinking. 'Perhaps we can work out who the mother is by eliminating who she isn't. We exclude all families where there's been a live birth recently or where the women in the home are past child-bearing age. We concentrate on families with daughters who aren't married.'

'That's assuming the mother is young. It's equally possible that the mother already has a large family and the thought of coping with one more was simply the final straw,' Sophie said. 'What do you think, Effie?'

Effie laid her cup on the table. 'How many women of childbearing age live on North Uist and Berneray? Hundreds, anyway. And that's assuming she didn't bring the child from Benbecula or one of the other Uists to throw people off the scent.'

'I think we should start by looking through our list of patients to see who was due to deliver about now,' Margaret suggested. 'The child is clearly at term.'

Effie looked doubtful. 'I'll give it a go but I

don't know how useful it will be. There are likely to be pregnant women on the island who have never come to see us.'

They looked at each other glumly. The task they'd set for themselves seemed impossible.

'We could cut the numbers down to begin with. Think, why would a woman give up her child?' Sophie suggested.

'Because she has no choice.' It was the first time Dolina had spoken since they'd started discussing the baby. 'Because she's frightened or thinks it's the best thing to do for the child.'

Margaret was surprised. Her crusty, Bible-preaching housekeeper was the last person she'd have thought sympathetic to the woman's plight.

'You're right, of course, Dolina. So what could those reasons be? Especially here?'

'Someone who can't cope. Whose husband has passed away and who is struggling to make ends meet. Someone who is worried she can't feed or clothe the child or keep it warm...' Dolina clamped her lips together as if sorry she'd spoken.

'That makes sense. No one springs to mind but let's try and make a list,' Effie said, looking pleased that she at last had something constructive to do. 'We can start by identifying any women whose husband has died recently.'

'Well there's—' Sophie started.

'Please. Don't say,' Margaret interrupted. 'When we do find the woman, it's better that no one knows who she is.'

Effie and Sophie exchanged glances. 'My dear, if you really think that the whole island won't know who she is almost as soon as we do then

348

you haven't learned very much while you've been here. This baby is going to be the talk of the town. They won't have had such juicy gossip since Dòmhnaill Eoghainn's bull went missing and was found in George Mor's field.'

'There's another possibility,' Margaret suggested. 'The mother could have fallen pregnant by accident. Perhaps she's been hiding her pregnancy from her parents. Or perhaps they found out and made her give it up.'

Effie and Sophie shook their heads. 'No. That wouldn't happen. As you can imagine, there are as many children here born on the wrong side of the blanket as there must be in Glasgow. The parents might be disappointed, angry even, but they always take on the child. There's many a man or woman whose aunt or big sister is really their mother. They look after their own here.'

A loud banging on the door interrupted their speculations and they all looked at each other as Dolina hurried to answer it. A few moments later she reappeared with a policeman following close on her heels.

Constable Watt was an older man in his fifties with a red veined face and a stomach that protruded over the top of his belt. Whatever else he'd been doing while they'd waited for him, he'd taken the time to shave. Seeing a policeman in uniform made Margaret feel slightly nauseous.

'I'd like a word with the doctors.' Constable Watt stuck out his chest. 'Alone.'

'Oh, get off your high horse, Ewan,' Dr Alan said, coming back into the kitchen. 'We're all here so you might as well say what you have to in front of us all. Dolina, would you mind fetching the constable a dram. Anyone else?'

When the women shook their heads, Dolina crossed over to the side table and poured a whisky for the policeman and Dr Alan.

'Thank you, Dolina. You may leave us.'

Dolina looked put out, but did as she was asked.

'I understand a baby has been found.' The constable took a large sip of his whisky before removing his notebook and pencil from his top pocket. He licked the pencil. 'Who found it?'

Margaret recounted the events of the night as succinctly as she could.

'And you have no idea who might have left it there?'

'Him, Ewan. Him. It's a boy,' Sophie interjected.

'Name?'

'You know our names,' Sophie said with obvious irritation.

'Name of the child.'

'He hasn't a name. At least, not one we know.'

'I need a name.'

'Then call him Ruaridh. That will do for now.'

'And no one has any idea who he belongs to?'

'No. We're just discussing who the mother might be,' Effie said. 'Poor thing. She must have been desperate.'

'When we find her she's going to be in serious trouble.' The policeman squared his shoulders. 'It's a criminal offence to conceal a pregnancy. I checked. I'm sure it must be another offence to abandon your child.'

'Whatever the reasons she left the child on my doorstep, I think we should wait to find out what they are before we pass judgement,' Margaret snapped, outraged that the policeman was more concerned with prosecuting the woman than finding her. 'We do need to find her, not so you can charge her or lock her up, but because it's likely she'll need medical attention. She could be out there bleeding to death.'

'The law is the law,' the policeman replied, unperturbed by her reaction. 'I don't make it, just uphold it.'

'You're not quite so keen on upholding it when it comes to the licensing laws, Ewan,' Dr Alan said quietly. 'Many's a night I've been out on a visit and seen your bicycle propped up against the wall of the Lochmaddy Hotel long after closing time. And as for the illicit still your brother has in his byre...'

The policeman glared at Margaret as if it was her fault the doctor had reprimanded him, no matter how gently.

'Dr Margaret is correct,' Dr Alan continued. 'We need to find the mother of this baby so we can ensure she gets the medical help she needs, and to see if mother and baby can be reunited. There's always a chance she's decided to do away with herself – if she hasn't done so already. We will need your help to look for her.'

'In fact, shouldn't you be doing that right now, Constable?' Margaret asked, acutely aware that time was passing. Every minute the woman was out there without medical attention might mean the difference between life and death for her.

'Look? And where do you suggest I start, Miss? There are hundreds of lochs and bogs – it would be like looking for a needle in the proverbial haystack. If she's thrown herself into the sea she'll wash up soon enough.'

'It's Dr Murdoch,' Margaret said, putting emphasis on her title. 'Until you find a body, you shouldn't assume she's planning to kill herself. You should assume that she's still alive and be looking for clues as to where she might have gone, starting with near my cottage.'

'Dr Margaret is quite right, Ewan. Gather some of the men and start a search. We'll find out soon enough who she is and why she felt the need to abandon her baby.'

He waited until the policeman had left before continuing. 'In the meantime we have to decide what to do with the boy. He can't stay here. We should send him to Glasgow.'

'Oh, let's not send the wee thing anywhere, Dr Alan,' Effie protested. 'The mother is bound to be charged then and might never get her baby back. He'll disappear into one of these children's homes and never be seen again.'

'None of this helps us decide what to do with the child now,' Sophie said, placing the feeding bottle on the table. The baby had had his fill and had fallen asleep again. 'I don't think we should even consider sending him to Glasgow for a week or two at the earliest.' She ran a feather-light fingertip across his cheek. 'Oh, he's such a sweet little thing.'

'Can't you keep him in the meantime, Sophie?' Effie asked. 'I'd take him myself but I've visits to do today. Donalda doesn't stay far away so it would be easy for her to bring milk over to the Manse. The mother could still come forward.

Then perhaps there will be no need to send the baby anywhere.'

Sophie looked down at the sleeping child in her arms. 'Of course I'll look after him, until you find the mother.' She tightened the shawl around him and stood. 'I'd better get him home. If you have any news you will let me know? The minister will want to do what he can.'

'Does she have children of her own?' Margaret asked after Sophie had left.

Effie and Dr Alan exchanged a glance. 'No, she doesn't,' Effie said, 'and it's been her cross to bear. But she's part of a large family and knows how to care for a baby.'

Dr Alan rubbed a hand across his jaw and pushed himself out of his chair. 'That's settled then. Now I need to leave to do the clinic in Berneray and you, Margaret, have surgery here.' He took his watch from his pocket. 'Starting in an hour.'

Chapter 33

The news that a baby had been found on the doctor's doorstep spread across the island with a speed that, even with her knowledge of how quickly the islanders learned what was happening in their community, still astonished Margaret. Every single patient who attended surgery that morning, and there were several more than usual, asked about the infant. One old lady, to Margaret's secret amusement, even suggested that the fairies had left it.

The day, which had started calm and crisp, had turned wet and blustery. Men from the township had been searching the lochs and moors all day without success and it would soon be dark. If the mother was out there somewhere and still alive, she might not be for very much longer.

Margaret was on her way in to the surgery after her home visits to write up her notes when she bumped into a distracted-looking Dr Alan in the hall, his dogs around his feet.

'Ah, Margaret. I was wondering where you'd got to. And where's Dolina when I need her? The police inspector from South Uist is here. He wants to speak to you.'

Margaret's heart jolted painfully. Dear God, Sinclair had finally realised who she was and told the police and – her heart gave another sickening lurch – possibly her father.

'What on earth is wrong with you? You've gone as white as a sheet. Here. Sit down, before you fall down.' He ushered her into one of the chairs in the hall that they used for the overflow of patients waiting to see the doctor. 'Put your head between your knees.' He patted her awkwardly on the shoulder. 'Dolina!' he bellowed. 'Where in God's name are you?'

Dolina emerged from the kitchen wiping her hands on a cloth. 'There's no need to shout. I was out getting some peats. What is it?' Her voice softened. 'Dr Margaret! I told you you didn't eat enough. Come away into the kitchen and have some soup. Dr Alan, don't just stand there gawping. Help me get her into the kitchen. What will the patients think if they see the doctor like this!'

Margaret raised her head and forced a smile. 'I'm all right, Dolina. It was just a moment's dizziness. Why don't you make the police inspector's tea?' She had to get Dolina out of the way so she could speak to Dr Alan in private. If she was about to be uncovered, she wanted him to hear the story from her first.

'A police inspector! At this time of day!' Dolina cried. As if there were an appropriate time of day for police to call. 'What does he want? Have they found that poor woman? Is she dead?'

Dr Alan frowned. 'He has come about that, not that it is any of your concern, Dolina. Now where's that tea? Or do I have to go and make it myself?'

Margaret grasped at Dr Alan's words. Of course! The policeman had come about the baby – not about her. She had to pull herself together.

'You'll not put a foot in my kitchen. The last time you tried to make some tea it was like dishwater. And the mess! Pigs in a sty make less.' Still muttering, she retreated, leaving Dr Alan and Margaret alone.

'Is it true? Has he come about the baby?' Margaret murmured. Thankfully the dizziness and the feeling of nausea were easing.

'So he says. He'd like to speak to you. Damn waste of time if you ask me.'

The relief made her head swim again. He wasn't here about her. At least not yet.

Dr Alan was still staring at her curiously. 'Shall we see what he has to say?'

Although the last thing Margaret wanted to do

was to come face to face with a policeman again, she had no choice. She told herself there was no reason to think he might recognise her or link her to a man accused of murder in Glasgow. If they were going to make that connection, they would have done so sooner. Nevertheless, her mouth was dry and her hands were still trembling.

The man who rose to his feet when they entered the sitting room was tall with cropped dark hair. To Margaret's surprise he was young, about her age. She'd assumed a police inspector would be older.

'My colleague, Dr Murdoch. Dr Murdoch, Inspector MacLeod.'

'Pleased to meet you, Dr Murdoch. Thank you for taking the time to talk to me.'

There was no hint of recognition in his expression or his voice.

'Please, sit, gentlemen,' Margaret said, relieved to find that her voice sounded normal. 'Have you found the mother? Is she all right?'

'I'm afraid we haven't. Not yet. We are still searching.'

'Then how can I help?'

'The baby was left on your doorstep. Any reason for that, do you think?'

'I'm a doctor and a woman. I would have thought that was obvious.' Yet she'd wondered the same thing. Why hadn't the woman left the baby outside Effie's house? Or the minister's?

'Did you see who left the child?'

'No. Whoever it was had disappeared by the time I got to the door. I suspect they waited long enough to see that I found the child before they left. The baby couldn't have been there more than a few minutes. It was a cold night yet his face was still warm.'

'If you do find out who the mother is you will tell us, won't you?'

'I will certainly tell you that she's been found. I don't see that I'd be able to tell you her name. Not if she comes to me as a patient. She would have the right to confidentiality.' Margaret glanced at Dr Alan. He shrugged his shoulders as if to say it was up to her.

The inspector intercepted the look. 'No, she doesn't. Not when she's committed a criminal act.'

Margaret lifted her chin and held his gaze. 'This was no criminal act, as you put it, Inspector. This was an act of desperation – ignorance at the worst. She must have been desperate to abandon her baby. The last place she should be is in police custody. It's not as if she could be considered a public threat!'

'That's not really up to you to decide. I'll have to make a report to the Procurator Fiscal. They are the ones who will make the decision whether to bring charges. My job is to determine whether she, whoever it is, did indeed conceal a pregnancy that led her to abandon her baby.' A flash of irritation crossed the inspector's face. 'Perhaps if Constable Watt hadn't been quite so assiduous about reporting it to me formally we might have been able to sort it between us, but he did.' The inspector seemed to catch himself. 'As was his duty.'

'I don't see how prosecuting the woman will help anyone.'

'As I said, that isn't up to you or me.' He leaned forward. 'But perhaps, if there were mitigating circumstances – although I can't think what they might be – that would help her case.'

'She must have had her reasons. We won't know what they were until we find her.'

Dolina brought in a tray of tea and plonked it on the table. She glared at the inspector before leaving.

'And the child,' Margaret continued, once Dolina had left. 'The baby. What will happen to him?'

'As I said, that's up to the court. Where is he now?'

'With Sophie Linklater, the minister's wife,' Dr Alan said. 'He's well cared for.'

'I should make arrangements to have him sent to Glasgow, although quite how I have no idea.'

'Surely you don't intend to take him away?' Margaret said quickly. 'He's settled there. Mrs Linklater is taking good care of him.'

The inspector looked relieved. 'If that's the case, then I don't see any need to change things. Not for the moment at least.' He smiled wryly. 'I can hardly take him to the police station in South Uist while arrangements are being made. However, if you do come across the mother can you give me your word that the child won't be returned to her?'

'Doesn't it depend on the mother's reasons for abandoning her baby?'

'Dr Murdoch. This woman left her child on your doorstep. It is clear to me that she does not want the responsibility of caring for him. If the child is returned he may be in danger. It is not up to you

358

or me to determine his future. I must make that clear.'

'If I do find out who she is I'll make sure she understands that she can't have him back. At least not yet.'

'In that case, I'm happy to leave things as they are.'

Margaret exhaled. She hadn't realised she'd been holding her breath. The man wasn't *totally* obsessed with rules.

'However,' he continued, 'if I discover the mother has had the child returned to her, or if I find out she's left the island, I shall hold you,' he looked directly at Margaret, 'responsible. Now if you'll excuse me, I should be getting back.' His expression made it clear that he had other, better things to be spending his time on, although Margaret couldn't think what they could possibly be – unless, of course, Dòmhnaill Eoghainn had stolen George Mor's bull again.

'I'm sure you must be run off your feet,' she muttered under her breath.

He looked pained. 'I don't make the laws of the land, Dr Murdoch, I simply enforce them.'

'But to even consider prosecuting a woman who was so distraught to find herself pregnant, she did the only thing she could think of to keep her child safe. Where's the justice in that? Are you not concerned with justice, Police Inspector?'

She was taking a chance needling him but she couldn't help herself. Once upon a time she'd had faith in the justice system. No longer.

He stood. 'I shall wait until I hear back from the Procurator Fiscal before I decide what action to take. However, if I discover by other means the name of the mother, I'll be obliged to interview her.'

'And if you do, I'd like to be there.'

'Fair enough.' He gave her a ghost of a smile before nodding in Dr Alan's direction. 'Thank you for your time, Dr MacLean.'

'I'll see you out,' Margaret said.

As she opened the front door for him he turned to her. 'I'm not an ogre, you know. I became a policeman because I believe in a safe, just world. I'd much rather be catching real criminals and hopefully, soon, I'll be doing exactly that. This posting is only for six months. All new inspectors have to do a stint in a rural community. I'll be taking charge in Inverness in the spring.'

Margaret cocked an eyebrow. What made him think she was the slightest bit interested? 'Don't let me keep you, Inspector.' She handed him his hat.

He gave her a long, hard look. For a moment she thought he was going to say something else, but then he tipped his hat, nodded, and left.

When the door closed behind him Margaret took several deep breaths, trying to slow her still-racing heart. Was this how it was going to be? Always living in fear, waiting for a knock on the door, expecting her children to be removed at any moment. But it hadn't happened so far, she told herself firmly, and may never happen. In the meantime she had her patients to think about.

Chapter 34

That evening Margaret's small kitchen seemed full to bursting with women. Apart from herself there was Sophie and the baby, Effie and Dolina, who for some reason stayed later and later every day. She might have given her seal of approval to Margaret's medical skills, but that hadn't appeared to extend to Margaret herself. The housekeeper was as taciturn as ever.

Yesterday Margaret had come out of her house on the way to the surgery and watched amazed as Dolina had stomped towards her carrying two heavily laden pails of peat. Margaret had hurried forward to take them from the older woman only to feel the full weight of her tongue.

'Away with you! I can manage!'

'Let me take one at least.'

'You'll do no such thing. The doctor carrying pails of peat! What would everyone say? Well, I know what they'll say. They'll say Dolina is getting past it – that soon she'll be ready for the poorhouse.'

Her words had bewildered Margaret. Although she knew the islanders feared the poorhouse as much as the people of Govan had, she was certain Dolina had nothing to fear. Dr Alan would make sure his housekeeper was looked after in old age.

But despite Dolina's sharp tongue and prickly

manner, having her to help had made a difference.

Dolina had made an enormous pot of tea which she set down on the table.

'You can go if you like,' Margaret told Dolina. 'I can manage from here on.'

'No indeed. Not when you have visitors.' She lowered her voice but not so much that everyone couldn't hear. 'Never met a woman so hopeless at looking after herself, never mind visitors.'

'Shall we go into the sitting room?' Margaret suggested, ignoring her comment.

Dolina sniffed. 'I'll put a fire on then. Waste of fuel if you ask me, when there's a perfectly good heat coming from the stove.'

Margaret had the distinct impression she didn't want them to go into the sitting room where she wouldn't be able to be part of the conversation.

'No, no need,' Sophie protested. 'It's cosier in here – especially for the wee one.'

Margaret noticed a quick, satisfied smile crossing Dolina's face as the women settled themselves into chairs.

'Any news of Ruaridh's mother?' Effie asked.

'Constable Watt *is* still looking for her? They haven't called off the search?' Margaret said, pouring the tea. So far he and the men he'd roped into help with the search hadn't found a body, nor had there been any reports of one washing up on the shore. That was hopeful. But neither had anyone come forward to claim the baby.

'Yes, PC Plod is still on the case. Not making himself very popular by going around asking all and sundry if they just happened to leave a baby on a doorstep.'

Effie held out her hands. 'Let me hold him for a moment.' When Sophie reluctantly passed the baby over, Effie took him with a broad smile and kissed the top of his tiny head. 'How could anyone give you up?'

Margaret cast a wary eye in Dolina's direction. The older woman had her back towards her, pretending to be immersed in cleaning the shelf above the fireplace. Given that Margaret had already seen her clean it earlier, it was clear that Dolina had no intention of going anywhere.

'In the meantime there is still the matter of what to do with the child. Much as I love caring for him,' Sophie murmured, holding out her arms to take him back, 'he needs a permanent home.'

'Apparently that will be for the courts to decide,' Margaret said. She repeated what Inspector MacLeod had told her.

'Courts, huh!' Dolina interjected. 'They know nothing.'

'I think if we have a suggestion to make about little Ruaridh then the courts will listen to what we have to say,' Sophie said, frowning at Dolina.

'But we're talking about keeping a child from his mother. Permanently. When we don't yet know why she gave him up,' Margaret said quietly. 'It's not a decision to take lightly. When I was working as a House Officer I had to do a stint in Gartnavel Royal – the asylum. There was a woman there, she never had any visitors, there didn't seem much wrong with her, but she used to wander up and down the corridor in the ward crying. I was puzzled so I looked up her notes. It turned out she came from a well-to-do family up north – obviously I can't tell you their name. She'd fallen pregnant as a young unmarried woman and they'd had her admitted to Gartnavel. Her baby was taken away and the mother had spent the rest of her years in the asylum. She never stopped longing for him.' It was one of the reasons she'd known her father could so easily have done the same to her.

'That's shocking!' Sophie said.

Dolina had stiffened, and a strange look crossed her face, but before Margaret could be sure what it was, she'd turned away and started scrubbing the already immaculate stove with renewed vigour.

'It would never happen here,' Sophie said. 'We look after our own.'

'Why does he have to go anywhere, then?' Dolina swung around. 'Why can't he stay here? There's bound to be someone on the island who wants a child to care for but can't have their own.'

Several pairs of eyes swivelled in Sophie's direction, then quickly away again.

'Even if there is someone, the child will still be removed from the mother on a permanent basis,' Effie said gently. 'I wonder if that can be right.'

'But if the mother is an islander and she must be, she could still see him,' Dolina continued. 'I think that's what she hoped. She would know her child is being cared for, without having to care for him herself.'

'I don't know,' Margaret said slowly. 'What if no one wants a child who has been born to a woman they know nothing about?'

'Look at him! He's as bright as a button,' Sophie said. 'Who could resist him?'

Right enough, the baby was looking up at Sophie

with bright blue eyes and waving his small chubby fists in the air, desperately trying to catch one in his mouth. He really was a beautiful baby. Sophie took one of his hands in hers and pressed it to her lips.

'I'm not sure it's up to us to decide the fate of a child,' Margaret said. 'At least, not until we know who the mother is.'

'Who better?' Effie said firmly. 'We have to accept that the mother may never be found. And even if she is, I doubt she'll be able to get him back. Supposing she wants him.'

Sophie looked up. 'Effie and Dolina are correct. Better we decide Ruaridh's fate than leave it to some court hundreds of miles away. There aren't many advantages to living on these islands but being so far away from the authorities is one of them. Being responsible for each other is one of the privileges as well as one of our burdens. I think we should let it be known that we are looking for a home for the child on the island.' She looked wistful for a moment, then gave her head a tiny shake. 'If you speak to Dr Alan, Margaret, I'll speak to my husband and tell them what we're thinking. Unless those two agree, it won't happen whatever we decide. Once we've spoken to them, we can think again.'

Dolina left off pretending to polish the hearth. 'It's getting late. Some of us have to get up to do a decent day's work tomorrow. The doctor needs her rest.'

'I think I'm able to decide when I need to go to bed, Dolina. But of course, off you go.'

Dolina glowered at the other women in the

room, made a noise in her throat and mumbled something about fetching Margaret's hot water bottle to fill.

The women stood and started gathering their coats. 'Well,' Effie said. 'I don't know how you put up with her and her moods.'

'She's not had an easy life, Effie,' Sophie murmured. 'She's had more than her fair share of trouble. And she's quite right. I've left my poor husband alone long enough. I doubt he can find his pyjamas without me to show him where they are – although they've been in the same place since we married. Men! He might be the kindest, most gentle man I know, but he hasn't a clue outside the church.'

After everyone had left and Dolina still hadn't come back through to the kitchen, Margaret went in search of her. To her astonishment, she found her sitting on the spare bed, holding one of Elizabeth's cardigans in her hand and weeping. Until now she had never seen the older woman show any emotion apart from irritation.

'Dolina, what is it?'

Dolina sniffed loudly and wiped her nose with the back of her sleeve. 'Och, don't mind me. I'm just a silly old woman.'

Margaret rummaged in her pocket, found a clean handkerchief and held it out to the older woman. 'Why don't you tell me what's the matter?' she said gently.

Dolina blew her nose loudly. 'I'll wash this and get it back to you. Now, it's time for me to get up the road.'

Margaret thought about pressing the older

woman harder, but everything in Dolina's de-
meanour told her she'd be wasting her time. And
who was she to pry? Everyone, including her
housekeeper, was entitled to their secrets.

'If ever you want to talk about anything – anything at all, you can talk to me. I promise you I
won't ever repeat it.'

Dolina straightened and pinned her with a hard
stare. 'Now what could I possibly have to tell
you?'

Chapter 35

In the end it wasn't any of their lists or the search
party that led to the discovery of Ruaridh's
mother. A couple of days after the women had
met, Margaret was asked to visit a young girl with
cerebral palsy who, according to the father who'd
sent the telegram, was burning up with fever. He
wanted, he said, either the nurse or the woman
doctor.

Effie offered to go, but she was due to do the
clinic on Berneray alongside Dr Alan, so it was
agreed that Margaret would attend instead.

The cottage where her patient lived was a couple
of miles across the moors from Lochmaddy. It was
an unusually warm and sunny day for the time of
year so Margaret decided to forgo Dobbin and
walk instead. It took a while for her to find the
house and she stumbled across it almost by accident. Like most of the croft houses here it was

close to the sea, it's back facing Eaval, the largest hill on North Uist. Almost hidden in a little dip in the land, it was isolated, with nothing to obstruct its view in any direction.

The father was sitting outside mending some creels. He stood up as Margaret approached and came forward to greet her.

'Thank you for coming so soon, Doctor. I'm Alec, Kirsty's father. I would have called you out a day or two ago, but I thought comfrey tea might settle things.'

It wasn't uncommon for the islanders to try their own remedies before giving in and calling the doctor. Although under the new scheme, visits from the doctor were free, habits of a lifetime where half-crowns were carefully put aside for the doctor – only to be used in an emergency – were hard to break.

'Where is Kirsty?'

Anxiety furrowed his brow. 'Ciorstag's inside. In bed. It's not like her.'

'Shall we go in and see her?'

He cleared his throat. 'She's not like others her age. She's a bit simple-minded, more like a child than a young woman. Her mother had a difficult time of it when Kirsty was born – the nurse thought her brain might have been starved of oxygen – she took so long to come out. Her hand's never been right either – but you'll see that for yourself.'

'Thank you for telling me. I'll be as gentle with her as I can.'

'I don't know what's wrong with her. I hope it's not the scarlet fever. Although I don't know where she could have got that.'

'I think it's best I have a look at her before we start thinking of what it could be.'

'Aye, well. I don't know what I would do if I lost her after losing her mother and her brother. She's all I have left.'

'Why don't I go and see her before we start imagining the worst?'

'Come on in, then.' He stood at the foot of a narrow stair and called up. 'Ciorstag, it's the doctor here to see you.' He added something in Gaelic, before translating. 'I told her I'm sending you up. She told me she doesn't want me there. Just go to the top and turn right.'

'Could you bring me a bowl of hot water to take up with me, so I can wash my hands?' Margaret asked.

Alec hurried away and as she waited for him, she took in her surroundings. The wallpaper in the hall was faded and worn, much like the rug running up the stairs, but there were a few feminine touches here and there, such as the faded pictures on the wall, that suggested that the house had once been loved and cared for.

When Alec returned, she took the basin from him and, with it balanced in one hand, walked up the stairs.

The bedroom was a bit of a mess. Clearly neither Kirsty nor her father were much interested in housework. It smelled of damp and, despite the sunshine outside, was chilly.

Kirsty was sitting up in bed, her face flushed with fever. She was about twenty with silky brown hair, large grey eyes and a heart-shaped face.

Although she was plump, she was also one of the most beautiful women Margaret had ever seen.

'Hello, Kirsty. That's a lovely name, by the way. How are you today? I'm Dr Murdoch but you can call me Dr Margaret if you like.'

'I know who you are. The new lady doctor.' Her speech was slightly slurred, her right hand twisted out of shape, and one shoulder slightly higher than the other.

'Now, you mustn't be frightened. I just want to have a little look at you. Your father tells me you haven't been well.' When she took out her stethoscope and placed the ear buds in her ears, Kirsty reared back in fear.

'Haven't you seen one of these before?'

Kirsty shook her head. 'Devil's horns.'

She had to remember that Kirsty probably thought and behaved like someone of a mental age well below her actual age. She should treat her as she would a child.

'They won't hurt you, I promise.' She removed the stethoscope and held it out. 'I can listen to your heart with this. More importantly, I can listen to your chest. I can hear if you have a bad cold – or flu, for example. You can try them yourself if you like.'

Kirsty shook her head.

'In that case, let me feel your pulse first.' She picked up Kirsty's wrist and felt the radial pulse with her two fingers. It was rapid and bounding. Everything pointed to Kirsty having an infection, but she still had to establish what was causing it before she could decide how to treat it.

'Now I do need to listen to your chest. Would

you like me to ask your father to come upstairs?'

Kirsty shook her head again, more vigorously this time.

'All you have to do is lean forward, lift your nightie for me and say ninety-nine while I put this,' Margaret pointed to the end of the stethoscope, 'against your back. Then I'll listen to your front. How does that sound?'

Kirsty still seemed reluctant but she did as Margaret asked. As she leaned forward, she winced.

'Is it sore when you do that?'

'My boobies hurt.'

Alarm bells were beginning to go off in Margaret's head. 'Why don't you lift your nightie at the front and let me see?'

Very carefully, Kirsty pulled up her nightdress. Her breasts were swollen, the left one hard and red with lines radiating off from the nipple. It was either a cancerous lump or a breast abscess. But Kirsty's nipples were darkly pigmented, something that usually happened in pregnancy.

Margaret sucked in a breath. Was it possible that she was looking at Ruaridh's mother? She was plump, and it was entirely possible that her father hadn't noticed she was pregnant – possible even that Kirsty herself hadn't been aware that she was until she'd gone into labour. Margaret had to tread carefully. She had to be sure before she jumped to any conclusions.

'When did you notice your breasts were sore?' she asked.

Kirsty shook her head. 'Don't know. They only got sore a little while ago after...' She clamped a hand over her mouth.

371

'After what, Kirsty? It's all right, you can tell me.'

She shook her head again. 'I'm not supposed to tell.'

Perhaps Kirsty's father had noticed she was pregnant. Perhaps it had been him who had made her give the child away. He might have felt that the two of them couldn't cope on their own.

'Kirsty, would you mind if I rolled down your pants so I can see your tummy?'

'No. I don't want you to. It's dirty. I'm a dirty girl.'

'I promise you I don't think you're a dirty girl. Let's just have a quick look.'

As soon as she peeled down Kirsty's pants and saw the line of pigmentation running up to her navel she knew her suspicions were correct. Kirsty had recently been pregnant.

'Very well, Kirsty, you can pull your pants up. You've been a brave girl.' She washed her hands, using the time to decide whether to speak to Kirsty or to tackle the father. Given her patient's mental age, the father had to be informed. She decided to speak to Kirsty first. She might never have another chance to get her alone.

'Kirsty, I think you have had a baby recently. Am I correct?'

'No. No baby.' She cast a frightened glance at the door.

'But Kirsty, I know you have. A doctor can tell, you see. Can you tell me what happened to it?'

Kirsty's face crumpled and she started wailing. Moments later her father appeared in the door-way. He said something to his daughter in Gaelic, but Kirsty kept sobbing, refusing to look at him.

'What's the matter with her? Did you hurt her? Did you say something you shouldn't?'

'Mr Stuart – Alec, I think you should sit down. I have something very serious I need to discuss with you.'

'Is she dying? Is that what you have to tell me? You had no right to say anything to her without me being there. You can see how terrified she is.'

'Kirsty is *not* dying, Alec. She will be better in a few days. However, it's clear to me that your daughter has had a baby recently. Probably within the last two weeks.'

'But that's crazy! Do you see a baby anywhere? Do you not think I would know if my daughter had a child. You're out of your mind, woman!'

'Alec, Kirsty most definitely has had a child. The temperature she is running is because she has mastitis, something women get after giving birth, often when for some reason they can't feed their child.'

'I know what mastitis is.' He turned back to his daughter and spoke rapidly in Gaelic. Eventually Kirsty stopped crying long enough to reply.

Alec's shoulders slumped and he leant his head against the door frame. 'She says it's true. She says it was born while I was away fishing. She didn't know what to do with it so she wrapped it up in a blanket – she's seen me do that with the early lambs often enough – and took it to the doctor's house and left it on the doorstep. She'd heard there was a new woman doctor who had children of her own and who knew how to save babies. She says she didn't want to keep it herself. Oh, Lord, how can this be? Kirsty doesn't have a man, at least not one I know of. I mean look at her – no one wants a simpleton, no matter how bonny.'

'Somebody must have made her pregnant. Can you ask her who?'

Alec turned back to his daughter. 'Ciorstag, you must tell me who you were with.'

But Kirsty shook her head, this time more vehemently than ever.

'Alec, would you mind leaving us alone for a few moments? I think it's best if I speak to Kirsty on my own.'

He hesitated, giving his daughter one more anguished look before leaving the room.

'I want you to tell me about the father of your baby, Kirsty,' Margaret said, once Alec had left.

'I told you, I don't want to say.'

'Your father has never touched you down below, has he?' Although she was almost certain Alec wasn't the father of Kirsty's baby, she had to ask.

'Daddy? Touch me there?' She pointed to her crotch and frowned. 'Don't be silly!'

'But somebody touched you there, didn't he? Somebody put his penis inside you and made a baby with you. I want you to tell me who it is.'

When Kirsty shook her head, Margaret continued, 'I'm a doctor, Kirsty, and that means you can tell me anything and I'm not allowed to tell anyone else. Do you understand? If you have a secret you can tell me and I'm bound, I mean I have to keep that secret for you. The only time I might have to tell is if someone is in danger and by telling I'll be able to stop them getting hurt.'

Kirsty was silent for a long time. 'He said he'd

take his gun and shoot me and Dad if I told,' she admitted eventually.

'Oh, Kirsty. Did someone attack you? Go on, you can trust me.'

'I told you! He said he'd shoot me. And Dad. And he will. I know he will.'

'All the more reason you must tell me who it is. Don't you see, Kirsty? He sounds like a very bad man. If you tell me who he is, I will do everything I can to make sure you and your father are kept safe.'

There was another long silence. 'I met him when I was out walking. He had his gun. It wasn't anyone I had seen before. I don't think he was from here. He was dressed differently. You know, kind of fancy. Like those men who come here from the mainland with their rods to fish the lochs and their guns to shoot the deer.'

She looked at Margaret. When she nodded, she continued. 'He told me he was looking for something to shoot. He was nice at first. He said I was pretty. He said he liked my eyes. His were funny. Then he put his arm around me and kissed me.' Kirsty pulled a face. 'I've never been kissed like that before, he put his tongue in my mouth and everything. I tried to push him away but he was too strong.' She began shaking her head from side to side as if to get rid of the memory. 'And then he put his hands down my pants. I didn't like that either. I knew it was dirty. Dad always said not to let a boy touch me there and dads are always right, aren't they?'

Margaret nodded again.

'I told him to stop, but he wouldn't. He took

my pants off and stuck his thing in me. It was sore and I cried, but he still wouldn't stop.'

So she had been raped. The poor, poor girl.

'Then he got up. That's when he told me if I said anything he would shoot me and my Dad. I'd told him I lived with Dad but he was fishing, did I tell you that?'

'No, but you've told me now.' Margaret took out a tissue and dabbed Kirsty's cheeks. Her heart bled for this young woman. Not a young woman – a child. Because essentially that's what she was. She couldn't imagine what she would do if someone ever did the same to Elizabeth. No, she knew exactly what she'd do. She'd tear him apart with her bare hands. 'Did this man tell you his name? Did he tell you anything about himself at all?'

'He said his name was Richard. That's all I remember.' Kirsty's lip started quivering again. 'I was scared...'

'You must have been, but there's no need to be frightened any longer. You've been very brave telling me all this. Is there anything else you can tell me? How did he look? Was he tall? Thin? You said his eyes were funny. In what way?'

Kirsty shook her head vigorously. 'I don't want to remember him. I don't want to think about it any more. He was a bad man.'

'Yes he was, Kirsty. A very bad man. But thank you for telling me.'

'And you won't tell the police? 'Cause I'll tell them you made it up if you do.'

'I think, at the very least, I should tell your father you were attacked. He'll want to look after you, to stop the bad man coming back. Not that I think he will come,' she added quickly, 'but it's best to be on the safe side. Your dad already knows you've had a baby and he's going to want to know who the father is.'

Kirsty chewed on her thumb. 'All right. If you think it's best. Tell him I'm sorry. I didn't mean to be a bad girl.'

'He won't think that for a minute.'

'It's the bad man who gave me the baby, isn't it?'

'Yes. I believe so.'

'I didn't know there was a baby growing in my tummy. I thought I was eating too much. Then one day when Daddy was at sea my tummy started to hurt. Then the pain went away. But it came back. And every time it came back it was worse. I didn't know what to do. I thought I was dying. I thought God was punishing me for going with the bad man. Then it came out. There was a lot of blood. And it cried. It cried a lot. I wrapped it in a towel to keep it warm. I'd seen Dad do that with the lambs. Then something else came out of me. It was attached to the baby. So I cut it. I'd seen Dad do that too. I boiled the knife in water first, like Dad did. And then the baby stopped crying. He was covered in blood. I thought he was dying. And then I remembered about you. I heard you saved a baby. So I wrapped him up and took him to you. I knocked on your door. I saw the light come on and I went away again. I knew you'd look after him. When I got home I cleaned up everything. It took ages and ages.'

'You did everything you could to make sure

your baby was safe. But what about your baby now? Don't you want to see him?'

'No! I know it's not his fault but I don't want him! He makes me think of the bad man! I thought you would keep him since you didn't have your own children with you. Sometimes when a sheep dies Daddy gives the lamb to another sheep who has lost her lamb and she looks after it just as if it was hers in the first place.'

Margaret's heart contracted.

'My children don't stay with me, Kirsty, because I can't look after them when I am working. If you don't want your son he'll be given to a new mummy to keep forever. You won't be able to get him back. Do you understand?'

'I'd like to see him sometimes. Maybe when he's a big boy and doesn't need so much looking after? I could play with him and take him back to his other mam after.'

It wasn't too different to the solution Effie and Sophie had mooted. But Margaret wasn't sure that Kirsty truly realised the implications of having her child permanently removed. 'Oh, Kirsty, I'm not sure that will be possible.' Margaret's pity was tinged with admiration. Kirsty had been raped, lived in fear of her attacker, given birth on her own, yet found the strength and courage to try and find a safe place for her child.

'Now you get some rest. I'll ask your father to get some cabbage leaves from the garden. He'll need to boil them in water for a minute or two then leave them to cool. When he's done that, you need to place them on your breasts. You might have to put your brassiere over them to keep them in place. Do that about four times a day. Do you think you can manage?'

Kirsty nodded. Although her face was still red and splotched with tears she seemed calmer.

'I'm going to have a talk with your father. I'll come back to see you in a few days but if the pain gets any worse, ask him to send for me or come to the surgery. It's really important that you do that.' Margaret touched Kirsty on the hand. 'Bye for now. I'll visit you again soon.'

She went back down the narrow stairs and into the kitchen. Alec was slumped in a chair, his head buried in his hands. The room was as untidy as Kirsty's bedroom. There were all manner of tools on the kitchen table, a badly darned pair of hand-knitted socks hung over the rail in front of the stove and pots and pans lay around unwashed next to the sink.

'Alec, you must have heard about the baby left on my doorstep. Did you really not consider it could be Kirsty's?' Haphazard though Alec and Kirsty's domestic arrangement was, there was clearly a strong, loving bond between them. It made it all the harder to understand how Alec hadn't noticed his daughter was pregnant.

He raised his head, his expression dazed and disbelieving. 'I had no idea she was carrying a child. And as for babies on doorsteps, I haven't heard a peep. I only got back from the fishing a couple of days ago and I've been working the croft since then.' His face was pale, almost ashen. 'Where is my grandchild now?'

Every word had the ring of honesty about it and Margaret believed him. He would need time to get his head around the thought that his daughter had had a baby without him knowing.

'Kirsty's son is with the minister's wife.'

He slammed his hands down on the table, making Margaret jump. 'Then we must go and fetch him.'

'I'm afraid it's not as easy as all that. Kirsty has committed a criminal offence and the police will want to speak to her.' She lowered her voice. 'It's possible, likely even, that they'll decide that it's not in the best interests of the child to be returned to her. Especially as it seems clear she doesn't want him back.'

'She was frightened, that was all! And what do you mean she's committed a criminal offence? Anyone can see she's not all there. If I had been at home, none of this would have happened.' He shook his head from side to side. 'I don't know why she didn't tell me. I wouldn't have been angry with her. That girl is my life.'

Margaret pulled up a chair next to him. 'What happened to Kirsty's mother?'

'Scarlet fever – three years ago. Took Kirsty's brother too.'

Alec had already borne so much and now this.

'Did she tell you who the father is?' Alec growled. 'By God, wait until I get my hands on him.'

'Alec,' she said gently, 'I think Kirsty was raped. In fact I am sure of it.'

'Raped?' Before he buried his head in his hands, Margaret saw the horror and anguish in his eyes. She watched helplessly as his shoulders shook with dry, heart-wrenching sobs.

'We need to tell the police,' Margaret said softly. His head shot up. 'No! I'll not have her shamed.' 'The shame is his, not hers.'

'That isn't how people will see it. Did she say who did it? I'll see to him myself. I'll make sure he never lays a hand on her, or anyone else, again.' He looked around wildly as if searching for his gun.

'The only thing she seems to be able to tell me is that his first name was Richard – although he could have given her a false name – and that she was certain he wasn't a local. She says if I tell the police she'll deny everything. She's frightened the man who did it will come after you and her if it comes out that she was raped. But I think we have to tell them.'

'Then they'll insist on questioning her. That Constable Watt might even arrest her! She won't be able to cope with that. You've seen how she is. Please, don't say anything. Hasn't she been through enough?'

'But whoever did it could rape again.'

He looked at her with wretched eyes. 'I'm begging you.'

'At the very least I have to tell someone I found the mother, Alec. They've been searching for her and it's not fair to let them continue when I know she's alive and well. And if we told the police she'd been raped, they might go easier on her about the baby.' She didn't want to add that the other thing that might make the authorities go easy on Kirsty, her simple-mindedness, might also be the very thing that kept them from returning her child.

She crossed over to the window and looked out towards the sea. It was one thing concealing

Kirsty's identity from the police when she hadn't known she was raped, quite another now. What if the man who'd raped her was still on the islands? Even if he wasn't, what if he attacked another woman? In which case wasn't it Margaret's duty to report what Kirsty had told her to the police? But what was the point in giving the police Kirsty's name? She couldn't, or wouldn't, identify her attacker. And Margaret knew without a shadow of doubt that as soon as Watt knew it was Kirsty, he'd be over here, frightening her with his ham-fisted questioning or even dragging her back to Lochmaddy to lock her in a cell. She couldn't let that happen.

What if she told them the mother had been found and that she'd been raped but without revealing Kirsty's identity? A wave of anxiety washed over her. If she did that they might require her to make a statement. How would she sign it? As Dr Murdoch? What would happen if she were called to testify in court? In which case she'd be adding perjury to her list of sins. Or – a shudder ran through her – her real identity would come out along with the knowledge she'd been practising under someone else's name. She would have to run again.

Why, oh why, couldn't it have been Dr Alan or Effie who had made this visit? She'd come to the islands thinking that she could do the job she loved while supporting her children and keeping them safe. She hadn't thought about the implications of the job she'd taken on. If she did the right thing, it would be her children who suffered. Was she supposed to sacrifice them, balance their happiness and her own against that of a woman she barely knew?

Yes, she realised with a dull thud of her heart, recalling the words Alasdair had used that day at the prison. Sometimes a person has to do the right thing, just because it is the right thing, and regardless of the consequences.

She turned back to Alec. 'All I can promise is that I'll speak to Dr Alan before I do anything else. If I can keep Kirsty's name out of it, I will. If I can't, then I will do my best to make sure she isn't charged with concealing her pregnancy or abandoning her child.'

'Then that will have to do. Thank you, Doctor.'

'Now, apart from the mastitis, there isn't much wrong with your daughter. If you can find some cabbage leaves for her and make sure she does what I said, that will make her feel much better.' She placed a hand on his shoulder. 'If she does say anything more about her attacker, do you promise to tell me? You mustn't go after him yourself. If you do, you may well end up in prison and then what would happen to Kirsty? She needs you. Now more than ever.'

Chapter 36

'I know who the mother of the baby is,' Margaret said to Dr Alan. They were in the treatment room, where she knew they were least likely to be overheard. She'd called him out of surgery telling him

383

she needed to speak to him on a matter of urgency.

Dr Alan felt in his pocket for his pipe and started to fill it. 'Kirsty Stuart.'

'How on earth...?'

'My dear, I don't have to be a detective to work it out. You went to see her on a home visit and on your return you tell me you found the mother.'

She sat down and told him everything Kirsty had told her, as well as Alec's insistence that she keep Kirsty's name to herself.

Alan set his lighter to his pipe and puffed for a few moments. 'Poor man. He loves that girl. He's been mother and father to her since his wife and son died. But if he thinks the islanders won't find out soon enough that Kirsty is the baby's mother, then he is deluding himself. If I worked it out so will others. At least they will as soon as the search is called off and we can't in all conscience let it continue.'

'Then Constable Watt will question her. Arrest her, even.'

'I'm very much afraid that is what will happen.'

'But we can't let him! Kirsty is terrified. I don't think she'll admit to being raped – and that's the only real defence she has for her actions.'

'What else can we do?'

On the way back from Kirsty and Alec's house, Margaret had mulled everything over and come up with what she hoped was a solution. 'We could tell Watt the woman has been found, but not give him her name. We have the right to withhold it under patient confidentiality, don't we?'

'We do. But I'm not sure how that will help. Her name will come out eventually and Watt will

384

learn it soon enough.'

Dr Alan was right. It seemed unlikely she could keep Kirsty's name out of it. However, she had to stop her from being charged and even arrested.

'I could go and see the police inspector. He seemed like a reasonable man. Maybe if I told him the circumstances he would pass that on to the Procurator Fiscal. Then they would drop the charges against Kirsty.'

'And the rape?'

'She can't identify her attacker, although she's certain he's not a local. She might remember more in time, when she's less frightened and traumatised. If she does, that would be the time for her to be questioned. There is one thing the inspector could do to try and find Kirsty's attacker. The baby was full term. That means the rape must have happened in the spring. I'll suggest he look at the hotel and shooting-lodge registers for that time period. Check the names to see if any of them are a Richard. Find out if any of the guests around that time have been accused of rape before. There's no point in him questioning Kirsty unless he has a suspect. I'll make him see that.'

'I'm not certain Inspector MacLeod can be made to do anything.'

Neither was she. Was she risking everything for nothing? 'I can but try. And while I'm on South Uist I can try and speak to Caroline's parents. Surely if they know how ill their daughter is, they'll come and see her.'

'This island is lucky to have you here,' Dr Alan said gruffly.

If he knew how reluctant she was to go to see

the inspector and how she'd deceived him and everyone else who had been so kind to her, he wouldn't say that.

But, like it or not, she was too involved to back out now.

Chapter 37

The journey to South Uist was as arduous and time-consuming as Margaret had suspected it would be. Dr Alan had let Watt know that the search could be called off while keeping Kirsty's name to himself. How long he'd be able to do so was anyone's guess.

Margaret had arranged for Johnny Ban to collect her from Lochmaddy that morning at seven, and he'd dropped her at Carinish. From there her journey had involved several boats and changes of hire car, the final one being when she crossed the ford from Benbecula to South Uist.

This end of the Uists was hillier than the north and there were parts where the road dipped perilously close to lochs on either side. She knew very little about South Uist. Only that the famous Flora MacDonald had been born here and that apparently Prince Charles had landed on Eriskay, the next small island along from South Uist, before being helped on his way to Skye by Flora.

To get to Lochboisdale and the police station they had first to pass through Daliburgh. There, Margaret asked the driver to take her to Yellow

Point with the request to return for her in fifteen minutes. She knew if she were to ask him to wait for her outside the McKinnons' house, it would only fuel gossip.

Caroline's parents' house – a newly painted bungalow – was set just back from the road. There were creels outside, as well as a boat that had been hauled onto dry land, probably to be repainted. She took a deep breath. If Caroline's parents were anything like hers, this would be a waste of time. Nevertheless, she had to try.

Her knock was answered by a middle-aged woman with dark hair and brown eyes. Margaret could see the resemblance to Caroline straight away.

'Yes?' she said. 'Can I help you?'

Margaret held out her hand. 'I'm Dr Margaret Murdoch – the winter assistant from Lochmaddy. I wonder if I could have a word?'

'From Lochmaddy?' Alarm flickered in her eyes. 'Is Caroline all right?'

'She is for the moment. But I do need to speak to you about her.'

Although the woman hadn't invited her in, she'd stood back. Margaret stepped forward, but as she did, the woman blocked her way. 'If there's nothing wrong with Caroline, then I have nothing to say to you – or to anyone for that matter – about her. If you've come to try and talk us round you've had a wasted trip. Caroline made her bed so she can lie on it.'

'I said she was all right for the moment. I didn't say there wasn't anything wrong with her. Look, may I come inside? I'm sure you don't want to

387

give the neighbours anything to gossip about.'

'They've had plenty to gossip about as it is, a little more won't make much difference.' However, she peered over Margaret's shoulder as if to check they weren't being observed. 'But I suppose you'd better come in. Colin is in the kitchen.'

A balding man was sitting at the kitchen table, mending a rope.

'Colin, this is Dr Murdoch from Lochmaddy. She wants to talk to us about Caroline. I told her it wouldn't do any good, but she insisted.'

Colin didn't even get to his feet. 'My wife is right. As far as we're concerned Caroline is dead,' he said, echoing the words her father had once said to her.

Margaret had had enough. 'Well, you'd better be sure that that's all right, because very soon she might well be.'

Her stark announcement, although one she hadn't intended to make, had the desired effect. Caroline's mother grabbed the back of the chair as if frightened she would fall without its support, while all the colour drained from Colin McKinnon's face.

Before they could recover, Margaret sat down at the table and explained about Caroline's condition.

'She never told us about this diabetes,' her mother said, starting to cry.

Margaret wondered if Caroline had ever had a chance to.

'You say she's going to have a baby?' Caroline's mother asked, between sobs.

'Yes. But I don't expect the baby to survive

much longer.' She hated being so brutal, but these two needed to be very clear as to their daughter's prognosis.

'That child will go to hell along with its mother,' Colin muttered.

'Oh, Colin, stop! That's our daughter you're talking about.'

'It doesn't change anything, Mary-Joan,' Colin said. 'She made her choice when she married out of her faith.'

Caroline's mother collapsed into a chair. 'We need to speak to Father Roberts. He'll know what to do.'

'I'll no' speak to him. He's the one that married them. He should never have agreed.'

'You do understand that it's not just Caroline's baby that will die. There's a good chance Caroline will too,' Margaret said. 'And it could happen at any time.'

'I don't mean to be rude, Doctor, but there's no more to be said on the matter. Now I'd like you to leave.' Colin picked up the piece of rope he had been working on and continued to unpick it.

Mary-Joan looked at her husband for a long moment and sighed. 'I'll walk you to the door, Doctor.'

Reluctantly Margaret got to her feet. She couldn't accept that they wouldn't try to see their daughter even if it was for one last time. But there was nothing else she could say or do.

At the door, Caroline's mother reached over to a jar on a shelf and pulled out a pound note. 'Please take this to give to Caroline. I don't want her to be without.'

Margaret stepped back, appalled. 'She needs her mother more than any money.'

Mary-Joan blew her nose on her apron. 'I know. Just give me a little time with her father. He loves her more than his own life.' She smiled sadly. 'Perhaps more than he cares for his own soul – he just hasn't realised it yet.'

In many ways Lochboisdale was like Lochmaddy. It had a harbour as well as a hotel and a couple of stores. The police station was on the main road. If it hadn't been for blue lamp on the front wall of the single-storey house, Margaret would never have known that's what it was. From the outside it looked like any other croft house.

She hoped Inspector MacLeod would be there and not out doing whatever police inspectors on the island did. If he was, she would wait. The hire car was returning to collect her at two, which gave her just under an hour.

The front desk was no more than a hole that had been cut out from one of the walls with the addition of a counter top. It was manned by a police sergeant who looked up with a mixture of irritation and curiosity when she entered. Clearly he wasn't used to having his day disrupted. She couldn't be sure whether he was pleased or annoyed by the break in his routine.

'Hello. What can I do for you? I haven't seen you before. Are you a tourist?' He pronounced the word more like towrist.

'I'm Dr Murdoch. I work in the practice in Lochmaddy. I've come to see Inspector Mac-Leod.'

'Have you, now? May I ask what it's about?'

'No. I'm afraid it's private.'

'Private. I'm sorry, Miss, I mean Doctor, but I'll need more than that if I'm to disturb the inspector. He's a very busy man.'

'And I'm a busy woman.' She glanced around at the empty station. 'I can't imagine that the inspector is run off his feet.'

'You'd be surprised.'

She would. 'Would you mind letting him know that I'm here to see him. I'm assuming he is in the building?'

'Now then, Miss. I wouldn't like to say.'

Margaret was tempted to lean over, take him by the scruff of the neck and shake him. She'd already had one difficult encounter that day and was in no mood for another. 'Just let him know I'm here.'

'Very well,' the sergeant said.

At that moment a door opened and the inspector himself walked into the room. 'Sergeant Connor, would you type this report for me? Oh, Dr Murdoch, what brings you here?'

'Could I have a word?' She glanced at the sergeant. 'In private.'

'Of course. Come into my office.' He smiled suddenly. 'Although "office" is too grand a word for it. Sergeant, please bring two cups of tea.'

'Before or after I type the report, Sir?'

'Before. Thank you. Two missing cows and a holed boat can wait for an hour or so. This way, Doctor.'

He was correct about office being too grand a word for his room. It was little bigger than a large cupboard, with only just enough space for a desk, a filing cabinet and two chairs. He was, she noted, a tidy man or else he hadn't been joking about the missing cows and there really wasn't much to keep him busy. She wasn't surprised. The islanders struck her as a very law-abiding group. As Dolina had said, no one ever locked their doors – even at night.

He waited until she was seated before he spoke. 'I'm assuming you've come to see me about the mother and baby,' he said. 'Unless,' and he looked almost hopeful, 'you have another crime to report?'

Her heart gave a nervous jolt.

'I have found the mother,' she admitted, 'but I don't consider what my patient did to be a crime. Whatever the law says.'

'I can assure you, Dr Murdoch, that it is a crime. Sad though it is, she will have to answer for her actions. In the meantime I shall call off the search.'

'Dr Alan said that he'd let Constable Watt know.'

The inspector leaned back in his chair and studied her through half-closed eyes. 'I'm sure you haven't come all this way just to continue the argument we had in Lochmaddy.'

Surreptitiously, she wiped her damp hands on the front of her skirt.

'In a way I have. You said that if there were extenuating circumstances, that might help my patient's case. What if there's more to how she got pregnant than she's willing to admit?'

'Perhaps you should elaborate.'

Sergeant Connor appeared with a tray of tea, which he laid on the table. 'Wife didn't give me any baking this morning, so there's nothing to go with it,' he said sounding genuinely regretful.

'Tea on its own will do just fine.' Inspector MacLeod smiled at Margaret again. 'I don't know about you, but I'll be twice the size I was by the time I leave here. The locals seem determined to fatten me up.' He held up the milk jug. 'Milk?'

'Yes please.'

He poured the tea with the air of a man who was used to seeing to himself and passed her a cup and saucer, before pouring his own. The china cup looked ridiculously small and fragile in his hands.

'Please continue, Dr Murdoch. You said there were extenuating circumstances. What might those be?'

Margaret hesitated, unsure of how to start. 'The woman you are looking for has a medical condition that can affect sufferers in different ways and to different degrees. In her case, it has interfered with the function of her right arm and leg. It doesn't stop her from walking, just gives her a noticeable gait. The moment anyone saw her they would know there was something wrong with her. In addition, and more importantly, her brain has been affected. She probably has the mental age of a child of around twelve. It would be easy for someone to take advantage of her. And that's exactly what appears to have happened.'

Now she had his full attention.

'You do see that you have to tell me more.'

Margaret sighed. 'She told me that she was out on the croft when a man struck up a conversation with her. She's pretty certain he wasn't a local, she thought it might be someone from the mainland over for the fishing or shooting.'

'Go on.'

'As I said, he stopped to talk to her. Despite her handicaps she is a very beautiful young woman. More importantly, she's very trusting. Why shouldn't she be? All the locals know her and her father.'

'Did this man attack her?'

'That's my understanding. All she would say was that he did something to her she didn't like. "Put his thing in her thing" was how she put it. She told him to stop but he wouldn't listen. Afterwards he told her that if she said anything to anyone, he'd find her or her father and put a bullet in one or both of them.'

'If she's telling the truth that counts as rape. Does her attacker have a name?'

'He only gave her a first name – Richard. And we can't be sure he gave her the right one. The problem is that she refuses to repeat the story she told me to anyone else. Neither do I think she'd be willing or able to point him out, even if she was brought face to face with him again. She's clearly terrified that he'll come back and carry out his threats – so terrified she took her baby to me and left him on my doorstep. I get the impression she thought if she could give the baby to someone else, she could forget the attack ever happened. And if she had kept the child, she probably knew her father wouldn't rest until he knew who the father was. He's very protective of her, as you can imagine.'

'If she was attacked then the person who did it needs to be apprehended and charged.'

Margaret leaned forward. 'But it would be her word against his. Furthermore, I don't think she would be able to testify in court. In fact, I'm absolutely positive she wouldn't be able to, even if she were willing.'

'You don't think she's making all this up, to protect someone else – the real father of her child, for example?'

'No, I don't think she's capable of doing that.'

'You do realise this means you have no option but to tell me who she is?'

'That's why I'm here. I'll give you her name on condition you don't interview her. I simply want you to tell the Procurator Fiscal to drop the case.'

His eyebrows shot up. 'You want a great deal, Dr Murdoch.'

'All I really want is to protect my patient.' She brushed away the uneasy realisation that that wasn't completely true. But, she reminded herself, if her own interests had been paramount she wouldn't be here at all. Besides, everything she'd told the inspector about Kirsty's reluctance to repeat her story and her vulnerability to withstand questioning was true. If Kirsty had been able, and willing, to name her attacker that would be an altogether different scenario.

'She's been through enough. I will promise you, if I ever find out who the man is who attacked her, I will tell you.' And, whatever the cost to herself, she would. 'The only help I can give you is that, going by the baby's gestation, the attack probably happened in the spring – some time in February. If this man was a visitor to North Uist he probably stayed in one of the shooting lodges

395

or hotels. It's not a busy time of year, so I imagine there will be a limited number of names in the registers.'

'Then I shall check them. However, if we find someone who fits the bill, we will have to interview your patient.'

'I understand. As long as I can be with her when you do.' If she were still here. If not, she knew Effie or Sophie would stand in her place.

When the inspector added nothing more, she continued, 'It's my understanding that there's a good chance of finding someone on the island who'll take the baby in permanently. Someone who will give him a loving home. If someone can be found, I'd like you to leave the child here, rather than sending him to a children's home on the mainland.'

'Let me get this straight. You want me to ask the Procurator Fiscal not to bring charges against this woman. You don't want me to interview her. And you wish the child to remain on the island.'

'Exactly.'

He thought for a long moment. 'I have your word that the child's mother cannot be held responsible for her actions?'

'You do.' She held her breath. This was when he might ask her to make a statement to that effect.

'And that if you discover anything that might lead to the identity of the man who raped her, you will tell me.'

'I promise.'

'Very well, Dr Murdoch. I shall do as you ask.'

'You will?' She'd never imagined it would be this easy.

'As long as we are agreed on my conditions?'
She nodded.

'And the woman's name?'

Still Margaret hesitated. But she had to trust the inspector. And as Dr Alan had said it was only a matter of time before everyone knew. The clincher, of course, was that charges couldn't be dropped unless they had a name.

So she told him.

Chapter 38

Margaret had just come to the end of surgery when Dolina told her that Dr Alan wanted to see her in the front room. As each day sped by with no further word from either Alasdair or Firth she became increasingly anxious. There had to be good news – and soon.

Dr Alan wasn't alone. Sophie and her husband were there with him. Her stomach flipped. Had something happened to one of her children?

'Ah, Margaret! Come in, come in!' When Dr Alan beamed at her, she relaxed. He wouldn't look like that if he had bad news for her.

She took a seat and waited for him to explain why he needed to see her. Sophie's normally cheerful expression was tight and anxious. She was holding hands with her husband.

'Now, Sophie and George have something they wanted to talk over with both of us.'

Margaret smiled in Sophie's direction and

waited for Dr Alan to continue.

'As you know they have been caring for Kirsty's child since we found him.'

'Yes.' Had they had enough? Did this mean the child was going to be sent away after all?

'I've had word from the Procurator Fiscal. They've decided not to bring charges against Kirsty,' Dr Alan continued, looking pleased.

'Thank goodness.'

'However, it is on condition that the child is not returned to her.'

'Poor Kirsty. I know she doesn't want to keep him, but I think she'd like to see him sometimes.'

'In addition, they've agreed to leave Ruaridh on the island, if suitable adoptive parents can be found for him. We all agree there's too many in children's homes as it is.'

'We want to keep him,' Sophie said quietly.

'I think it's a perfect solution,' Dr Alan said, smiling broadly.

'Are you sure, Sophie? George? It's a big decision,' Margaret asked.

'George and I have talked about it. It's not a decision we came to lightly. We haven't been blessed with our own children...' she took her husband's hand, 'until now.'

The minister cleared his throat. 'Sophie loves the wee lad.' He looked at his wife. 'I've taken to him quite a bit too.'

Sophie nudged him in the ribs. 'Taken to him? Away with you! You're as besotted with him as I am.' She turned back to Margaret. 'Normally George, as her minister, and I as the minister's wife would have gone together to broach the subject of adoption with Kirsty, but it wouldn't be right if we are the ones who want him. We don't want her to feel forced into anything.'

'You'd like me to talk to her?'

'Yes. We think that would be best,' Dr Alan said.

'If she agrees we'll go and see her and her father ourselves,' Sophie said. 'To tell them that we'll be happy for Kirsty to see Ruaridh whenever she wants and to reassure her that he'll want for nothing.'

'And if she doesn't agree?' It had to be said.

Sophie's grip on her husband's hand tightened.

'We've prayed that she will,' her husband replied, looking into his wife's eyes. 'But if she doesn't, we'll have to accept that God has different plans for him – and for us.'

It was irregular, but the alternative was a children's home for Ruaridh and she had no doubt that Kirsty wouldn't want that. The Linklaters would make excellent parents and Kirsty would still be able to see her son from time to time.

Margaret stood. 'I'll go and see her this afternoon. I'll let you know what she says as soon as I return.'

Margaret had expected Alec to be out fishing, but it was he who opened the door to her knock. The strain of the past weeks was clearly etched on his face. He stepped aside, wordlessly inviting her in. Margaret put her medical bag down on the kitchen table.

'Is Kirsty in, Alec?' Margaret asked.

He nodded. 'Aye. In the sitting room, putting on a fire. I'll call her for you.'

Margaret put a hand on his arm. 'In a minute.' She nodded towards the table against the wall. 'Why don't we sit down?'

The lines on his brow deepened but he did what she requested. He sighed and rubbed a hand through his hair. 'Every knock on the door, I expect the police to be outside to arrest my daughter.' He looked up at Margaret.

'That's partly why I'm here. The police have Kirsty's name – I had to give it to them – but the Procurator Fiscal isn't going to press charges against your daughter, so no one will be coming to arrest her–'

'Thank God.'

'However,' Margaret made sure she had his attention before she carried on, 'there is something else I need to discuss with her. It's about her son. You probably know we're calling him Ruaridh.'

'It's a fine name.' Alec shifted in his seat. 'I've thought about the child – my grandson – night and day. Kirsty and I will manage to take care of him. It won't be easy but...'

'That won't be possible, I'm afraid,' Margaret said gently. 'One of the conditions about dropping the charges against Kirsty is that Ruaridh is not returned to her. The court has the power to place the child in an orphanage unless suitable adoptive parents can be found. I'm so sorry, Alec.'

His face darkened. 'How can they just take a child from his mother? Who gives them the right?'

'Unfortunately, Kirsty gave them the right when she left Ruaridh on my doorstep. I know she did it not just because she was frightened but because

400

she knew she couldn't look after him, and she told me the last time I saw her that she doesn't want him back.'

'She doesn't realise what she's giving up.'

'However, there is an alternative solution – if Kirsty's agreeable, that is.'

'Hello.'

Neither of them had heard Kirsty enter the kitchen, but now she stood in the doorway, her good hand twisting the folds of her dress.

'How are you today, Kirsty?' Margaret asked.

'Better. I don't feel so hot. My boobies aren't so sore either.'

'Can we go upstairs so I can have a look?' As she stood, Margaret squeezed Alec's shoulder. 'We'll talk more before I leave.'

When she finished examining Kirsty, pleased to find that her temperature was normal and the sore red, hard bit on her breast much reduced, she asked her to get dressed.

'We need to have a chat.'

'All right.'

'Let's stay up here where we can't be heard. Now, Kirsty, I need to ask you some more things about the baby.'

Kirsty's face turned bright red. 'He's with the minister's wife. Daddy told me.'

'How do you feel about that?'

Kirsty was silent for so long that Margaret began to wonder whether she'd forgotten her question. 'I think it's good. The minister's wife is kind. She will look after him. Better than me.'

'You know it's unlikely you will get your baby back?'

'I gave him away.'

'Yes you did. Because you hoped he would be with someone who could care for him.'

'And because I didn't want Daddy to find out.'

'And now your daddy knows?'

Kirsty looked baffled. 'I don't want him back if that's what you're asking – least not all the time – but I would like to see him sometimes.'

'Oh, Kirsty. I know you do. But you do know if he is adopted you will never be able to take him back to live with you?'

'When you say adopted, do you mean given to another mummy to keep forever?'

'Yes. To someone who will love him and look after him.'

'But I would never see him again?'

'That depends. I think we should include your father in this discussion.'

They went downstairs where Alec was waiting. 'How is she?' he asked.

'Improving. Another day or two and she'll be fine.'

'Good. I'm glad.'

'Alec, we need to finish our discussion. And I think it's best if Kirsty is involved. Do you mind if I sit?'

'Of course not. Where's my manners? Forgive me, Doctor, I've had a lot on my mind.'

'Now, you know Kirsty's baby is being looked after by the minister's wife?' Margaret said when they were seated.

'Yes. She's a good woman. I'm glad it's her that's looking after him.'

'As I said, the police aren't going to take Kirsty's

case any further, but they've made it quite clear that the child should not be returned to Kirsty.'

'I keep telling you, I don't want him back,' Kirsty said. 'I don't think I can look after him.'

'We'll do it together, *mo ghràidh*. I can still remember how to change a nappy. I've looked after you all these years, haven't I?'

'I know you think you can look after him. But what happens in the summer? When you go back to the fishing?' Margaret said.

'I won't go back.'

'Then how will you support both Kirsty and the child?'

'We'll manage.'

'Oh, Alec, whether you give up fishing or not, they won't let Kirsty keep the child. There is another solution. There is a couple who don't have children of their own, I can't say who yet, who would dearly love to keep him. They know Kirsty is Ruaridh's mother and would be happy for her to see him whenever she wanted. I believe they would make very good parents to Ruaridh and I think when you know who they are, you'll agree.'

'We don't even get a say?'

'You do. That's why I'm here. You could still appeal to the court, but there is a good chance that they will remove Ruaridh from Kirsty – they might even decide to prosecute her after all – and if they do remove him, he might go to the mainland to be adopted. In which case neither you nor Kirsty will ever see or hear about him again. But I know that the couple who wish to adopt him would be happy for you both to keep in touch with him. Now, there is a chance that they might move away one day and take him too, you should understand that, but I think it's unlikely. They both have good jobs here, although the wife will give hers up should you agree to let them have Ruaridh. They have a lovely, big house and more importantly – plenty of love to lavish on him.'

Alec scratched his head. 'I don't know. Maybe. Depends on who the couple is.'

'I can't tell you that at the moment. I want you and Kirsty to talk about it some more. I'll come back in a few days and if you are thinking you might let this couple have him, I can tell you who it is before you make a final decision. How does that sound?'

'It sounds as if we have no choice,' he replied glumly, before standing. 'Thank you, Dr Margaret, for everything you've done for us.' Margaret stood too, still unsure of whether she had helped or betrayed the two people standing in front of her. She took her young patient's hand. 'Kirsty, have a think about everything we've talked about. I need you to understand one very important thing, however. If you agree that this couple can take Ruaridh, you will never, ever be able to take him back.'

Her next visit was to Caroline. It didn't escape her that one woman had given her child away while another was risking her life just for the chance to hold her child in her arms.

This time her young patient didn't come to the door when she heard the sound of Dobbin's hooves and, for one terrible moment, Margaret wondered whether she was inside and unconscious, having slipped into a coma.

But when she went inside it was to find Caroline sitting in a chair, her knees covered by a blanket and her husband by her side reading to her. Caroline's face was pale and drawn, and she had clearly lost more weight.

'Oh, Dr Margaret. We never heard your horse. Otherwise we would have been at the door to greet you.' When Caroline made as if to get out of her chair, Margaret hastily told her to sit back down.

'You and Donald are as bad as each other – not letting me do a thing. See how good I'm being?'

It didn't matter how good Caroline thought she was being – one look at her was enough to tell Margaret that her condition was deteriorating.

She examined Caroline before pressing her Pinard stethoscope over her belly. The child's heartbeat was strong. She almost wished she hadn't been able to hear it and that the child had died. That way she could deliver the baby and Caroline would have a chance. The effect the pregnancy was having on her diabetes and consequently her health was already irreversible, but it was still possible that, if no longer pregnant, Caroline might have a few years left. However, the longer the pregnancy continued the less likely that was.

'Baby's heartbeat is normal,' she said, replacing the Pinard in her bag.

'That's good, isn't it?'

The poor, poor woman still didn't fully understand how grave her situation was.

'Caroline, sooner or later the baby will begin to suffer the effects of your diabetes. I need to test another sample to see how that is, but I'll do that once I have you in the antenatal annexe. I want to admit you to there so we can keep a closer eye on you.'

Caroline's eyes filled with tears. 'But then I'll be away from Donny. I don't sleep well when he's not here.'

'Nevertheless it's the best place for you. Or you could still go to Glasgow.'

'What will they do there that you can't do here?' Donald asked. 'You told me there wasn't anything. Have you changed your mind?'

'No, I'm sorry. Nothing has changed. There is nothing the doctors in Glasgow can do for Caroline that we can't do here. And that is very little. All we can hope for is to try and keep Caroline and her baby alive as long as we can.' And to try and save her life once the baby died, which it almost certainly would. She didn't like being so frank with the couple, but they had to know what they were dealing with.

'I don't want to leave my home,' Caroline cried.

'I know you don't, but as your doctor, I'm saying that you need to. If you won't go to Glasgow you have to come into the antenatal annexe, where I can keep an eye on you. Have you had any fainting spells?'

Donald looked at his wife, who gave him a pleading look in return.

'She doesn't want me to tell you, but she has,' Donald said. 'Yesterday. I gave her some sweet tea as you told me to and she felt better after a while.' He turned to his wife. 'You need to listen to the doctor. If she says you should go to hospital, then

406

you have to go. If you won't go to Glasgow, you must go into Lochmaddy.'

'I want to stay with you.'

'Och, I'll be there as often as they let me. Please, *mo ghràidh*, do this. If you won't do it for yourself, do it for me.'

Caroline closed her eyes for a long moment. 'Very well. I can't fight you both. Can I come in tomorrow?'

'Yes. But no later. Can you take her, Donald? I don't want her walking.'

'Aye. I'll take her. I'll find someone to give us a lift on their cart. And if I can't, I'll just have to carry her all the way in my arms.'

Margaret didn't like to leave Caroline at home even overnight. But on the other hand, there was actually very little they could do for her on the antenatal ward – except carry out a Caesarean section if the baby did start to become distressed. She almost wished she'd insisted Caroline go to Glasgow – that way she'd be someone else's problem. She gave herself a mental shake. Glasgow or here, the outcome would likely be the same. At least here Caroline was in familiar surroundings – and with her beloved Donald.

Chapter 39

A gentle hand on her shoulder woke Margaret from a deep and dreamless sleep. Dolina was standing over her, the light from the small paraffin lamp she was holding casting a ghostly glow over her sharp features. Margaret swallowed a shriek just in time.

'What is it, Dolina?' She pushed the blankets aside. Dr Alan was away attending a meeting in Stornoway so she was on call, but it was rare to be disturbed during the night. Margaret fumbled for her alarm clock and peered at the time. Midnight! It felt as if she'd been asleep for only minutes. It seemed the moment Dr Alan left the island everyone had come down with something. She'd been run ragged all day.

'Oh, Doctor, I'm not sure how to tell you.' It was only the second time Margaret had seen the usually taciturn woman upset. And more than upset: she was clearly distraught.

Alarm spiralled down Margaret's spine. 'Tell me what?' She bolted upright and gripped the older woman's arm. 'Tell me what, Dolina!'

The wind howled, rattling the window-frames as if trying to shake them loose.

'It's Libby. She's not well. They sent one of the neighbours to come and tell us. He's ridden all the way from Grimsay.'

'Did she say what's wrong?' Margaret launched

herself from the bed.

'No. Just that she needs a doctor. And her mother.'

Margaret was throwing on her clothes as Dolina spoke. Why did Dr Alan have to be away? 'I need to get to Grimsay. Now. What's the quickest way?'

'The tide's on the way in. The neighbour said that someone would meet you with a boat at Carinish pier. You finish getting dressed and I'll send word to Johnny Ban.'

'Go! Hurry! Tell him there's no time to waste.'

When Dolina left, Margaret finished getting dressed. She could hardly do up the buttons of her cardigan, her hands were shaking so much. What could be wrong with Elizabeth? Scarlet fever? Whooping cough? An accident? Dear God, she could be dead already!

She sucked in a few deep steadying breaths. Panic wouldn't help her child. But damn this island. Damn the lack of modern facilities, the lack of transport, damn the fact there was no way she could telephone Sandbank to find out about her child.

She hurried downstairs and automatically checked her bag. As she knew it would be, it was fully packed with everything she might need for an emergency. It was an unbroken rule. After every call-out, everything that had been used was replaced.

Dolina appeared back at the door. A rumpled-looking Johnny Ban was standing by the door of his car. As soon as Margaret stepped outside the wind almost knocked her from her feet. There was no chance any of the ferries would be able to arrive or leave until the storm died down.

'Get me to Carinish as fast as you can,' Margaret said.

He muttered something in Gaelic.

'What's he saying?' Margaret asked Dolina.

'He says he'll drive as if the devil himself were after him.' Dolina gripped Margaret by the shoulders. 'I'll pray for you and the wee lass.'

The journey seemed interminable despite the fact that, true to his word, Johnny Ban drove the car as if the devil himself were after them, which in a way, Margaret thought despairingly, he was.

Peter was waiting with his boat at Carinish Pier, rain dripping from the rim of his hat and down his face.

'Is she...?' She couldn't bring herself to complete the sentence.

'She's poorly, but she's still alive,' he replied. 'Flora is with her.' He helped her into the rocking boat.

'James?'

'He's right as rain. We kept him away from his sister as soon as we realised something was wrong.'

Thank God. She didn't know how she could bear it if both her children were ill.

'What's her symptoms?' Margaret asked, forcing herself to think like a doctor and not a mother.

'She's burning up. She's had a cough these last few days, all the children have, so we didn't think anything of it. But yesterday she wouldn't get out of bed, wouldn't eat anything. Flora wanted to call you but I persuaded her to wait a day. God,

410

I'm sorry. I should have listened to the wife. She has more experience of these things than I do.'

He should have called for her before now and it was on the tip of her tongue to tell him so but he looked so dejected she bit back the words. If anyone was to blame it was her. She should have fought harder to keep her children with her. But there was no point in thinking about what should have been, she had to get to her daughter.

The boat struggled to make headway against the combined force of the wind and the waves but at last they were pulling up outside Sandbank. Margaret jumped out of the boat before Peter could lift her ashore, uncaring that she had to wade the last few feet.

Flora came hurrying out of the house, her normally neat appearance ruffled. 'You're here. Thank God.'

'How is she?' Margaret panted.

'She's not good. I've done everything I can think of. Kept her cool, bathed her forehead, tried to make her drink, but...'

Margaret didn't wait to hear the rest. She burst through the front door, taking the stairs up to her child two at a time, not stopping to acknowledge the children sitting on the stairs, their faces white with anxiety.

Elizabeth was lying in the bed, her face flushed with fever. She didn't respond when Margaret called her name. She resisted the impulse to cradle her child in her arms and quickly felt for a pulse. It was rapid and weak.

'It's all right, Elizabeth. Mummy's here,' she said past the lump in her throat. 'Everything is going to be fine.'

She grabbed the stethoscope out of her bag.

Her daughter's eyes flickered. 'Mummy?' she whispered.

Thank the Lord. She hadn't slipped so far away that she didn't know her mother.

'Could you lift her?' Margaret said to Flora, who had followed her up the stairs. 'I need to listen to her chest.'

Flora did as Margaret asked. Elizabeth was floppy and unable to hold herself upright.

Margaret pressed the bell end of the stethoscope to her daughter's chest and listened. There it was – the unmistakable crackle of pneumonia.

Pneumonia wasn't always a death sentence, she told herself. Elizabeth was a strong child – a healthy child before this and she'd been well looked after. She slid the bell of the stethoscope over her child's heart. It was still beating strongly, although rapidly.

'What can we do?' Flora whispered.

Margaret pulled Elizabeth into her arms and nestled her child's head against her breast. 'There is nothing anyone can do for her,' she said, 'except keep her cool and wait for the fever to break. And pray.'

'Shall I send a telegram to Toni to let Alasdair know?' Flora whispered.

Margaret hesitated. Alasdair would want to know his child was ill, but telling him would be pointless. By the time they could get word to him, Libby would have either recovered or... She couldn't – wouldn't – think of the or.

'No. It will only worry him when there is nothing he can do.'

It was the longest night of Margaret's life. As the wind continued to howl and the rain spattered against the window panes, her world shrunk until it was just her and her child. She bathed Elizabeth repeatedly, murmuring to her, telling her that she was there and that everything was going to be fine. She knew the next hours would either see the fever break or... Once again she pushed the alternative from her mind.

As night turned to day and back to night, Elizabeth's breathing grew more and more laboured.

'Hold on, my darling,' Margaret whispered over and over. If anyone's love could protect a child, surely hers would. Her eyes fell on Alasdair's fob watch on the bedside table. She picked it up, rubbing the gold case between her fingers.

Alasdair, help me. If you can hear me, pray to your God to save our child's life.

She brought the watch up to her ear and listened to its tick-tock. Faith, it seemed to say with every movement of the hand.

She knelt by the bed and, still clutching the watch, rested her head on top of her knotted hands. 'Margaret, it's going to be all right,' she could hear his voice as surely as if he were in the room beside her. 'You just have to have faith.'

She prayed, then, asking God to forgive her many faults, her lies and deceit, to punish *her* if He would, but please, please not to take her child.

Light was filtering in through the windows when a small voice called to her. 'Mummy?'

Her daughter was awake and calling for her.

413

She scrambled to her feet, her stiff muscles pro-testing. She sat on the bed and stroked the damp hair from her child's forehead. 'You're awake. How are you feeling?'

'I'm thirsty, Mummy. Can I have some water?'

The simple request made Margaret want to laugh out loud. Her daughter was going to be all right. Her prayers had been answered.

She stayed with Elizabeth for the next two days, only leaving her to spend some time with James. Dr Alan had returned from his night away and sent a telegram telling her to stay as long as she wanted. He would manage until she was ready to come back to work. Her daughter, as many child-ren did, improved rapidly and soon was taking food and demanding to be let out of bed.

On the third day, she had a surprise visitor. Flora came into the bedroom to whisper that there was an odd-looking woman demanding to see her. 'I told her if it's the doctor she's wanting then she should call Dr Alan. But she insists it's you she wants to see.'

Elizabeth was sleeping so Margaret put down her book and followed Flora downstairs. She was surprised to find Dolina in the kitchen.

'Dolina! Is everything all right?'

'That's what I've come to find out. Dr Alan says she's on the road to recovery, but I've come to see the wee one for myself.' She thrust some-thing at Margaret. 'I brought her a present.'

It was a little hand-knitted teddy bear. Mar-garet swallowed the lump in her throat.

'She's going to be all right. She's sleeping

peacefully now.'

'I'd like to see her,' Dolina said stubbornly. 'I haven't come all this way just to hand over a toy.'

'Of course you haven't. Come upstairs.' Margaret held out the teddy bear. 'You give it to her yourself.'

Elizabeth was still sleeping but when Dolina stroked her face with a gentle finger her eyes flickered, then opened. 'Hello, Dolina,' Elizabeth whispered.

'Hello, *mo ghràidh*. How are you feeling?' Dolina smiled and perched on the side of the bed.

'Better,' she said. 'Am I at Mummy's house?'

'No,' Margaret said gently. 'You're still at Aunty Flora's. But I'm not going anywhere until you're better.'

'What about the other sick people, Mummy? Don't they need you?'

'They have Dr Alan and the nurses to look after them. They can do without me for a while longer.'

Elizabeth rubbed her eyes and sat up. 'Are you going to stay here too, Dolina? 'Cause I'd like that.'

Dolina blinked rapidly. 'I'm sorry, pet, but I have to go back and see to Dr Alan. I just wanted to give you this.' She tucked the teddy bear into Elizabeth's arms.

'Oh, he's beautiful!' Elizabeth hugged the toy to her chest. She looked up at Dolina. 'Will you read me and Teddy a story?'

'I can tell you a story if you like.'

'Yes please,' Elizabeth said. She moved into the older woman's arms and settled herself against her. 'It's okay, Mummy. You can go for a bit.'

Margaret went to sit in the kitchen while she waited for Dolina to come downstairs. After a while she heard her heavy footsteps coming down the stairs.

'That child needs to live with you,' Dolina said. 'They both do. They need their mother.'

'I know, Dolina. I can't leave them again. I'm going to take them back to Lochmaddy with me. Dr Alan will understand. There must be someone who will look after them while I'm at work.'

'I can take care of them.'

'What about Dr Alan?'

'He'll manage. He'll want you to stay too.'

'And when I'm out on call?'

'They can either come and stay at the Big House or I'll make myself a bed on the floor and sleep at the cottage.'

'I can't afford to pay you much.'

'I don't need much. You and I can manage between us. I'll continue seeing to Dr Alan and the patients too, of course.'

Margaret didn't know if she could trust herself to speak. 'I'll have to discuss it with Dr Alan, but if he agrees that would be wonderful. Thank you, Dolina!' To have her children with her all the time would make such a difference. Dolina sniffed. 'Aye, well. It's not good for a child to be kept from her mother.'

'Did you never want to get married, Dolina?' She couldn't help taking advantage of this newer, softer, side to Dolina. She might pretend to be as tough as old boots but Margaret was increasingly certain that behind that crusty exterior was a soul in pain.

Dolina flushed. 'I don't see what concern that is of yours. Do I ask you things about your personal life? No!'

Margaret could have bitten her tongue. Dolina might have mellowed towards her, but deep down she was still the same prickly individual Margaret knew and, surprisingly, had come to love.

'Sorry. Forgive me. You are quite right. I shouldn't pry.' Perhaps Dolina had been in love with someone and he was killed in the war? Or perhaps she'd been in love with someone who didn't love her in return? One day, she hoped, Dolina would trust her enough to tell Margaret her story.

'I'm going to take the children back to Lochmaddy to live with me,' Margaret told Flora over a cup of tea after Dolina had left and Elizabeth had gone back to sleep.

'I understand. I'm sorry I didn't care for Libby better.'

'Oh, Flora. Of course I don't blame you! These things happen regardless of how well we care for our loved ones. But I see now I was wrong not to keep them with me. I could never forgive myself if Libby had ... if something had happened to her and I wasn't with her.'

'Will Dr Alan let you keep her with you?'

'If he won't, then I'll have to leave. I'm not sure where we will go, but I do know I'll never be separated from my child again. Not ever.'

'We will miss them. The children will take it hard.' Flora's hand dropped to her belly. 'Although I have something in here that will take their minds off your children leaving us.'

'You're pregnant?'

'Yes.' Margaret didn't need to ask if Flora was sure. After three children she would know.

'Congratulations. I'm happy for you.' She paused. 'As long as you're happy for yourself?'

Flora's face lit up. 'I always wanted a brood. So does Peter. There's more than enough love in this house to go round.'

'You are so right about that.' Margaret went around to Flora's side of the table and hugged her.

'Oh, I nearly forgot,' Flora said when they'd moved apart again, 'the postie delivered a letter from Mairi a wee while ago while you were upstairs with your visitor.'

'Good news?' Margaret hardly dared hope. There were just over six weeks left before Alasdair's case went to court.

'It could be. For you, at least. Remember Mrs Murphy? And how she was able to give Toni and Mr Firth one of the names of the two men she saw. Hugh McCulloch it was. Toni and his pals have been trying to find him. A week ago McCulloch's body washed up in the Clyde. His throat had been cut.'

'Dear God! It wasn't Toni...?'

'Heavens, no!' Flora smiled grimly. 'Just as well your Alasdair is locked up, otherwise they might be saying he did it.'

'Who do they think did kill him?'

'The police aren't saying, but everyone thinks it was Billy Barr. He never believed Alasdair was guilty and swore he'd get the man who was.'

Margaret hated to think a man had been murdered, a man who might well be alive if the police had taken Mrs Murphy seriously or believed Alasdair. However, she couldn't help the way her heart was thrumming, the joy flowing through her veins.

'Surely now they have to listen to Mrs Murphy?'

'You would think so.' Flora laid a hand over Margaret's. 'I know it's hard but all we can do is wait.' She smiled again. 'But I have a feeling it's all going to turn out all right.'

Margaret returned to Lochmaddy at the end of the week. Elizabeth was recovering well and, although Margaret and Flora had agreed she should stay indoors for a few days yet, was almost back to her usual lively self. There had been no more letters from Mairi, and Margaret burned with impatience. At night she dreamed that Alasdair's name had been cleared and that he was on his way home to her. She felt happier than she'd done for months.

As soon as she reached Lochmaddy she went to the antenatal annexe to check up on Caroline.

She was shocked by the young woman's appearance. She was barely conscious and still clearly pregnant. Donald was by her side, holding her hand.

'How is she?' Margaret whispered, picking up the chart at the end of the bed. Caroline's blood pressure was dropping, her heartbeat and respirations rising. The baby's heartbeat, however, was still there.

'Not good.' He looked at Margaret with anguished eyes. 'It won't be long now, will it?'

'No,' Margaret said softly through the tightness in her throat. 'I don't think it will.'

Donald blinked rapidly. 'How's your wee girl? We heard she was poorly.'

'She's much better. But she was very, very ill. It's why I couldn't be here.'

'I know. I'm happy your child was spared.'

At that moment two people walked in. Caroline's mother and father. They nodded to Margaret and took a seat at either side of their daughter's bed.

Donald lowered his voice. 'They've been here all week. Caroline knows. She was awake when they arrived and they talked. I think it's made her more peaceful.'

Margaret felt tears prick the back of her eyes. She squeezed Donald's shoulder. 'I'll be back to see her this evening.'

When she left the annexe she went in search of Dr Alan. She found him in the consulting room. Once more the ubiquitous pipe was filling the room with smoke.

'I've just been to see Caroline,' she said. They shared a look. No words had to be exchanged. Despite what Dr Alan had said about life and death being part of a doctor's lot, she knew he would hate losing Caroline as much as she did. Every ill patient felt like a personal battle, a battle no doctor wanted to lose.

'Dr Alan,' she said, after a moment. 'I've decided to have the children come to live with me in the cottage.'

'Of course, of course.'

'It will either mean having them here when I'm

out on a call or having Dolina stay over at my house.'

'Don't need a full-time housekeeper anyway. Quite able to look after myself.'

Margaret doubted that. Dr Alan probably had little idea how much work went into the preparation of meals, laundry and all the other myriad of tasks that went into keeping a home warm and clean.

'Be married soon anyway,' he added with a little smile. 'Might take advantage of you being here to nip down to Glasgow and tie the knot! Cecilia has been hinting it's time for long enough.'

He'd kept that to himself. 'I didn't know you were engaged!'

'Didn't know myself. Until yesterday. Sent her a telegram and got her reply straight back.'

'You proposed to your wife-to-be by telegram?'

'How else was I supposed to do it? Can't take two weeks off to ask her in person, now can I? Especially when I've just been away!'

In that case he should have invited his fiancée up here and proposed to her then. Perhaps he thought if she saw the place for herself she wouldn't have agreed to marry him.

'Has she ever been here?'

'No. But I've told her about it.'

'You think that's enough?'

He looked at her quizzically. 'Yes. Don't you?'

She wasn't quite sure how to reply to that. 'Where's she from?' she asked instead.

'Edinburgh. So she'll be used to the wind.'

Margaret almost laughed. A girl from Edinburgh might be used to the wind, but surely she wouldn't be used to the lack of comforts on the island. But, as she was finding out, the people themselves went a long way to make up for that.

'And she's a doctor. Used to rough conditions.' Margaret had learned that the more emotional Dr Alan was the fewer words he used, but to have never mentioned he was courting and that she was a doctor!

She held out her hand. 'Congratulations. I hope you'll both be very happy.'

Elizabeth and James moved in with her the following weekend. Although they were sad to leave Sandbank, Elizabeth in particular was thrilled to be living with her mother again. It would be harder for James, Margaret realised sadly, when he kept asking for Flora. She'd been more of a mother to him recently than she had been. However, she trusted that in time, he would feel as secure in her arms as he did in Flora's. But on the whole, he was a happy, contented child and she had hopes that yet another change in his short life wouldn't be too traumatic for him. Especially when she'd spend all her spare time making sure he and Elizabeth felt loved and secure.

'Your new teacher is going to be Miss Mac-Lennan,' she told Elizabeth as she watched James toddle around the kitchen peering under sinks and into cupboards. 'You'll like her.'

'I don't care about school. I have you. I'm going to grow up to help people just the way you do.'

'In that case you'll have to go to school. A doctor needs to do well so she can go on to university.'

'Oh, I don't want to be a doctor! I want to be a

nurse. I want to tuck people up in bed and put cloths on their forehead and ... what else do nurses do, Mummy?'

'They do lots, my darling. They work very hard.'

Elizabeth puffed out her small chest. 'I work very hard. I feed the chickens and milk the cow and get water from the well. Lots of things. And I never get tired.'

Margaret pulled her daughter into her arms and breathed in the scent of grass and sunshine from her hair. 'So you do, love. So you do.'

Chapter 40

As winter deepened, the days continued to shorten until there were only a few hours of daylight each day. But the cottage that had once seemed dark and gloomy was now filled with laughter and joy. With Libby and James with her again, Margaret wondered how she could have ever been parted from them. True to her word, Dolina took care of them whenever Margaret had to work, and the children adored her.

The only blot in her happiness was that neither Mrs Murphy's statement nor the murder of the man she'd identified had led to the police reopening Alasdair's case. Nor had they been able to locate the second man. There was just a month to go before the trial.

Kirsty had agreed to let the Linklaters keep little Ruaridh and saw him regularly. The police were still keen to find the man who had raped her, but as yet had come up with no potential suspects. Margaret thought it unlikely they ever would, and supposing they did, that Kirsty would ever be able to testify against him. With the arrival of winter came the storms, and often at nights the wind shook their little house, rattling the windows. Inside, however, it was warm and cosy. Taking advantage of Margaret's presence on the island, Dr Alan had arranged to take some time off to go to Edinburgh to marry his fiancée and was to return with his bride after a short honeymoon in the capital. Margaret still thought he should have waited until the summer to bring her here.

At the end of November there was a ceilidh in the village hall. Margaret hadn't attended any of the previous ceilidhs that had been held while she'd been on the island but when Effie had mentioned this one, her daughter, now completely recovered, had begged to go. 'Please, Mummy. I've never been to a grown-up party.'

'Very well. This once. But we have to leave when I say so, all right?'

Elizabeth started bouncing on the tips of her toes. 'What shall we wear? Can I put lipstick on?'

'No indeed,' Dolina said from behind them. 'Children don't wear lipstick.' Her expression softened. 'Besides, you are too pretty to need any of that nonsense on your face.'

The question of what to wear to the ceilidh had been troubling Margaret. She had only brought one dress with her that might do, but it was navy and plain – not quite right for an evening's entertainment. As for Elizabeth, she'd sprouted since

424

coming to the islands. No doubt due to the fresh air and wholesome food she'd been having.

Dolina had left the room and when she came back she was carrying a length of Harris tweed in purples and pinks. 'You can wear this as a stole,' she said, thrusting the garment at Margaret.

'Oh, it's beautiful! Is it yours?'

'Yes. But I have no longer any need of it. An old woman like me doesn't need to dress up to go to a dance but a young woman like you should have something nice to wear.'

'I couldn't. It's yours. You wear it!'

'Are you coming to the dance, Dolina?' Elizabeth asked, bouncing from foot to foot.

'If I did, who will look after young James here?'

'He can come too, can't he, Mummy?'

'He's far too small to go dancing.'

'I could bring him,' Dolina said. 'All the children will be there. We could stay for an hour or so, or until he gets sleepy, then I could take him home and put him to bed.'

'You wouldn't mind?'

Dolina cleared her throat. 'I said I would help you, didn't I?'

'Thank you, Dolina. You are very good to us.'

Dolina made a noise in her throat that sounded as if she was holding back tears. 'There's no need to go all soft.'

'In that case, thank you.'

'So yes, Libby, I'm going to the dance.' Dolina smiled and all at once Margaret could see that she must have been an exceptionally beautiful woman when she was younger. 'And why not? Do you think these old pins can't do a jig any more?'

Elizabeth flung her arms around Dolina's legs. 'You're coming to the dance! Mummy, Dolina is coming to the dance.'

For a moment tears glistened in Dolina's eyes. She blinked rapidly. 'Who will look after you and James if I don't? Make sure you're wrapped up in bed all cosy when the time comes.'

'Isn't Mummy going to put me to bed?'

'Of course I will.'

'Mummy might be dancing. We wouldn't want to spoil her fun now, would we?' Margaret could have sworn she saw Dolina wink.

Elizabeth opened her mouth to protest but before she could, Dolina continued. 'That reminds me, do you know how to dance the Scottish country dances?'

'No.' Elizabeth giggled. 'Will you teach me?'

'Of course, but first I have something for you too.'

'For me?'

'I couldn't give your Mummy a present without giving you something too, could I? Now wait you here.'

Dolina disappeared off again.

'Can you dance those dances, Mummy?'

'I used to be able to. But it's a long time since I danced.'

'Dolina will teach you too.'

Margaret hid a smile. A more unlikely scenario she couldn't imagine. 'I hope so. Let's have something to eat before we get ready.'

Dolina returned as they were washing up. 'You should have left that for me.'

'You have to get ready, too. And you still have

426

to teach me to dance!' Elizabeth said.

'Silly me. Of course I do.' She placed a brown paper package tied up in string on the table. 'I would have wrapped it in fancy paper if I could have found some.'

'Can I open it?' Elizabeth asked.

'Yes. Let me help you with the string.'

A few moments later, Elizabeth pulled out a dress in colours similar to the stole Dolina had given Margaret. But where her wrap was made of rough Harris tweed, the dress was more like gossamer than wool. It must have been knitted with the tiniest needles.

Elizabeth held it to her. 'It's the most beautiful dress I have ever seen. Did you make this for me?'

'I made it for a little girl just like you.' Dolina welled up again. 'She never got the chance to wear it, but I know she would have been happy for you to have it.'

Margaret swallowed a lump in her throat. Whoever that dress had been so lovingly and painstakingly made for must have meant a great deal to the older woman. It and the stole were clearly made to match.

'Can I try it on?' Elizabeth asked.

'Yes. After your bath. I've kettles on the stove and you can have your bath in front of it. Then you can put your dress on and I'll show you a dance or two.'

'I've got something for you too,' Elizabeth said. 'I'll be back in a minute.' She scarpered away.

'Are you sure, Dolina?' Margaret asked gently. 'Are you sure you want Elizabeth to have that dress?'

427

'Why wouldn't I? There's no one else it will fit so well.'

Before Margaret could say anything more, Elizabeth came running back. She held out her hand to Dolina and opened her fingers. Alasdair's watch was lying in the palm of her hand. 'Mummy gave me this so I wouldn't be sad. I think you're sadder than I ever was. And Mummy isn't so sad any more either. It belonged to my Daddy. You put it against your ear when you are missing someone and it's like listening to their heart. Go on. Try it.'

Margaret did her best to hide her dismay. Elizabeth was going to give Alasdair's watch away – the only thing she had left of him!

Dolina took the watch and held it to her ear. As she listened to its tick-tock tears flowed unchecked down her cheeks. 'You would give me your daddy's watch,' she said. 'I have never been given a present before. Never mind such a fine one as this.'

'My daddy would be happy for you to have it,' Elizabeth said.

Did her daughter realise that giving it away would be for keeps?

'I can't keep this,' Dolina said, thrusting it back at Elizabeth. 'It's too precious.'

'But you must! Otherwise I won't keep the dress you gave me and I want to.'

'Tell you what,' Dolina whispered. 'I'll hold on to it for a little while. Just until I feel less sad. Then you can have it back.'

'All right. Is it time for my bath?'

Dolina and Margaret shared a smile over the top of Elizabeth's head. The older woman had managed the situation perfectly. Nevertheless, she brought the watch up to her ear one more time, listening intently before putting it safely in her pocket.

The town hall was thronged with people by the time they arrived. It seemed as if the whole of North Uist was here. There were certainly enough horses and carts. It had been one of the cold but clear winter days that had continued into the evening, and the sky sparkled as if studded with a thousand diamonds. A table had been set up along one side of the room and was groaning with food. The women of the island must have been baking and cooking for weeks.

Gone were the stout boots and wellingtons. In their place were little heels and best dresses. Even the men had been scrubbed to within an inch of their lives. Most were wearing suits – albeit like Margaret's dress showing signs of age – and if they didn't have a decent enough jacket, they wore newly knitted jumpers over clean shirts.

The children were there too. Some running about and bouncing with excitement, but mostly on their best behaviour. Margaret recognised Chrissie, who was there with her baby wrapped in a shawl and the focus of much admiration.

As they walked towards the table where Sophie, Effie and their husbands were waiting, several people smiled and called out a greeting, patting Elizabeth on the head and taking James in their arms to exclaim over. Libby's Gaelic was good enough already to answer simple questions and Margaret had learned enough to say 'good evening' and 'I'm well, thank you. How are you?'

'You look gorgeous,' Effie said when they arrived finally at the table.

'So do you,' Margaret said truthfully.

'Are you going to dance?'

Margaret smiled. 'I doubt Libby is going to let me get away with sitting in a corner.'

She danced an eightsome reel and a strip the willow. The unaccustomed exercise made her breathless and hot.

Knowing her children were safe under the eagle eyes of Dolina, she went outside for some fresh air. She found a boulder and sat down, pulling her knees to her chest. The sky was clear, the stars shining as bright as diamonds on a bed of velvet. Was Alasdair thinking of her? Somehow she knew he was.

Hearing footsteps behind her, she turned to find Dr Alan standing there. She scrambled to her feet. 'Is there an emergency? Do you need me to cover for you?'

'No, my dear.' He touched her on the shoulder. 'I thought you'd want to know. Caroline passed away a short while ago.'

'Oh no,' she whispered. 'The baby?'

He shook his head. 'We did everything we could but we knew it would end this way.'

'I wish I could have done more.'

'You're too hard on yourself, my dear. In the time you've been here, you've achieved a great deal. And because of you, Caroline didn't die alone. Her parents and her husband were right there with her.' He looked over her shoulder. 'I'm going to let Sophie and George know. Will you be all right?'

Margaret couldn't trust herself to speak so she simply nodded. Dr Alan was right. No one should die alone. At least Caroline hadn't.

One by one the people she'd come to care for came outside to find her. First was Effie, who said nothing but sat down beside her and joined her looking up at the stars. Then came Elizabeth, who plonked herself in Margaret's lap and leant against her. Hard on her daughter's heels came Dolina, holding James on her hip. Moments later they were joined by Sophie, holding little Ruaridh. They all stood quietly. Even James was silent – his big eyes taking in the enormous sky.

'Are you all right?' Sophie asked after a while.

'Of course she's not all right,' Dolina snapped. 'She's crying. No one cries when they're all right.'

Margaret looked around at her new friends who had in a short space of time become more of a family to her than her own parents. Between them they held her heart in their gentle hands.

'No, I'm not all right.' She swallowed. 'Not right now. But something tells me that one day I will be.'

A few days after the ceilidh Dr Alan left for Edinburgh to marry his bride. Margaret now had sole responsibility for all the patients on the island, but the prospect no longer held any fears for her. What did worry her was that there were just three weeks to go before Alasdair's trial and still Firth hadn't enough evidence to secure his release.

She had just helped Dolina put the children to bed when there was a loud banging on the door.

She sighed. She was on call, which was why Dolina would be staying the night. Even when she wasn't, Dolina appeared intent on spending every spare moment she could at Margaret's cottage. She only hoped that when Dr Alan got married his new wife would keep Dolina on and not wish to employ someone younger.

When she was on call and Dolina was in the house, the older woman insisted on answering the door, telling Margaret she would soon dispense with any 'time wasters'. Not that there were many of those. The islanders rarely called for the doctor unless they were really worried. In which case it was almost a certainty Margaret would be going out.

She checked her hair in the mirror, tucking a stray lock behind her ear. It was growing quickly and she should really take a pair of scissors to it.

The banging started again and Dolina's heavy footsteps hurried to the door. She could hear her muttering as she passed. 'Don't folk know there are children in the house? They'll be getting a piece of my mind.'

There was the sound of a man's voice, one she thought she recognised.

'This is no time to be calling on the doctor,' Dolina was saying. 'Not if there's nothing wrong with you. She was about to get herself ready for bed. She needs her sleep.'

Margaret thought it best she rescued whichever poor soul was getting a tongue-lashing from her over-protective housekeeper.

'Who is it, Dolina?' she asked, walking into the kitchen. To her dismay, Dr Sinclair stood there, apparently unperturbed at Dolina's hostile attitude.

'Dr Sinclair! What can I do for you? If you've come to enquire about Caroline, I'm afraid she passed away a few days ago.'

'Caroline?' His brow furrowed.

'The young pregnant woman with diabetes.'

'Oh, her! No, that's not why I've come to see you.' He glanced over at Dolina. 'Perhaps we could speak in private?'

A chill ran up her spine.

Dolina harrumphed but retreated, pulling the door behind her but, Margaret noticed, leaving it slightly open.

'Do you have a patient you wish to consult me about?' Margaret asked, still praying his visit was nothing more than a professional one.

'Consult *you* about a patient?'

'Yes, well, I can see no other reason for this visit.' But she could. Oh God, she could.

Dr Sinclair sank into the chair beside the Rayburn and without asking permission, lit a cigarette. He exhaled slowly.

'Dr Martha Murdoch? Eh?'

Her heart gave a sickening thump. 'Excuse me?'

'There is no need to pretend. I know exactly who you are.' He leaned forward, his cigarette dangling between his long fingers. 'You see, the last time we met I couldn't get it out of my head that I'd seen your face before. I just couldn't remember where. Last week I had to go to Glasgow for a meeting at the university and while I was there I thought I'd look through photographs of past graduates. And lo and behold! There you were. Sandwiched between the real Dr Murdoch and Dr Lillian For-sythe. Your hair was different, longer and blonder, but there was no doubt it was you.'

Feeling as if her legs were about to give way, Margaret hung onto the back of a kitchen chair for support. 'I don't know what you mean.'

'Oh, but I think you do, Dr Bannatyne.' He leaned back in his chair and took another draw of his cigarette. 'So I began to wonder. Why would Dr Bannatyne be pretending to be someone she wasn't? Then it came back to me. The murder of the gang member. I only paid attention to that because they mentioned Alasdair Morrison's wife was the daughter of Bannatyne the shipbuilder and had qualified as a doctor. Even then it crossed my mind you were bringing the profession into disrepute, but I soon forgot all about it.'

Margaret's throat was so dry she couldn't speak.

'I decided to do a bit more investigating. I tried to locate the real Dr Murdoch. Didn't take me too long to find that she was in India – had been there for years. But, funny this, there was no finding Dr Bannatyne. Or Dr Morrison if that's what you called yourself. She had disappeared.' He stubbed out his cigarette and lit another one. 'And lo and behold she turns up on a remote Scottish island under a different name!'

There was no point in denying it. 'Why are you here?'

'Now let me see. How much trouble are you in?' He held up his forefinger. 'Firstly, you are impersonating another doctor – does she even know?' Margaret shook her head. 'Because if she does, she'll be in all sorts of trouble herself. And

434

what about the good Dr Alan? What about him?'
Margaret shook her head again. 'Because if he
did, *he'd* be in all sorts of trouble too. Now where
was I?'

Margaret answered his question with a lift of
her eyebrow.

'But why disappear? Actually, that part I do
understand. So embarrassing to be the wife of a
murderer. But why take a different name? Why
practise under an assumed name when you must
have known the risks you were taking? Made me
wonder if William Bannatyne knew where you
were. Surely a daughter doesn't take her children
and run from her parents? Especially when those
parents are the Bannatynes. The very people who
could best protect her from the press and the
scandal. Unless they were complicit. So I made
some more enquiries. Didn't take me too long to
discover that there was bad feeling between you
and your father.'

'Did you see him?' Margaret's head was spinning. If Sinclair had, her father could be here at
any moment. Images of the children being pulled
from her arms, her in gaol, or in an asylum,
flooded her head. She couldn't let that happen.
She needed to get away. But how? There wasn't a
ferry off the island until tomorrow.

'No. I did try. Unfortunately he was too poorly
to receive visitors, or so the maid said. Quite
insistent she was.'

Her father was ill? Ill enough to stay at home?
She'd never known him to take time off before.
She chased away the feeling of unease. Her father
didn't deserve her sympathy and she had more

435

pressing matters to consider. But for whatever reason, thank God, Sinclair hadn't managed to see her father. If he had, she had no doubt, her father would have turfed him out on his ear – and then come here himself. Or, more likely, started proceedings to have the children removed from her.

'I have nothing to say to you.'

'Really? Are you sure?' When she was quiet, he continued, 'On my way back, I began to think. Here we have a Bannatyne hiding in our midst. And the Bannatyne family have more money than they know what to do with. Your father's shipyard is busier than ever, I understand. Something to do with events in Europe?'

'Why don't you just say what you've got to say?'

'I can't imagine he, or you, would be too happy if I went to the GMC and explained there was a doctor, being paid a salary, who was working under an assumed name. They take a pretty dim view of things like that, you know. You'd almost certainly be struck off. Maybe even go to prison. Then what would happen to those children of yours? Elizabeth and James, I believe?'

'What do you want?' she asked through frozen lips.

'I thought I should offer to come to some arrangement with you. As you know doctors here are paid a salary, but it's a pretty poor one. Unfortunately I had to give up private practice, an unfortunate incident you understand, and this was the only job I could get. Why Dr MacLean chooses to work here when he doesn't have to, is beyond me.' He contemplated the end of his cigarette. 'I do like the finer things in life. Particularly decent holidays and fishing. And all that tends to cost more than a simple doctor like me makes.'

'You've come here to blackmail me?' She could hardly believe it. Exposing her through legitimate indignation because she was practising under a different name was one thing, blackmailing her was quite another. The man was despicable.

'I wouldn't call it blackmail – such a nasty word – more like us helping each other out.'

'I don't have money, whatever you think.'

'No, perhaps not, but your father does. I might not have managed to see him, but I could still write to him.'

All at once she felt flooded with rage. She'd been harassed from pillar to post by men and she'd had enough. She wanted to stay here, with the people who had become her friends. The thought of ripping her children away from the people they'd grown to love, only to go into hiding somewhere else, and with no money and no way to earn more was unthinkable. This man, with his supercilious smile and sleazy manner, would not get the better of her.

'I won't be giving you a penny,' she said. She sat down on the chair and looked him in the eye. 'You may be aware there is a young woman who lives here who was raped recently. She won't, as yet, identify her attacker. But I think she will. It's fairly easy to persuade her of things.' She hoped God would forgive her for saying this. 'She did say that the man who raped her was well dressed, like one of the men who come to the island to shoot or fish. In fact the man she described sounds a lot like you. And, if I remember correctly, the day you visited me to tell me about Caroline, you told me you came down to this side to fish whenever you got the opportunity. Perhaps you were in Lochmaddy the day Kirsty was attacked?'

He laughed. 'You can't be serious! I've never found a reason to take a woman against her will.'

'But will people believe that? Especially if this woman points you out as her attacker. And as I said, I think she could be persuaded.'

Now she had wiped the smile off his face. 'But that's outrageous. You know as well as I do, I had nothing to do with any attack on any woman.'

'Perhaps,' she said mildly. 'But even the accusation will taint your reputation, won't it?'

'You wouldn't dare.'

'Oh yes, I would. You've already discovered that I'm a woman who is prepared to bend the rules for my own purposes.'

'No one would believe a woman who has deceived everyone.'

'Aye they would.' The voice came from behind her. Margaret whirled around. Dolina stood in the door, her arms folded over her chest. 'Especially if I tell them I saw you with this woman one day.' The older woman had clearly been listening through the slightly open door. How much had she heard? 'People would believe me. And if they believe me, they'd believe the doctor here.'

Dr Sinclair laughed again but this time it was without conviction. 'Why would they take the word of an old crone and an about-to-be-disgraced doctor over me?'

'It's a funny place, this island. People can give

their neighbour an earful, they can fall out with each other, but in the end we look after our own. And if I say you were the man I'd seen talking to this young woman one day, then I'm as certain as I can be that one or two would back me up.'

Dr Sinclair's hands were shaking as he lit another cigarette. 'You'd perjure yourself? Don't you know you could go to prison for that?'

'I've been in worse places,' Dolina said grimly.

Dr Sinclair stumbled to his feet and tried to smile. 'It was only a friendly chat. A quid pro quo, if you like. But if nothing's doing, then,' he shrugged, 'it was worth a try.'

Margaret stood too, unsure of whether her legs would support her. Something wasn't right. He'd given up too easily.

'What is your first name?'

'What the hell do you want to know that for?'

She took another step towards him. He was standing directly under the gas light. 'It isn't Richard, by any chance?'

'It's Roderick, as it happens.' But he had paled. She took a step closer until she was only a foot or so in front of him. She'd never noticed it before but now she could see he had one green eye and one blue. It was very rare. Could she have stumbled across the truth?

'The victim said the man had funny eyes. And you have heterochromia.' Her mind was racing. It was entirely possible he'd given Kirsty a different name. Indeed if he'd intended to rape her all along that is exactly what he would have done. But Sinclair was a doctor! It was unthinkable. Nevertheless, she recalled their conversation about

Caroline. His dismissal and contempt for the islanders – the way he viewed them as less than human.

Dolina walked across to the door and flung it open. A gust of damp evening air rattled the windows. 'Now you'd better leave before I take you by the scruff of the neck and throw you out. I may not look strong, but these arms are a lot more used to hard work than yours.'

Dr Sinclair stared at Dolina as if she were from another planet. He straightened the lapels of his jacket and, with a shake of his head, let himself out.

As the door closed behind him, Margaret started shaking and couldn't stop. Dolina said nothing, but placed the kettle on the stove and calmly began to make a pot of tea.

'How much did you hear?' Margaret asked.

'Enough to know that that man knows something about you that you wish he didn't.' Dolina heaped tea leaves into the pot and set it on the stove. 'I've known about you for a while now.'

'What do you mean?'

'I was laying the fire with some old newspapers. There was a photograph in one of them of a man who had been arrested for murder. I recognised him immediately. The same man that's in your wedding photograph.'

'Why didn't you say?'

'What was I going to say? You'd taken a different name for a reason. Either he was guilty of murder and you were trying to protect your children, or he wasn't and you had other reasons for coming here.'

'He's innocent.'

A ghost of a smile crossed the older woman's face. 'I've no doubt he is. I can't imagine you'd be keeping letters under your pillow from a man guilty of murder. Neither would those children be the way they are if they were fathered by an evil man.'

'But you didn't tell Dr Alan?'

'I thought about it. I knew if I did he would have to let you go. And that man needed your help.' She cleared her throat. 'The folk here like you. Say you treat them kindly. That counts for a lot in my book.'

'And knowing all that you would still lie to save me? I can't be sure Sinclair did what I accused him of.'

'Aye. If it came to that.'

'Oh, Dolina, why?'

The housekeeper cleared her throat. 'Because you and the bairns are the nearest thing I've got to a family. Because I know what it is like to be down on your luck and to have no one to turn to. I'm no' daft. I saw that something was troubling you since the very day you arrived.'

'I thought you didn't approve of me.'

'Aye, well, to be honest, I didn't, not at first.' She sighed again and took the chair recently vacated by Dr Sinclair. 'The thing is I never had much truck with women doctors – all doctors come to that. With the exception of Dr Alan, that is. Now there's a real gent.'

'You had a daughter, didn't you?'

Dolina looked at her sharply. 'Not so daft either, are you?' She exhaled deeply. 'How did you know?'

'A few things. But it was when you gave the dress to Libby I really guessed. No one holds onto a dress belonging to a child for years unless it means something to them. And it was beautifully knitted and put together. Anyone could see it was made with great love.'

Tears flooded Dolina's eyes and she wiped them away impatiently with the back of her hand. 'That lass meant everything to me.'

Margaret couldn't be sure if, even now, Sinclair was planning to go to the police or to her father. He couldn't go to Dr Alan, who wouldn't be back from his honeymoon until tomorrow afternoon – if the ferry even managed to sail. She had tonight to decide what to do. In the meantime, she owed this woman so much, she could at least listen to her.

'What happened to your daughter?' Margaret asked gently.

'It's been a long time since I spoke about her. To be honest I'm not sure I ever spoke about her. That's the worst of it. With no one to remember her with it's almost as if she never existed. It's almost as if I dreamt her.'

'Tell me, Dolina. Tell me. We'll remember her together.'

Dolina sat down and stared into the distance for a long while, a small smile hovering on her lips. 'She was a lovely wee thing. Not that she lived very long.'

Margaret stayed quiet, sensing that Dolina needed to recount her story in her own time. 'I was one of ten,' she said eventually. 'We lived on

Barra.' It was a small island off the coast of South Uist. 'We didn't have much. My father was always poorly and struggled to provide for us, so as soon as I was fourteen I went to Glasgow to take up a post as a housemaid. I know I don't look like much now but back then I was pretty. Pretty and big-headed. I imagined that Glasgow was like people think of New York or London – I thought it was made of gold. I had no intention of staying a housemaid forever. I believed that something,' she smiled wanly, 'or someone would come along and I'd make my fortune. Then I'd come back or at the very least send lots of money home. I imagined myself stepping off the ferry, dressed in the best money could buy,' she shook her head slightly. 'In those days the best meant something shop bought and not hand-knitted or passed down from one child to the next. I was the fifth sister so you could imagine my clothes were pretty worn by the time they got to me. My mother was a great knitter, but we didn't even have sheep in the end to get the wool.'

A spatter of rain hit the window and Margaret hid a shiver. She had a good idea of what was coming.

'And I did like Glasgow – at first. Everything about it amazed me – not that I got to see that much of it. The house I was sent to was in Kelvinbridge, not as grand as some, but grand enough. There were only two maids, so we had to do all the work between us. We got up at five and often weren't in bed until after ten. We had one afternoon off a month and I'd go out and wander the streets no matter the weather. The pay was poor too. I knew I'd only have a few pennies to send to Mam and Dad but I still believed something better was going to come along.

'I met him in Kelvingrove Park. My hat blew away and he chased it for me and brought it back. He was so handsome, so well dressed, I knew immediately he wasn't for me. But we got talking and he was kind and he didn't try anything funny. We met a few afternoons after that and I told him that I wasn't happy at my place – not that the people there weren't kind enough, but that the pay was so low and I wanted to do better. Of course he agreed – a pretty girl like me, he said, should have the world at her feet.' She paused, a wry smile hovering over her lips. 'I can hardly remember the girl I was back then. One who would believe whatever she was told.'

Margaret said nothing, knowing that if she interrupted, Dolina might never finish her story and knowing at the same time that it was important for the older woman to do so.

'There was no job. But I kept meeting him. I was in love and I thought he loved me. I was certain that we would marry. Of course, when I told him I was pregnant he disappeared. I didn't know what to do. I was ashamed. Then Mam wrote to say they were all going to Canada. They'd get help with fares and the boys had been promised jobs. She wanted me to come with them. How could I? I was going to have a baby. I should have told her but I couldn't. I didn't want anyone to know. So I told her I was going to stay, that I had met someone, that we were going to get married. I thought he might still come back for me. I couldn't believe that he'd been lying all that time.

'They went. I looked everywhere for Michael – that was his name – but I couldn't find him, nor anyone who knew him. I doubt now that was even his real name. I tried to hide the fact I was going to have a baby from my employers and I managed for longer than I'd hoped, but of course they found out and I was dismissed. I only had a small bit of money saved–' She shook her head. 'You don't need to know what I did to survive. I knew I had to keep the little money I did have for when the baby was born.'

She smiled. 'Dawn – that's what I called her – was so beautiful. I loved her straight away and I knew I would do anything and everything to keep her safe. But I couldn't. Not for long. I ran out of money and then there was only one thing for it. I had to take her to the poorhouse. They took her in but they wouldn't take me too. I got a job as a maid. I had to pretend I didn't have a child. They wouldn't have taken me on if I'd said. I saw Dawn sometimes, but not as often as I wanted. For three years I kept thinking and thinking of what I could do so we could be together again. I thought if I could save somehow I could get enough together for a small place for the two of us.' She shook her head. 'I started knitting the dress, imagining Dawn wearing it when she was older – when we'd be together again. I know I was dreaming, but I had to make myself believe it.' Tears were running down her lined cheeks. 'Then one day I went to visit Dawn and they told me she was dying. They hadn't even sent me a note to tell me she was sick.'

Margaret's heart ached for her. She took

Dolina's hand and for once the older woman didn't pull away. 'It was a woman doctor who saw her. She didn't realise how sick she was to begin with. Dawn was still alive when I got there, but only just. The doctor wouldn't let me see her. Said she couldn't be upset. By me! Her mother! I couldn't even say goodbye. If she had to die she should have died in my arms. I should have been with her. I'll never forgive myself or that doctor for that. Most of all I'll never forgive myself. Me and my stupid pride. I should have told my Mam as soon as I knew I was going to have a baby and that the father had run off. She would have been disappointed, but she would have taken us in. We would have been all right.'

'You did the best you could,' Margaret said gently. She thought of the dress Dolina had given Libby, the love and care that had gone into every stitch and how the older woman had kept it with her all these years.

'I know how terrible it is to think you are going to be separated from your child.' Margaret told Dolina what her father had threatened. 'I was terrified when I thought I might lose my children. I don't know if I could have borne it. But when Libby was ill, I thought about what I had done, taking my children away from their grandfather and how it would have been my fault if she died. I—' She couldn't continue past the tightness in her throat.

The two women sat for a while, each lost in their thoughts.

'Aye well,' Dolina sniffed and smiled wanly. 'We did what we thought was best at the time. I made a mistake. A mistake I'll pay for until I'm cold in the ground. But you still have your two children and we need to see that it stays that way.'

Chapter 41

It was over.

She'd spent the night unable to sleep, knowing she had no choice but to reveal what she suspected. She wasn't sure whether Sinclair was the man who had raped Kirsty but if there was the smallest chance he was, she had to tell someone. He couldn't be allowed to continue to practise, whether he was guilty or not.

As soon as she reported the conversation she'd had with Sinclair, the truth about who she really was would come out. Then there was every likelihood that she'd be arrested too. Her father would find it easier than ever to take the children from her. She had to make sure that didn't happen.

But what to do? She could take the children and hide at Flora's, but that would be the first place they'd look for her, in which case Flora's part in her deception would come to light. But leave here she must.

Dolina had helped her pack and their suitcases were waiting by the door. If she could only keep the children safe until she got on the ferry they might still have a chance. Her plan was to telegraph Lillian in the morning and ask if she and the children could stay in her house in Perthshire.

Every moment she expected a knock on the door from Constable Watt, but when morning came and there was no sign of him, she wondered if she had been correct about Sinclair. He hadn't gone to him to report her. Whether he was frightened that if he did she would accuse him of blackmail or whether it was because he was guilty of raping Kirsty, she couldn't be sure. Despite what she'd said to him, Margaret knew she would never lie about him being the man who raped Kirsty. She couldn't do that to a man if there was a chance he was innocent and even more, she couldn't and wouldn't entice Kirsty to lie. But, regardless of Sinclair's innocence or guilt, she had to go to Dr Alan and tell him the truth of what she suspected and about herself and her own situation. What would happen after that she didn't know.

When she told Dolina she was leaving the island, she'd insisted on coming too.

'What about Dr Alan?' Margaret had asked.

'His wife will keep house for him now. And if she needs help she'll be wanting someone younger.'

'He'll be lost without you.'

'*You'd* be lost without me. Never met a woman so hopeless at looking after a home before. And you'll need to get work. When you do, you'll need someone to care for those poor bairns.'

It had been easier to give in than argue. Besides, Dolina was right, Margaret would need help. And, if she were honest, she'd become used to having the elderly woman around even though, despite her revelations, she'd reverted to the grumpy Dolina Margaret knew so well. But loved all the same.

As soon as she'd telephoned Lillian, she went to see Dr Alan. If he noticed her agitation, he gave no sign of it. Instead, he insisted on introducing her to his new bride. She was a surprise. Instead of the willowy woman Margaret had conjured up in her imagination she was sturdy, open-faced, relentlessly happy and clearly delighted to be wherever Dr Alan was. They spent an excruciating hour – for Margaret at least – chatting before Cecilia excused herself, clearly intuiting that Margaret wished to speak to Dr Alan alone.

He listened to her story without interrupting. She told him everything: why she'd become estranged from her father in the first place, about Alasdair's arrest and her father's demands, his threat to remove the children from her, and that she had come here accepting the post under an assumed name because it was the only way she could keep her children safe. Finally, she told him about Dr Sinclair and his attempt to blackmail her and her suspicion that he might be the man who raped Kirsty.

'Well, now,' Dr Alan said when she'd finished. He spent a few moments packing his pipe, waving her into silence when she repeated how sorry she was to have deceived him.

Eventually the pipe was filled to his satisfaction and he took a few deep puffs. 'Would you have told me all this had Dr Sinclair not threatened to expose you?'

'Probably not,' Margaret admitted. 'I knew you would have no option but to dismiss me if I did and I had nowhere else to go. But I am telling you now, not because Sinclair might expose me, although the prospect terrifies me, but if there is the slightest chance Sinclair did rape Kirsty, he has to be put where he can't hurt anyone else. Even if he didn't, he's not fit to practise.'

'I'll tell Inspector MacLeod what you suspect. He'll need to interview him.' He shook his head. 'I hope to God your suspicions aren't true.' He studied Margaret, his forehead knotted. 'The thing I like the least is that you didn't tell me who you really were before now. A doctor has to be above reproach – you do see that, don't you? If we don't trust each other how can we expect our patients to trust us?'

'I do see that,' Margaret said miserably. 'I've already packed.'

'Now hold your horses, young woman. Where will you go?'

'A friend has a cottage in Perthshire we could use for a while.' On her way to see Dr Alan she'd telephoned Lillian from the post office. Her friend had been surprised, but pleased to hear from her. Lillian's baby, another boy, had been born just after Christmas and was a perfect angel. Although Lillian was clearly agog to find out what Margaret had been up to, Margaret had kept the call short, asking whether it was still all right to use the Gate-house and would Lillian mind awfully keeping it secret that she was there. To her relief her friend had been quick to agree.

'Dolina is coming with us,' she added.

Dr Alan's eyebrows shot up. 'She is? Well, well, well.'

'I could ask her to stay until you find someone else?'

'No, if Dolina wants to go I'll not be the person to stop her. Cecilia has someone she wanted to bring, a long-serving servant of the family, but I thought she would put Dolina's nose out of joint.' His gaze sharpened. 'You will look after Dolina, won't you?'

'I promise.'

'And what will you do for money?'

'Whatever I need to. I'll find a way to make enough to keep us. Even if it means scrubbing floors.'

Dr Alan smiled for the first time. 'I'm not certain your domestic skills are up to it, dear.'

'I'll do anything. I'm not scared of hard work.'

He puffed some more. 'You *are* a qualified doctor, aren't you?'

'I am. I wasn't lying about that.'

'Of course you are. You couldn't have looked after the patients half as well as you did if you hadn't been.' He relit his pipe. 'You do know I can't keep you on beyond the end of February whatever I decide now? The funding stops then, regardless.'

'I know.'

'I don't agree with what you did but I can understand why you did it. Now here is what I suggest. I could tell the authorities that Dr Murdoch has had to leave but that Dr Bannatyne has taken her place for the last couple of months. I won't tell the GMC what I know.'

'It's very, very kind of you and far more than I deserve, but I'll still have to leave. As soon as Sinclair is questioned, I am certain he'll tell the police about me. Then you'll be in trouble with the

GMC for keeping me on. You've been so good to me. I couldn't do that to you.' She blew her nose. 'The worst thing is knowing I'm letting you and the people here down. I know how difficult it will be for you on your own.'

'Been on my own for years.' He smiled. 'Besides, I'm not on my own any more, am I? Cecilia admitted she'd like nothing better than to help me out.' He turned a deep shade of crimson. 'Before the little ones come along.'

'In which case,' Margaret said sadly, 'I can't even justify putting you at risk so I can stay to help. There is no other way. I'll have to go. If I don't, there is still the likelihood of my father discovering where I am.'

'Very well then, if you must. You will be sorely missed.' He cleared his throat. 'I hope that husband of yours manages to clear his name and that one day you'll come back to see us.' He stood and crossed to the bureau, removing a sheaf of notes from the drawer. 'This is your salary up until the end of the month and a little more on top.'

'I can't take it – at least not all of it.'

He pressed the notes into her hand and smiled. 'Take it, girl. Save you having to scrub floors.'

Tears sprang to her eyes and she dropped a kiss on his forehead. 'Sometimes,' she said, meaning it, 'I don't know how I came to be so blessed.'

He waved her away. 'On you go, girl. On you go. Don't you know I have a wife waiting for me?'

452

Chapter 42

A week later the four of them were settled in the house in Perthshire. The children, especially Libby, had been heartbroken to leave the place that had become home to them, but Margaret had promised that she would take them back to see everyone as soon as she could. It had helped a great deal that Dolina was with them. Leaving had been hard on Margaret too. She'd come to love the place and the people who made it their home. There was no time to visit Flora and Peter, so she sent them a letter, explaining she had had to leave, but promising to write as soon as she could. There were only thirteen days left before Alasdair's trial, and Margaret despaired. Whatever the risks, she had decided she would be there. She couldn't let him face it without her.

She was sitting by the fire reading to the children when Dolina showed Simon Firth in. He was as scruffy-looking as ever and if possible paler than the last time she'd seen him. The small patch of eczema she'd noticed the first time they'd met had expanded and was now covering the best part of the right side of his face. Her heart plummeted. He did not look like a man who was coming to tell her good news.

But when he smiled her heart lifted.

'Mrs Morrison, I am so very pleased to see you again. Might we speak in private?'

Dolina took the children by their hands and led them away.

'You have news?' she asked.

'I do indeed. Do you mind if I smoke?'

'Not at all.'

'Now. I gather you know that the body of one of the men mentioned in Mrs Murphy's statement, a certain Hugh McCulloch, was fished out of the Clyde. And that he'd been murdered?'

Margaret nodded.

'The police believe that Billy Barr was the perpetrator and are currently searching for him. What you may not know is that shortly after McCulloch's body was discovered, a Christopher Boyd turned himself in. He admitted that he was the man with McCulloch the night Tommy Barr was killed. Naturally, he claims that he, Boyd, had nothing to do with the lad's death but that he didn't think Billy Barr would worry about that and with McCulloch's death, he feared Billy would discover his name and come after him too. But the other thing he said was even more interesting. He said that he'd gone to your husband's lawyer to confess before McCulloch was murdered. Boyd had heard the men of Govan were asking questions that he knew, sooner or later, would lead to him.' He smiled at Margaret. 'It appears your husband has some very loyal supporters.' He nodded approvingly, then frowned.

'So I paid a visit to Johnston. He should have pounced on this new witness and I wondered why he hadn't. It seemed odd at best, negligent at the worst.

'I have to say I wasn't impressed by your Mr

454

Johnston. He reminded me of a worm wriggling on the end of a hook. He denied that Boyd ever came to see him, but I don't believe him. If I find proof Boyd did, Johnston will face charges. At the very least if he had gone to the police with this new evidence McCulloch might still be alive.'

'Did you speak to his secretary, Miss Donaldson?'

Firth shook his head. 'She arranged the appointment, but she wasn't there when I saw Johnston.'

'Talk to her. Ask her about her appointments diary. She adores Johnston but she's a stickler for order. If Boyd did visit you can be sure she kept a note.'

'Then I will. I believe we have enough with Boyd's confession, but I don't want the prosecution finding holes in his evidence. What I can't understand is why Johnston would risk everything by lying. Not when he could be so easily found out.'

Margaret stood and started pacing. Her mind went back to everything Johnston had said, the speed with which he'd agreed to a trial, his determination that Alasdair should plead guilty, the way her father had known the details of the case against Alasdair. The truth struck her like a hammer blow. 'Dear God, my father got to Johnston. When exactly I don't know.'

'Can you prove that? It would help if you could.'

'I'll go and see my father. I'll make him tell me.'

She continued to pace, her excitement building. This was the news she'd been waiting for! 'Tell me, what do you think my father's chances are of having me committed to an asylum?'

455

Simon looked at her, a wry smile playing on his lips. 'I doubt I've met anyone saner.

'And of removing the children from me?'

'That's more difficult to say. If your husband is cleared of charges, none at all would be my guess. And if your father is implicated in suppressing evidence, then he'd be fortunate not to be facing charges himself.'

Her heart was still racing. 'What now?'

'I believe there is enough evidence to have Alasdair released on bail while matters are being looked into.'

The joy that had started as a circle of light around her heart widened and spread until she felt consumed by it.

Firth held up a finger. 'However, your husband won't agree. He takes a different view.'

He dug in his pocket and brought out a crumpled letter and handed it to her. As always, her heart leaped when she saw the familiar writing. She tore open the envelope.

My dearest

I have asked Firth to give you this and if he has you will also know that we believe soon my name will be cleared and I will walk away a free man. You probably wonder why I haven't sought bail. I want to have my name cleared in court. I want to walk away from here with my head held high, with the world knowing that I am innocent. I need others to know that they should trust in the law.

My love, when we meet again it will be when I have been declared an innocent man. I hope you understand why I need to do this.

*I count the days and hours until I can be with you.
I swear we will never be parted again.
Your loving husband
Alasdair*

She read it again before turning back to Firth.
'This is no less than what I expected from him.
But isn't he taking a chance?'

'I don't believe so. Williams and I would prefer
it not to go to trial, but I have no doubt Alasdair
will be cleared of all charges and, if I have my
way, receive an apology from the police and the
Crown Office.'

The next morning, determined to confront her
father, Margaret took the train to Glasgow, leaving the children behind with Dolina and promising that she would see them soon.

Before she left, she settled the children on either
side of her.

'Libby, remember when I said that Daddy had
to go away for a while?'

'Pa!' James said and clapped his hands. She
wondered how much he remembered of Alasdair.
Elizabeth buried herself against Margaret. 'He's
been away a very, very long time.'

'Yes he has. He didn't want to go, you know
that? He never wanted to leave you and James
but it was something he had to do.'

'Is he coming back to us?'

'He is. My darlings, we are all going to be together again. Hopefully very soon.'

'Will he remember me?'

'Oh, my sweet girl, of course. He's thought about

you and James every day while he was away. Your face, every inch of you is imprinted on his mind. He could no more forget about you than forget his own name.'

Elizabeth giggled then. 'Imagine forgetting your own name. He'd be a very silly daddy if he did that.'

Glasgow was covered in snow when, her fury still burning bright, Margaret arrived at the house in Great Western Terrace. She prayed her father would be here and not at their home in Helensburgh, but if he wasn't, she would demand to be driven to Helensburgh.

The maid let her into the house. It no longer felt like home – it hadn't for a while. Nevertheless, as the familiar smells of beeswax assailed her nostrils, she felt a pang of longing for her childhood so intense it almost took her breath away.

'Oh, Miss Margaret, it is good to see you. We never thought someone would manage to get word to you,' Betty said, taking her coat.

'Word to me? About what?'

'About your father. Him being sick.'

'My father is sick?' Only then did she remember what Dr Sinclair had said about her father being too unwell to receive him. Surely he couldn't still be ill?

'The master is very poorly, Miss. Madam is with him now. Shall I let her know you are here?'

'No. I'll just go up.' She took the stairs two at a time, pausing to catch her breath outside her father's bedroom door, before knocking and marching straight in.

The curtains were closed and it took a while for

Margaret's eyes to adjust to the semi-darkness. Her mother was by her father's bed, sewing by the light of an oil lamp.

'Margaret!' she murmured, placing her embroidery aside and rising. 'My dear. It is so good to see you, so good of you to come. How did you know?' She took Margaret's hands in hers and kissed her on both cheeks. It was as if she'd only seen Margaret a couple of days earlier and that all that had happened was only a figment of Margaret's imagination.

'How is he?' Margaret asked, removing her gloves.

'I'm not dead yet. I can still speak for myself.' The voice came from the bed. Softer, quieter, less forceful than she remembered, but still with that unmistakable ring of authority.

She crossed to his side and looked down at him. He was far thinner than he'd been the last time she'd seen him, his grey skin stretched across the bones of his face. Lying in bed he looked smaller, almost vulnerable, and the anger she'd nursed towards him for so long faded. She'd thought she'd shout at him – pummel his chest with her fists – scream at him. Now all she felt was a detached pity.

'How are you, Father?'

A spasm of coughing prevented him from answering for a while. 'You're the doctor. You tell me.'

She took his wrist in her hand and felt for a pulse. It was weak and rapid. Judging by her father's flushed cheeks and over-bright eyes he had a fever too. 'What does your doctor say?'

'Bloody fool says I've bronchial pneumonia.'

'I suspect he's right.'

'Says there's nothing to be done. I'll either survive it or I won't.'

'He's correct there too.'

'He also says your father has a tumour on his lung,' Margaret's mother whispered. 'He doesn't think he has more than a year, if that.'

Margaret absorbed the news for a few moments. Her father had cancer. It would kill him if the pneumonia didn't.

'Where is my grandson? Is he here?'

So no mention of Elizabeth, then. Her father might be dangerously ill, but he hadn't changed.

'They are in a safe place. Where you can't get to them.'

A spasm of coughing kept him from speaking for several minutes. 'For God's sake, Margaret, bring them to me. Do you really intend to keep my grandson from me, even now? When you know I'm dying?'

'I know what you did, Father.'

'What are you talking about, girl?'

'I know you arranged to have evidence suppressed that would have helped free Alasdair and I suspect you paid Johnston to do the same.'

'I warned you I would if you didn't sign the children over to me.'

'Then you admit it?'

'What difference does it make now?'

So she was right! Until this moment she hadn't been certain. A wave of hot anger washed over her. 'Alasdair could have hung! He was innocent – and you knew that!' Her pulse was beating hard in her throat. 'You separated him from me and the children for no reason. Was there no limit to your wickedness?' She was shaking so much she could barely speak. 'But you've lost, Father. Despite everything, you have lost. Alasdair can prove his innocence beyond doubt. Nothing you or anyone else can do will prevent that from happening.'

Her father's expression hadn't changed. 'So what did bring you here? Did you hear I was dying and decided to come crawling back looking for your inheritance?'

'You know me better than that, Father. I don't want your money.'

He shook his head. 'You've always been a fool. But despite your foolhardiness, you've always managed to get what you want, haven't you? You have a lot more Bannatyne in you than you care to think. In other circumstances you might have been a worthy successor for the business.'

'If I'd been born a man, you mean?'

A glimmer of a smile crossed his face. 'You're tougher than many men. If your fool husband had agreed to my offer of a job, you could have been running Bannatyne's alongside him.'

'Is that all you can say? No apology? You should be getting down on your knees begging my and Alasdair's forgiveness.'

Her father didn't reply. Not even being within touching distance of death would make him admit he was wrong.

'Bring me the boy,' he grunted.

'You can see him soon. You can see them both. When I decide the time is right.'

Her father struggled into a sitting position.

'God damn it. I want to see James Fletcher now!'

'When you've recovered from your fever. Not before. And,' she warned, 'I'll be bringing Elizabeth to see you too. She is not to feel as if she is of no consequence. So you'll pay her attention or I'll remove both children immediately and won't allow you to see them again. I'll be with them all the time to make sure.'

If possible her father's face flushed an even deeper red. Then he gave a small laugh. 'As I thought. Underneath you're not so different to me, after all.'

A few moments later, her father's eyes closed and Margaret and her mother stepped out of the room and into the drawing room next door. 'You *will* bring the children to see us?' Margaret's mother asked. 'I long to see them again.'

'I never wanted them to grow up not knowing you. But you made your choice. You must have known that Father intended to have them live with you – that he intended to take custody of them. How could you have agreed?'

'You think your father asked my opinion? He hasn't done for years.'

'Why do you let him treat you the way he does? Why did you never stand up to him? You could have divorced him – people do these days, you know. It's not as if you mix enough with society to give a fig if they ostracised you.'

Her mother flushed. 'Do you really think it would have been that easy? I have no money of my own and no means of earning it. If I had left your father I would have been destitute – and he would

462

never have allowed me to see you children.'

'But you could have left when we were grown up. He couldn't have stopped us from seeing you if we chose.'

Margaret's mother sank into a chair. 'I loved your father once. He wasn't always like this. Oh, he was always determined to succeed, always used to getting what he wanted – not so different to your young man. But when the boys were killed something in your father died too. Something died in both of us. All the joy went out of life. We'd lost both our sons. Life could never be the same after that. The world is endlessly grey without them and I, for one, look forward to the day when I can join them.'

A memory came flooding back. They'd been in Helensburgh. Fletcher and Sebastian had still been alive. It was the long, hot summer just before the war. Although on the cusp of becoming a woman she'd still been a child – the protected, loved and spoilt only daughter. Back then they couldn't imagine the bloodbath that was to come. Instead, there was an air of excitement – everything and everyone seemed more alive, more vital. Her father had taken a rare day off work and they'd all gone out on her father's boat, sailing it across to Largs, Fletcher and Sebastian shouldering each other out of the way as they took turns at the helm. She remembered sunshine, a picnic, bees, happiness. She, Sebastian and Fletcher had swum in the sea while her parents had watched benevolently. It was the last time she could remember her mother being happy. The last time she could remember them all being together.

'You still had me,' Margaret whispered. 'I missed Fletcher and Sebastian too.' She swallowed hard. 'I'll always miss them.'

Her mother's eyes glistened. 'You were always such a happy, self-contained child. You didn't seem to need anyone or anything.'

But she had. When her brothers had died she'd needed her mother just like her own children needed her.

'I have no right to expect you to forgive me,' her mother continued. 'I've let you down – I know that. I should have been a better mother to you. I wanted to be – I just couldn't.' She looked at Margaret, her face wet with tears. 'I wish our lives could have been different. If I could change the past I would. Please give me the chance to make amends now.'

Margaret's heart softened. How could she refuse? There had been more than enough bitterness.

Over the next few days Margaret took turns with her mother by her father's bedside. There was little either of them could do except try to lower his fever with cold cloths and aspirin. She sent her father's chauffeur for the children and Dolina and soon they too, wide-eyed and a little dubious, were ensconced in her parents' house.

Eventually the fever broke and her father began to recover. It would, Margaret knew, be only a short reprieve. Although she doubted she could ever forgive him, she couldn't bring herself to keep the children from him. Not when he didn't have long left.

At first they were stiff with him, a little fearful. But as the days passed and they spent longer with him, to Margaret's surprise, the children quickly overcame their initial awe of her father and he kept to his side of the bargain, directing the odd question to Elizabeth and apparently listening attentively to her answer. While Elizabeth remained wary of him, James Fletcher, with his usual indiscriminate affection for anyone who was kind to him, adored him. He would sit up next to him on the bed and demand to be read to. Whenever her father stopped, he would bossily insist that he carry on.

But if James was her father's clear favourite, Elizabeth was Margaret's mother's. The change in her mother was astonishing and if Margaret hadn't seen it for herself she would never have believed it. Gone were the pallor and listlessness she'd come to associate with her mother over the last years. Instead was a middle-aged woman full of vigour. It was as if whatever life was leaking out of Margaret's father had found its way into her mother, reinvigorating her.

She no longer spent time in Helensburgh and, even more surprisingly, retreated to her room only for a short nap after lunch. Then she would rise and insist on taking the children for a walk in the Botanic Gardens, sometimes accompanied by Margaret, sometimes on her own. Margaret knew that it was largely due to Elizabeth and James' demanding, amusing and loving presences constantly around her.

This is how it should have been, Margaret thought. The children should have always had the love and affection of their grandparents.

But, despite a softening in her father's attitude, Margaret couldn't quite forgive him, was still wary of him. She doubted that the hurt, mistrust and anger she felt whenever she looked at him would ever truly disappear.

In the meantime, reassured that her father wasn't in immediate danger of dying, she took the children to visit Mairi and Toni. They spent a couple of happy hours together before Margaret and the children took their leave. She wanted to see Peggy too.

Her old servant and her mother were delighted to see her, and Peggy scooped the children into her arms, soaking them with her tears. Mrs McQuarrie had deteriorated in the time Margaret had been away and Margaret knew that she, like her father, was not long for the world.

Before they left, Peggy thrust a letter into her hand. 'This came to the flat a few days after you left when I was still settling things. I didn't know where to send it so I kept it with me.'

The letter was addressed to Mr and Mrs Morrison although Margaret didn't recognise the handwriting. She opened it to find a banker's draft for fifty pounds and a letter. She and Alasdair, the letter read, were now shareholders in a fast-developing pharmaceutical company. This was their first dividend, and the writer – a Mr Jack Winter – anticipated that there would be many more to follow. He thanked Alasdair once again for loaning him the money that he'd invested in the company. *'We're putting most of the profit back into research. As a shareholder I'm sure you'll agree that's best. I am looking forward to showing you what we are doing and should you manage to come to New York I'd be delighted to see you.'*

She should have had more confidence in Alasdair's investment. If only this letter had come six months ago, how different everything might have been.

The following afternoon, when her mother had taken the children shopping for new clothes – she'd been aghast at the children's wardrobe – and Margaret was sitting by her father's bedside, he cleared his throat.

'I'll not live to see the summer.' He gave her a sly smile. 'You do know that James Fletcher will still get everything.'

'He's only a boy.'

'Which is why I've made you executor!' There was a note of triumph in her father's voice. 'You can't turn your back on Bannatyne's now.'

'I know nothing about running a shipyard, Father. Even if I had any interest in doing so.'

'The shipyard needs to continue. We'll be even richer if war comes.' He dropped his voice. 'There will be more jobs than ever before for the people of Govan. Let the shipyard go into decline and you'll be doing them out of a livelihood. I can't imagine that's what you want.'

'Still determined to get your way, Father? Who is running it now?'

'Ferguson. He does all right, but he has no imagination. Besides, he's not getting any younger either. The firm needs new blood.'

'Then find a new manager. There's bound to be someone amongst your thousands of employees.'

'No one I can trust as much as family.'

'You of all people have no right to talk of trust.'

'That husband of yours can run things.'

'He could, whether he would want to is another matter.'

She turned her back on her father. Fat blobs of snow slid down the window pane. She watched the people hurrying to get back home. A tram trundled along the road, stopping to pick up passengers. A man stood on the street holding out his hands in the universal sign of want and a few feet along from him was another. There were many more just like them – women too – on the streets of Glasgow. The people of Govan and beyond needed the work the shipyard could bring. She and Alasdair could yet do a great deal of good. Bannatyne's under their control could make so much difference to so many lives.

She turned away from the window and towards her father. 'I will speak to Alasdair. But this is how it is going to be. If Alasdair wants to be involved in the shipyard then you will sign over full control of your businesses to him and to me. You will have no more to do with any of it.'

'Over my dead body.'

'It is your choice, Father. But believe me when I say it will be the only way Bannatyne's will continue and prosper.'

Chapter 43

Margaret sat in her position at the front of the public gallery, nibbling her lower lip. Under her gloves her hands were perspiring. It had been just over three months since she'd seen him, and she'd changed. So would he have. A man couldn't spend time in prison in fear for his life and not be affected.

And despite Firth and Alasdair's confidence, it could all still go wrong. Boyd could yet retract his confession.

Firth, wearing a new suit and a dazzling white, stiff-collared shirt, his hair neatly combed and with no evidence of ash to be seen, was already at the table. In the formality of the court room he seemed to have increased in both height and presence. Mr Williams, Alasdair's advocate, was beside him, a striking and imposing figure in his black gown and horse-hair wig.

Yesterday, Margaret had received a letter from Dr Alan. Sinclair had been arrested and questioned, but Kirsty couldn't, or wouldn't, identify him as her attacker. It seemed the police might never know for certain who had raped Kirsty. However, Sinclair had left the island and so far hadn't reported her to the GMC.

She heard a rustle and smelled a whiff of expensive perfume and looked up to find Lillian, looking every inch Lady Lillian in her wide-brimmed hat and matching velvet dress in deep burgundy. 'Couldn't let you go through this on your own, darling.' She squeezed Margaret's shoulder. 'Forgive me for not coming to you before?'

Mairi, who was sitting next to Margaret, jumped to her feet to give Lillian her seat but Margaret grabbed her hand and pulled her back down. 'Stay where you are,' she whispered, 'Lily can sit next to you.' An embarrassed Mairi sat back down, forcing Lily to take the chair next to her. 'It's good to see you, Lily,' Margaret said. 'May I introduce my dear friend Mairi?'

Moments later they were joined by a plumper, equally beloved figure. 'Said we'd hold true,' Martha said, sinking into the seat on Margaret's right and taking her hand.

'When did you get back?' Margaret asked, tears pricking behind her eyes.

'Lily wrote to me a month ago.' Martha leaned across Margaret and glared at Lillian. 'She should have written to me the moment Alasdair was arrested. I would have come then. Jumped on the first ship I could.'

'I have something I need to tell you,' Margaret whispered. Her friend might not be so affectionate, or supportive, when she learned how Margaret had appropriated her name.

'It can wait. Hush now, they're coming in.'

Alasdair, wearing the suit Margaret had bought and left for him at the prison, was ushered into the dock. The only evidence of how he'd suffered was the new silver strands in his dark hair. He searched the room for her and when their eyes met, he smiled. The world disappeared until it was only the two of them. The years slipped away until it was as if they were back in the bar where they'd first met. The arrival of the judge in court broke their gaze. Dr Marshall, the doctor who believed that Alasdair was correct not to remove the knife, was first in the witness box to give his evidence, followed by Mrs Murphy. She repeated what she'd seen in a calm, no-nonsense voice, reiterating that yes, she was certain she hadn't been mistaken, that of course she would have come forward sooner had she known there was any possibility that they had imprisoned the wrong man, she would have been able to say the accused wasn't one of the men she'd seen running away, and really, did anyone think that she, a lifetime churchgoer, would ever lie on the stand? Then it was Christopher Boyd's turn. He admitted he had been there with Hugh McCulloch when an argument had broken out between him and the murdered man. Once again he said he had no idea that McCulloch was going to stab the victim until Tommy Barr had fallen to the ground. He would have stayed to help but he was certain nothing could be done for the lad, and besides, he had been scared he'd be charged along with McCulloch. There was a deathly silence in the court when he finished by saying that after thinking matters over, he had gone to Alasdair's lawyer to confess, had been told Johnston would be in touch, but had heard nothing more. When asked why he hadn't gone straight to the police to give himself up, he admitted that he had hoped that Johnston would agree to defend him in return for his confession.

471

Next was Mr Johnston, who denied that Boyd had ever approached him. He was allowed to stand down while Miss Donaldson was called to the witness box.

She, albeit reluctantly, told the court that Boyd had indeed come to see Mr Johnston and that she remembered him well. They didn't get too many of his sort seeking assistance from someone of Mr Johnston's calibre and standing. She had tried to turn him away but when he'd said that he had information that would help Johnston free his client, Alasdair Morrison, she had ushered him in straight away. As she spoke, she kept her eyes averted from her former employer.

A sorry-looking Johnston was recalled to the stand. He admitted that Boyd had come to see him but claimed that he hadn't believed his story. When asked by Alasdair's advocate why he hadn't gone to the police, Johnston had blustered but had no convincing reply. Mr Williams told the jury that the solicitor was facing an inquiry and that he had reason to believe that the father-in-law of the accused had made several large payments to Johnston's account.

At this there was a roar from the public gallery. Cries of 'shame' and 'Bannatyne the Bully' could be heard clearly. Margaret wanted to bury her flaming face in her hands, but remained straight-backed.

When Johnston left the witness box, an irritated-looking judge told the jury that there was no case to answer, that the prosecution should have known that, and that Alasdair should be found not guilty and released immediately with no stain on his character. It happened so quickly, Margaret could hardly believe it was all over.

A cheer went up and everyone stood. Margaret tried to reach Alasdair but she was pushed by the crowd towards the door. Men stepped forward and lifted Alasdair aloft and carried him outside. Margaret stood back and smiled. A part of him would always belong to the people – just as a part of her did. The rest was hers and the children's. But the essence of her and him – the important, secret, part – belonged to each other.

The crowd followed Alasdair outside, dragging her along in their wake and separating her from her friends. Outside, hundreds, if not thousands, lined the streets, in some places several yards deep. And not just from Govan. They'd come from as far as Dumbarton, all having downed tools for a couple of hours so that they could welcome the man to whom they owed so much.

A hush descended and the crowds parted silently until there was a path straight from where she stood to Alasdair. Somehow he had persuaded the men to put him down. Her breath caught in her throat as they walked towards each other. As Alasdair passed them, the men, almost as one, doffed their caps. The looks they gave her weren't quite as friendly.

Then he was standing in front of her, his blue eyes boring into hers. 'My love,' he said simply, his voice hoarse.

'I need to ask,' she said raising her voice until it carried across the crowds. 'Can you still love a Bannatyne?'

'I love you.' Suddenly he grinned. 'I will love

you until the day the breath leaves my body and probably long after.'

He picked her up and whirled her around. A ripple of applause spread through the crowd and Margaret blushed.

'My love. My love. I wasn't sure I would ever hold you again,' he murmured into her hair when he put her down.

He smelled of him. His mouth tasted of him. His hard body was exactly the way she remembered. God, how she longed to be alone with him, their arms wrapped around each other.

She stood on tiptoes and whispered what she'd been thinking – what she wanted – in his ear. He laughed and picked her up as if she were as light as a feather. 'I think we've wasted enough time, don't you?'

'More than enough. But first there are two small people who are longing to see you.'

Acknowledgements

This book owes thanks to many people, some of whom have passed away. My grandfather, Peter Morrison, worked at the Glasgow shipyards between the wars, making his home in Govan. It was he who told me that the returning WWI soldiers were promised a land for heroes. When this promise failed to materialise and with the Glasgow smog affecting his children's health, he took his family back to his childhood home on North Uist where he worked as a crofter and fisherman. He was also a visionary – a keen writer of letters to the *Stornoway Gazette* – and at one time attempted to resettle the abandoned Monach Islands with his family. After four years, with no other families to provide support, he was forced to admit defeat and returned to Grimsay. Sandbank, the house of Peter and Flora, is the house I remember visiting as a child, where I lived as a teenager and of which I still have many happy memories. It is still largely as I describe it.

My mother was a midwife in the fifties, (a 'Green Lady', as they were fondly known because of their green uniforms) and she spent several years working in the most poverty-stricken parts of Glasgow. Although the National Health Service had come into being by then (based on the model nat was originally implemented on the islands) conditions had changed very little for the poor. Sadly she passed away many years ago, and I only have a few recollections of the stories she told me. She remains however, my inspiration. Fortunately I was able to quiz some of the women who worked with her – in particular my aunt Liz, now a very grand age and living in Australia, and my mother's great friend, Catriona MacKinnon, who still lives on South Uist.

A GP in North Uist for many years, the late Dr John MacLeod, or Dr John as he was better known to the islanders, did much to further the health of the islanders as did his father, Dr Alex, before him. My Dr Alan, of course is fictional but I hope I have shown in him some of the qualities required of an island doctor! My thanks also go to Lorna MacLeod, a nurse herself and Dr John's widow, with whom I spent a lovely afternoon drinking tea and listening to her stories of both Dr Alex and Dr John and their experiences on the island – a book in itself!

Govan has changed since my grandfather worked and lived there – the shipyards that once stretched along the length of the Clyde have vanished. But there is a fabulous little-known museum in the building that once housed the management of Fairfield's shipyard, if you're tempted to find out more. Although in my book, I say there wasn't a hospital in Govan, many people will of course know that there was, as well as one in nearby Linthouse. I hope I will be forgiven for denying their existence.

My thanks to the Govan Reminiscence Group

who kindly invited me to attend one of their meetings. What is clear from their memories, is that while many people in Govan were desperately poor, there was a much valued sense of community – and laughter.

Thanks also to my agent Judith Murdoch and to the wonderful team at Little, Brown, in particular my editor Manpreet Grewal and the copy-editing team headed up by the ever-patient Thalia Proctor.

Finally, I'd like to acknowledge the help of friends and family, who unstintingly gave their time to help me with edits. Flora, Mairi, Isabel, Stewart – I owe you big time.

This Large Print Book for the partially sighted, who cannot read normal print, is published under the auspices of

THE ULVERSCROFT FOUNDATION